NIGHT WATCHER

Chris Longmuir

To Martin
Enjoy
Chris Longmuir

B&J

Published by Barker & Jansen

Copyright © Chris Longmuir, 2012

Cover design by Cathy Helms www.avalongraphics.org

ISBN: 978-0-9574153-0-0

This book is dedicated to Liz and Betty who give unfailingly of their time to read and comment on all my books.

PART ONE

July to September 2008

1

Mist shrouded everything except for the Discovery's skeletal masts pointing long bony fingers into the sky. It was an omen. He had come to the right place.

There had been so many places since he had last been in Dundee, but he doubted anyone here would connect him with the skinny little lad ejected forcibly from his birthplace, and sent to a borstal far away. They were no longer known as borstals though, secure accommodation, that's what they called them nowadays. As if the name made any difference. They were still the same brutal lockups they had always been.

Smiling grimly, he pulled his collar up and the brim of his hat forward until only his eyes showed. He turned his back on the glass frontage of the station and shuffled in the direction of the pedestrian bridge.

It was not there. Confused, he stopped and stared. Everything had changed. He did not like change, it unsettled, immobilized him. He turned in a slow circle. The Discovery was behind him, its masts now barely visible. Hazy lights from Tayside House's tower building pierced the mist, over to his right, and in front of him the dual carriageway – but no pedestrian bridge.

He sent a silent plea to the voice asking him what he should do. But the voice had been silent for some time now, demonstrating its disapproval, because he had acted on his own initiative before he left Newcastle.

The voice had not told him to end the social worker's life, nor had it instructed him to set fire to her office. But at the time he had been thinking clearly and, knowing he had to vanish, it had seemed sensible to leave no clues to where he had gone.

A cluster of people waited at the edge of the road and, although he did not like crowds, he followed them across both carriageways when the lights changed.

He was in familiar territory now, and his panic subsided as he started to walk up Union Street towards the familiar City Churches at the top.

A faint smell of smoke accompanied the grubby piece of paper and the bottle of pills as he pulled them out of his pocket. On the paper was written the directions to the hostel and all the instructions he needed to start the job the social worker had organized for him. Dumping the pills in the gutter, because he did not need them anymore, he followed the directions on the paper.

The hostel was no different from any other hostel; a grey, unwelcoming building, full of strange noises, strange smells, and even stranger people. He never felt safe in these places but it would have to do until he found something that suited him better.

That had been six months ago; six months of rest and regeneration, since the completion of his last mission in Newcastle. After it was completed the voice had told him to return to his roots in Dundee, but ever since then, the voice had remained silent. Despite this, his faith never wavered. He was convinced there must be a reason why the voice had guided him to this place.

Over the last week, he had been aware of his increasing restlessness. He was nervy and jumpy, forever fidgeting, unable to remain at peace for more than a few minutes at a time. This was a sure sign that the time was almost here.

As the days passed a fever engulfed him; his body burned and his skin itched. Insects burrowed below his flesh, eating him from the inside. Only one thing could quieten them and that was the completion of his next mission.

But though he continued to wait for instructions, the voice did not speak to him.

The waiting was more than he could bear and in desperation he followed several women, searching for the evil within them. But it soon became obvious to him they were not evil, only silly or misguided.

Then he found this one. She was not silly or misguided. Nor was there any other excuse for the bad things she did. But still, he doubted, for although he had followed her every day for the past week and hoped she would be the one, the voice was silent.

Tonight, after leaving the department store from the back entrance in the alley, she walked confidently towards the street, unaware she was being watched.

He waited until she reached the street, then rose from the depths of his secret hiding place and followed her.

When she arrived home her house was empty. No husband waiting tonight. But the voice was silent and had not yet confirmed that she was the chosen one, and without the voice, he could not act.

He followed her again when she left the house later that evening. He watched as she visited the man. He heard the argument and saw the despair in the man's face when she left. And he was there at the end – at the killing time.

And he knew that if it were not for the woman, the man would not be dead.

Surely now the voice would come. It could not fail to see that this woman was evil through and through.

'Where are you? Where are you?' The question echoed through his brain although no sound issued from his lips. He did not need to speak aloud for the voice to hear him, for it was tuned into his thoughts.

As if in answer to his plea the voice responded. 'The evil that women do cannot be allowed to continue.' It roared through his head so loudly he had to clamp his hands over his ears.

When the voice quietened and started whispering to him, that was when he knew he had been right to think this woman was the chosen one. And now his mission was clear to him. He had to watch her and prevent her from doing further evil.

He slunk off into the darkness, back to his hiding place. It was time to plan what form his mission would take.

2

'It's over. Finished. Can't you get that through your head?' Nicole's hand was on the doorknob.

'No!' Dave lunged towards the door preventing her from leaving. 'It can't be. We love each other.' His voice faltered.

Nicole looked up at him and laughed. 'Love,' she said. 'No it was never that. Attraction maybe, lust certainly. But never love.'

He reached for her, entwining his fingers in her blonde hair. 'But I gave up everything for you.' He fought the tears pricking behind his eyes. Men didn't cry.

'Then you're a bigger fool than I took you for.' Nicole shook his hand off and glared at him through icy blue eyes.

'But you said you loved me. You said if I promised to divorce my wife, you'd divorce Scott and marry me.'

'Words, words.' Nicole laughed harshly.

His eyes filled with tears, and he ran his fingers through his short brown hair. 'You knew I'd phoned her to say I was coming home to talk things over.'

'That's your problem, now get out of my way, and go back to your wife. At least she wants you.'

For a moment Dave wanted to put his hands round her lovely white neck and squeeze. But damn-it-all, he still loved her. 'I can't live without you, Nicole.' He despised himself for having to plead.

'Tough,' she said, pushing him aside.

Despair flooded through him and he stood away from the door. 'I won't be responsible for my actions if you leave.'

'You do whatever you have to do.' Nicole hesitated in the doorway before stepping through it into the darkness of the corridor. 'But I'm going and I'm not coming back.'

He followed her. 'Don't go,' he said, catching the entry

door before it swung shut, but she was already running up the street to her car.

He watched until she was out of sight. Then, swearing loudly, he kicked the door shut and thumped the corridor wall with his fist. An upstairs door opened sending a sliver of light through the gloom of the landing. 'Nosy sod,' he shouted and the door closed.

He massaged his hand as he entered his own flat. It seemed empty without her. Picking up the framed photograph, he caressed the face with his fingers. But even her laughing image seemed to be mocking him and he laid it face down on the table. His fingers lingered on it for a moment, wanting to turn it over again, but he could not bear to see the mockery in her eyes.

Anger surged through him, his fingers tightened on the frame and he threw the picture across the room. It hit the wall and boomeranged back to him, coming to rest at his feet. He ground his foot on top of it, and then covered his face with his hands. Life hardly seemed to be worth living without her.

The sound of the doorbell woke him out of his misery. No one ever came here except her. She must have returned.

'I knew you'd come back,' he said, opening the door and stepping out into the corridor.

The door at the end was open, although he was sure he had closed it when he came back. A faint light from the street filtered in, but the hallway was empty. The stairs at the other end of the corridor were shrouded in darkness. There was no movement or sound from them, so he knew it had not been one of his upstairs neighbours who had rung his doorbell or left the outside door open. It must have been Nicole with one of her unpredictable changes of mind. His heart lightened. She had come back but had not stayed. That meant there was hope for him and their relationship, for he knew she was like a bird beating its wings in a headwind, blowing this way and that, ruled by the turbulence of her emotions.

He ran down the corridor to the front door. If he could

catch her he would persuade her to stay. But there was no Nicole and her car had gone.

His shoulders slumped and the weight on his heart returned.

Tears blinded his eyes so he did not see one of the shadows on the stairs detach itself and move towards him.

And he did not expect the ligature round his neck as he turned to enter his room.

The sound of Dave's voice echoed behind Nicole as she ran up the street. Even when she tumbled into her car she imagined she could still hear him shouting, and entreating her to return. The car roared into life, and with an ear-splitting screech of tyres, she drove off, even though the temptation to turn back, to tell him it was all a big mistake, was overwhelming.

Tears trickled down her face as she drove. She had not meant to get so involved with Dave. It had just been a bit of fun – just another one of her affairs. But he had not seen it that way, and she had been drawn into a relationship that frightened her with its intensity.

She had tried to end it gently, without causing him hurt. That was the way she usually ended her affairs. But he was having none of it, and eventually, she had come to realize that she would have to be brutal. However, what she had not banked on was this feeling of something having been ripped out of her.

It was too dangerous to continue though. It had to end. Scott was not a fool and sooner or later he would have become suspicious.

She had been with Scott since she was fifteen, and she could not imagine life without him. He was overbearing, opinionated, and he often made her feel worthless and like a child again. She should have been happy with him, but there was a void, an ache that constantly needed to be filled, and she did that through casual affairs with other men. It boosted her self-confidence – made her feel needed.

Maybe if they'd had children she would not have this urge. But Scott had taken care of that, forcing her to have an abortion when she was fifteen.

'You must have it,' he had said, 'or it's prison for me.' It was the after effects of the abortion that ensured she would never have a child.

Nicole turned into the gate and drove up to the house. It was in darkness. Scott was not home yet. She was grateful for that because she was sure her mascara must be streaked and her eyes swollen.

Entering the house through the kitchen door, she kicked off her stiletto-heeled shoes and eased her cramped toes on to the coolness of the tiles.

She crossed to the sink and splashed cold water over her face, before pouring some into a glass and gulping it down. Leaning against the sink for a moment, she stared uneasily into the darkness outside. Then, shivering, she left the glass in the sink, padded out of the kitchen and through to her bedroom.

It only took a moment to shrug off her clothes, but she paused before releasing her breasts from the too tight bra. They were large, firm and shapely, but she was unable to see that because Scott always mocked them.

'You're like a Jordan look-a-like,' he often said in a tone of disgust, although she was sure she was not as well endowed as Katie Price. And when he was being particularly cruel, he would compare them to the udders of a cow.

She jumped into bed and pulled the duvet over her head, unsure whether she was crying because of Scott's dissatisfaction with her body, or because she had lost Dave.

It was much later before Scott returned home, and it pleased him to see Nicole's blue, Porsche Boxster, tucked up safely in the garage. She was at home, where she should be.

A smile flickered at the corners of his mouth as he walked silently to the bedroom. He stood for a moment considering whether to wake her but decided against it. He really was not in the mood for sex tonight and would rather savour the successes of the evening.

Raising a hand to the back of his neck he tugged at the elastic ponytail holder and shook his hair loose. It swirled around his head before settling, in dark-brown waves on his shoulders, hiding the diamond stud in his left ear.

He was an attractive man, and he knew it. His chin jutted out more than most men's, but that did not displease him because he thought it made him look masculine. If there was any fault with his features it was his nose which was slightly off-centre, making his face look a bit less than symmetrical.

He undressed, and walked over to the window, staring out at the darkness and the vague reflection of his body. At least it was still firm and muscled, like the body of a younger man. Not like Nicole, who was running to flab and needed to diet.

Making a moue of distaste he crossed to the bed, slipped under the duvet and, turning his back on Nicole, closed his eyes. He fell asleep still smiling and thinking about everything that had happened earlier.

3

Bill Murphy stamped out of his ground floor flat in the run-down Victorian villa. He had not invited Evie, his ex-wife, but when she had turned up at his door with a skinful of booze he had not had the heart to turn her away. Then after she passed out on the sofa he knew he had to get out. She had caused him enough grief already. So, in case he ended up doing something he would later regret, he covered her up with a duvet and left.

His anger simmered below the surface as he got into his beat-up red Fiesta, and for a moment he thought about curling up on the back seat and sleeping there, but it was too close to Evie, and the night was chilly.

There was nothing else for it. He would go into the office. With a bit of luck, he would be able to get some shut-eye in the staff room.

Headquarters car park was as full as it was during the daytime but Bill managed to squeeze his Fiesta into a tiny space at the end. He straightened his tie and ran his fingers through his unruly brown hair as he strode towards the building.

The vestibule was empty and he glanced briefly towards the main office where a glass fronted wall separated the horde of desk-bound, white-shirted staff from contact with the outside world. A constable raised his head and waved a greeting. Bill waved back before inserting a number into the entry keypad. While he waited for the door to unlock he wondered idly whether the glass was bomb-proof.

The upper corridors had that strange hollow feeling of an empty building and there was no one in the detectives' room. A computer hummed quietly on one of the desks and every now and then its screensaver beeped. A coffee mug and a

half-eaten sandwich lay beside it. Bill felt the cup, it was still
warm.

'Where is everybody,' he muttered, rubbing the bump on
his nose – the aftermath of a thump from a bottle. 'It's like
the bloody Marie Celeste in here.'

The staff room was also empty, although there was a
stink of curry and an empty foil container on the coffee
table. Bill stretched out on a sofa, but he was too tall to fit it
and his feet dangled over the end. After a fruitless attempt to
get comfortable he reckoned enough was enough and
wandered down to the ground floor to share a joke and some
gossip with the night shift officers.

It was the usual madhouse in the duty room: phones
ringing, voices raised, officers rushing in and then out again.

'Damn it,' Max, the duty inspector said to Bill. 'The
town's gone mad tonight and I don't have a single officer to
spare if anything comes in.' He looked at Bill curiously. 'I
didn't know you were on duty tonight, but I'm bloody glad
you're here. All the other detectives have been called out.'

'I'm not on duty but seeing I'm here . . .' Bill let the
sentence dangle.

Max grinned. 'I'll take that as an offer.'

'Sure,' Bill said. He had known Max since their training
at the police college at Tulliallan Castle and had a lot of
respect for him.

Max hurried off in the direction of a gesturing telephone
operator while Bill turned to the coffee machine and tried to
persuade it to dispense a cup of the usual sludge, but the
machine was not playing and refused to part with a drop.

'Bugger it,' muttered Bill. He would have gone home if
Evie hadn't been there.

'Remember what you said?'

Bill hadn't heard Max come up behind him and he turned
with a jerk. 'What was that then?' He stared gloomily at the
empty paper cup.

Max carried on as if Bill hadn't said anything. 'There's
been a 999 call from a hysterical woman. The operator had a
bit of difficulty making sense out of what she was saying.

But apparently, she's terrified to go outside her front door because of a disturbance at her block of flats . . .'

'A domestic, just what I need.'

'It might be a bit more than that,' Max said. 'She says she thinks there's a body hanging from the banisters over the stairwell.'

'Hysterical, you said? You sure she's not a nutter?'

'Nutter or not, it needs to be looked at. Are you up for it?'

Bill crumpled the paper cup and threw it into the bin. 'You got somebody to come with me?'

'If I did I wouldn't need to ask you to go. But I'll get one of the cars to join you as soon as they're clear.'

The address was in Lochee, known as Little Tipperary because of the influx of Irish immigrants, seeking work in the jute factories, in the nineteenth century. Now, Lochee had been swallowed up by Dundee, being bypassed on its south side, cutting it off from the main traffic flow and allowing it to retain its small town image.

During the day Lochee High Street was like any other small town High Street, with smaller shops jostling for space beside slightly larger ones. Here you could find traditional bakers and butchers shops as well as a supermarket and a local Woolworths. But at night the place had a derelict feel, due in part to the heavy steel shutters on shop doors and windows – a sign of more turbulent times.

Bill parked his car on the double yellow lines at the kerb. The tenement building, flanked by steel-shuttered shops on one side and an undertakers on the other, was in darkness. After rummaging in the glove compartment to find a torch, he got out, crossed the pavement in two strides and pushed the heavy front door. It opened onto a long dark lobby. At the end of the lobby was the stairs. And in the flickering torchlight, the body that hung there seemed to dance and twist.

Bill shivered. Bodies always had that effect on him. No

matter how many he saw he never got used to death.

He wished the reinforcements would hurry up. It was bloody eerie standing here on this dark staircase with only the John Doe for company.

And where was the hysterical phone-caller? You would have at least thought she would have been here to meet him.

Oh, well. Better make himself useful. Tightening his grip on the torch he shone it upwards to illuminate the face then wished he hadn't. It was purple and contorted and the tongue protruded out of one side of the mouth. There seemed little doubt the man was dead, but Bill climbed the stairs anyway and reaching over the banister pulled an arm up and felt for a pulse. There was nothing, except the cold, clammy feel of dead flesh.

The wail of a police siren announced the arrival of the police car. Two uniformed policemen joined him in the lobby.

'Bloody high time,' Bill said. 'Better phone it in. Tell them we need the police surgeon here, and make it fast or else we'll be here all night.'

'Right you are, sir.' The older guy in the uniform turned and ran out of the lobby.

The second uniform looked sick. He was a fresh-faced lad, hardly old enough to be shaving yet, Bill thought. Probably fresh out of police college and not yet hardened to the job.

The first uniform clattered back up the lobby. 'The doc's on his way,' he said. 'But shouldn't we be asking for the SOCO team as well?'

'Call out those scene of the crime buggers and we'll definitely be here all night. But I suppose we'll have to, although it looks like a straightforward suicide to me.'

He peered along the landing at the closed doors wondering which one the hysterical phone informant was hiding behind.

'Should we cut him down, sir?' The second constable looked as if he would rather be anywhere else but there.

'It might be best, lad,' Bill said. 'The doc's not going to

be able to do much with him up there. Once you've done that see if you can find a bulb for that bloody light.' Bill nodded at the dangling flex. 'And then the pair of you can do a bit of door-knocking upstairs and find out if anyone saw anything. I'll try the doors down here.'

There were only two doors in the lobby, and one of these was slightly ajar with a sliver of light slanting out. Bill tapped, then pushed it open, saying, 'Anyone there?' His feet crunched on glass and he bent down and picked up the framed picture which lay shattered on the floor. His stomach turned over as he looked at the image of the woman's face.

'Evie,' he muttered, staring at the mischievous blue eyes and blonde hair.

The churning in Bill's stomach eased, the nausea receded and his vision cleared.

He had thought for a moment it was a photograph of Evie. She had the same eyes, the same blonde hair and the same expression. But it was not Evie. It was someone he had never seen before. Still, the likeness gave him a shiver.

The slam of the outside door jolted him. 'Where's the body, then?' The voice was gruff and unfriendly.

Bill sighed and placed the photograph on the table. He had hoped that it would be Doctor Armstrong. She was far gentler in manner than Chisholm, who was obviously past his sell-by date and it showed. But he pasted a smile on his face and turned to meet the old curmudgeon.

'He's at the back of the lobby, doctor.' He did not dare call the police surgeon by his first name as he would have done with Rose Armstrong.

'Hmph! How'm I supposed to see anything back there.' Whisky fumes wafted from his breath.

Bill frowned. The constable apparently had not located a light bulb. 'I can take a bulb from the flat, or we could move the body inside, whichever you prefer. Body's been moved anyway so it doesn't really matter.'

'Who gave you permission to move the body before I got here?'

'Didn't think you'd want to examine it while it was still

dangling from the stairwell. And anyway, what if he'd still been alive?' Not that there had been any doubt in Bill's mind that the man had been long gone.

'Hmph! Just shine your torch on it, that'll do.'

The doctor bent down. He felt for a pulse in the wrist and then the neck; held a mirror to the mouth; placed his stethoscope on the man's chest, and then stood up.

'Dead as the proverbial doornail,' he said. He polished the ends of his stethoscope and slid it into his pocket. 'See you at the post-mortem.' He grinned for the first time.

The bugger knows how much I hate post-mortems, Bill thought grimly. No wonder he was smiling.

Bill returned to examine the John Doe's flat while he waited for the SOCO team to arrive. It was going to be another long night.

4

The Mile was quiet, with only the hum of far-off traffic from Princes Street breaking the early silence. Julie plodded upwards, savouring the freshness of the morning air and the feeling of peace that would vanish as the day wore on.

A slight breeze caught the edge of her gypsy style skirt, swirling the end of it – where the grey merged into pink – around her legs, revealing the straps of her Egyptian style, high-heeled sandals, winding upwards to her knees. Her pink top, cinched round the middle with a grey belt, was the exact same shade as the pink at the bottom of her skirt. While the silk jacket draped over her arm matched the silver-grey of the material before it merged with pink.

If it had not been for the aura of sadness that surrounded her she might have been beautiful, although interesting would have been a more accurate description. Her features were regular, an oval face with a slightly pointed chin, lips neither too thin nor too full, straight blonde hair brushing her shoulders, eyes a misty greyish-blue. But her eyes had a dispirited look, her step lacked bounce, her shoulders drooped and – hidden under the long sleeves of her pink top – her arms bore multiple scars, evidence of the dark place she had been in for the past year.

This sadness had been part of her life for so long now she found it difficult to hang onto former happier times. However, there was a glimmer of hope because Dave had phoned earlier in the week to say he intended to come home so they could talk things over. When he came, it would be up to her to persuade him to stay. Surely all their years of togetherness and their love for each other – which Dave had momentarily forgotten in his obsession with that woman – would count for something.

There was no need for Julie to come into the art gallery so early, but ever since Dave left she had been restless, sleeping little and waking early.

The flat was like a morgue without him there, and she was glad to leave it behind. Besides, she liked the Royal Mile at this time of the morning when it was too early for the sightseers who would later throng its narrow steep street, jabbering in a multitude of tongues, and snapping photos with their obligatory cameras.

The gallery was in a prime position; one of the last buildings before the castle which, perched high on its rock, overlooked Edinburgh. And it would not be long before the first of the tourists arrived, to 'ooh' and 'ah' over the paintings and sculptures.

Julie leaned against the door while she rummaged in her bag for the keys. Her hair spilling forward to obscure her vision caused her hand to still, and brought a sigh to her lips as she remembered how Dave used to run his hands through it, lifting the strands and winding them round his fingers. He had a weakness for blondes. That bitch in Dundee was a blonde as well. She compressed her lips and angrily shoved her hair back behind her ears. He was tiring of her though, she was sure of it, and now her patience had been rewarded and he would soon be home. Still thinking of Dave's return she pushed the heavy double doors open.

Adrian had not arrived yet, which was nothing out of the usual, and Julie busied herself pulling the dust covers off the exhibits. She looked up when the old-fashioned bell that hung over the top of the door, tinkled. Her welcoming smile faltered when she saw the policewoman.

'Can I help you?' She supposed policewomen were allowed to appreciate art as much as anyone else.

'Mrs Julie Chalmers?'

'Yes, that's me.'

'Is there somewhere we could talk?'

Julie stared at her. A feeling of apprehension tightened her chest. 'Have I done something wrong?' she asked, although she could not think what it could be.

'No, no. It's not that. It's just that what I have to say may be a bit upsetting and you might want to sit down.'

'Well, I can't leave the gallery unattended until Adrian gets here, so maybe you'd just better say what it is you've come to say.'

The policewoman pulled a notebook from her pocket and looked at her notes. 'Your husband, would he be David Chalmers?'

Julie nodded, her throat suddenly dry. 'We're separated,' she whispered. 'I haven't seen him for over a year. Has he done something?'

The policewoman looked up from her notebook and stared into the space over Julie's right shoulder. 'I'm afraid I have some bad news for you.' She hesitated. 'It's your husband. He's dead.'

The strength went out of Julie's knees and her fingers tightened on the dust sheet she was holding.

'Dead?' she repeated. 'But he can't be.' It was impossible. He was too young. But there was no mistaking what she had heard. 'Has he been in an accident? Was it his car? I always told him he was foolish to buy that sports car.'

'No, it wasn't an accident. I'm very sorry to have to tell you that he was found hanged last night. It would appear that he took his own life.'

The room spun as a wave of dizziness overwhelmed her. 'But Dave wouldn't do something like that. He's a Catholic,' she said as if that explained everything.

'I'm sorry,' the policewoman repeated, fidgeting with her notebook and shifting her feet.

'How? Where?'

'He was found hanging in the stairwell of the building where he lived. Apparently, he had an argument with a lady friend earlier. One of the neighbours reported he seemed quite disturbed when she left.'

Julie's head spun as darkness descended and the air diminished. She struggled for breath and a band of pain tightened around her chest. The word 'Bitch' punched itself into her brain over and over again.

'Do you want to sit down?'

As the mists in her head cleared, Julie became aware of the policewoman's arm around her.

'No, no, I'm fine,' she muttered, 'I'll be all right now.'

The door swung open and Adrian staggered in with an enormous canvas.

'You should see this, Julie,' he said, leaning the painting against the wall. 'It's absolutely marvellous.' He hesitated when he saw the policewoman. 'Oh, I say, we haven't had a break-in, have we?'

'No.' Julie shook her head. 'It's Dave. He's dead. They're saying he hanged himself.' Her voice broke on the last words and a tear slid down her cheek.

'Oh, you poor thing.' Adrian scurried to her side and wrapped his arms around her.

'I'll go now,' the policewoman said with relief.

Adrian nodded. 'I'll see she's all right.'

'Oh, Adrian. Why would he do a thing like that?'

Adrian's arm tightened around her. 'Who knows why anyone does anything,' he said.

Julie stiffened, pulling away from him, and in a flash of anger, said, 'It's her fault. She's a bitch. I always said she was, but Dave wouldn't listen. And now, she's killed him.'

'You don't know that.'

'Yes, I do. The policewoman said he'd been disturbed after a quarrel with her. He wouldn't have hanged himself if it hadn't been for that.'

'You're upset, Julie. You don't know what you're saying.'

'She should be made to pay for what she's done.'

Adrian looked at her helplessly. 'You ought to go home, Julie. I'll manage the gallery myself today.'

'Home?' Julie said bitterly. 'It hasn't been home since Dave left. And now he'll never return.' She dashed a tear from her cheek with the back of her hand. 'No, Adrian. I don't want to go home. I'll stay here, at least I won't be alone in the gallery.'

The rest of the day passed slowly. Julie went through the

motions, smiling at customers, attending to their needs, trying not to think about Dave, and trying to suppress the anger building within her.

'That's the fourth time you've dusted the bronze fisherman.' Adrian was looking at her with a worried frown on his face. 'I really do think you ought to go home.'

Julie polished the sculpture a fifth time. 'I've been thinking,' she said, without looking at him. 'I should go to Dundee and sort things out.'

'But you've been separated from Dave for the best part of a year now. Can't his lady friend do it?'

'I'm his wife, Adrian, not her. It's up to me to see that things are done properly.'

'But won't it be awkward if she's there?'

Julie's anger flared to a frightening level, and she struggled for breath before saying, 'I hope she is so I can make her face up to what she's done. But I know she won't be.'

'You're in shock, Julie. Go home and rest, you'll feel better for it.'

He plucked her silk jacket from its hanger in the small office they shared and handed it to her.

Julie's shoulders drooped with defeat. Maybe Adrian was right, maybe she would feel better tomorrow, but she doubted it. Shrugging on the silver-grey jacket and knotting a filmy, pink scarf round her neck, she gathered up her Radley handbag.

'Until tomorrow then,' she said, aware of Adrian's worried eyes on her as she left the gallery.

Her heel caught on a cobble as she crossed the road to the narrow pavement. An elderly man caught her elbow. 'That was a near miss,' he said and she smiled her thanks to him, although her thoughts were elsewhere.

The Mile was crowded now, voices yabbered on all sides of her in different tongues and dialects, but she did not hear them. Passing The Hub, she glanced across at the French Bistro just beyond the junction. One of Dave's favourite eating-places. They had been there that last day. The day he left.

It was May Day and he had seemed strange all that day. The sun had been shining and they had eaten lunch while they sat on the terrace and looked down through the iron railings to Victoria Street, far below. But he had only picked at his food, chasing it around the plate with his fork, just eating the occasional mouthful. It was not like him.

'Are you ill?' she had said 'Sickening for something?'

'No, no, I'm fine.' He concentrated on his plate, avoiding her eyes.

Walking down the Lawnmarket afterwards, she had slid her hand into his. He hadn't resisted, but he hadn't clasped it the way he usually did.

His silence made her uneasy and she filled it with inane chatter about anything and everything until they reached the end of The Mound and turned into Princes Street with its heaving crowds.

'Let's go into the gardens,' he said as they passed the National Gallery. 'It's quieter, and there's something I need to tell you.'

The gardens, stretching the length of Princes Street, were at a lower level than the main thoroughfare giving the impression of a sheltered oasis in the midst of the hubbub of city life. They found a spot on the grass to sit, away from the packed benches and wandering visitors.

'I've met someone,' he said, plucking at a blade of grass so he did not have to meet her eyes.

Julie drew a shaky breath and bit her lips. She did not want to hear this.

'She's interesting, dynamic and beautiful,' he continued.

'Do I know her?' It was an effort for Julie to speak and her voice did not sound like her own.

'No, she's not someone you know.' He plucked at the grass. 'She's called Nicole and we're in love.' At last, he looked up. 'I've rented a flat in Dundee and I've left my suitcase at the station. I won't be coming home.'

That was when she had screamed at him, letting loose the emotion that had been churning inside her since his first words.

But he had simply looked at her and walked away.

His words still echoed through her brain, the world slowed, the sun was less bright, and everything her eyes could see was imprinted in Julie's mind, coming back again and again to haunt her.

She leaned against the window-frame of a tartan shop, closed her eyes and saw once more – the young lovers sprawled on the grass; the elderly couple walking past, his stick clicking on the path; the boy kicking his ball; the baby in the pram; the sparrow picking at a crust; the tiny spider climbing a blade of grass – Dave walking away from her.

Rummaging in her bag for her mobile phone, she flicked it open and dialled Adrian's number. 'I won't be coming in to the Gallery tomorrow,' she said. 'I'm going to Dundee.'

Julie felt as if she had been in a trance since the policewoman broke the news to her. Time passed slowly and the night seemed endless.

She slid into that dark place she thought she had left behind, where the pain inside her had been so great the only thing that relieved it was the physical pain she inflicted on herself with a knife – carving her arms over and over again, then picking at the scabs that formed to prevent the cuts from healing.

The psychologist who counselled her had explained that the physical pain from self-harming was something she used to mask the torment inside her and that the only way to stop would be to find a replacement for that physical pain.

It made sense, so she started going to the gym, punishing her body with a drastic exercise regime. But it was when she started running that things gradually grew better. She ran and ran until she broke through the pain barrier. Then she pushed further until she thought she was on the brink of death.

That was when she started to come to terms with her inner anguish and became calmer. She stopped cutting herself and started to lead a comparatively normal life again, although the ache for Dave was still there.

But the pain had returned, taking her back to that dark place, and now she was in Dundee harbouring thoughts of vengeance against the woman she held responsible for Dave's death. How she'd got there was a blank. She could not remember going to the station, getting on the train, nor even how she got to Dave's flat. But here she was, sitting in his living room and talking to his landlady.

The woman sighed. 'Such a sad time for you,' she murmured.

Julie nodded, although she had not taken in the sense of the words. Her feelings were too raw.

'If there's anything I can do?'

'There is one thing,' Julie said, and then hesitated because she did not know where the idea had sprung from, nor did she know if it was what she wanted. 'Can I keep the flat on?' There it was, out in the open, whether she wanted to or not. 'Just for a short time,' she added.

The woman hesitated. 'That's a bit awkward,' she said. 'You see I've promised it to the girl upstairs. She's got a young baby and she finds the stairs difficult.' Her voice tailed off. 'I can let you have her flat if you like. It's the same as this one, two rooms with a curtained off kitchen area.'

Julie nodded. The ghost of Dave would probably haunt her if she stayed in this flat. Upstairs would be better. 'That's very kind,' she said.

'When do you think you can move his belongings?' The woman, clearly embarrassed, looked away from Julie. 'It's just that I have to let the girl upstairs know when she can move in.'

'Probably within a week, two at the most,' Julie said, 'will that suit your arrangements?'

'Yes, that will be fine,' the woman said. 'I'll leave the inventory here so you know what to leave behind.' She looked round the room. 'He doesn't appear to have any furniture of his own so the flat shouldn't be too difficult to clear.' She shifted her feet, restlessly. 'I'll leave you to it then.'

'Yes,' Julie said.

After the woman left, Julie sat in the ancient moquette armchair. This was where Dave sat, she thought, running her hand over the chair arm. A puff of dust flew upwards, tickling her nose, making her sneeze.

She pushed herself out of the chair, raising another dust cloud. It wouldn't take long to pack his belongings. He didn't have much, only his clothes. He had never returned to collect all the other things he'd left behind in Edinburgh, which was why she'd always been so sure he would come home.

Tears gathered in her eyes, forcing themselves past her eyelids to trickle down her cheeks. Why did he have to do something so stupid? Why didn't he just come home? Things could have been sorted out.

But it had been beyond sorting. She had known that for months.

She remembered the parting. 'Why do you have to go?' she'd shouted, unable to control her voice.

'It's no use,' he'd said. 'We can't go on like this. It's not honest.'

'You're the one who's cheating.'

He had just looked at her and walked away.

'She's not worth it,' she'd screamed after him, but he hadn't heard her. Now she couldn't even say, 'I told you so.'

Julie laid a suitcase on the unmade bed. She opened it and started to pack his clothes: two suits, four shirts, four ties, seven pairs of socks. He had always liked fresh socks, couldn't bear to wear the same socks two days running. Two pairs of shoes, seven boxer shorts, he'd never liked briefs. No pyjamas.

He had always worn pyjamas with her, except for the honeymoon period. Tears gathered in her eyes. He must have still been in the honeymoon period when he'd had that last argument with Nicole.

The photograph of Nicole lay, alongside its smashed frame and shards of glass, on the table. Julie's eyes kept flicking past it, willing it not to be there. She didn't want to see it, but it would not go away.

She snapped the locks of the suitcase shut then roamed the flat, checking the inventory, and making sure she hadn't left anything of Dave's behind.

But there was still the photograph.

She sat on the edge of the bed and stared at it. Her hand reached out and picked it up, shaking the fragments of glass free. If it hadn't been for this woman, Dave would still be alive. The beginning of a plan started to formulate in her head. Nicole wasn't going to get away with stealing someone else's husband and driving him to his death. Julie was going to make sure she paid.

She slipped the photograph into her pocket. When it was all over, when she'd done what she had to do, she would burn it.

5

Chief Inspector, Andy Turnbull toyed with a pencil. 'You're sure it was suicide.'

'I'm as sure as anyone could be. It looked as if he'd tied the rope to the banister and then thrown himself over.' Bill Murphy closed his eyes in an attempt to block out the image of the hanging man's face. He would be glad when this case was closed.

'Forensic results?'

'Nothing suspicious there.'

'What about the post-mortem?'

The chief inspector leafed through a few pages of the file until he found the report.

'It just confirmed what I'd already surmised.'

'And the Procurator Fiscal?'

'He agrees. He's not pursuing it any further.'

Andy tapped the open file with his pencil. 'Any joy trying to trace the mystery woman?'

'No. Apparently, they had a ding-dong of a row that all the neighbours heard. But he was still alive after she left. According to them he was swearing and kicking walls so they stayed out of the way.'

'You sure none of the neighbours knew who she was?'

Detective Sergeant Bill Murphy nodded his head. 'The guy on the top floor said she was a classy piece of stuff, but that's all we know. He had a wife in Edinburgh, though, so I got the local force to inform her.'

Andy closed the brown cardboard file. 'I guess that's it then.'

Adrian had learned never to open his front door without

checking who was outside, but when he looked through the peephole it took him several moments to realize that the woman standing there was Julie.

He unfastened the safety chain and pulled the door open. Then, clutching his chest in a melodramatic gesture, said, 'Oh my! What have you done to yourself?' He hardly recognized his voice as his shocked eyes took in Julie's haggard expression, cropped hair, and supermarket jeans and sweatshirt. This was not the girl he knew. This was some stranger who inhabited her skin and had robbed her of her ebullient nature.

Julie patted the sleek, short hair clinging to her head like a brown skullcap. 'I don't know if Nicole has ever seen a photo of me so I needed to change my appearance.'

'Why?' Adrian regained control and, removing his hand from his chest, gestured for her to come in.

A blanket of misery passed across Julie's face. 'I don't intend to let Nicole off with what she's done to Dave. He didn't deserve to die, but she does. So I'm going to Dundee for a time. Just long enough to make sure she suffers.'

Adrian stepped back from the look on Julie's face, then took hold of her elbow and guided her into the flat. 'That's silly. How many Julie Chalmers do you suppose there are? She'll know who you are by your name.'

Julie laughed bitterly. 'I'm not that stupid,' she said. 'I'll go back to my own name. I'll be Julie Forbes.'

'It's a pity you hadn't become Julie Forbes when Dave left you.'

'He was going to come back to me.'

'You wish.'

'He was. I know it. Why else would he phone me to say so?'

A tear rolled down Julie's cheek.

'We'd loved each other for such a long time – ever since we were at school together – and love like that just doesn't die.'

Adrian sighed. It was clear to him that Dave had moved on, but Julie had stayed put. And because of that, she was in pain.

'Sit down for a while, love, and make yourself at home. I'll get you a glass of wine, you'll feel ever so better after it, and I've got a rather decent Chablis chilling.'

Julie perched on the edge of the pink brocade sofa twirling the glass between her fingers. It was obvious to Adrian she'd only accepted it to please him.

'This is not the best idea you've ever had.' Adrian sat cross-legged in front of her. His silk pyjamas were a shade darker than the carpet.

'Are you listening to me?'

'What?'

'I said – this is not the best idea you've ever had.' Adrian frowned. 'If you want more time off then, by all means, take it. Sam can fill in at the gallery. He's in between shows at the moment.'

Sam was Adrian's partner. He had just finished a long run at the Playhouse where he'd had bit parts in several musicals.

'How much time?'

'Take a few months, relax, have a holiday. Whatever. You'll soon feel better. After all, you can't be sure Dave was coming back to you, and given a bit of time you'll get over him.'

'That'll give me time to do what I have to.'

Adrian groaned. 'Not a good idea.'

'It won't take long. And if I'm in Dundee it'll just be like a holiday.'

The stubbornness in her voice convinced Adrian she would not be deflected from her purpose.

'I doubt that,' Adrian said drily. 'I don't know what you intend to do, but it doesn't sound good. However, I can see that nothing I say will change your mind.'

Julie laid her wine glass on the coffee table and stood up. 'I'll phone you now and then to let you know what's happening.'

Adrian opened the door for her.

'Take care.'

He stood there for a long time looking down the stairwell before sighing and closing the door. Despite his concern, over what she was planning to do, Julie was a decent person and he hoped she would come to no harm.

Julie's determination did not waver until she moved to Dundee on a thundery August afternoon. Lightning split the skies as if nature itself was admonishing her.

Wet, weary and dispirited she looked round the flat she had been so desperate to rent. How would she ever settle in this bare, dingy place that she now had to call home? Wrapping her arms around her body, she shivered. The only time she had ever felt anything like this damp, clingy cold was when she had been standing beside Dave's grave.

Thoughts and memories of Dave haunted her even though this had not been his flat, for she only had to look at the floor to imagine him in the one downstairs. Her hand tightened on her damp handkerchief as a fresh wave of tears threatened to overwhelm her. She could not back out of her plan; she had to go through with it. She owed it to Dave.

But the plan was little more than a desire to punish Nicole for causing Dave's death, and how she was going to go about it was less clear. She supposed that the first thing to be done was to meet Nicole and become her friend – that was a laugh – get the woman to trust her, and once that was done she would be in a better position to exact vengeance.

Finding Nicole had been as simple as finding the High Street department store, Patrick Drake's, where she worked. The store was massive, so it was quite easy for Julie to hang around, watching and waiting for Nicole.

For three weeks Julie followed her – in the store, around the town, and back and forth to the car park. Julie's only regret was that she had sold her own car as well as Dave's. Damn, she wished Dave had told her Nicole lived in the country, but it was too late, both cars were gone, and she would need all her money now she was no longer working.

Meeting Nicole was slightly more difficult. It wasn't as if

the woman was a sales girl, she was a director of the firm.

The idea, when it came, seemed so simple. It would be risky, and it might not work, but it was worth a try. And, if it did not work, the most it would cost would be her life – and that no longer had any value now that Dave was gone.

Nicole was feeling more vulnerable than usual when she arrived at the store. Scott had been particularly nasty that morning, undermining her confidence with his sarcastic wit, which was always at her expense.

It was at times like this that the burden of guilt over Dave's death was most acute. When she broke up with him she had never imagined he would be so foolish as to take his own life. Nor had she imagined how much she would miss him.

Bracing herself, she entered the store through the revolving doors of the main entrance and strode through the ground floor display area. It was time to assert her authority as an assistant director.

'Who is responsible for this display?' Nicole turned to the floor manager. 'It's the work of an amateur. Get it sorted.'

'Yes, Mrs Ralston. I'll see to it right away.' He snapped his fingers at a salesgirl. 'You heard Mrs Ralston,' he said. 'See to it.'

Nicole stifled a smile and walked away. There had been nothing wrong with the display, but exerting her authority helped boost her self-esteem.

She took the lift to the executive floor, deposited her briefcase and ventured out again. There was nothing to be gained by skulking in her office feeling sorry for herself, and the only way to keep staff on their toes was by regular inspections.

Working her way down, from the top of the store to the bottom, she ended up at the restaurant on the basement floor.

'The coffee wasn't up to your usual standard this morning,' she said to Betty who was in charge. 'See that it's better tomorrow.'

Betty continued to wipe the servery top. 'That's probably because I had to keep an eye on the grocery floor as well. When are you going to get a locum manager while Karen's off ill?'

Nicole frowned and her self-esteem plummeted. Betty never gave her the respect that was her due, but she had been with Drake's for a long time and it would be difficult to get rid of her. 'It's in hand,' she said brusquely. She wasn't about to tell Betty that the only people who had applied so far had been worse than useless.

'Hmph,' Betty said. 'I've heard that before.'

'Just concentrate on your job and leave me to do mine.'

Nicole stalked off through the grocery aisles. It was just as she reached the swing doors to the exit that she felt the prickle at the back of her neck. The feeling she was being watched. She swung round expecting to see Betty glaring after her. But no one was there.

Julie swung the Marks and Spencer bag containing the thick padded jacket. Something, that in normal circumstances, she would never have bought. She thought it would cushion the blow.

She had been trying hard not to think about the risk she was about to take and what the result might be. But now, her hand gripped the carrier bag with unnecessary force and thoughts about what she intended to do filled her mind. She broke out in a sweat. The plan was madness. She should give up before it went any further.

Her feet slowed as she neared Dock Street and her destination. She stopped at the pavement's edge across the street from the car park. It wasn't too late to change her mind. She could turn right and head for Tayside House or retrace her steps up Commercial Street. Closing her eyes for a moment she pictured Nicole's face and smug smile. If she gave up now Nicole would never pay for what she had done to Dave. So, wiping her hands on her jeans, she forced herself to cross the road. She could not turn back now. It was the only way.

The car park covered a large area of ground which was partially beneath the approach roads to the Tay Bridge. Most of it was in the open, but there was a smaller area at the rear which included some parking spaces underneath the road bridge, and beyond that a central grassy area with park benches. The furthest away parking spaces gradually reduced in height as the road above descended from the bridge until only smaller vehicles or motorbikes could use them.

She sidestepped as a car darted out from the exit. It narrowly missed her and the oncoming traffic before it sped up the slip road to the Dock Street dual carriageway. It would have been ironic if she had been hit here. The driver in the next car raised his eyebrows in an unspoken question, but she shook her head and hurried towards the spaces under the bridge's approach road.

Once she was in the shadows she stopped and leant on one of the supporting pillars to catch her breath. Traffic rumbled above her head, but she was hardly aware of it and it did little to impinge on her thoughts or her mood.

She found what she was looking for in one of the furthest away parking spaces, where the section of the roadway above only cleared the top of the sports car with a few inches to spare. Julie smiled grimly when she saw it. How much pressure, she wondered, would it need for a knife to pierce the hood's fabric? And a scratch on the electric-blue bodywork would show up a treat. Running her hand along the shiny surface of the Porsche Boxster, her fingers itched to do the damage. But Julie drew back. She had other plans for Nicole: plans that did not include petty vandalism. When Julie paid her back she would make sure Nicole knew why.

The late afternoon sun was shining down into the compact open area beyond the parking place. Often she had sat there watching Nicole come and go. Nicole had never noticed her. But today was different. The watching brief was over and it was time to put her plan into action. So she withdrew into the shadow of one of the pillars. Her position was ideal for what she had in mind. Nicole would have to drive past this pillar to the exit.

It was over an hour later before Nicole came. Julie listened until her heels stopped clicking on the tarmac, the car door slammed and the engine revved. She risked a quick look and saw the wheels start to move. It was time.

Counting under her breath as she had done every night this week until she had got the timing right, Julie closed her eyes and stepped out in front of Nicole's car.

6

A frisson of excitement shot through him as he watched the other one step in front of the woman's sports car. His heartbeat quickened in time with the motorbike engine which throbbed between his thighs. His palms were sweaty in his leather gauntlets and a fine mist gathered inside his visor.

Such an emotional reaction surprised him. But gradually his pulse slowed and he started to wonder why the other one would have done such a thing.

Once he had identified the chosen one, it had been like it always was when he was on a mission. He had followed her, learning her routines, watching her, and remaining unseen.

But he had not anticipated the other one; this other woman who also watched and followed his chosen one. Why would she do that? Was she also on a mission?

A mist seeped into his brain and he shook his head to clear it. He had to retain clarity of purpose, and surely he would have known. God would have told him.

But the other one was there and there was no doubt in his mind that she also was watching and waiting. Intrigued, he had followed them both.

And now this! There was no reason for it. To deliberately step out in front of the car was an act of stupidity.

Nicole, that was her name, was shaking as she got out of her car. It would only take a moment to rev the engine of the motorbike and send her flying into purgatory, just as she had done with the other one. But he restrained himself. It was too early and there was much to be done. She had not suffered enough.

He revved the motorbike engine and sped past her as she bent over the body.

7

The stiletto heel of Nicole's shoe snapped when she floored the brake pedal. Her heart pounded and adrenalin zipped through her body. Christ, there was no way she'd be able to stop the car before she hit the bloody woman. There was a thud and the engine cut out as the car shuddered to a stop. Nicole stared unbelievingly through the windscreen. But the woman was no longer to be seen.

The knot of sickness gathering in Nicole's stomach rose until she tasted bile at the back of her throat. She must have hit her. She tried to get out of the car but was overcome by a severe dose of the shakes. Closing her eyes Nicole rested her head on the steering wheel.

Where had the woman come from? One minute she'd been driving out of the car park as usual and the next there was this woman right in front of her car. Damn it, maybe she'd killed her.

If only the shaking would stop she would be able to find out.

She gulped in a mouthful of air. Deep breathing, that was the answer. It always helped her when she had to present her ideas to the board. But this was not a bloody board meeting. This was something entirely different. Something she had never experienced before.

Gradually her breathing calmed and she gained enough control of her nerves to stumble out of the car. Swearing under her breath, she hobbled around the bonnet. And that was when the shakes hit her again, for the woman was lying on the ground. And she wasn't moving.

Nicole dropped to her knees. Grasping the woman's wrist she felt for a pulse, but couldn't find it. Either she was dead or she hadn't found the correct spot. She sat back on her heels, feeling vulnerable and at a loss. What would other people do in a situation like this?

A motorbike roared past and she stood up, waving her hands at the rider to stop. But he kept going.

Sinking back to her knees, she placed her hand on the woman's chest. She couldn't detect anything. Then she placed her fingers on each side of the woman's neck – that was what actors in television dramas did – and could have cried with relief when she eventually found a pulse. Just at that moment, the woman's eyelids flickered and she moaned.

'Stay still. It's all right,' Nicole said, although it wasn't all right. She would lose her licence over this and it wasn't her fault. The woman should never have walked in front of the car. 'I'll phone for an ambulance.'

'No! I think I'll be fine if you help me to my feet.'

'But you might have broken something.'

The woman grabbed Nicole's wrist in a vice-like grip, preventing her from standing up.

'No, you don't understand. I can't be taken to hospital. I just can't.'

Nicole, catching a glimpse of fear in her eyes, wondered what she was afraid of. And if she didn't want an ambulance how would she react to police involvement? It would be interesting to find out.

'The police have to be informed about accidents and they'll probably insist on a medical check up.'

The woman's eyes widened. 'No, you mustn't. I'll be all right if you just help me up.'

'But it's an accident. I have to report it.'

'No!' She struggled to a sitting position without releasing her grip on Nicole's wrist.

'Why not?'

'Because he'll find me, that's why.'

'Would that be so awful?'

She laughed bitterly. 'Awful doesn't come into it.'

Nicole's brain raced. Maybe she wouldn't lose her licence after all. But, if she left the woman here and someone else found her, she would really be in trouble for not reporting the accident.

'You can let go now.' Nicole tapped the fingers that grasped her wrist. 'I won't do anything you don't want me to.'

The woman closed her eyes and a flicker of something passed over her face. Nicole supposed it was relief.

'But I can't leave you sitting here.' Nicole wobbled as she stood up, stared for a moment at her ruined shoes and then kicked them off. Reaching out her hand, she said, 'Hold on to me and when I pull, grab hold of the front of the car and push yourself up.'

Grasping her under the arms Nicole heaved, but she was heavier than she expected and she almost fell when the woman slipped sideways.

'I'm sorry. I don't seem able to help myself much.'

'That's all right.' Nicole gritted her teeth as she struggled to regain her balance. If the bloody woman couldn't stand maybe she would have to send for an ambulance after all. But one final heave had her on her feet.

'My bag.' The woman started to lean over.

'Don't!' Nicole grabbed her. 'I'll get it. But let's get you sitting down first.' Nicole, afraid to let go of her in case she fell, helped her to the passenger seat in the car.

'Thanks,' the woman murmured, closing her eyes and allowing her head to flop back against the headrest.

Nicole scooped up her shoes, threw them into the car, and then bent to rescue the bag, but the jacket inside it had spilled out and one of the sleeves was firmly pinned beneath the front tyre. Bloody lucky it hadn't been her arm, she thought, as she reversed the car to release it.

'I'm afraid your jacket's probably ruined.'

'It doesn't matter.'

'Don't you care?'

'No.'

'Where's your car? I'll drive you over to it.'

Something about the woman was making Nicole feel uneasy.

'I don't have a car.'

If she didn't have a car what was she doing in the car park? It didn't lead anywhere.

A chill slithered down Nicole's spine.

'You meant to jump out in front of a car,' she accused. 'Why the hell did you pick mine?'

The woman shrugged. 'It was there and you were driving faster than most of them.'

The weariness in her voice intrigued Nicole and she remembered a time when she too wanted to finish everything. She had a sudden urge to help this woman. Maybe by doing this, she would have done something worthwhile.

'What's your name?' She turned the key in the ignition.

'Julie,' after a moment's hesitation she added, 'Forbes.'

'Well, Julie,' Nicole said with a glow of satisfaction because she was doing something nice. 'You're in no state to take yourself anywhere so I'll drive you home. Just tell me where.'

'You're so kind.'

A slight smile flickered over Julie's lips and, once again, Nicole felt a tinge of unease.

8

Julie suppressed a smile at Nicole's sharp intake of breath when the car slid to a halt outside the tenement.

'This is where you live?'

'Yes, I was lucky to get this flat. It came vacant when a previous tenant topped himself.' She glanced sideways at Nicole but quickly masked it by pretending to have problems unbuckling her seat belt.

Everything was working out beautifully. The staged accident had hurt a bit and she would probably have some bruises to show for it, but the puffa jacket had cushioned the blow. Lucky she had thought of that. And now Nicole was on a guilt trip. And it was about to get worse because Julie had brought her back to the place where Dave had died.

'I'm not making a good job of this,' Julie said breaking into Nicole's trance. 'But my shoulders are sore and I can't get it unbuckled.'

Nicole leaned over and pressed the release button. The belt shot up almost hitting Julie in the face and making her jerk backwards. Nicole didn't seem to notice and she hadn't switched the engine off. Was she getting ready for a quick getaway?

Julie eased herself forward in the seat but made no move to leave the car. Nicole was not going to get off as easily as that, she thought grimly. She hadn't risked her life to let her escape now. It was of the utmost importance that Nicole accompanied her upstairs, so the moan, when she moved, would have to be good.

Julie twisted in her seat and reached for the door handle. 'Ow!' She gasped and clenched her teeth. She hadn't needed to act, the pain in her shoulder and hip was all too real.

Nicole frowned. 'You sure you haven't broken

something?'

'Not entirely,' Julie said, willing Nicole to get out of the car and help her. 'But I think it's only bruising. I'll be able to judge better when I get inside.'

Nicole sighed and switched off the engine.

'I'd better help you.'

Not before time, Julie thought, but only said, 'Thanks, that would be very kind of you.'

The entry door swung shut behind them and Julie, leaning heavily on Nicole's arm, shuffled along the corridor leading to the stairs. Nicole slowed as she drew level with the door that had been Dave's. Julie saw a flicker of panic in her eyes, and couldn't resist saying, 'That's where he lived.'

Nicole flinched. 'Who?'

'The tenant I was telling you about, the one who topped himself.' Julie steered Nicole towards the stairs. 'Hanged himself just there,' she said, pointing to the stairwell. 'They said he tied the rope to the banister on the landing up there and then jumped.'

A vision of Dave, legs dangling, body swaying and face contorted rose in Julie's mind. She shuddered and blinked back the tears pricking behind her eyelids. For, although she could feel Nicole cringing at her side, thinking of Dave was hurting her more than Nicole.

'Does it bother you?' Nicole's voice was strangely quiet.

Julie shrugged. 'Not really. I didn't know him and I don't believe in ghosts.' In her mind, she apologized to Dave for denying him.

'My flat's one up.' Clenching her teeth she climbed the stairs. It was time to build on Nicole's guilt and sow the seeds for the relationship with her that was essential for Julie's plan to succeed.

'This is it,' she said, watching Nicole's expression. The flat was a replica of the one downstairs with which Julie was sure Nicole must have been familiar.

Nicole's expression didn't falter. 'If you're sure you're all right I really should get back . . .'

'Don't go just yet.' Julie's brain whirled trying to think of a way to prevent Nicole from leaving. 'I was going to make a cup of hot, sweet tea – for the shock, you know – but I don't know if I can handle the kettle. It's my shoulder, you see.' Slow down she told herself, she was starting to babble.

'You really should see a doctor,' Nicole said. 'You may have dislocated your shoulder.'

'No! No doctors!'

'Why ever not?' Nicole sounded exasperated.

'I daren't do anything that could lead to him tracing me.'

A spark of interest flared in Nicole's eyes. 'Why would seeing a doctor lead to your being traced?'

'He works for the health service, you see. He has access to medical records.' Julie embroidered on the lie she had started in the car park.

'Would it be so awful if he traced you?'

Julie shuddered. 'If you think these bruises are bad you should see the ones he's given me. I've had broken arms, black eyes and once he even broke my jaw. So the answer is yes, it would be awful if he found me. He'd probably kill me.

'It wouldn't be so bad, but I left a damn good job in Aberdeen – I was the manager of a fancy goods store – and I had to leave it all behind. I can't even access my bank accounts or he'd know where I was. And if I don't get a job soon I don't know what I'll do.'

Julie had chatted with Betty who worked in the restaurant and knew that Drake's Department Store needed a food hall manageress. She hoped Nicole would take the bait.

Nicole poured the tea she had made into two china mugs. She ladled several spoonfuls of sugar into Julie's. 'Here, get this down you,' she said, 'it'll help with the shock. And then we can talk about how I can maybe help you.'

Julie suppressed a shudder. She hated sweet tea.

Three weeks later, in mid-September, Julie started work as manageress of Patrick Drake's food hall and, as she complimented herself on succeeding with the first stage of her plan, she plotted out the next stage. But it would be a long, slow process and would require a great deal of guile and all her resources to become Nicole's friend.

PART TWO

November 2008

9

He had been following her for more than four months and now felt he knew her better than she knew herself.

She was an evil woman and the voice had instructed him to watch her. It was his mission in life to ensure she did not grow too strong and destroy everyone.

He could not allow her to grow stronger. That would be disastrous. So he watched and waited And although he made sure she could feel his presence, she never saw him. But he was certain she knew, certain she could feel him there, always behind her, always watching. He could tell by the way she looked over her shoulder, particularly when she was somewhere quiet, or in a dark and lonely place.

It was quiet now, in the garden of her house: the kind of quiet where the wind holds its breath, and small animals of the night freeze into silent watchfulness.

The ground was soft beneath his feet, but not too soft. There would be frost tonight. He could feel it in the air and see it reflected in the bright ring imprisoning the moon in its hazy grasp. But he must depart before the grass silvered round his footprints, for he must not leave any trace of his presence, except for the shiver down her spine.

He hid in the dark shadows of the shrubbery, merging with them until he became a shadow. The aroma of frosted earth nipped his nose mingling with the odour of the decaying blackbird lying at his feet. He inhaled deeply, savouring the fascinating mixture of smells. There was nothing more fragrant to him than the smell of death and decay.

He watched her enter the house, fumbling in her bag for the key. As usual, it had slipped to the bottom, merging with the pens, nail scissors, combs and the other bits and pieces that jumbled about there.

He knew what was in her bag, just as he knew what was in every room of her house and every inch of her office. He knew what she had in her dirty washing basket at this very moment, and was familiar with the smell of her and everything she used. He could close his eyes and know she was there just from her perfume and her more intimate body smells.

She felt safe at home. This was her castle, her protection. She had not yet suspected it had been invaded, and that even here he was watching.

That would soon change, for the time was drawing near.

The house was in darkness, a brooding, pulsating darkness that pleased him. However, he knew the light in the lounge would come on in a moment for she always followed the same routine. He prepared for this by moving further into the shadows. He did not want her to find him here. Not yet anyway. But the temptation to let her know he was watching her was strong tonight. He wanted to destroy the illusion that even here, where she thought she was safe, there was nowhere she could go to escape him.

But the time was not yet right.

The light spilled out over the grass and he watched as she emptied her briefcase onto the table and sorted through the papers, selecting the ones she wanted to work on. Her workload seemed heavy, but he did not feel sorry for her. He knew that those with power had to pay a price. And that price was linked strongly to the expectations of those who were even more powerful. She had chosen what she wanted to be. But he knew this was not enough for her and she wanted even more. She wanted to be the one who would exact the price. He could not allow that to happen because then, she would take over everything.

Power! The word buzzed in his brain like a saw. When she did attain the power she desired he would have to stop her before it became too great and swallowed everything in its path.

She dimmed the lounge light, flicked on a table lamp,

pulled a chair over to the table and, resting her chin on her left hand, started to read. A halo of light surrounded her, making her dark-blonde hair glint with the reflected glow. It straggled onto her shoulders where it separated into strands which seemed to have no connection with each other. The fingers of her right hand opened and closed in a restless rhythm and eventually, she moved her hand upwards, reaching into her hair to tease the ends round and round her fingers.

He wondered whether she could sense his presence and if so, why she never closed the curtains or put blinds on the windows. But she was arrogant. She probably assumed she could not be overseen here, where she felt so safe. She had probably chosen to live in this house because of its location in the countryside, its high walls and electrically operated gate, which, she foolishly thought, provided her with privacy.

The house reflected the woman. She called it a bungalow, but it was larger with wings and extensions sprawling in all directions. It was ostentatious and smelled of money, just as she did.

And yet, it was vulnerable in its isolation in the same way that she was vulnerable. She was feeling vulnerable now. He could see it in the little girl lost look that only appeared when she thought she was alone. At these times she appeared to be on the verge of crying, but never actually gave in to it. In any case, he had come to the conclusion the vulnerability was a façade, another tool she used to wield her power. He had seen her using it, so he knew. There were times when she presented her vulnerable image to others, but when she did so she would wait until she had the other person's sympathy, then she would stamp on them. Flatten them. Disintegrate them. He was not going to fall into that trap.

It was the power image, the one she presented at work that had marked her out as the one. The voice in his head reminded him of those other women who had encroached on his life – women who had no right to be powerful, just as she had no right to be powerful. He had not known about the vulnerable part of her in the beginning. Although initially this vulnerability had confused him and played games with his mind, it was not long before he realized it was a trick. In some ways, it made the plans he had for her even better.

God had given him his gift of being able to identify Satan's chosen ones. He had also provided the voice to instruct and give him permission to act. But his calling to God's service weighed heavily on him.

Sometimes he wanted to be like other men, seeking out the beautiful, those with style, those who attracted him. But he knew this was not possible for him because he was not like other men. He had no option but to accept God's will – and God had chosen this woman and instructed him to watch her.

Light wafted over the trees in the orchard, shimmering over the leaves like some ray from an alien spacecraft and he knew a car had entered the gates and would appear round the curve in the drive in just a few moments. He merged further into the shadow of the bushes where he would not be seen, although he knew this was not a necessity because he was invisible. Still, it was always better to play safe because he never knew when his cloak of invisibility would fail him and, if the husband discovered him, he did not know what would happen.

The car crunched to a halt in front of the door. A spray of loose stones pattered off the ornate tiled entrance with bullet-like precision. The engine had barely stopped before the man unfolded himself from the driving seat unaware of his shadow which expanded upwards and outwards until it was a giant phantom shape, dancing and jumping behind him.

Doors slammed, and from where he crouched he could see the woman collect her papers and stuff them in her briefcase. He could almost hear the pitter-patter of alarm in her breast for she was afraid of her husband. Why he did not know because she feared no one else.

She was only halfway out of her chair when the door of the lounge thudded open. He could hear the jumbled sound of raised voices and see the anger in both their faces.

It was good to see her suffer.

He thought for a moment the husband was going to strike her and was disappointed when he did not. Maybe if the husband knew about the other man he would.

After a few moments she slammed out of the room and he imagined her running down the central corridor. He timed it in his mind and knew the exact moment the light would snap on in the kitchen, for the woman and her husband always fought about the same thing, her failure as a housewife and her shortcomings in seeing to his needs.

Often he felt like applauding the husband for his efforts to make her bow down to a higher authority. But she never really relinquished her power to him. Her anger was evidence of that.

His brain hurt with the buzzing of the power word and he pressed both hands against his head. He had to stop the saw rotating and grinding its message into the core of his being, and it would only stop when he had completed his mission. She had to be stopped from increasing her power.

That was why his mission was to stand here in the cold, darkness of the night and continue watching her. She must not increase her power any further or they were all doomed.

10

Julie ignored the dagger of pain that knifed through her chest every time she breathed. She jogged on, punishing her body and legs with each step she took. It helped to quieten that other pain. The pain she felt every time her thoughts turned to Dave. The pain that never seemed to lessen despite the passage of time.

She seemed to have been running forever and hadn't noticed when the dusk turned into darkness. Or when the moon decided to look down on her with an enigmatic gaze that was less visible tonight because of the shimmering haze surrounding it. Once she'd thought the face of the moon was friendly, that it smiled down at her. But that was in the past. Now she was thankful for the haze so she could not see its baleful frown.

In her present mood, she was glad the streets were dark and empty and, apart from the distant hum of traffic, silent except for the thud of her feet. She concentrated on that tiny pocket of noise, measuring each thud to the beat of her heart, the only spark of life in the deadness of her soul.

Julie's feet faltered in their stride when she reached the gate leading to Balgay Park and the observatory and, although she often ran there during the daytime, at night the shadows were deep, appearing to shift and change shape.

She had shadows of her own with which to cope: terrible shadows that had changed her life out of all recognition. They had become part of her life when the blackness gripped her heart, threatening to overwhelm her. It was a seductive blackness, which beckoned to her, tempting her to tread paths she was reluctant to follow.

Her breathing slowed, although the pulse beat vibrating inside her ears and resounding through her head did not quite silence the whispered invitation of the trees for her to join them. The sharp aroma of wood and leaves tantalized her nostrils, inviting her into their dark embrace. Afraid she would succumb to the temptation, afraid she would be swallowed up by the darkness, she turned her back on the park gates and started to run.

She was not ready to face the dark alone. She needed street lights in the same way she needed her bedroom lamp when she was sleeping. It was silly, she knew, but she had a feeling that if she let the dark swallow her she would be finished.

The street sloped gradually upwards. Icicles of air invaded her mouth, chilling her teeth and freezing her throat. Each breath jabbed icy needles into her lungs before exiting in painful gasps which echoed through her head like a drumbeat. But she couldn't stop running, pushing herself past her limits until she was no longer conscious of the effort of putting one foot in front of the other. She ran in a semi-conscious state, neither seeing nor feeling until she came to the roundabout and saw the sprawl of Ninewells Hospital below her.

The large, modern complex, glowed, rather like an over-illuminated Christmas tree, a parody of the pain it contained. This was where they might have taken Dave if they had found him in time. But they hadn't, and she blamed Nicole for that.

Julie shook her head, refusing to allow the tears to gather. Instead, she thought of Nicole. Pain rose in her chest like a clenched fist, rising to her throat until she gagged. The hate resurfaced. An overwhelming, all-consuming hate, for Nicole, the woman who had taken him from her and whom Julie held responsible for his death.

Turning her back on the hospital complex, she forced her feet to run back down Glamis Road and on into Arran Road.

A car cruised by, slowing as its headlights washed over her, but she did not look up and it picked up speed again until its red tail lights disappeared round the next bend in the road, leaving only the smell of its fumes in Julie's nostrils.

On she ran, from one street light to the next, with only the sound of her pounding feet for company. The short gasps of her breath rasped in time with the strange singing noise in her ears, as once again she pushed herself to her limits.

She was concentrating now on putting one foot in front of the other, like a child learning to walk, and still, she ran. It was the only thing to do to muffle her inner pain.

Her thighs and body ached each time her Reebok-shod feet slapped off the flagstones in a rhythmic pattern that resounded in the quiet evening air. If she stopped now she might not have the energy to start again, but the lights at the Loons Road junction were in her favour and she jogged across.

Lochee High Street had its usual complement of late night revellers and kids, bunching in groups, trying to outdo each other with a show of bravado.

Julie, however, was so turned into her inner thoughts and pain that she was deaf to their catcalls and jeers.

Knowing she was almost home if the flat she rented could be called home, she slowed her pace until she came to a stop. Leaning over, she placed her palms on her quivering knees. Greedily she gulped in knife sharp air which seared its way into her lungs, while her whole body trembled, forcing her to lean against the wall.

The cold grabbed her neck and breasts. Her clothes clung damply to her skin in a chilling embrace while her cap of brown hair sculpted itself wetly to her head. Sweat trickled down her forehead. She blinked it away from her eyes for fear it would initiate the tears she was trying so hard to prevent.

Gradually her breathing became more even and the pain lessened.

Shivering, she turned into the doorway leading to her flat.

The outside door swung shut and the darkness of the lobby and stairwell swallowed her. Icy fingers of panic clutched at her, grabbing her chest and squeezing. In her mind's eye, Dave swung slowly in the stairwell waiting for a rescue that never came.

She stood, unable to move, reluctant to push herself forward, but not wanting to go back outside. And, although she knew it was only the stair light bulb which must have popped again, and that Dave was not really there, it did not help the irrational burst of fear engulfing her.

'Don't be silly,' she muttered to herself, more to hear her own voice than anything else. 'There are other people living in the building. They would hear if anything untoward happened.' She had no idea what this nameless happening might be, and they had not heard Dave when he needed their help. Stretching out her hand, she slowly felt her way along the hall until she reached the stairs and then, grasping the banisters, pulled herself upwards to safety.

After what seemed an eternity, she fumbled her key into the lock and stepped into the austere security of her flat.

The harsh light from the bare electric bulb in the middle of the room bounced off a table, two cheap moquette armchairs and a two-seater sofa.

The sink and a baby Belling cooker sat in an alcove which should have been covered by the curtain which hung limply to the side, but was not, because Julie hadn't bothered to pull it shut.

A tiny bedroom held a tumbled, unmade bed and two suitcases containing her clothes, which she had never fully unpacked during the three months she'd been living here.

She loosened the laces of her Reeboks, prised them off, stepped up onto the bed, and bouncing over it in two steps jumped to the floor and into the tiny toilet and shower room. Tearing her clothes off, she slung them onto the bed stepped into the shower and turned on the taps. The ice-cold water needled her skin, shocking it into another kind of pain. A physical pain, reminding Julie she was still alive even though Dave was dead.

She pressed her head to the wet tiles while the water gradually heated. Dry sobs overtook her. Her body, racked with painful spasms, shuddered uncontrollably.

Gradually she brought herself under control, but the emptiness of the shower with no Dave to press in beside her, rub her back and make glorious soapy love, reflected the emptiness in her heart. There was nothing but her own wet body and the memory he had loved someone else, and that love had led him to eternity. An eternity where there was no room for Julie.

Julie turned her face into the flowing water, letting it run down and over her, and repeating the vow she had made over and over again. 'Vengeance shall be mine.' Julie was not sure where the quotation came from, but it seemed apt and she recited it again. 'Vengeance shall be mine.'

11

Nicole, fighting the tears pricking behind her eyelids, ran blindly down the corridor.

The bastard was always doing it, making her feel guilty, telling her she wasn't looking after him properly. He wanted a skivvy, a doormat who would jump to his bidding, not the independent woman that Nicole had become.

'But why should I?' she muttered, throwing open the kitchen door. Giving vent to her pent-up anger, she slammed it shut behind her. It made her feel slightly better, although she knew Scott would complain later. 'I don't bloody well care,' she screamed, knowing he couldn't hear her.

She clattered the wok onto the hob of the cooker and splashed some oil into it, leaving it to get hot while she hurriedly selected a bottle of wine and rummaged in the fridge. Thank God for instant food. She threw the ingredients into the pan, shaking it, so they merged and mixed into an attractive concoction.

The gas flame licked around the bottom of the pan until the oil began to smoke, making the mixture sizzle and spark. Nicole adjusted the flame, stirring, shaking the pan, and muttering over the brew, like a witch casting a spell that would make Scott a more understanding man. And it would, because after he had eaten he would mellow and be his usual charming self. Then maybe, just maybe, they would make love in the massive bed she'd had specially made for them. And the lovemaking would be all the better because of the fight they'd had. There was something about a good fight and a dominant man that made her as horny as hell, although she would never tell him that.

She shook the wok for the last time, then lowered the gas beneath it even further so she could leave it long enough to rummage in the kitchen drawer for the silver cutlery. Grabbing a pair of linen napkins, she ran through to the dining room and started to set the table wishing, not for the first time, that Scott would at least share some of the chores. But the wish was a non-starter because he never would. It was not in his nature. She was out of breath by the time she'd stopped rushing between the dining room and kitchen and had time to inspect the table, dim the lights and put a match to the candles. The wine glasses glinted in the candlelight, the crystal throwing facets of the glow upwards and outwards. Surely Scott would have nothing to complain about this time. Surely it was as near perfection as he could expect.

Resentment flared, burning in her chest like the flame of the candle, as she thought of how critical he could be even when everything was perfect. Not for him a cold or reheated meal prepared by the daily maid and left in the fridge, a TV dinner on his knee in front of the television, or a casual meal at the kitchen table. It had to be something special prepared by his wife's own hands and served on the dining room table with good wine, the best silver and candles flickering in the antique candelabra. But, Nicole had to admit, now the table was ready it had a certain feel of class and it helped her forget her more earthy roots.

It was those roots which made her vulnerable to Scott's criticism and exposed the lack of self-esteem she successfully hid from everyone else. Scott knew only too well how to undermine her tough exterior, and he delighted in seeing her revert to the insecurities of her childhood. But tonight she was damned if she was going to give him that pleasure.

Scott was where she expected him to be, sprawled on the lounge sofa with his shoe-clad feet resting on a cream, silk cushion.

'Dinner's ready,' she murmured, walking to him and leaning over to kiss his forehead.

He reached up and grasped one of her wrists. Tightening his grip, he twisted until she was forced to her knees.

'Not before time. One of these days I'll come home and it'll be on the table waiting.'

Releasing her arm he swung his feet to the ground and stretched to his full height, making her crane her neck to see his face. He smiled at her, the tenderness in his expression transforming him into the Scott she loved.

'Come on then,' he said, 'what are you waiting for? Now it's ready we'd better eat it.'

Scott attacked the food on his plate with a ferociousness that reflected his attitude to life. It was as if there were a fire and an anger burning within him that needed to be stoked. She watched him, surreptitiously, but it would not have mattered if she had laid down her fork and stared. He would not have noticed.

Sometimes she wondered about her feelings for him. Although she was sure she loved him when they were writhing in each other's arms at night, she was not so sure afterwards, when he turned away from her. She wanted him now with a desire that warmed her, making her glow with the depth of her need for him. It reminded her of earlier times when her passion was for him alone. Times when she did not need other men to fill the emptiness that crept over her more frequently now. An emptiness she never seemed able to fill.

She remembered him as he had been sixteen years ago when first they met. She'd loved him then with an unquenchable passion and couldn't quite believe it when he had wanted to marry her. He'd been older and more experienced than the other boyfriends she'd known. And she had been a sexually-naïve, fifteen-year-old child who thought herself grown-up. She remembered thinking he had seemed so sophisticated and mature and she couldn't understand why he had wanted her, an awkward, skinny girl who was too frightened to speak and couldn't believe he was real. Even now he was still handsome, although he had passed his forty-first birthday. His features were strong and well-defined, with a straight nose overshadowing lips which were on the full side and a chin that jutted outwards a little too far. And she knew, without him raising his eyelids to look at her, that his eyes were dark brown with a sensual, magnetic quality that seemed to hypnotize and fascinate. They could sparkle with anger, smoulder with lust or penetrate with a glare. But above all, they could paralyse with a stare rather like a snake hypnotizing its prey. His eyes were what made his face so attractive and alive, and she often felt they were what held her to him.

Forcing herself to look away she glanced at the window, although it was too dark to see outside. A slight movement made her put her fork down with a clatter. She half rose from her chair.

'Something wrong?' Scott looked up from his plate.

'No . . . well, I'm not sure . . . I thought for a moment someone was outside.'

Scott pushed his chair back and strode to the window. 'Who'd be out there? We're not expecting anyone, are we?'

Nicole did not want to provoke him, so she said, 'I probably imagined it, but I could swear I saw the shadows move.'

'How can you see shadows move? That's impossible. Anyway, it's too dark out there for you to have seen anything, but I suppose I'll have to go out and check.' He threw his napkin on the table and strode out of the room.

'It's not really necessary,' she murmured, but he was gone.

A few minutes later he tapped on the window and she could see the outline of his face as he pressed it to the glass. His lips moved and she could just make out the words. 'There's nothing out here.' She nodded in response and hoped his foray outside hadn't made him angry.

He vanished from sight, reappearing in the dining room with a wide smile on his face. 'Silly little woman,' he said in a disparaging tone, and she knew he was all right.

However, she was not.

The resentment rose in her like a tide of bile because he had assumed the role he enjoyed most, that of protector and master of the house. She wished he had just stayed angry.

She could cope with that, but not this, never this, the patronizing, belittling attitude he adopted towards her, which made her feel he was laughing at her.

She fought against her anger. If she allowed it to take over it would spoil their evening together and he would stomp off, in the sulks, to one of the spare bedrooms. After all, it was not as if she didn't know why he had to act the way he did. She knew only too well. It was his way of suppressing his feelings about her being the main provider, the payer of the bills, the breadwinner, whilst he churned all his profits back into his software business in a determination to be the biggest and the best. On paper, he was probably a millionaire, but that was only figures it was not the folding stuff. And so he took it out on her.

'Sit down and finish your dinner,' she said, modulating her voice so he would not detect the resentment. 'Then we can have a brandy in the lounge. I managed to find a rather nice one in that specialist wine shop that's just opened.'

The rest of the evening passed without any further unpleasantness, although now and again Nicole shivered as she imagined watching eyes in the darkness outside. She said nothing to Scott, not wanting him to make any more disparaging remarks about silly, nervous females.

Later, in bed, when he reached for her she fleetingly thought of turning her back to him, but as usual her love for him, or lust, she was not sure which, flared through her body with a heat that made it pliable and moist. Opening her arms she pressed her body against his, twining her legs around him so he could not escape her. In this, at least, she could retain her power over him.

The moon filtered its silvery glow through the bedroom window dusting everything with an eerie frosting. Nicole had wanted him to close the curtains, but Scott refused. 'You're like a little cry-baby afraid of the dark,' he taunted and, although she'd glared at him, she hadn't argued.

Nicole had been acting strangely tonight. First, there had

been her anger – although he'd rather enjoyed that – and then her insistence that there was a prowler outside. He could almost smell her fear and it gave him a perverse pleasure to ridicule her. It was for the same reason he had made her sleep with the window open and the moon shining on their lovemaking. There had been a moment when he'd thought she would refuse, but she didn't. She never did.

Scott liked the quiet of the night, the dark, and most of all the solitude. It was restful and allowed him to be the man he had always been. Recently he'd felt swamped by Nicole who seemed to be an entirely different person to the girl he had married. He lay in the dark and acknowledged just how tired he had become of her voice, her demands and her needs.

A moonbeam bathed Nicole's face, spreading upwards to silver the hair fanned over the pillow in frosted strands. She was almost beautiful in a sensuous kind of way, although it was a beauty that no longer appealed to him.

A flash of anger stirred in his gut. It appealed to other men though, and he was sure she was making a fool of him again. If he found out who it was he would take care of him, in the same way he'd taken care of the last one.

Scott turned over, so he didn't have to look at Nicole puffing the air out of her mouth in the beginnings of a snore, and wondered where the little girl he had married had gone. He had to admit though, that she was still fantastic in bed, even if her breasts were too full and her hips too curvy.

His thoughts turned to his last visit to Manchester and to Emma. Now there was an attractive girl, small and with the body of an adolescent, for although she was twenty-one, she looked fourteen. His wife certainly could not compare with Emma, because Nicole's body had developed a voluptuousness that did not appeal to him.

He only stayed with Nicole because of her success and her ability to bring in a top salary. In some ways it made him feel less of a man, but although he was usually reluctant to admit this, it also made her indispensable. It was Nicole's money that left him free to invest and expand his own business, but the day would come when he didn't need her anymore and then it would be goodbye Nicole, and he could plan a future with Emma.

Nicole muttered in her sleep, turning over and slinging her arm around his waist. It felt alien and uncomfortable, sending a shiver through him. Gently he lifted her arm off his body and slid out of the bed. A lock of hair flopped over his face and he reached onto the bedside table feeling for a scrunchie to fasten his hair behind his head in its familiar pony-tail.

Soft carpet pile tickled his toes while cool air bathed his skin. He tucked the duvet around Nicole's naked body and, reaching for his bathrobe, crept out of the bedroom.

The house throbbed with silence as he walked barefoot to his study. Once inside he swung gently in his swivel chair and powered up the computer. It came alive with a steady hum, the screen flickering in the dark, competing with the moonlight. Scott turned his attention to the chat rooms. There was no competition. He would rather communicate with his computer than watch the moon any night.

Several hours passed before he returned to the bed he shared with Nicole.

12

She had seen him. He had not meant to let her see him. But, remembering the startled look in her eyes, he shivered with pleasure.

There had been scepticism in her husband's eyes when he crossed the room to look out the window. The man had not seen him though. He was too quick and clever for him.

Now he lay on the earth under the windowsill inhaling the smell of mould until it filled his nostrils and intoxicated him with its aroma. But he knew he could not stay there because, even though the husband did not believe, he was coming outside to look. He could not let the husband see him, or he would lose his hold of fear over the woman.

Tree branches beckoned to him from the orchard and he slid beneath their protective arms. He slipped from tree to tree until he reached his own special tree: the one with the massive, spreading branches reaching over the wall, allowing him access to the grounds.

He lay along a branch, moulding himself to it until he was almost a part of the tree itself. He watched the husband leave the house and enter his territory: the territory of the night and of the dark.

The husband was a fool. A simpleton who could not even check the grounds properly, and never suspected his presence here in the tree. So, he watched and waited while the man pranced around and made faces at his wife through the window.

Fool!

Snakelike, he slid out of the tree and crawled to the window when the man returned to the house. The woman was not pleased. He could see it in her face. But she bowed down to her husband and hid her feelings behind a mask.

He waited and watched. He saw her use her sex to enslave the man. It was the way she wielded her power. Afterwards, he saw the husband escape from her bed. He did not blame him. The man probably sensed her power, her desire to enslave him and make him do things against his will, like the evil deed he had done for her that dark summer night which now seemed so long ago.

He continued to watch, for this was when the real demons appeared. He could see them on her face as she slept. They made her toss and turn, although she did not wake until after the man returned to sleep beside her.

The man would tame her demons for a time. But they would come back again because she had the power.

Only he could kill the demons for all time. And he was the only one who could take her power away from her. It was his mission. Given to him by God.

A slight breeze ruffled through the trees and bushes, the night was almost over and soon it would be dawn. Like all nocturnal creatures, he would have to leave. So he sidled into the orchard, up the tree and over the wall.

He had things to do before dawn.

13

Patrick Drake's Department Store was one of the most impressive buildings in Dundee. It spread over a whole block of the High Street with large display windows in three streets, and reached backwards, almost to Whitehall Crescent, at its rear. Not only did it occupy so much ground space, but it also stretched upwards for five stories and down for one. If you counted the bottom basement, where there were heating ducts and a conglomeration of pipes and wires servicing the upper regions, then the store extended downwards for two levels.

Julie had been working there for the past two months, thanks mainly to Nicole's guilt trip over the accident; she was in charge of the food hall which occupied most of the basement floor. The restaurant which took up the rest of the space was managed by her friend Betty, whose cooking skills brought a steady stream of customers downstairs. There was also the coffee shop one floor up, in one corner of the ground floor, which served the best of coffees, a selection of teas, and tempting cream cakes.

Julie always arrived at the store in the morning before any of the other section managers, although there was no need for this. She liked to ensure that her section was ready when the doors opened. Besides, it gave her the chance to have an early cup of coffee before getting down to the business of the day.

Early morning staff entered through a rear door at the back of the building. The alley leading to this door was vastly different from the sparkling appearance of the frontage and was invariably strewn with papers, rubbish, and condoms left behind by the previous evening's amorous seekers after privacy.

At the rear of the alley, beyond the door, a stone staircase descended to the subterranean depths of the lower basement. Two large iron rubbish skips leaned against the railing which separated the stairs from the main body of the alley and, depending on the day of the week, these were either overflowing or almost empty. However, they never lost their stink of rotting produce and other unidentifiable smells that made Julie think something had died and not been buried.

Julie had tried holding her breath as she walked up the alley, but could never hold it long enough, so she compromised and held it, just before she came to the door.

Lately, a tramp had taken up residence in the alley, probably because it was reasonably quiet and dark at night and provided shelter from the cold wind that rushed up the River Tay. The security staff did their best to move him on, but he always returned, and each morning he seemed to be huddling ever nearer to the door recess.

This morning he looked frozen as he squatted on the frosty pavement in his huddle of tattered clothing, paper and cardboard, over which he had pulled a dirty blanket.

Julie shivered at the thought of how cold he must be and feared that some morning she would find him beyond help.

Most of the staff seemed frightened of him and gave him a wide berth, but Julie did not share their fear and could only pity him. Maybe that was because she'd been accustomed to tramps in Edinburgh, sitting in Princes Street with their backs against shop frontages, their begging bowls, or whatever they were using for begging bowls, in front of them. Despite being used to them though, she'd always had a niggling feeling that no one should have to beg, and she often suspected that what they wanted was money for drink or drugs. So, while she was sorry for them she never threw money in their caps, although she sometimes slipped them a bar of chocolate or a sandwich.

This tramp, however, did not have a begging bowl or a cap or anything else in front of him. He was just there, a miserable bundle of rags, inviting sympathy rather than fear.

Julie's heels clacked off the paving stones, throwing an

echo upward between the buildings the alley sliced its way through. It was deserted except for the tramp and herself.

She paused as she drew level with him. For some reason she always expected him to look up and acknowledge her presence, but he remained bundled in his makeshift bedding giving no indication he knew she was there.

A flurry of wind teased at the edge of her coat making her shiver. She wondered how he must feel as the awfulness of being cold and having nowhere to go forced its way into her consciousness. But he was always there no matter how bad the weather. This alley was his, although he never argued and never objected when the security guard came out and hustled him on his way. He simply moved on, although they all knew he would be back once the store closed down.

The tramp, in his cocoon of blanket, paper and cardboard, was motionless as Julie walked past him, and for a moment she wondered if he was still living.

An unwanted memory of Dave flickered and returned to haunt her. It seemed that one day he had been a living, breathing man and then, in the blink of an eye, he'd been gone.

The bundle heaved slightly and she knew her fears were groundless, although it reminded her of the level of her obsession with death. An obsession she knew would consume her until she laid Dave's memory finally to rest. And that would never happen until she had dealt with Nicole.

A bell was cemented into the stone of the door surround, a large grey button attached to a heavy electric cable that reached upwards and vanished into the building somewhere above her head. She pressed it and, although she couldn't hear anything, imagined the sound wriggling its way up the cable and into the building.

'Morning, Julie. All ready for a new day then?' The security guard who opened the door smiled at her.

She smiled back. She liked Harry, he was quiet and gentle, although perhaps a bit too sensitive for the job.

'He still there then?' Harry nodded at the tramp. 'Poor

bugger, I'll have to move him on soon. Still, it'll be a good hour before Madam puts in an appearance so I'll let him sit for a while.'

'Better not let her hear you call her Madam.' Julie grinned up at Harry. 'Or she'll have your guts for garters.'

'I think she has them already.'

A tired look flitted over Harry's pleasant features.

'I'm getting too old for her shenanigans and that's the truth, Julie. If it wasn't that I needed this job I'd walk out, but if I did where would I get another one.' He shrugged his shoulders and closed the door. 'If it weren't for my wee Rosie . . . '

Julie put her hand on his arm. 'I know, Harry. But her bark's worse than her bite you know.'

Julie didn't really believe this, she'd seen the way Nicole treated Harry. She tightened her grip in what she hoped was a comforting squeeze.

'Maybe if you told her about Rosie, maybe she'd be more understanding.' Even as she said it, Julie knew it wouldn't make any difference to Nicole it would only make her treat Harry worse than she did already because she would know his weakness.

Harry shook his head. 'I don't think that's a good idea, she'd only use it against me. Anyway, I don't particularly want to let her know about Rosie and listen to her nasty comments.'

Julie let go of his arm. 'I suppose you're right.'

She sighed. Depression flooded through her in a wave of sadness that left her with a hollow sensation in the pit of her stomach. At least Harry had his Rosie. She had nothing, only a memory. She would have given anything to have had a child to care for, even one like Rosie. Suddenly she was in desperate need of her usual fix of coffee. 'I'll see you later, Harry.'

'You won't tell her, will you?' Harry muttered behind her.

Julie turned her head to look at him. 'No, I won't tell her, Harry. Your secret's safe with me.'

'You be careful, Julie. You may think she's your friend, but if she gets anything on you, she'll use it. Don't you be telling her any of your secrets.'

'I'll remember that,' Julie said. She had no intention of allowing Nicole to know any of her secrets, but she couldn't tell Harry that.

The heels of Julie's shoes clattered with a comforting noise as she walked along the flagstones of the empty corridor. A creak startled her and she glanced over her shoulder, but no one was there. She shrugged and hurried on, although she couldn't help wondering what mysteries the other doors in the corridor hid. She suspected they led to store cupboards or maintenance areas, although one of them probably led to the sub-basement which was not accessible to the sales and store staff.

The door at the end of the corridor swung shut after she pushed through it and emerged onto the mid-landing of the staff staircase. At the bottom of the stairs was the food hall and beyond that the restaurant; while the coffee shop was upstairs on the store's ground floor.

Julie went downstairs because she knew the coffee shop wouldn't be ready for business yet. Betty, who saw to the restaurant, would have the kettle boiling and the coffee pot on, and she desperately needed the cup of coffee she'd been promising herself.

'Hi, Betty,' she greeted the cook-cum-restaurant manager. 'D'you have a paper cup of coffee for our visitor while you make me one of your lovely special coffees.'

'Here you are.' She passed the paper cup to Julie. 'Mind it's hot.'

'Ta,' Julie said, turning back the way she'd just come. 'Won't be a mo.'

'You shouldn't encourage him, you know,' she heard Betty shout to her retreating back.

'I know,' she said, 'but I can't see the poor blighter freeze to death, now can I?' Julie didn't wait for Betty's response.

When she reached the outer door she hooked it back so

she could get in again. 'Here,' she said, 'That'll heat you up before you have to move on.'

The blanket heaved and a thin, blue-veined hand emerged. 'Ta, Miss. You've a good heart.' He grasped the cup.

'I brought you this as well.' Julie dropped a packet of sandwiches in the direction of his lap. She'd taken them from one of the shelves in the food hall. They would never be missed.

The tramp lifted his head and, although she could not see his face, she looked into his eyes which were the palest shade of blue she had ever seen. There was no expression in them and they reminded her of glacier ice. They were the eyes of someone who had given up and had nothing left to live for.

She shivered. He always made her feel cold as if she was sharing the cold that was within him. Turning, she almost ran back into the store, not relaxing until the door slammed behind her.

14

The wind increased during the night keeping the worst of the frost at bay. It blew through the trees in the orchard making the branches shake and rustle while the swaying bushes joined in the chorus. It swooped and gusted and whistled round the house, rattling the roof slates and window frames. A far off shed door clattered open and shut, with ever-increasing thuds and bangs.

Nicole slept badly, waking several times throughout the night, imagining some hidden menace within the depths of the shadows. Every creak and rustle seemed like an intruder. She could not rid herself of the feeling she'd had the evening before that she was being watched. Even now she could still see that shape at the window, the one that had seemed more solid than a shadow.

And yet, Scott had investigated and said there was nothing. But there was something outside, she knew there was. Scott just couldn't see it.

When she was a child she had been afraid of the dark. Afraid of the ghosts and goblins lurking in cupboards and dark places. Afraid of the shifting shadows that moved in the night. Afraid of her uncle who visited her bedroom when her parents were asleep. And more afraid to tell anyone about it, particularly Scott.

However, she had not been bothered by a fear of the dark for a long time, not since her marriage anyway. That was why she was convinced someone had been outside, in the garden, spying on her.

Last night Scott had laughed. He had accused her of being paranoid after he'd looked for what he had implied was an imaginary intruder. So she wasn't going to wake him up now and risk his ridicule again. Instead, she buried her head beneath the duvet and snuggled close to his back, knowing that as long as he was beside her she was protected.

The slamming of the front door jolted her out of a dream where she was fleeing down a dark street, chased by something shadowy and featureless. The fear lingered and gripped her, and she was relieved to see greyish daylight filtering into the bedroom. She realized the door must have been slammed by Marika, their daily maid, and not some fearsome creature from her nightmare.

The bedside clock indicated it was too early to get up. But her back ached from tossing and turning, and she was cold because Scott had pulled the duvet over himself leaving her exposed. Grasping the end of the quilt she tugged, but Scott grunted, pulling it back until once more she lay uncovered. She aimed a punch at the middle of his back, but then thought better of it, not wanting to be on the receiving end of his wrath. Scott was never at his best first thing in the morning.

'Selfish bastard,' she muttered, swinging her feet over the side of the bed.

Padding to the bathroom she showered quickly. It was a task rather than a pleasure and, after pulling on her clothes, she went through to the kitchen.

The maid looked up from where she was crouched in front of the dishwasher.

'You up early this morning?' Marika's Polish accent was not so pronounced as it had been when she came to work for them two years ago. 'You want I make you some breakfast?'

Nicole shuddered at the thought of food. It was too early.

'No, Marika, I'll just have a cup of coffee.'

She sat on one of the kitchen chairs, placed her elbows on the table and cupped her chin in her hands while she watched Marika manipulate the percolator.

'You all right, Mrs Ralston? You not look well.'

'I didn't sleep too well, Marika. I'll be fine after some coffee.'

Steam rose, bringing with it the strong aroma of Nicole's favourite blend as the maid poured the black liquid into a cup. She brought cream from the fridge, but Nicole shook her head. 'I think I need it black this morning, Marika. It'll help me wake up.'

The maid compressed her lips. 'You be better going back to bed and sleeping it off. You no good at work like this.'

Nicole's mouth twisted into a wry smile. 'You're probably right, Marika, but I can't. This is Mr Drake's day at the store and he doesn't make allowances for illness or anything else.'

Marika snorted. 'Illness, is that what it is?'

'It's not a hangover,' Nicole snapped, feeling the heat of her anger flood her body. Marika was starting to become too familiar, but she couldn't afford to lose her, for then there would be only herself and Scott. 'I'm sorry, Marika, I'm just on edge because I couldn't sleep.'

Marika shrugged her shoulders. 'Mr Ralston, he like some coffee?'

'No, let him sleep. He'll get up when he's ready, but you can tell him I've gone into work early.'

Nicole gulped the last of her coffee and stood up. 'Oh, by the way,' she said, as if she had only just thought of it, 'you didn't notice if there was anyone skulking about outside, I suppose?'

'I no see anyone.' Marika lifted Nicole's cup and turned to the dishwasher. 'You think someone out there?' She looked out of the window.

'No, no of course not. It was just that I thought we had an intruder last night. It doesn't matter.'

'What I do if intruder come back?' Marika frowned.

'Tell Scott, if he's still here, or call the police, of course.'

'Of course,' Marika muttered.

Ralph, the big ginger tomcat was sitting on the bonnet of Scott's BMW again. Nicole stopped to tickle him behind his ears and he purred in appreciation, a loud, rumbling noise as if Ralph had an engine tucked inside him.

'You'll get chased, Ralphy boy, if Scott catches you there.'

Nicole knew how much Scott hated paw prints on his

cars, but then, if he couldn't be bothered to garage the damn thing when he came home, it served him right.

Nicole kissed Ralph on top of his furry head before she walked round the corner of the house towards the two double garages which she had often considered labelling his and hers.

The door slid up without a sound when she pressed the button of her remote control. She stood for a moment considering before she threw her briefcase and handbag into the low-slung electric-blue sports car. She needed the ego boost this morning and the Porsche Boxster would give that to her. It was the car that infuriated other drivers, particularly men when they saw a woman driver. She was in the mood to annoy men this morning.

The hum of the tyres on the tarmacadam road had a soothing effect on Nicole. She relaxed, enjoying the wind whipping at the scarf she'd bound round her hair and the envious glances of other drivers. A lorry driver honked his horn as he drove close to the rear of her car, but she just grinned, pointed one finger skywards and pressed the accelerator to leave him trailing far behind her.

The wind caught her throat bringing tears to her eyes, but she drove faster and faster enjoying the adrenalin rush the speed gave her. It was like everything else in her life, the more risk there was, the greater the thrill.

The huge Michelin wind turbines came into view, their blades rotating lazily in the breeze, and she was forced to slow down as she caught up with the tail of traffic leading into the city centre.

The slow moving vehicles failed to dampen her pleasure after the exhilarating drive. Despite this, there was an element of relief when she pulled into the car park and manoeuvred the Porsche into her usual space, underneath the overhanging carriageway of the approach road to the Tay Bridge.

Still intoxicated by the drive, she was almost at the store before she remembered she had forgotten to close the Boxster's hood. 'Bugger it,' she muttered but carried on walking. She would get a staff member to go and put the hood up later. Maybe she would get Julie to do it. After all, Julie owed her big time for getting her the job.

The main doors to the department store were not yet open so Nicole was forced to enter the store by the rear entrance. She usually avoided this way in if she could, because the dirt and untidiness, the rubbish skips, and above all that bloody tramp who had taken up residence at the back of the store never failed to disgust her.

She clenched her teeth as she passed the tramp and, although she avoided looking at him, she could feel his eyes following her. Something would have to be done about him. He would have to be removed.

The key to the back door had slipped to the bottom of her bag and she leaned against the door as she rummaged for it. She could have rung the bell, but she wanted to catch that lazy bastard of a security guard skiving off when he should be working. He was old and past it, and if she'd had her way he would have been out on his arse a long time ago.

A gust of wind rippled down the alley sending bits of paper dancing in the air and rustling at the rubbish in the skips. For a moment Nicole thought she sensed a movement towards her, but when she glanced at the tramp he was still in the same place. Grasping the key she slid it into the lock, turned it and swung the door open until it was wide enough to let her enter. She slipped inside and quickly closed it again.

The electric bulbs in the corridor were too high up to provide much more than dim lighting. One of them hissed, spurted and flickered, sending odd shadows bouncing into the recesses. Nicole tutted her disapproval, although she was used to this, and had no intention of improving the lighting in a part of the store the customers never saw.

Light spilled out through the open door of the room the security guard used when he was doing duty at this entrance, and she could hear the Radio Tay announcer giving the latest news update. Tiptoeing along the corridor until she came level with the door, she peered in.

'Just as I thought,' she snapped, 'reading the newspaper when you should be working.'

Nothing infuriated Nicole more than someone not pulling their weight. She had worked hard and sacrificed a lot to get where she was and knew that every minute counted in the workplace. She was generous with staff who worked to her exacting standard but had no time for those who did not. It was not the first time a business had failed because of the laxity of some of the staff.

'I'm sorry Mrs Ralston, but there's nothing else to do when I'm waiting for staff to arrive.' Harry hastily folded the newspaper and pushed it across the table.

His whining annoyed her. Always making excuses, always saying he was sorry. She would make him sorry all right before she was finished with him, lazy sod.

'Nonsense,' she snapped. 'There's always something to do. That alley's a disgrace for a start.'

'I'm not a cleaner,' Harry mumbled, not meeting her eyes.

'I don't give a damn what you are or what you aren't. And there's that tramp. He's always there. It takes the tone of the place down. Get him moved on and if I catch him there again I'll hold you responsible.'

'Yes, Mrs Ralston. I'll do it right away.'

Nicole turned and marched down the corridor. She was ready for her coffee now.

15

Harry waited until Nicole vanished through the door at the end of the corridor before bending down and rummaging under the table. Good job she hadn't noticed his shoes were off or she would have flayed him. She'd already criticized his shirt and jacket this week – as if he could help it if they were slightly worn – so finding him without shoes would have suited her just fine. It would have given her an excuse to bawl him out again.

Finding his shoes he slipped his feet into them, grimacing slightly as the left one pressed on the corn on his little toe. Babs said he should go to the chiropodist, but where was he to find the extra money to do that? So instead he tried to poke the corn out with nail scissors and made it worse. He would be damned lucky if he didn't end up with a poisoned toe.

The dizziness struck him again when he stood up. It always did if he'd been bending down too long, although nowadays the time seemed to have shortened. Maybe if he didn't have so many worries it would clear up, but that bloody Nicole Ralston did not help matters having it in for him the way she did.

It wasn't as if he had ever done anything to harm her or go against her, she just seemed to have a down on him. It had got so bad that guilt had become his normal reaction anytime she was near him, although he was sure he'd nothing to feel guilty about. But it didn't stop him jumping when she crept up behind him. As if that wasn't enough, he'd developed this twitch at the side of his eye which, he was positive, gave him a shifty expression. He could feel it twitching now simply because he was thinking about her.

He leaned against the table until the swimming sensation

in his head settled down and the room stopped spinning. But he dared not stand too long for fear Nicole returned and found more fault with him. All it needed was for her to come back and check if he had moved that poor bugger of a tramp out of the alley. If he was still there, he dreaded to think how she would react, although he could guess.

As soon as he left the warmth of the guardroom for the draughty corridor a paroxysm of shivering engulfed him. He pulled his jacket tighter and, turning his collar up, limped to the back door.

The sound of his shoes on the flagstones echoed eerily down the passage, joining with the far off rumble of water pipes from the basement and the sound of the light bulb fizzing overhead. A smell of perfume hung in the air, tantalizing and teasing with its fragrance.

He wished he could buy perfume like that for Babs. She had a hard time looking after Rosie and she didn't get many treats, but he knew it was probably far too expensive for his pocket even for a special gift at Christmas. Still, he supposed there were other things he should be thankful for. After all, they had his pay every week and a roof over their heads, not like that poor homeless bugger camping out in the alley.

Harry hooked the door back, thinking the fresh air would clear the smell of Nicole from the corridor before he went back inside. He stood for a moment looking at the ragged bundle sitting against the wall of the alley. At first glance it just looked like a heap of rubbish except for the tips of blue-tinged fingers hanging on to the edge of the rags, holding them close round the unseen body, so that hardly any skin was exposed to the air.

Poor sod, he thought, it must be awful to sink to that state. After all, he's a human being just like the rest of us.

'Come on, mate. The boss lady says I have to move you on.'

The bundle stirred, bleary, blue eyes stared up at him with a bleakness and desperation Harry hoped he would never see again.

After the fraction of a moment, the tramp tried to

scramble to his feet while still grasping the blanket tightly around his head and body. Grunting, he almost collapsed against the wall, and Harry could hear the rasp of his breath as he struggled to pull himself up.

Harry thought the tramp wouldn't be able to push himself away from the wall without falling down again, but after swaying to and fro several times, the mountain of rags started to shuffle in the direction of the street.

'Wait a minute,' Harry said, rummaging in his pocket. He pressed a pound coin into the blue fingers that protruded from the rags. 'Get yourself a cup of tea or something. It'll heat you up.'

The tramp nodded and shambled off.

Harry looked at the rest of his change, rattling it in his hand before he stuck it back in his pocket. Oh, well, he thought, that's my packet of fags for today up the spout. Still, it won't kill me and it'll please Babs because she says I smoke too much. Sighing, he went through the door, releasing the hook holding it open, and let it slam shut.

The warmth of the guardroom was welcome after the cold air outside. Harry risked putting the kettle on and plonked a teabag into the mug he took out of the cupboard on the wall.

It was not much of a room, not like the Hollywood versions he had seen on the telly, where security guards sat in a posh room with a wall of computers so they could watch all parts of the building. He had to be satisfied with a sink, cupboard, hard chair and table. At least it was warm. But that was only because some of the heating pipes from the basement passed through this room before entering the complicated system of ducts and ventilation passageways winding tortuous routes through the upper floors of the building.

He drank his tea quickly while he checked his notebook for outstanding jobs to be done. Then he started checking the casual security staff who patrolled the departments. They only started work when the store opened and they finished when it closed. But Harry, as the regular man, had a responsibility for checking the maintenance of the building and instructing the maintenance and cleaning staff.

First things first, he thought, and depositing his cup in the sink he left the guardroom. Stopping at a door halfway along the corridor, he opened it and peered down the stone stairs into the murky depths of the lower basement.

'You there, Neil?' he shouted. He did not particularly want to go down the stairs because he was not familiar with the layout and feared he might lose himself among the conglomeration of pipes that, as far as he knew, stretched the entire length and breadth of the store. This was the domain of electricians, plumbers and odd job men, not security guards.

A door slammed somewhere in the depths and he shouted again until he heard the shuffle of feet.

'D'you not hear me shouting?' Harry addressed the man in the oily dungarees who surfaced out of the gloom.

'Sorry, boss. I was in the middle of something.'

The man who spoke was tall and thin with a slightly emaciated look about him. The ends of his lank brown hair clung to his neck and he blinked myopically as he looked up towards the stronger light in the corridor. He was not young and he was not old. In fact, Harry had great difficulty trying to think what age he was for he could have been anything from his late twenties to late forties. He always meant to ask him, but only when the time was right and the time had never been right.

'Okay,' said Harry. 'Just wanted to check if you'd done anything about those scrabbling noises Ken reported hearing in the ventilation ducts on the top floor.'

Neil stared up at him from his position at the bottom of the stairs. 'Yeah, I did that earlier this morning. There were some droppings, could have been mice, but more likely rats, so I set some traps. Better tell Ken and the others not to go poking in the vents. Those traps are strong.'

'Rats?'

'Sure, rats.' Neil stretched his mouth into a grin. 'You know, those wee furry things. The store's full of them, they wouldn't need me otherwise. Don't worry though they won't come out when the store's full of customers, believe it or not, they're shy wee blighters.'

'If you say so,' Harry muttered. 'Well, keep an eye on it then. We don't want to be overrun.'

'Sure will, boss. Sure will.'

Harry closed the door to the lower basement and shuddered as he went up the corridor. He would be glad to get up into the hustle and bustle of the store even if he did have to face up to Nicole.

16

The restaurant at the rear of the food hall was functional. It was there to serve the busy shopper and housewife who daily examined the shelves for all the little luxuries that other grocers and food shops did not think profitable enough to keep. However, Julie encouraged the food hall buyer to invest in these non-profit making luxuries, for they were as much the loss leaders in the department store as cut prices were in other shops. Julie was a wise enough section head to understand that those who came to see what luxuries were on offer at reasonable prices would also wander through the rest of the store and be tempted to buy.

Julie's first port of call in the morning was always the restaurant. Despite its functional appearance – formica-topped tables and modern-looking plastic chairs, which were more comfortable than they looked – it did a good trade, mainly because Betty and her staff were excellent cooks.

Julie had been sitting at one of the corner tables for ten minutes before Betty brought her coffee over.

'Thanks,' she said. 'I need that to get me going this morning.'

She took an appreciative sip of the hot liquid. There was no doubt about it, Betty made the best cup of coffee in Dundee. If anything could have kept Julie in Dundee after her task was completed it would have to be Betty's coffee.

'That smells good.' Nicole slumped into the chair beside her.

Julie started. She hadn't heard her coming and it was important that Nicole should continue to believe Julie was her friend. If she did not remain alert, Julie thought, there was always the danger she might say or do something to give herself away and reveal her true feelings. As it was she suppressed the upsurge of antagonism to smile warmly at the woman she despised.

Betty had suddenly found some urgent cleaning behind the servery but that did not prevent Nicole from shouting across the room.

'Cup of coffee, if you don't mind – and hurry because I'm desperate for it.'

Betty straightened up and made a noise in the back of her throat that was halfway between a humph and a grunt, but she poured the coffee and brought it to the table.

'I could swear that woman doesn't like me.' Nicole grinned at Julie. 'Not that I care. Nobody ever likes the boss, do they?'

'Oh, I don't know, it's just the way Betty is. She likes to get on with the work and doesn't like to be delayed.'

Julie looked over Nicole's shoulder and caught sight of Betty's glare of disbelief. If Nicole hadn't been sitting beside her she would have laughed, but she didn't dare.

'Well, I suppose it's a good thing somebody likes working.' Nicole stirred her coffee. 'I've just come from a session with Harry. Now there's one useless, lazy lump of a man if ever I saw one. Give me half a chance and I'll get rid of him.'

'Harry's not that bad,' Julie murmured. 'It's just that he's afraid of you and it always puts him at a disadvantage.'

Nicole snorted. 'You know your trouble, Julie? You're too nice a person. You never speak ill of anybody.'

Julie ignored the comment and smiled down at her coffee. That's rich, she thought, coming from the one person I would gladly see in Hell, so it's just as well you can't read my thoughts Nicole, or you would shrivel up and die.

She glanced over the rim of her cup. 'You don't look so good this morning. Is something wrong?' Julie's voice indicated nothing but concern.

'Is it that obvious? I'll have to perk up before I meet with Patrick. I can't let him see me under the weather.'

'Hangover?' The note of concern was still in Julie's voice, but she hoped Nicole was suffering.

'Maybe a hair of the dog might cure it. I've got a little something in my locker if you want it.' Patrick would just love Nicole smelling of drink.

'No, no. It's not that. It's just that I didn't sleep well last night.'

Nicole lapsed into silence and both women sipped their coffee. 'What with the wind and the prowler and all.' Her voice had lost its usual confident tone and sounded strained.

'Prowler?' Julie couldn't help feeling curious.

'I thought I saw someone outside my window last night, but Scott says I just imagined it.'

'And did you? Imagine it, that is?'

'I don't think so.' A faraway look appeared in Nicole's eyes. 'It seemed real last night.'

'What did he look like?' Julie had trouble catching her breath. This was more than she'd hoped for, a real live prowler, whether or not it was in Nicole's imagination. She could build on that. Use it to destroy her.

'I don't know. I didn't see him.'

'What d'you mean you didn't see him? How did you know he was there if you didn't see him?' Julie almost stuttered in her excitement.

'Well, he was like a shadow. Only his shadow was deeper than all the others and it moved when it shouldn't have.' Nicole shuddered.

'He was there. I know he was there, but Scott wouldn't believe me.'

'Mmh,' Julie kept her voice calm. 'Did Scott do anything about it? Apart from ridiculing you, that is.'

'He went outside and looked, but he said there was nothing there and that I must have imagined it. He accused me of being paranoid.' Nicole sounded breathless and panicky.

Better and better, thought Julie. 'That's interesting,' she said.

'What d'you mean, interesting?' Nicole's forehead creased into a frown as if she was having difficulty understanding.

'Well,' Julie said, 'if you look at it logically it seems odd.'

'You think I'm paranoid too. Well, thanks a lot.' Nicole started to stand up.

Julie put a hand on her arm. 'No, hear me out. It's odd because you say you live in a house that's secure and that your grounds are almost impregnable to intruders, and yet Scott saw nothing. Doesn't that suggest something to you?'

Nicole relaxed back into her seat. 'What d'you mean?' she whispered.

'Well.' Julie was enjoying herself. 'Someone must have let him into the grounds and if it wasn't you who could it have been?'

'Scott,' Nicole murmured.

'Snap. Take it a bit further. Scott went out to look and found nobody, yet you're convinced there was someone there. So why did Scott not see him?'

'Because he didn't want to see him.'

'You've got it, Nicole.'

'But why would Scott do that?' There was genuine puzzlement in Nicole's voice.

'Think about it, Nicole. Scott's away from home a lot, isn't he?'

Nicole nodded.

'Maybe he's got an interest somewhere on his travels.'

Julie watched the understanding creep over Nicole's face. It had taken her a while to latch on to what Julie was suggesting, but she was getting there.

'You don't think. Oh, but it's not possible . . . Scott would never . . .'

'Wouldn't he? He's a man isn't he?'

Anger twisted Nicole's face. 'If that's his game he needn't think I'll give him a divorce. I've invested too much in this marriage, I'm not going to give up now.'

'Maybe that's why you've got an intruder then.' Julie sat back and waited for the penny to drop. It didn't take long.

'Well if he thinks he's going to put a private detective on to me to catch me out, he's got another think coming.'

She hesitated, as another thought seemed to strike her.

'Or, if he's out to frighten me because of some sick game he's playing, that's not going to work either.' And with that, Nicole picked up her briefcase and handbag and left the restaurant without a goodbye or a backward look, which was just as well or she would have seen Julie's smile of satisfaction.

Stupid bitch, Julie thought, I hope that has given her plenty to think about.

She turned back to her coffee and drained the last of it before going up to the servery and saying to Betty, 'Well, I think I deserve another coffee after that session.'

'Sure, Julie. I'll get it for you.' Betty turned and poured it. 'What's up her hump then?' she said as she handed it over. 'I've never seen her in such a state before.'

'Nothing of any importance, Betty. I don't think we need to bother about Nicole for just now.'

17

How dare Scott try to frighten her! Nicole was not convinced with Julie's theory that she was being watched to provide evidence for a divorce. But she did know that Scott was capable of playing games. After all, he had plenty of practice in games playing and devising new games for development by his software company. But if this was a game, it was a sick one.

She stormed to the lift. The lift wasn't there, and that made her even angrier. She stabbed her finger onto the button while in her mind she swore at Scott. If he'd been here she would have torn his eyes out. But he was not here which was just as well because it would give her time to calm down, although if that bloody lift didn't hurry up there was little hope of that.

She pummelled the lift doors with her free hand swinging her briefcase with the other as if she intended using it as a weapon. It made little difference. The doors remained closed, blocking her progress, while she fumed in front of them.

Eventually, when the lift doors slid open they did so with a suddenness that took her unawares and she almost fell inside.

Gathering herself together she inserted her pass key for the top floor, waiting until the doors slid shut before practising the deep breathing exercises that were supposed to help with her stress levels.

As she struggled to regain control she forced herself to think about Scott in a more rational way and decided she would play it cool and look for a way to turn the tables on him.

She smiled. It was a smile that did not reach her eyes. If

he wanted to play dirty she was a past master at the art and she would easily get the better of him.

Nicole, once more the model of the perfect manager, smart, professional and controlled, left the lift on the top floor.

This was where the unseen business of the store was carried on. It housed the accountants and other finance staff, a couple of public relations officers and a legal adviser.

A set of glass doors at the end of the corridor led to the conference rooms, the boardroom and the executive offices. Only the Managing Director and Assistant Managing Directors had offices beyond these doors.

She paused in front of her own office and looked with pride at her name on the door – Nicole Ralston, Assistant Managing Director – she had come a long way since she started work in the store as a shop assistant. Patrick was to be thanked for that. Once he spotted her potential she'd been on her way up and she'd made the most of her opportunities. Of course, he no longer wanted her in the way he previously had, although there was still the odd occasion. However, he had grown to rely on her ability and expertise.

She wondered briefly whether he knew about her and Ken, but then shrugged the thought away. Patrick spent more time in some of his other stores nowadays and was not here often enough to be fully aware of what was going on . . . and yet . . . he was sharp.

A slight whisper of air touched the back of her neck and she knew she was no longer alone in the corridor, but before she could turn to look, Ken grasped her shoulder, pushed aside her hair and kissed her on the nape of her neck.

'Not here,' she muttered, pushing him away. 'Patrick's due today and I don't think he'd approve.'

He stroked her neck with a single finger while his soft brown eyes reflected a mute plea and his face developed that little boy lost look that always succeeded in making her insides churn.

'No,' she said, her voice little more than a whisper while ghostly fingers crawled over her skin making her shiver with desire. She could see from his face that he knew the effect he was having on her.

He pushed her office door open, guiding her through it. 'Is this any better?' His voice deepened with a husky quality that told her he wanted her.

She pushed the door with her foot until she heard it click shut.

'Not really,' she whispered as she turned towards him.

Her arms circled his neck and she teased her fingers up through his hair, perfectly aware of the effect it would have on him.

'Patrick's just as liable to come in here when he arrives and he'd go berserk if he caught us. You know he would.'

'I don't know anything of the sort.'

Ken slipped his hands inside her jacket and pulled her blouse out of the top of her skirt.

His hands caressed her skin. Her nerve ends tingled with a need she didn't quite understand and she had difficulty suppressing the scream rising within her. Sex with Ken was always frantic and noisy, and she knew that although she wanted him it was too risky with Patrick due at any moment.

She pulled away from him. 'No, you mustn't. Not here. Not now.' She tucked her blouse back into the top of her skirt. 'It's too dangerous.'

Ken pouted, his face even more like a child's. 'It's not fair, you always do this to me.'

Nicole stretched out a hand and stroked his face. 'Later,' she promised. 'Now you must go to your own office. You don't want Patrick seeing you like that.'

Ken left the room, but Nicole knew he was not pleased. She would make it up to him after and she knew just how to do that.

Sighing, she picked up her briefcase from the floor where it had fallen when she had put her arms around Ken. She threw it on the desk, snapped the locks open and pulled out the papers she had tried to work on last night. She sank back into her leather upholstered chair and attempted to concentrate, but it was hopeless.

She stood up and stretched, raising her arms above her head in an attempt to loosen her muscles and get rid of tension. Then she paced across the room and around her desk, stopping to look out of the window. She had a good view of the City Churches and the Overgate Centre. Patrick was worried about the Centre which was a swish shopping mall. He was afraid it would take away too much business. That was why he wanted them to formulate trading plans. The trading plans Nicole could not get her mind to concentrate on.

Patrick had already hinted that economies would have to be made and he might have to downsize the staff. Nicole had no wish to be a loser in that situation. She knew that even if it came to a fight between her and Ken about who was to be kept on, she would fight her corner with the same ruthlessness that had put her there in the first place. And, if Drake's went down the tubes, there was always the possibility of opportunities in the mall which, rumour had it, was planning an extension. Absentmindedly she tapped the window with her fingertips.

A pigeon swooped down, landing on the windowsill with the grace of a ballet dancer. He cocked his head to one side and tapped the glass with his beak.

Nicole stroked her finger down the glass. 'Looking for your breakfast biscuit are you, Freddie?'

She smiled at the bird. Even as a child she'd always had a soft spot for birds and small animals. They were weaker than she was and no threat to her. She didn't have to be in competition with them and could drop the tough exterior she'd had to develop to survive in the business world.

Only she knew how difficult her professional role was to maintain, and how vulnerable she really was.

She walked to her desk, slid a drawer open and extracted two digestive biscuits from the top of an open pack. Returning to the window she pushed it open, crumbled the biscuits between her fingers and scattered the crumbs on the ledge.

'There you go then, Freddie. Enjoy.'

A smile played over her lips as she watched the bird peck at the crumbs before flexing his wings and soaring off again. Nicole watched him for a moment and then slid the old-fashioned casement window closed.

If only life could be as simple for her as it was for Freddie. She leaned her forehead on the cool glass, her eyes absently scanning the crowds below. The sensation of being watched sent a chill up her spine as she focused on a shabby figure in a long raincoat staring back at her. He stood, leaning against Primark's wall, not quite part of the bus queue. As she fixed her gaze on him, he turned and shuffled off.

Her nerves stretched like piano wire and tension returned to her muscles.

Was this a part of Scott's game? Or was she starting to imagine things?

She shrugged. If she allowed fear to become part of her life, Scott would win. She had no intention of allowing that and knew, if she played the game, she would get an opportunity to turn it back on Scott.

It seemed no time at all after she returned to her desk to work that the telephone rang.

'Mr Drake wants you in the boardroom.'

His secretary's voice always annoyed Nicole, it was mellow and polite, giving no indication of the woman's feelings. In fact, Nicole wondered if she had any or whether she was just an attractive robot who was programmed for perfection.

Nicole gathered up her papers. The presentation was as ready as it was possible to be in the timescale allowed for the piece of work, but she was edgy. She would explain it was still rough and required some development, but that it was the outline of something that could be exciting and successful.

Nicole had no doubts about her ability to sell herself and her ideas so she walked smartly up the corridor and into the boardroom.

Ken was already there and Patrick gave a small frown as

she entered. A small piece of her confidence eroded, but she smiled at him and took her place at the large oak table. Nicole ignored Patrick's secretary but nodded briefly at the chief accountant, a public relations officer and the legal adviser as she opened her briefcase and took out a file.

'We all know why we are here,' Patrick said as he opened the meeting. 'The company has been experiencing problems and we need to address these positively. That will require the combined efforts of you all.'

He paused as if debating with himself whether to talk further but seemed to decide against it. Turning to Ken, Patrick said, 'Mr Moody has been explaining his ideas to me, therefore, I thought we would start with his presentation. It's all yours, Ken.'

Patrick placed his elbows on the boardroom table and steepled his fingers as he looked, with an expression of eagerness, in Ken's direction.

Ken opened the folder in front of him and took out several acetates placing one of them on the glass top of the overhead projector. Switching the machine on he started to speak, sketching out his ideas and overall plan.

Nicole's mind wandered and it was difficult for her to concentrate. She had psyched herself up for her own presentation, so was anxious for Ken to conclude his.

But, as Ken continued to talk, a feeling of incredulity crept over her. She shook her head unable to believe what she was hearing because they were her ideas and her plan he was putting forward as his own.

The bastard, she thought, remembering all the times they had played the 'what if' game and tossed ideas around. He couldn't have thought this up on his own. He must have deliberately stolen her ideas for himself.

18

Julie lingered over her second cup of coffee appreciating the creamy taste and texture of a brew well made. The drink soothed and warmed her, and she relaxed for the first time since arriving in Dundee. She had once been a happy natured person, but all that changed when Dave left. Then, after he died she'd been so tied up in her grief and her plans to hurt the person who had brought so much suffering into her life, there hadn't been room for anything else. However, now that she'd been able to strike back at Nicole, even if it was only in a small way, it seemed to have lessened the pain.

Her peace of mind wavered slightly as she thought of Nicole's husband Scott. On the few occasions Julie had met him he'd been polite, although a bit standoffish. She suffered a slight twinge of guilt. For all she knew he was a decent man who deserved a better wife. Maybe she shouldn't use him to get at Nicole, particularly as he was probably as much sinned against as Julie was.

She pushed the guilt feelings away as she rationalized her actions to herself. What she'd suggested to Nicole wouldn't actually do him any harm. He had already accused his wife of being paranoid so he would probably think any reaction of hers just proved his point.

And anyway, Nicole had been so concerned about this phantom watcher, who was probably just a figment of her imagination, it had been too good an opportunity to miss. I wouldn't mind being a fly on the wall at Nicole's house tonight, Julie thought, with a certain amount of grim satisfaction.

'What are you smiling at?' Betty lifted her cup and wiped the table with a wet cloth. 'You'd think you'd just seen your dream man.'

'You've got men on the brain, Betty. Where would I find a nice man here, I ask you? Unless you mean Harry, of course.' Julie watched the guard as he paraded between the aisles of the food hall.

'Some seem to manage all right.' Betty looked in a meaningful way at the lift doors which had just swished shut behind Nicole.

'Careful, Betty,' Julie warned, 'idle gossip could lose you your job.'

'Well, anyway.' Betty sniffed and gave the table another rub. 'I can't stand here chatting to you all day. Some of us have work to do.'

Julie knew Betty wouldn't stay offended for very long. And, not wanting to annoy the older woman further, she waited until Betty vanished into the kitchen behind the servery before she stood up and left the restaurant.

The store was still quiet, but it wouldn't be long before the aisles she was inspecting would be mobbed with customers. Julie wanted to make sure everything was in order. She beckoned to a salesgirl and pointed out an empty space on one of the shelves. The girl nodded and mumbled something about the late arrival of stock.

'I don't care,' said Julie, peering at the girl's name badge, 'Debbie. Put something in its place until the stock arrives. Customers don't like to see empty shelves. It annoys them and puts ideas in their heads that the business might be going downhill. Always remember, no customers, no job.'

Debbie stared at her with eyes magnified by her spectacles, although there didn't seem to be any acknowledgement of what Julie was trying to tell her. It reminded Julie of an old saying of her granny – the lights are on but no one's home – which was what she used to say when describing a friend of Julie's who was a bit wanting in the intelligence stakes.

Julie sighed. Where were all the keen girls who wanted to learn a trade when they were looking for salesgirls? If this one was any example heaven help all businesses.

It wasn't as if Julie had any interest in department stores

or food halls or selling, but she could still give her best to the job, so it shouldn't have been too difficult for the sales assistants.

'Oh, go on. Just put something on the shelf,' she snapped. 'I don't want to see it looking like this when I make my next inspection.'

'Yes, Miss Forbes.' Debbie gave her a terrified look and scuttled off.

Before continuing with her inspection, Julie made a mental note to speak to one of the more senior sales assistants.

Out of the corner of her eye, she saw Harry on the stairs and knew he was on his way to open the main door to the store. Other people could open the side doors and minor entrances, but Harry liked to attend to unlocking the large revolving doors. Julie sometimes watched him and she guessed it made him feel important to turn the key, test the mechanism and then welcome the first customers of the day.

Julie hurried through the rest of her inspection and ended up where she usually did, outside the door of her office. She opened the door and switched on the light. It illuminated the small cubby hole of a room with a harsh brilliance that only intensified the stuffy atmosphere. The office, a rather grandiose title, had no window and was only large enough to contain a desk, chair, filing cabinet and her computer. Nevertheless, when she entered her own private space she always experienced a feeling of relief, which could often be so intense it almost swamped her.

There was only one message on her answering machine. However, it was an unexpected one. Adrian never phoned her at work. In fact, he never phoned at all. Not since she'd explained to him that this was something she had to do, although she hadn't been too specific about what that something was.

He had understood how Dave's death affected her and had been sympathetic. 'By all means,' he'd said. 'Take some time off. I'll hold your job for you.' However, he hadn't understood why she needed to come to Dundee, nor why she needed to work beside Nicole. Nor had he understood her need for revenge, preferring to think it was an obsession or morbid curiosity.

Julie remembered him, standing in the smaller gallery with the light from the long windows shining behind him making his fair hair look white in the sun. 'What you are planning is sick, Julie.' He fingered his bow tie in a gesture that was all too familiar when he was feeling uncomfortable. 'This woman is of no importance. Forget her.'

'I can't, Adrian. She killed Dave.' Julie's voice had been harsh and unforgiving as she met Adrian's stare.

'Dave killed himself, Julie. You have to accept it.' He laid his hand on hers. It was soft and warm and Julie could almost feel the sympathy oozing out of him.

'But he wouldn't have if it hadn't been for her.' Julie knew she was right, although she knew Adrian would never understand because he didn't have a vengeful nature.

Adrian looked at her with those piercing blue eyes that seemed to see right through her. 'Well, if you must, you must. But I still think you are making a mistake.'

And now, after three months, he had phoned her.

She realized with a little pang of guilt that she'd never tried to contact him since she left Edinburgh and he must be wondering about her. Lifting the phone, she dialled the number. An unexpected reluctance to speak to him crept over her, probably because she knew of his disapproval. Maybe he wouldn't be there, she thought, and in the next moment, maybe I should just hang up. However, the receiver at the other end was picked up on the second ring as if he'd been waiting for her call.

'Julie, I was worried about you, particularly when you didn't phone me. Nothing's happened, has it?'

'I'm fine, Adrian,' she said.

'You're not depressed, are you? You know with Dave and all.' He sounded awkward as if he had trouble mentioning Dave's name.

'No, I'm not depressed. I'm doing just fine.' Fine, fine, it echoed in her brain as if this was the only thing she could say. But she was not fine and wouldn't be until she had finished what she came here to do.

'When are you coming back? The gallery needs you.'

Julie thought longingly about the gallery, the paintings, the sculptures, the works of art. Things she loved working with.

'Not yet, Adrian. I haven't finished what I came here to do.'

The silence hung between them neither willing to break it. At last Adrian said, 'You're not still looking to pay that woman back, are you?'

'Of course, I am.' Her voice was crisp with a certainty she was not particularly feeling and she could feel her hands warm and sweaty.

'It's not like you, Julie. It's turning you into something you're not. It'll destroy you if you're not careful.'

'I don't think so.' She cradled the phone between her neck and shoulder as she wiped her hands on her skirt. 'Is that all you phoned to say? I'm busy, you know.' She hated herself for the brusqueness in her tone. Adrian was a good friend.

'No, that wasn't all. I just wanted to tell you that Sam's started a new show, so I've had to employ a temporary replacement for the gallery. The job's still yours,' he added hastily. 'The only thing is, this temp is very good and would be willing to stay permanently.' He paused. 'However, I've told him you'll be back at the beginning of January, but if you're not then I'll consider making his job permanent.'

'What you're telling me is that, if I'm not back by January, I don't have a job at the gallery anymore.' Julie's voice was harsh. She loved the gallery and would mourn the loss of a job where she had built up specialist knowledge in the art world. There wouldn't be many other jobs like it. However, she had an unfinished task and until she'd dealt with Nicole she could not consider leaving Dundee, even for the luxury of working in an Edinburgh gallery.

'That's right,' Adrian said and hung up.

19

Ken was on a high as he elaborated on his plans for increasing the store's potential and Nicole was powerless to stop him. But underneath her calm exterior, she seethed. Her fury intensified as she watched Patrick's sharp eyes glitter with interest, but she knew it was no use complaining. Patrick admired sharp practice and would rightly deduce that Ken had stolen a march on his nearest rival. No, she would just have to outsmart him and rescue what little she could.

Patrick looked what he was, a successful businessman who was only one step removed from a con man. He was tall and angular with a full head of white hair and a sharp, pointed face, with nose and chin to match. His aquiline features might have given him an aristocratic look if it had not been for the habitual cunning expression, which gave the impression he was plotting something. He had been good to Nicole over the years, but she had no illusions about him and knew he would discard her if he thought she was of no more use.

His attention remained focused on Ken with such an intensity that she almost expected his pointed nose to twitch at the smell of success, and when he finally glanced in her direction she sensed that he was aware of her discomfiture and knew exactly what was going on.

'And you, Nicole? You have formulated some plans for me as well?'

His eyes glinted and there was a hint of malice in them.

Nicole knew Patrick wouldn't tolerate anyone who failed to deliver. She also knew how ruthless he could be. So she removed her elbows from the table, leaned back in her chair, and smiled with a confidence she was far from feeling. If she was to come out of the game ahead of everyone else she would have to convince Patrick she still had control.

'You've just heard my plans.' She stared straight at Patrick. 'Ken and I decided that rather than work on opposing plans that would take up time and resources to test out, we would work jointly on a plan with the aim of succeeding in the least possible time frame. The plan would, as a result, have a greater chance of success.' She moved her gaze to Ken. 'We drew lots to see who would present it and Ken won the toss of the coin.'

Patrick's thin lips stretched into a smile that was almost vulpine while his eyes flicked between Ken and Nicole.

'Good thinking,' he said.

Nicole knew that she'd scored for the time being. But she also knew from Patrick's expression that he was perfectly aware of her ruse. Of course, now he was aware of the competition between them he would use it, and wouldn't care if he destroyed both of them in the process. Nicole, however, had never considered herself a loser and had no intention of giving up what she'd fought so hard to attain. If Ken could stay on top with her that would be well and good, but if it came to one or the other of them she would see Ken going down the tubes first.

Patrick wound up the meeting, impressing on everyone that a rationalization of all his businesses was in process and that this would inevitably mean some downsizing and job losses. He gathered up his papers and informed them he had two more meetings that day. However, if they all worked hard on the project that had been presented, and if it was a success, he was confident this particular store could survive. With that threat hanging over them, he left.

Nicole waited until the lift doors closed and then turned on Ken. 'What the hell was that all about?' she hissed. 'Those were my ideas and fine well you know it.'

'Not here!' Ken glanced over his shoulder. 'Somewhere private and I'll explain.' He took her arm and manoeuvred her along the corridor and through the door into her office.

'You had no right to steal my plan,' she spat, as soon as the door was closed. 'No right at all. It would have been all the same if I'd told Patrick what you did. That you don't have any ideas of your own so you've to steal someone else's.'

Ken backed her up against the desk. 'Patrick wouldn't have cared and you know it. Anyway, I did tell him it was your plan, but he wouldn't listen, just told me to get on with the presentation and not make excuses for you.'

'Excuses for me?' Nicole's voice almost failed her. 'Since when have I needed you or anyone else to make excuses for me, and anyway, I don't believe you. Patrick would have enjoyed saying that himself. He wouldn't have left it to you.'

'No, that's not right, and you know it. Patrick's game has always been to play people off against each other. Nothing would suit him better than if we were enemies. That way he gets the best of both of us because then we'll always be trying to outdo each other.'

Nicole was conscious of the edge of the desk cutting into the tops of her legs and Ken's grasp on her arms. She could smell his breath as he leaned over her, a mixture of smoke and the mints he continually sucked, his face twitched and his eyes darkened with desire.

'We don't want to be enemies, do we, Nicole? We don't want to play into Patrick's hands. That would mean we'd both lose out.' He bent her arms behind her as he pushed her back onto the desk. 'What we want to do is play our own game,' his voice came in short gasps, 'and you were magnificent in there. It let Patrick know just where we stand.' His knee pressed between her legs prising them open. 'What d'you say, Nicole? Do we work together?'

'Yes, we'll work together.' Nicole's voice was husky as she pulled him into her, but only as long as it suits me, she thought.

Before they left the store, Patrick handed his briefcase to his secretary, a tall, aloof blonde who accepted it without question. He didn't bother to stand aside for her, but pushed through the revolving doors, expecting her to follow him. They could have waited inside because the Rolls hadn't yet arrived. But he needed some fresh air after the claustrophobic atmosphere of the meeting upstairs which, he had to admit, had been slightly more interesting than usual.

He'd made a good choice when he brought Ken on board as an assistant director. The younger man reminded him of himself when he'd been Ken's age, ambitious, cunning, and with a hunger to get ahead at all costs. He was a good match for Nicole who also had those qualities. Both of his assistant directors would do anything to get ahead, just as he would have done and would still do.

He smiled to himself as he thought of Ken's presentation, so obviously Nicole's work he would have recognized it anywhere. She had been furious. He could see it in her eyes and her body language. Still, he had to admire the way she'd handled it, he couldn't have done better himself.

Maybe he would send her a dozen red roses with a congratulations message. It had been a long time since he'd sent her roses, but then she was not as young as she was in those days.

The Rolls Royce pulled into the kerb. The liveried chauffeur got out and opened the door for him. 'Thanks, Frankie,' Patrick said, stepping into the back seat of the car. His secretary handed the briefcase to Frankie before sliding into the back seat beside Patrick. He laid his hand on her knee, inching the material of her skirt up until it rested on her bare flesh, although his hand might not have been there for all the response she made. The car pulled out into the traffic and Patrick gave one last glance up at the store to where the executive offices were. He wondered briefly what Nicole and Ken were doing at the moment, although he had a good idea. The silly fools thought they'd kept their affair a secret, but there were no secrets that Patrick was not party to.

He turned his attention to his secretary. It would be an hour before they reached the next store and he knew how he was going to fill the time.

20

Ken whistled as he walked down the corridor, but before he passed through the glass doors leading to the general offices, he stopped, checked his tie was straight and adjusted his collar. It wouldn't do for the clerical assistants to notice his clothing was in disarray.

The soft buzz of conversation fizzled out as he strode into the room.

'Hi, girls,' he said. 'The meeting's over so it's back to the grindstone.'

He smiled; a boyish grin that he knew girls and women responded to. It was his trademark.

Plonking his briefcase on the edge of one of the desks he brought out a folder. 'Think you can get that done for me today?'

The senior administrative assistant plucked the folder from his hand. 'The typists are busy on the new production details so I'll do it myself,' she said. 'I wouldn't want you to be disappointed.' She leaned close to him so that he could smell her perfume.

He inhaled deeply. 'Is that a new perfume, Evelyn?' He swayed slightly. 'It makes you irresistible.'

One of the younger girls turned her face away and became engrossed in her computer as she tried to hide a smile, while Evelyn's face developed an interesting shade of pink. She pulled away from him, but he followed her around the desk and took hold of her hand.

'I just wanted you to know I appreciate your dedication to the job,' he said. 'And I'll make sure you're not forgotten if things change around here.'

Ken had no doubts that the clerical staff knew exactly what was going on and what was being considered simply because they handled everyone's typing.

'Thank you, Mr Moody.' Evelyn turned an even deeper shade of pink before she moved back to her desk. 'I'd better get started if you want this today.'

She settled down in front of her computer and started to type, but evidently remembering something, she looked up just as Ken was leaving. 'Oh, by the way, you don't happen to know if Mrs Ralston's free yet?' Her fingers poised in mid-air.

Ken turned and leaned against the doorframe. 'She's out of the meeting if that's what you mean, but I'd leave her in peace just now, I think she's working on her project.' He lowered his voice, and said, 'And to tell you the truth I don't think she's finding it very easy.'

'Yes, of course, Mr Moody.' Evelyn's fingers busied themselves on the keyboard. 'Look back in a couple of hours and this will be ready for you.'

Ken left the lift on the fourth floor and wandered round the china department. Shining crystal winked and gleamed at him from spotlessly clean shelves while plates, cups and saucers, glowed warmly under the concealed lighting. He stopped to admire the Doulton ornaments in their revolving glass cabinet, but the one he had hidden away in the stock room was not among them. It was a special limited edition, a present for Claire's birthday.

As he wandered he smiled and chatted to the various assistants, asking about their sales targets and whether these were being met, while at the same time encouraging and praising them. He liked to create the impression among the floor staff that he was interested in them and their departments and he was fairly positive he succeeded in this. He was sure every member of staff thought he had their interests at heart whereas, if there was a cutback, he really didn't care much who it affected as long as it was not himself.

Reaching the stairs he decided to walk down to the electrical department. Claire was fancying a new refrigerator and he thought, provided she chose the correct model, he could do a deal with the sales rep when he came to the store next week.

Ken stepped off the stairs to be met by the section head, a cold, austere woman who was immune to his charms.

'Your wife was here earlier,' she said. 'Told me to tell you she would be in the coffee shop if you turned up.'

'Thank you, Miss Smithers.' Ken did not bother smiling because he knew it would have no effect. The woman was a dragon and he could never fathom why her sales figures were always so good.

The ground floor coffee shop was busy, but Claire had managed to get a corner table at the rear of the seating area. And, although she had to admit the coffee and cakes were excellent, she did not particularly want to be here. But she had to wait for Ken somewhere and this was as good a place as anywhere else in the store. Besides, she needed to kill some time before collecting Catriona from the nursery. Catriona was the baby of the family and she wouldn't trust anyone else to collect her, not like Jake and Charlie her six-year-old twins who preferred to go home from school with their best friend Davie and his mother.

Claire was tempted to leave the store and would have done so if she had thought it would make Ken wonder why she hadn't waited for him. But she'd always waited for Ken, had done it all her life and he was used to it. Besides she knew Ken so well she was sure that however strange he thought her leaving was, it wouldn't trouble him. In any case, she didn't want to wander the streets.

She was on her second coffee before Ken turned up looking as if he had swallowed a whole churn of cream, and she could just guess which particular cat had supplied it.

Her eyes narrowed as she watched him smiling at the customers while he weaved his way between the tables. He always thought she never knew about him and his affairs and when she did tackle him he acted like the injured party with that little boy lost look she had originally found so attractive.

Now that she was older and wiser she was well able to resist it.

However, she was getting tired – tired of him and his affairs. It was time to thwart his little diversions even if it meant she might lose him, but somehow or other she didn't think she would.

'I thought you were going to meet me in the electrical department?'

She used both hands to place her cup in the saucer, afraid that the anger starting to swell within her would make her hands shake. Anger did that to her and if it was fierce enough her entire body was liable to shake with emotion. But Claire had spent her whole life trying to control her emotions and she'd developed certain defence mechanisms that probably didn't do her blood pressure much good.

'Sorry, love.'

Ken bent and kissed the top of her head. 'The meeting dragged on and on. I thought it was never going to end.'

'Really!' Claire squirmed away from him. 'Funny, but I saw Patrick getting into his car when I arrived.' She looked at her wristwatch. 'It must be about an hour ago.'

Ken sat down opposite her and gave her his wide-eyed innocent stare which Claire knew was the prelude to a lie.

'Patrick didn't stay for the full discussion. He said what he had to say, a bit of a pep talk really, and left. We had to carry on and discuss what plans we would have to come up with to ensure the store remains open.'

'I'm sure.' Claire's voice could have sliced concrete.

Ken wriggled slightly on his chair. 'What does that mean?' He no longer sounded so sure of himself.

'It means I know exactly what you've been up to,' she snapped, 'and I tell you here and now I'm not putting up with it any longer. No more excuses, you finish it and you finish it now, or I'm gone.' Claire gathered up her handbag and stood up. 'Now,' she said, 'or you'll never see me and the kids again.'

Holding her head high and ignoring the curious stares of the other customers she stalked out of the coffee shop and through the perfume department, not stopping until she emerged from the swing doors onto the pavement. Her exit was so speedy she almost collided with an elderly couple on the way in.

'Sorry,' she mumbled, hesitating for only the briefest moment, before mingling with the crowds and hurrying to the car park.

21

The dark held him in its grasp. He luxuriated in the thick, pulsating blackness smelling of must and decay.

Scratching noises and the scrabble of tiny paws whispered to him as he stood in this, his special place. He stretched his arms until his fingers brushed the raw brickwork of the wall pressing against his back.

He held his crucifixion pose for a moment, imagining he was Christ, before relaxing and sliding down into a sitting position.

It had been an interesting day.

He leaned back against the wall in the corner where the dark was most intense, and dug his teeth into his bottom lip, chewing and grinding. He did not feel his teeth tearing at his own flesh.

He had often wondered whether it would make what he did more enjoyable if he could experience the pain they felt in the final stages of the game. But, when you are busy doing God's work it would be a sin to experience enjoyment as well.

His hands flexed as he thought of the woman and her powers.

He had watched, from one of his secret places, as she dominated all those poor fools in the boardroom. It amazed him that they could not see through her evil spell, and he was convinced she was getting stronger.

And then there was that gross scene in her office where she tempted the other man with the sins of the flesh. And he, poor fool, succumbed, unable to see she was wielding her power over him.

Fools, all of them, and she was getting stronger and stronger as each minute went by. It would soon be time. But first, she had to feel the fear.

Fear of the dark. Fear of the shadows. Fear of the unknown. Fear was such a positive emotion: one to savour while he went about his business.

He stretched first one leg and then the other. His knees cracked with the effort. It was always the same, he thought, as he rotated his ankles to relieve the aches and the stiffness he was plagued with after he had spent some time in the cramped space of the ventilation shafts.

It was dark in there as well. It was like being enclosed in a coffin, the only difference was it did not have closed ends which meant he could move undetected almost anywhere in the store and spy on anyone he chose.

He shivered with pleasure as he thought of the fear that could be generated if only they knew about the shafts.

He liked the shafts – they were almost as comfortable as this deep, dark place he had selected as his resting place. A place where the sun never shone and daylight could not reach – a place where he was alone with his thoughts and his plans.

The only problem was his plan was not going as he had intended.

Last night she had felt his presence. Although he had not meant it to be so soon she had seen his shadow at her window, and the slow growth of fear in her breast had started. She knew he was watching her, silently, invisibly. The shadow in the dark – the shape-shifting shadow – always out of reach, but near enough to cause fear. That fear should have taken seed last night, and by today it should have been growing.

It had started out well, but now, after listening to the other one, she was convinced her husband was behind it. The insult of it. Spittle gathered at the corner of his mouth. His fury rose clutching him in its hot grasp until he shook and clenched his teeth.

He was greater than her husband or any of her minions. And he would prove it. Oh yes, he would prove it.

22

It had been a bugger of a day. Nicole's eyes stung with tiredness as she sifted through the papers on her desktop and gathered together what she needed. She packed them in her leather briefcase and clicked it shut. After a final look around, she pulled the door of her office closed and turned the key in the lock, before heading down the corridor to the glass dividing doors. Barging through them she almost collided with a workman in a dirty tan boiler suit.

She glared at him. 'What are you doing here? This is the executive floor.'

The man stood motionless, looking at her with impassive light blue eyes.

'Sorry, miss, but the security guard said I had to check this floor.'

There was something about those eyes that made her uneasy. It was as if he was talking to her, but not really seeing her.

Her insides shrivelled and she suddenly wished that someone else would appear. Anyone. Even Harry would have been welcome.

'Where is the security guard?' she snapped, pulling herself together. It wouldn't do to let this unsavoury looking workman know he had unsettled her.

'Downstairs, miss, in the guardroom.'

His eyes did not waver.

'So why are you doing his job up here?'

'It's the traps, miss. I have to check the traps.'

'Traps? What traps?'

'The ones I had to put in the ventilation shafts. For the vermin, you see.'

Nicole shuddered. 'Vermin? What vermin?'

She was aware she was repeating herself and her annoyance increased.

No emotion showed on the man's face, and his voice was calm and measured. 'It was because of the noises, see. Scrabbling noises the typists said. So the traps were put in, and now I need to check them. See if anything's been caught.' He paused as if thinking. 'Probably nothing there. Probably just the typists' imagination, but I still have to check.'

'Well, couldn't you do it later? After everyone's gone home.'

Nicole gritted her teeth. The man was so slow and deliberate she was sure he didn't have all his senses.

'Sorry miss, but I thought everyone was gone.'

His eyes appeared opaque giving the impression there was no intelligence or understanding behind them.

Nicole glared at her watch.

'Damn, is it that time already?' Glancing at him dismissively, she started to walk to the lift. 'Well, I suppose you'd better get on with it then, but make sure you don't make a mess.'

'Yes miss,' he said.

Although Nicole was reluctant to admit it, even to herself, the workman had startled her. She had this odd prickle at the back of her neck, the one she'd experienced frequently over the past few weeks. It was the strangest sensation which made her feel as if someone was watching her. It made her wonder if his eyes were following her as she walked away from him.

Thankfully the lift doors were open when she reached them but, although she tried to resist it, she couldn't help glancing back along the corridor as she entered. She just had time to register that no one was there before the doors swished shut.

A laugh, half hysterical, half giggle, escaped from her lips. Scott was maybe right when he told her she was becoming paranoid, she really must pull herself together.

The basement food hall was gloomy and deserted when

she got out of the lift. Only the security lighting was on, and it did little to illuminate the vastness of the area other than creating pockets of shadows, which seemed strangely menacing.

The back of Nicole's neck was prickling again and she hurried past the aisles of food that led into the darkness of the interior. Reaching the door that led to the stairs she slipped through it and clattered upwards to the middle landing. The security guard would be in the guardroom in the back corridor so once she left the stairs she would be safe.

'Harry?' she shouted as the stair door clanged shut behind her. 'Where are you?'

The light in the corridor fizzed and spluttered making the shadows dance.

Her heels clacked on the stone floor and she was halfway to the guardroom before Harry's tousled head peered round the corner.

'You've been sleeping,' she accused. 'Didn't you hear me shout? I need you to let me out.'

'Yes miss,' he said, although she knew as well as he did that she could have let herself out.

'And while you're at it, you can walk with me up the alleyway.' Nicole hated saying it, but she could not shake this irrational fear she had that she was being watched. 'I just want to make sure you've got rid of that tramp,' she added as if this would explain her request.

'The tramp's long gone.'

Harry opened the heavy iron door and stood back to allow her to leave the building. Despite the sturdiness of the door it made no noise as it swung shut, apart from a soft click as the lock engaged.

A street light shone down the alley, not quite reaching the corners and alcoves. Nicole's anxiety increased and, although Harry was at her side, she kept looking into the shadows expecting someone or something to materialize and take them both by surprise. She could have been in an alien world if it had not been for the muffled noises of pedestrians going about their business and the steady hum of traffic drifting towards them down the deserted alley. Nicole did not feel safe, and for a moment she wondered if she had made a mistake asking Harry to walk with her. After all, what did she know about him, apart from the fact she didn't like him.

Her footsteps quickened until they reached the main street. It was like entering a different world. A vibrant world. A world with people and cars and buses, and everything else that signified she was in a city centre. A world where she could be safe again.

The tension seeped out of her body leaving her feeling slightly faint, and there was an ache where her muscles had slackened.

'I won't need you anymore,' she said in the sharp tone of voice she reserved for people like Harry and, without looking back at him, she joined the stream of people on the pavement.

The shadows at the end of the wine row shifted and moved as Julie straightened from her crouching position. It had been at least three minutes since Nicole had vanished through the service door to the stairwell leading to the rear of the store. Nicole wouldn't be returning now, so Julie felt safe enough to leave her hiding place.

She'd made it a habit never to leave the store before Nicole, although she wasn't sure what good it did apart from giving her the satisfaction of observing the other woman's unease as she passed through the gloom of the empty building. Her mouth twisted into a smile as she remembered Nicole's frequent glances over her shoulder. Maybe Nicole wasn't wrong about her feeling of being watched, because Julie constantly watched her, making sure she always knew what the other woman was doing. She didn't want to miss the chance of taking her revenge on Nicole if the opportunity arose.

Julie bent down, and lifting her coat from where it lay on

the floor she slipped it onto her shoulders. If she hurried she would be able to follow Nicole to the car park and observe her reaction when she saw her beloved car. Julie shivered with anticipation as she thought of the pleasure it had given her when she'd gouged it with the small penknife she kept on her keyring. It had been worth missing lunch to perform that tiny act of revenge.

She could still hear the screeching noise the knife made as it bit into the shining blue paintwork of Nicole's favourite possession. It echoed in her head, setting her nerves on edge, making her close her eyes until a vision of the knife biting into Nicole's flesh forced its way into her consciousness.

Her eyes snapped open at the force of her vision. She shivered. Hate had taken her to depths of emotion that frightened her with their intensity. Even now she was never entirely sure if she could carry out everything she wanted to do. Nor was she sure she wanted to sink to the level of Nicole's depravity.

Her fingers caressed the penknife in the depths of her pocket. It was like caressing Dave. 'My dad gave it to me.' His voice echoed in her head. 'It's all I have left of him.' And now, it was all she had left of Dave.

The corridor echoed with her footsteps as she ran to the back door, almost colliding with it as it opened.

'Sorry, Julie.' Harry grasped her arm as she staggered backwards. 'I didn't know you were behind the door.'

Julie leaned on his arm, quickly regaining her balance. 'That's okay Harry, I should have taken more care, but I didn't expect anyone to be coming in at this time of night.'

A fleeting smile crossed Harry's sad features. 'I was just seeing Mrs Ralston up the alley, seemed a bit nervous like, she did.' He held the door open for her. 'Would you like me to walk you up to the main road, as well?'

'No, I'll be fine. Who'd bother me here when a good shout would bring people running to see what was happening?'

'You sure, Julie? It's no trouble like?'

'I'll be fine, Harry.' Julie turned and gave him a wave as

she walked towards the street.

Harry watched her for a moment and then entered the building. As soon as the door closed behind him Julie started to run. She couldn't be very far behind Nicole now.

A sense of unease crept over Nicole and for a moment she was hesitant to enter the gloomy area of the car park. The car bays, dark caves under the overhanging roadway, made a perfect hiding place for muggers and car thieves. Suddenly Nicole remembered she had forgotten to send someone to put up the hood of her car. The spurt of fear that her precious car might no longer be there overcame her nervousness and she ran towards her parking space.

An exiting car roared past her in a cloud of exhaust fumes and a cheeky toot of the horn. She jumped sharply to the side of the path with a muttered, 'Cheeky bugger.'

A disturbing thought crept into her mind. He must have seen her in his headlights, but he'd kept coming straight at her. She shook the thought away. No one would be foolish enough to mow a pedestrian down in an empty car park. She hurried to her sports car, which the menacing car's headlights had illuminated as it drove past.

At least the car was still here, although her feeling of unease had not decreased. She imagined eyes watching her and glanced nervously over her shoulder, but all she could see were shadows. The sooner she got out of here the better, she thought, rummaging for the car key in her handbag.

Her key was in the door lock before she spotted the dark shape on the driver's seat, but she was used to rubbish being dumped in her car when she forgot to close the hood, so she leaned over ready to scoop it out onto the ground.

Her hand closed over the shape before she realized what it was.

A shudder rippled through her body, freezing her, before an involuntary scream, shrill and despairing, erupted from her throat.

23

Wind soughed in one side of the glass shelter and out the other. Harry gripped the edge of his jacket, where it was missing a button, pulling it closer to his body. It had been a long day and the bus was late. A good job Babs was easy going, although she would have kept Rosie out of bed because she knew the child would not go to sleep until he had kissed her goodnight.

Rosie was Harry's only child and she was never far from his thoughts. He closed his eyes now, picturing her. She was growing fast, but to Harry she was, and always would be, a child. He loved her with an intensity that shut out everyone else, even his wife. Harry carried the guilt of this on his shoulders, but Babs understood and was in agreement that Rosie had to come first. As a result, she gratefully accepted any little morsel of love Harry had left over.

When Rosie was born, Babs became depressed and refused to look at her.

'I've failed you,' she'd said.

It had taken all Harry's persuasive powers to convince her that, as far as he was concerned, Rosie was perfect. Babs now loved Rosie as much as Harry did, but neither of them had been able to forget her initial rejection of the child. And, as a result, Babs had slipped further into depression. She accepted everything Harry did and said without argument in an effort to atone for her failure to produce a perfect child.

Harry accepted her penance, although he had no complaints – Rosie was his child and would always be his child.

The bus was quiet. It was too late for the teatime rush and too early for the late night carousers to have left the pubs yet. Harry slumped into a corner of the back seat where he could close his eyes against the darkness of the night, and the darkness that was within his soul.

His brow creased with the weight of his worries. What would Babs say if he lost his job? Rosie wouldn't care. She would have her dad at home with her. She had no worries, but Harry worried for her. How would he be able to look after her? It was not as if she would ever be able to leave home, so he had to make sure her future was safe. How could he do that without a job?

Damn that Mrs Ralston. He had been all right until she took a pick at him, and now she wouldn't leave him alone. 'Do this, Harry! Do that, Harry! You haven't done this, Harry! You haven't done that, Harry!' His mouth moved silently as he mimicked her.

What did she expect from him? He was doing his best, wasn't he? Only it wasn't good enough for the perfect Mrs Ralston. She was one God Almighty bitch and he was at a loss to know how to manage the situation and please her. If the truth be told there was no pleasing her.

Dark despair settled over Harry each time he realized his days were numbered.

'Hello Harry, my love.' Old Mrs Dempster from the end of his street swayed down the aisle of the bus and plonked herself into the seat beside him. 'Saw your Rosie today. My, but she's getting big. Soon have to watch out for the boys I reckon.'

The aroma of unwashed skin and urine wafted around Harry and he almost gagged, although that might have had as much to do with the suggestion of boys as the smell.

'Have to watch these Mongols, you know. Sex mad they are.'

'Rosie is a girl with Downs Syndrome, Mrs Dempster, and she's definitely not sex mad.' Harry's voice was stiff with anger. He hated it when anyone referred to Rosie as a Mongol.

'Well, whatever.' The old woman's eyes gleamed. 'You'll still have to watch her. Don't want her bringing home any surprises now, do you?' The malicious gleam in her eyes matched the sting of her comments.

Harry held on to his anger. It was something he'd got used to doing over the years since Rosie was born, although it was getting harder as he grew older. It was like holding down a tidal wave of emotion, one that was getting increasingly difficult to manage, and the pressures surged within him in an effort to find release. But release was not an option for Harry because he was afraid of the explosive effect of lowering his flood barriers. So he did the only thing he could do, he gritted his teeth, scrunched further into the corner of his seat and tried not to listen to the droning voice of the woman who sat next to him.

He thought of Rosie, his Rosie. Rosie with her oriental features, the innocence of her expression, the way her almond shaped eyes crinkled at the corners when she smiled at him, and her chunky body that became as light as a fairy's when she danced for him.

If things had been different she could have been a ballet dancer. But Harry knew that would never be possible for Rosie because things were not different and there was always the problem of acceptance.

The world was a cruel place for girls like Rosie. Harry sighed, knowing there wasn't much of a life for his daughter outside her family, but on the other hand, he would never lose her.

The bus trundled to a stop outside the few shops that serviced the council estate and was known by the grandiose title of the Greenfield Shopping Centre.

Mrs Dempster lumbered to her feet in a wave of nauseating aromas. 'I'll get you down the road,' she said to Harry as she turned backwards to lower herself to the pavement.

Harry grasped the icy rail and stood for a moment until she was well clear.

'I have to go to the shop,' he mumbled, not wanting to walk with the old woman and her accompanying smells.

She snorted as she tightened her coat collar around her neck. 'Don't know what you want to shop there for,' she complained, 'dirty, Paki bugger. I wouldn't touch his stuff if you paid me.'

Turning away from Harry she stumped off up the road. 'Don't blame me if you get salmon thingie,' she called over her shoulder. 'Serve you right for shopping there.'

Harry stood for a moment watching her shuffle off down the road. He should have gone with her, there were dark areas where any of the local yobbos might be lurking and he would never forgive himself if she came to harm. Still, he thought, it would be a brave one who tackled old Mrs Dempster for she had been known to inflict serious damage with the handbag that hung from her arm like a leather weighted cosh. In any case, she wasn't his responsibility, so he turned away and walked into the deserted shopping square.

The jangle of discordant music drifted through the pub door as he passed it and, because they were a rough lot, he hoped the drinkers were too busy with their pints and nips of whisky to look outside. He limped in the direction of the mini-supermarket, passing dilapidated shop fronts, boarded up windows and graffiti-covered walls on his way to the only lighted windows in this barren area.

The shop, when he entered it, was not much warmer than the square outside, but the owner greeted him with his usual expansive smile.

'You in for your usual?' he asked. 'Wee Rosie's treat?'

Harry slumped against the counter. 'That's right, Ali.' Everyone called the shopkeeper Ali, and Harry was no exception, although he was perfectly aware the man's name was Vijay. It was a hangover from the time of Vijay's arrival in Greenfield when the kids all called him Ali Baba. 'Some humbugs for Rosie, she loves them and I wouldn't want to disappoint her.'

Vijay still sold sweets in the old fashioned way which was why Harry preferred to buy them here. He didn't trust all these pre-packaged sweets, they weren't the same, didn't have the same flavour for one thing. So now he watched as Vijay pulled a jar from the shelf and weighed the sweets on old fashioned brass scales.

'You look tired, man.' Vijay didn't look up from his task. 'Saw you limping when you came over the square. You okay man?'

Harry forced a smile. 'Yeah, I'm okay. Just have this bloody corn on my toe, can't get it to go away.'

'You try corn plasters, man. I give you good ones, better than the chemist.'

'Yeah, okay, anything's worth a try.' Harry paid for his purchases and smiled again at the shopkeeper. 'See you later, Ali,' he said as he limped out of the shop.

The curtains twitched as he walked up the garden path and light spilled out onto the neglected garden. The house was a typical council house with two small bedrooms and a bathroom upstairs, and living room and kitchen downstairs. It wasn't in particularly good condition, but nevertheless, Harry was proud that he lived in a house rather than a flat as most council tenants did. He fumbled for his key, but the door opened before he got there.

'You'll get the cold, Rosie,' he protested as he pushed her inside, 'and anyway, you shouldn't come to the door in your pyjamas when you don't know who'll be there.'

'But I saw you coming,' she told him. Harry was thankful that Rosie's speech was good and not like some of them at the Day Centre.

'I might have had somebody with me.'

'But you didn't and I've been waiting for you for such an ever so long time.'

'Yes I know, love.' He pushed her into the living room as he kicked the outside door shut. 'What you thinking about, Babs? Letting her come to the door like that.'

'When could I ever stop her from doing what she wanted?' Babs' voice was soft and gentle.

He had never heard her raise it and he often wondered if she was capable of anger.

She held out her arms to her daughter. 'Come on Rosie, your daddy's here now so we can get you to bed.'

'Wait, wait,' Rosie squealed. 'I need to show him my

new dance step.' She pirouetted around the living room in her pyjamas which made her stocky body look even more ungainly. However, she was light on her feet and there was a grace in her movements.

Harry applauded. 'Excellent. That calls for a wee treat,' he said and handed her the sweets.

'You're the best daddy in all the world,' Rosie said as she grabbed the paper bag.

'Off to bed now,' Babs told the excited girl. 'Daddy'll come up once I've tucked you in.'

Familiar tears pricked at the back of Harry's eyes and a lump gathered in his throat as he watched them leave the room. He was afraid for them. Afraid of what the future might bring.

He had a sudden vision of the tramp who sat in the alley and wondered if it might come to that. His shoulders slumped as the reality of his position hit him, his lack of power and his inability to get his problems sorted out.

Babs shouted from upstairs. 'She's bedded and looking for her goodnight kiss.'

'I'm coming,' Harry said, forcing a smile to his face.

He hugged and kissed his daughter with a desperation that made her eyes widen. 'Go to sleep now, Rosie,' he said, 'and I'll see you in the morning before I go to work.'

'Yes, daddy.' She snuggled further under the covers and closed her beautiful almond shaped eyes.

Harry blinked away the tears that had been threatening to overwhelm him all day. How could he face Babs tonight when he was so upset about the possibility of losing his job? Babs, who had never harmed anyone and was always so gentle and understanding. There were enough worries and sadness in his wife's life already. How could he add to it?

Harry forgot his corn as he stumbled down the stairs and opened the front door.

Babs followed him out. 'I've got dinner in the oven for you,' she called to his retreating back.

'Sorry love, I'm not in the mood,' he shouted over his shoulder, as he vanished up the dark street.

24

Julie slowed when she reached the end of the alley, but even then it was not enough and she almost collided with an elderly couple as she turned onto Whitehall Street.

'Sorry,' she said.

The breath whistled out of her throat in a wheeze as she struggled to regain her composure.

'And so ye should be.' The old man scowled. 'Running out of the alley like that, ye near knocked us down. A woman of your age should know better, it's not as if ye're a lassie.'

'Hush, Charlie, she didnae mean it. Did ye no, hen?'

The woman smiled apologetically and, grasping her husband's arm, pulled him along the street.

'C'mon, or we'll miss the start . . .' her voice faded as they turned the corner and continued along Whitehall Crescent.

There were more people than usual hurrying along the pavement. Some were coming from the direction of the railway station and some from the car park under the Tay Road Bridge which lay just beyond Tayside House.

They formed a constant stream of bodies that met and merged in front of the massive building that towered over the city like a watchful sentinel of the ruling Council.

She could only guess that some pop star or celebrity was appearing at the Caird Hall.

Julie weaved her way through a mass of people hurrying in the opposite direction.

Sidestepping to avoid a couple who seemed intent on pushing her out of their way she narrowly avoided bumping into an old busker with an accordion.

She veered sharply to her right, battling through the

crowd where more than once she collided with passers-by, but she sped on to cries of, 'Canny up there.' 'What's all the hurry?' 'Watch where ye're going.' Or the more prevalent, 'Get oot o ma fuckin road.'

Intent on catching up with Nicole, she paid no heed to any of them.

Tayside House loomed in front of her. She sped past the metal mesh barriers which denied access to the escalators, and then through the short tunnel that connected the buildings on either side. With the multi-storey tower now at her back Julie gripped her shoulder bag close to her body and started to run.

A combination of breathlessness and despair clutched at her insides. She was determined to catch up with Nicole, although afraid she wouldn't unless Nicole had been hindered by the throng of people as well.

Nicole drew her hand back in disgust. The feathers were stiff and cold. As stiff as the body they clothed. She bit her lip as another scream threatened to erupt.

'Is something wrong?' The voice came out of the darkness behind her.

She jumped and shrank back against the side of her car.

He was tall and fairly young, although his face was in shadow.

He raised a hand in a reassuring gesture.

'I heard you scream . . .' his voice tailed off, 'but if you'd rather I went . . .' He turned and started to walk away.

'No! No!' Nicole pulled herself away from the side of her car. 'It was just the shock, you see.' She struggled to regain control of her breathing. 'I . . . I wasn't expecting it and it took me by surprise. It's something horrible and it's on the front seat.' She looked at the black object. 'I don't want to touch it again.'

He looked over her shoulder. 'What the hell is it?'

'I don't know, but I think it's dead.' She wanted to cry and her body stiffened as she held back the tears.

Leaning into the car, he grasped the tip of a wing and held the blackbird up so that it dangled, wings outspread.

'How the bloody hell did that get there?'

He looked at it for a moment and then threw the body into the shadows.

'Some bloody sick buggers going about,' he muttered.

The dull, thudding sound of the bird hitting the ground vibrated from her head into her body, leaving an aching nauseous emptiness behind. The silence that followed was even more disturbing.

'Will you be all right now?'

The stranger's voice jarred her back from the black void into which she'd been sinking.

'I . . . I think so.' She glanced at the driver's seat in her car, still seeing the body lying there, although she knew it was gone, thrown into the dark recesses of the car park.

'Here. I'll wipe your seat for you.' He pulled a handkerchief from his pocket and gave the leather a vigorous rub.

He fidgeted for a moment and she sensed he wanted to leave.

'I'll be fine now.' She sat in the seat with a jaunty confidence she didn't feel. 'Thanks for your help. I don't think I could have touched that thing.'

Her foot pressed hard on the accelerator. The wheels spun, and with a roar of the engine, the car sprang forward.

Looking back over her shoulder as she slowed for the exit she noticed he was still standing where she'd left him.

Julie's footsteps slowed when she reached the car park and she slipped behind one of the overhead carriageway's support pillars. From this position, she could see Nicole standing beside her car although she couldn't hear her or see her face clearly. The young man Nicole was chatting to bent over the car and then made a peculiar throwing motion.

Trust her to find a man, Julie thought, even in a car park. She was like a cat in heat. They seemed to smell her out.

Julie sidled round the pillar trying to get a better view. But she was still too far away to hear anything and had to be content with standing in the shadows and watching.

She wanted to move nearer but was afraid to in case she was seen. Gripping her arms around her body, she was oblivious to everything around her except for Nicole.

In this state of mind, it felt as if she were in a world apart, a strange place made up of shadows and fear, where revenge was the controlling force that held her in its grip and wouldn't let her go. A world where she was an automaton pre-programmed for a task that was impossible for her to complete. A world where she didn't really like herself anymore but found it impossible to change and become the old Julie.

The stutter of a nearby motorbike engine roused her from her reverie in time to see Nicole slide into her car, roar the engine and take off with a wheelspin that put her on a collision course with a pillar.

Julie caught her breath, but Nicole straightened the car and drove out of the car park.

Too bad, she thought, a dent in her bonnet would have given Nicole something to think about.

The drive home seemed twice as long and, apart from an occasional car travelling in the opposite direction, was more deserted than usual. Wind tore at Nicole's hair as she drove and her body shivered uncontrollably. She pressed the electric hood control, but nothing happened. It had always worked before and considering the cost of the car it shouldn't have failed. But her driving was erratic and the car wasn't responding in its normal way. The engine spluttered and stuttered and occasionally a red light flashed on the dashboard. She shrank lower in her seat as the vulnerability of her situation struck her and, although she loved her sports car, she was now wishing she'd taken the Saab this morning.

Turning her head to look over her shoulder was becoming a habit, like a tic that was uncontrollable. She didn't want to do it, but even though her car mirror told her there was nothing there, still couldn't prevent herself. Most times when she looked, there was only the dark, winding, country road behind her, although, early in her journey, a tailgating car made her break out into a sweat until it roared past with an angry honk of the horn.

Nothing else seemed to be moving on the road and she listened to the stutter of her engine with growing alarm. The single headlight of a motorbike dazzled her as it reflected back from her mirrors.

'Dip your light, you fucker,' she muttered under her breath in an attempt to stop the burst of nervous reaction that left her quivering.

Reaching for her handbag on the seat beside her, she fumbled with the clasp.

'Bugger, bugger, bugger,' she muttered as her slippery fingers struggled with the catch. She must have travelled miles before the bag eventually opened. She wiggled her fingers down past her purse and chequebook, past the comb and makeup bag, past the plethora of junk, rummaging for the remote control, which somehow or other always seemed to slip to the bottom. Scott continually told her she shouldn't keep it in her handbag, but then, when did she ever do what Scott said, or anybody else for that matter. Even as a child if she'd been told to do one thing she would do the opposite.

Her fingers had only just closed over the remote when the motorbike screamed past her car in a choking cloud of dust. The fumes still lingered in her nostrils when she pressed the remote button and the gates to her property slid open. She drove through them as fast as she could and only breathed properly again once they closed behind her.

The long winding drive up to the house had never before seemed so hostile and deserted and when she reached the garage she was reluctant to leave the car. Not that the sporty model provided any protection, but at least it offered her a degree of mobility. Besides, the security lighting was off and the garages were in darkness. The logical part of her brain told her it must be a fuse, but the other part, the irrational side of her, feared the worst. She imagined shapes in every shadowy corner and footsteps in every rustle of the shrubbery.

The wind whistled through the orchard, bending tree boughs and shaking bushes. Leaves rustled and moved. Shadows danced. She remembered stories of a big cat stalking through the Angus countryside and saw gleaming green eyes in the darkness among the trees. She thought about the moving shadow outside her dining room window last night, and as each fear joined to other fears, she grasped her body with shaking arms and shrank into the seat of her car.

Long before Scott arrived home she froze into an immobility that she found impossible to break on her own.

The lights from Scott's BMW splashed over Nicole as he drove up to park beside her. Even then she still couldn't move. She heard his door slam and the crunch of his feet approaching.

'Bloody hell,' he said. 'You've scraped your car. How the hell did you manage that?'

She looked up at him with a mute plea in her eyes. Couldn't he see she was distressed? What was wrong with him?

'Well, are you going to sit there all night? Get your butt off the seat and have a look.'

He bent down and traced his finger along the length of the car.

'That'll cost a pretty penny to put right,' he grumbled. He pulled the door open, grasped her arm and pulled her from the car.

The top part of Nicole's body moved, but her feet and legs were reluctant to follow, and it was only when her face was in danger of coming into contact with the gravel that she managed to regain her balance.

She leaned heavily on Scott's arm, pressing her body into his. Shudders turned her into a quivering weakling. Hot tears pricked her eyes threatening the defences she had so carefully built around herself over the years.

But Nicole would not cry. She hadn't cried since she was a child and, although she had difficulty quelling the threatened flood, she did not cry now.

'What the hell's wrong with you?'

Scott tightened his arms around her. 'Been in an accident or something?'

Nicole could sense Scott's perplexity. He wasn't used to her needing him in this way, although she could discern that in some strange way he was enjoying it.

'It's been a horrible day,' she muttered. 'Horrible things have happened.' The flood was in danger of breaking.

'Can't have been that bad.' He patted her, treating her like a child or a pet animal. 'Come on into the house and have a drink. You'll feel better.'

He guided her to the side door, flung it open and flicked the light switch. With both hands still on her shoulders, he pushed her gently into the kitchen.

She froze. Stared. Shrank back into his body.

A scream pushed its way up from her throat. She bit her lip until the blood came, to prevent it escaping, but was unable to stop the tortured groan it turned into.

25

Julie gathered her coat around her body, holding it tightly closed at the neck to keep out the cold blast of the wind. This is stupid, she thought, as she walked back towards Tayside House. Adrian was right, her obsession with revenge was eating at her, turning her into somebody even she couldn't recognize. It made her feel dirty. Maybe she should give it up, go back to Edinburgh, forget Nicole ever existed, forget Dave. Ah, but how could she forget Dave. A tear trickled down her cheek, solitary and cold, just like she was. In fact, she thought she would never be warm again. How could she give up on Dave? It was a betrayal of everything that was important for her. And yet, it was destroying her, for with Nicole's destruction came her own, and she knew that with victory there would also be defeat.

Depression gripped her and she wanted to slide into the darkness. Maybe it would have been better to join Dave instead of following this course of revenge which was all consuming and was bound, in the end, to destroy her.

Julie stumbled back the way she had come, barely conscious of her surroundings, oblivious to a junkie busker with his outstretched hand and an accordionist who only seemed to know one tune.

She knew she should return to her flat and jog the poison out of her system. But there was no one waiting for her there, and her flat would be empty and cold. Despair gripped her. Tiredness seeped through her body, sapping her energy. She wanted to lie down, to sleep never to wake, to join Dave wherever he was now.

Her feet slowed, and when she left Tayside House behind her she turned in the direction of Whitehall Crescent and Donovan's pub.

It was warm inside and it buzzed with noise and life, however, she was on her third vodka before she started to revive and relax.

She had never been much of a drinker before Dave died, but that had changed. Maybe it was the poison eating away inside her that made the difference or maybe it was just missing him. Missing his teasing about how prim and proper she was. Missing his laughter – laughter that always jolted her out of a bad mood. Missing his arms around her. Missing him just being there.

'Another vodka.' She waved her glass at the barman.

She twirled her stool around and leaned her back against the bar while she sipped her drink and watched for a table to become vacant so she didn't have to perch on the bar stool that was just a little too high for comfort. Knowing she would have to be quick, she was ready when the crowd at the corner table started to move; and lifting her drink she crossed the room and slipped into an empty seat.

'My, you were quick off your mark. We almost collided.'

He was medium height, had shoulder length hair, narrowed eyes that seemed to see right through her; several heavy gold chains round his neck and a fistful of finger rings that made her wonder how he managed to lift his glass.

'Get you another drink, love?'

'No thanks.'

She turned away from him hoping he would take the hint.

'Oh well, whatever,' he said, sitting down and placing his glass on the table. 'Here on your own, love?'

She looked over to the barman, but he was deep in conversation with a man at the end of the bar. Their heads were close together as if whatever they were saying to each other shouldn't be overheard.

'I'm waiting for someone,' she said, hoping he would believe her and leave her alone.

'That's okay, love. I'll just keep you company until he gets here.' He pushed her glass over to her. 'Drink up, love and I'll get you another.'

A hand reached over and took the glass from her just

before it reached her lips. 'I think that drink's contaminated.' The man from the end of the bar smiled down at her. 'Hoppit, Sammy, or I'll run you in and don't you bother this lady again, she's with me.'

'Sorry pal. Didn't realize she was your bird.'

Sammy's eyes darted around the bar looking for a way out that would not damage his reputation.

'Drink somewhere else, Sammy. I don't want to see your face around here again.' He held a finger up to the barman who came over with another drink. 'Wash this one away, Stevie. I don't think it would be healthy to drink it.'

'Sure thing, Bill.' The barman grinned at Julie. 'You'll be safe enough now.'

'What the hell,' said Julie, not sure what had just happened.

Bill slid into the seat beside her. 'I'd better sit down in case chummy comes back.' He held out his hand. 'I'm Bill Murphy and I just saved you from a fate worse than death.'

He grinned at her with a grin that was so infectious she had to smile back.

'What is this fate you saved me from?'

Her eyes appraised him. He seemed nice in a pleasant sort of way. Attractive, but not too attractive, with his brown hair and eyes and slightly misshapen nose suggesting he might have been in a fight at some time.

'Stevie saw him spike your drink. Says he's done it before to girls who don't have anyone with them, and he doesn't want the pub to get a bad name.'

'Oh.' She swirled the vodka in her glass. 'I see.'

She looked up at him from under her lashes. She liked what she saw. She also liked the note of quiet humour in his voice. Instinctively she knew that this was a man to be trusted.

She relaxed, and for the first time in months, Dave was not at the forefront of her mind.

26

It was the kind of night he liked. Where even the stars were hidden behind a cushion of darkness which enveloped everything, leaving the whole world in shadow, although some shadows were deeper than others. It was in these deeper shadows that he sought anonymity to observe the one he had been ordained to watch.

He was there in the car park when she found his first gift. He watched her reaction. Savoured her fear.

Ah, that was the delicious part, the fear.

But her show of bravado irked him, even though he realised this was just one of her many pretences because she would not want it to be known that she was afraid. For he knew that this woman, like all of her kind, ruled by inducing fear in others.

There was still much more for him to do, although the night was not yet over, nor were all the gifts yet received.

The motorbike felt firm and solid between his legs as he waited and watched in the shadows of the cars.

He knew he was not the only one watching the woman and, although it puzzled him why the other one had followed Nicole and spied on her, he watched her as well.

The other one intrigued him. She claimed to be the woman's friend, but she was not. He could see it when her eyes followed the woman's movements. There was hatred there, a deep, dark hatred. If the woman ever saw it he knew she would make the other one suffer.

However, he did not have time to ponder about the other one for he had more work to do before the night was over.

The motorbike had been a good choice, and the biker it had

belonged to no longer had any need for it. It was powerful and he had no trouble arriving at her house before she did, despite her speed and recklessness. He slid into the shadow cast by a tree. He liked the orchard. It was dark and full of interesting rustles, noises and smells. Small animals and insects crawled here, things of the earth rooting and foraging in the dank, clammy soil, hiding from the light just as he did.

He was almost sorry when he heard the whirr of the electric gate. He drew himself further into the shadows as her car headlights shimmered through the trees with tentative, probing fingers that seemed to bounce off every leaf and branch threatening to expose him.

She drove up to the garage and, although the door rumbled up with the same noise the entrance gate had made, still she sat on in her car like a statue petrified for all time.

He knew why she sat there. She was afraid. He could almost taste her fear. The fear he had induced.

He was tempted to make his presence known, but she had not yet received her other gifts. The gifts he had left earlier.

The big ginger cat circled the tree. The cat was his friend. It was accustomed to his presence and often sought him out on his visits. He bent to stroke it. 'Pretty pussy,' he mouthed, although nothing came out of his mouth except a greyish, filmy vapour that made him think of ectoplasm.

The cat purred its welcome and rubbed itself against him. His hand stiffened. However, he resisted the urge to pull the cat to him and tighten his grip.

'Later, cat. Later,' he mouthed, before straightening up to turn his gaze towards the woman.

He was still watching when the man arrived and it was as he expected, the man ridiculed her and argued with her. The man even pulled her from the car. But, when she choked back her scream – ah, that was the highlight of the evening.

He moved closer. Close enough to see the terror on her face. She liked his little gifts, he could tell.

Later when she called the police, he left. It was time to return to his lair.

27

The scream bubbled up inside Nicole, trying hard to force its way out of her throat, making her bite her lips until they bled to prevent the sound erupting. She tried to step back, but Scott's body blocked her way. She shrank into it, merging with him until they were almost one. He stiffened, but whether that was because of what was in the kitchen or whether he was resisting her, she didn't know or care. She was glad he was with her.

'What the fuck,' he said, the breath of his words whispering through her hair.

Nicole turned, burying her head in his tweed jacket so she wouldn't have to see those little furry shapes with their staring, dead eyes. Little bodies lined up on her kitchen floor, looking as if they had taken part in some weird ceremony. She knew, without touching them, they would be as cold and stiff as the bird she had found in her car.

'That's it,' he muttered above her head. 'I've said before he's a menace, always chasing birds and making a mess. And now this. That cat's got to go, I'm not standing for any more of his shit.'

'It's not Ralph.' Nicole removed her tear-streaked face from his jacket. 'Don't you see it must be that prowler I saw last night. The one you didn't believe was there.'

'Nonsense. This is just the kind of thing that cat would do; murder poor defenceless creatures and drag them through the cat flap as a present for his mistress.' His eyes mocked her. 'Get rid of the cat and you won't have any more bodies.'

'You've never liked Ralph, have you? But you're wrong this time. It's not Ralph, it's someone trying to frighten me and they're doing a damned good job.'

Nicole pulled herself away from Scott. 'I want you to call the police.'

'I'll do no such thing.' Scott thrust his chin out in the belligerent way he had when he didn't agree with her. 'And make a laughing stock of myself? You must be joking.' He pushed her in the direction of the door to the hallway. 'Take yourself off to the lounge and I'll get rid of the bodies.'

'Leave the bodies right where they are,' Nicole snapped as anger surged through her with a flash of heat. 'I want the police to see them exactly as they are. Too bad I didn't keep the bird I found in my car tonight.'

'Bird?' Scott raised his eyebrows and looked at her with an odd expression on his face.

'Oh! Not that you'd be interested, but someone left a dead bird on my car seat tonight. When it was in the car park, I might add. Did Ralph do that as well?'

'Coincidence.' His voice was offhand. 'Pure coincidence. Still, if you're determined to make a fool of yourself calling out the police don't let me stop you.' He squared his shoulders, thrust out his chin and stalked out of the kitchen.

After Scott left, Nicole stood, just inside the kitchen door, looking in fascinated horror at the bodies on the floor. A squirrel – spreadeagled, with its tail bushed out behind – it lay alongside a stoat and the pet white rabbit that belonged to the boy on the farm a couple of miles along the road. Each one had their limbs outstretched in a mad sacrificial pose. Ralph couldn't possibly have caused this carnage.

A breeze tickled the back of her neck arousing her senses and she had a sudden awareness of the open door behind her that led out to the blackness of the garden and the orchard.

The urge to run out into the dark and punish the murderer of these poor animals was almost too great to resist. But she knew that would be foolhardy. She tried to scream her defiance at whoever was out there, but could only summon a croak. Her limbs were leaden. She looked out into the darkness and it was as if she were floating above herself, separate from her body while every rustle and whisper out there was a threat.

Knowing she had to shut the door if she was to stay safe Nicole forced her hand to grasp the doorknob and push the door. Only after it clicked shut and she turned the key in the lock was she able to breathe easily again and lose the out of body feeling.

She forced herself to move, picking her way around the edge of the kitchen so she didn't have to pass too closely to the bodies. Her breathing quickened until she was almost hyperventilating and she had to stop for a moment to grasp the edge of the sink. The stainless steel was cool on her fingers as they tightened until they were white and bloodless.

The tiny bodies mocked her and she was unable to stop looking at them. Who could do such a thing?

She shivered. Unwelcome twinges of fear plucked at her nerves as if they were violin strings playing a dirge.

Nicole was not sure how long she stood, frozen to the kitchen unit, with her hands glued to the sink. Maybe he was out there now, spying on her. She forced her eyes away from the bodies and looked at the window, but saw only the darkness outside. A darkness, pulsing with evil. An evil prepared to take the life of small creatures. Would it stop there? Or was her life at risk as well? Was this a warning?

She pulled herself away from the sink and sidled along the front of the kitchen units until she reached the wall-phone. Her hand was like lead and it took her all her time to grasp the phone and dial. Scott would not like it, but she had no option but to call the police because she had no way of knowing what was outside watching and waiting for her.

Bill Murphy leaned back in his seat. She'd said her name was Julie. It was a nice name to match the woman who had it. He watched her over the rim of his pint glass as he sipped the lager he shouldn't have ordered. He was on-call tonight and should have stuck to the cokes, but he didn't want her to think he was a wimp.

Bill liked what he saw, nice features, short dark hair, sad grey eyes that lit up when she could be persuaded to smile, nice figure, conservatively dressed.

At first, she'd seemed like a startled fawn when he had come over, but after he'd got rid of that slimeball, Sammy, she seemed to relax. He suspected Sammy had spiked her drink but didn't really know. However, it was a great way to introduce himself, and she was well rid of that boyo.

'You don't mind me sitting here?' he said, hoping she wouldn't ask him to go. He would have liked to put his arm around her, but somehow she didn't seem to be that kind of girl.

Julie swirled the vodka in her glass.

'Yes . . . I mean no . . . I don't mind.' Her face took on a pink tinge and she shifted position in her seat until she was slightly further away from him.

'If you're uncomfortable, I'll go.' Bill held his breath waiting for her reply.

'No . . . it's all right. It's just that I thought I might see someone I knew here tonight.' Her eyes roved around the bar in a restless search for familiar faces.

'That's all right then.' Bill wasn't usually so tongue-tied, but this woman was having a strange effect on him. She seemed so vulnerable and restless as if she had something worrying her, while an aura of sadness cloaked her, bringing out every protective feeling he had.

The noise of voices and background music mixed and mingled, soaring around them as they sat there, but the silence between them was impenetrable.

Bill sensed a fear in her. It showed in the way she sat and the way she gripped her glass and clasped her shoulder bag to her body. His instincts told him she was in emotional turmoil and didn't know how to handle it. It made him wonder if he'd made a mistake sitting down beside her, but he wasn't sorry he had.

'Another drink?' He reached for her glass and stood up. Maybe another drink would relax her, although he had a feeling she'd had quite a few already.

She nodded, looking up at him with those large startled eyes, although she just as quickly looked away again as if she regretted letting her guard down.

'She come in here often?' Bill asked the barman.

'I've seen her now and again, but she's not a regular.' Stevie placed a glass in front of Bill. 'Doesn't usually talk to anyone except for an older guy who comes in occasionally. In fact, there he is now.'

Stevie took Bill's money and rang it up on the till. 'Cheers mate, I don't think you're going to get far with that one.'

'Thanks, Stevie, I'll bear that in mind.'

Bill squeezed his way through the crowd until he reached the table in the corner where Julie sat. The man who had joined her was quite a bit older and had a down at the heel look. He seemed to be a man who had seen better times.

'What you drinking, mate?' Bill said as he slid Julie's glass over the table.

The man half rose from his seat. 'Oh, . . . I didn't know you were in company, Julie. I'll be off and leave you in peace.'

'No, no, Harry. You sit where you are.' Julie patted his hand. 'You don't mind, do you, Bill? It is Bill, isn't it?'

Bill did mind. He minded a lot, but he didn't want to contradict Julie and perhaps spoil the start of a burgeoning relationship.

'Of course not,' he said, wondering how long Harry would stay. 'Sure you don't want to have a drink, mate?'

'No, I'm fine. I'll stick with my beer.' Harry smiled apologetically. 'I don't really drink much, you know, but I had to get out of the house or I don't know what I'd have done.' He looked into his glass as if he was expecting it to give him the answer. 'It's been a rotten day.'

Bill's mobile vibrated against his leg, which was just as well because he could hardly hear the ringing tone over the racket in the pub. He groaned when he took it out and checked the number. 'It's the office,' he explained as he got up, 'but it's too noisy to take it in here – bloody nuisance,' he muttered under his breath as he pushed through the crowd to the door.

The street outside was windy and Bill looked for a quiet doorway to take the call. Frowning, he listened for a few moments before saying, 'Can't someone else do it? I've got something good going here.' His frown deepened as the voice continued. 'Bugger you,' he said, 'I'll make sure I return the favour sometime, with bells on.'

Bill pushed his way back to the table. 'Sorry, Julie.' He tried to smile. 'Got to go. Duty calls.' He paused. 'Can I see you again, or maybe phone you?'

'I don't know.' Her voice sounded husky. 'We don't really know each other.'

She looked away from him and turned to speak to Harry.

'Damn! Damn!' he muttered as he left Donovan's. 'I didn't even get her phone number.'

The Coca-Cola can he kicked clattered along the street and bounced off the wall. It made him feel slightly better, although not much.

Julie watched Bill leave the pub. His shoulders had slumped when she turned away from him. Now, as she watched him, he seemed to have a dejected look, rather like a dog who had been kicked. For a brief moment she wanted to run after him, but she didn't.

'Why'd you give him the brush off?' Harry gave her a quizzical look. 'He seemed a nice enough chap.'

'Yes.' Julie's voice was slow and thoughtful. 'But I don't know him. He could be anybody. Besides I don't want complications in my life.'

She gulped her drink trying to rid herself of the guilt that was flooding through her, because, when Bill had been with her she hadn't thought of Dave once. Her eyes clouded with the suggestion of tears as she turned her thoughts to Dave. As long as he was part of her, even in death, there was no room for anyone else.

28

The twins, Jake and Charlie, were being tucked into bed when Claire heard Ken's car pull into the driveway. 'Cuddle down now,' she said in a calm voice that masked her annoyance. 'It's just your Daddy coming home.'

Jake struggled upright. 'Wanna get up,' he mumbled, although his eyes were almost closed.

'Hush now,' she said laying him down again. 'You'll see him in the morning.'

Jake sighed and pulled the covers under his chin. Claire gave him a quick hug.

'Me too.' Charlie leaned forward out of the bottom bunk.

'As if I'd ever miss you, chum.'

Claire bent down and gathered him to her in a quick hug before releasing him onto the pillow and pulling his quilt over him.

'Don't close the door.'

Claire smiled. Charlie liked to play at being tough, but he was still afraid of the dark. 'I won't,' she promised. 'Go to sleep now.'

The room next door was smaller, not much more than a box room, but it was big enough for Catriona who was the baby of the family.

Claire peeped into the small cot bed where Catriona lay, her little mouth blowing bubbles while she slept, and dropped a light kiss on her forehead. 'Sleep now,' she said, as she softly closed the door behind her.

The click of the door latch acted like the release button for her anger. She had hardly taken two steps along the landing before the pain in her stomach erupted, gnawing at her like some animal trapped, trying to find a way out where no way out existed.

Claire gasped and sat on the top stair until both the pain and her anger were under control. She had never liked displays of violent emotions thinking that, in some way, they were demeaning. Therefore, she'd been taken aback at the strength of her feeling about Ken's latest extra-marital adventure, unable to understand why this one was any different and why she disliked Nicole as much as she did.

It might have helped if she'd been able to claw Nicole's eyes out, but that was not Claire's style. Although she was no longer sure what her style was. Maybe it was calm, civilized, or simply just long-suffering. A sudden thought struck her. Maybe she enjoyed being a martyr. It was not a pleasant thought, but she still couldn't bring herself to lose control.

Claire took several deep breaths before standing up and walking downstairs to where she could hear Ken moving about in the kitchen. She leaned against the doorjamb and watched him as he rummaged in the fridge, wondering when he was going to acknowledge she was there.

Ken stripped the ring pull off a can of beer and, turning, he kicked the fridge door shut with his heel, smiling at her at the same time.

'You're home then!' Claire bit her lip and kept her voice low, although she wanted to scream at him.

Ken looked at her over the top of the can as he put it to his mouth and drank. His eyes flickered and he blinked as if he was trying to hold something back.

The hard knot of pain gripped Claire's insides again.

'You bastard,' she muttered, her voice sibilant with disgust. 'You've been with her, and you have the cheek to come back here as if nothing's happened.'

'Don't know what you mean.' Ken's eyes widened proclaiming his innocence.

'Oh, come off it. You know exactly what I mean.' Claire's voice had risen. 'You've been with that blonde tart. I can almost smell her on you.'

All her suppressed feelings exploded in a surge of anger and she thumped the door with her fist. She stared at her hand unable to believe she had reacted so violently. But the pain from the blow was real. Her eyes widened with fright at her lack of control and she modulated her breathing to restrain her emotions. As she regained her composure a hard knot settled in her gut like a stone weight.

'You've got it all wrong.' Ken's smile was smug. 'I've been with Patrick all night. We were discussing my plan for the store.' His smile broadened. 'He likes my ideas and I'm only safeguarding our future.'

Claire stared, wanting to believe him. He didn't have his little boy, hangdog look though, so maybe this time he was telling the truth. 'You won't want your dinner then,' she said as she left the kitchen, 'just as well because I turned the oven off two hours ago.'

Her control only lasted until she reached the bathroom. Locking the door she sat on the toilet seat, and grabbing a towel buried her face in it and wept.

'It's the RSPCA that's needed on this one, not us.' Annoyance still niggled at Bill because of the call out. The car engine whined, contributing to his mood, as he stared out of the window at the enveloping blackness of the country road. 'And what's more, why does it need a detective sergeant and a detective inspector to handle this one? Surely the uniform boys could've done it.'

'You finished grumping yet?' Andy manoeuvred a cigarette between his lips while he steered the car with his other hand. 'Bugger it,' he muttered, as the dashboard lighter slipped out of his fingers. 'Might at least have waited till I got it lit.' He sucked the unlit cigarette. 'I needed a drag, I did.' His face, normally glum, took on an expression of intense sadness.

'Thought you were giving it up. Anyway, you didn't answer me. Why us?'

'Because she's a hotshot business woman who has clout with the Chief Constable. That's why.'

Andy spat the cigarette out of his mouth. 'You think I

like this any more than you do?'

The two men lapsed into an uneasy silence until they reached the massive iron gates that protected the house and grounds. Andy rolled his window down, pressed the buzzer on the gatepost and announced, 'Police,' when the tinny electronic voice demanded to know who was there. The gates swung open, closing again after they had driven through.

'Impressive security,' muttered Bill.

Gravel crunched under the tyres as the car rolled gently to a stop in front of the house. Andy unfolded himself from the driver's seat and hoisted himself out into the fresh air. Bill, who had developed pins and needles in his left foot, opened the passenger door and stretched his legs out of the car, sitting for a moment while the blood prickled back into his foot.

'I wish you'd get a bigger car,' he said as he stood up. 'How you can bear to drive this midget of a thing beats me.' Bill knew the car, a vintage Ford, was Andy's pride and joy.

Andy glowered at him. 'Time to stop moaning and get down to business,' he snapped.

'I suppose,' Bill replied. He was chancing his luck with Andy now, and he knew it. Although they had an easy relationship with each other, there was only so much Andy would tolerate from him.

A tall man with dark brown, wavy, shoulder length hair answered the door. His features were strong and masculine belying the single diamond stud earring he wore in his left ear, which might otherwise have given him an effeminate look.

'I'm sorry to have troubled you, officers,' he said, 'but my wife's in a bit of a state. She's been a bit nervous lately, seeing shadows round every corner.' He led them into the house. 'My wife's in the lounge.'

He turned to face them when they reached the door of the lounge. 'I forgot to introduce myself, I'm Scott Ralston.' He held out his hand and gripped Andy's and then Bill's hand in a strong grasp.

Bill never really trusted people who deliberately strengthened their grip for handshakes and he instinctively disliked this man who impressed him as being just a little too smooth.

'And this is my wife, Nicole.'

Scott flung open the door of the lounge. 'Here are the policemen you sent for, my dear,' he said. The tone of his voice indicated his disapproval.

The woman curled up in the corner of the massive white sofa was younger than Bill had anticipated and quite pretty except for the redness of her eyes making it obvious she'd been crying. Her hair was dark blonde, and her suit was rumpled where she had lain on it.

'Thank goodness you've come.' She blinked tears away from her eyes.

Bill's hands clenched and he shifted his weight from foot to foot. He was reminded of Evie, his ex-wife, who could always get him to do things he didn't want to do. This woman had the same expression and her likeness to Evie was disturbing. Something else niggled at the back of his mind, but he couldn't quite put his finger on it.

The woman looked at him. Tears glistened on the end of her eyelashes, but she dashed them away with the back of her hand before they could roll down her face.

Her actions were so like Evie's it was almost frightening. And, although she didn't look as helpless as Evie, she had that same look of vulnerability. Bill had felt such a fool when he'd realized that Evie's vulnerability was simply an act to manipulate him into doing whatever she wanted.

Heat built up under his shirt and he could feel the familiar tightening of his skin as if his body was too big for its covering. He did not know what to do with his hands so he rammed them into his pockets. Whatever happened tonight, he wasn't going to fall into the trap of feeling so sorry for her he would do anything to stop her crying.

Bill pulled his notebook out of his pocket and opened it. He cleared his throat. 'You reported that an intruder was threatening you.' He did not mean it to sound intimidating, but his voice was loud and hoarse, mirroring his resentment at being called out on what he considered a trivial complaint.

The woman grasped a cushion to her body in a defensive motion and glared at him, making it obvious she was used to more courtesy when she was being addressed. Her husband, perched on the arm of the sofa, dwarfed her, increasing the impression of her vulnerability.

Bill remembered how Evie used to affect him when she was upset, and he wondered why Scott Ralston appeared insensitive to his wife's distress. Maybe he was used to it and maybe he'd become impervious to her emotions in the same way he had with Evie. It's all I need, he thought, another neurotic woman.

Bill sensed Andy watching him and modified his voice. He had no right to be judging this woman, even if she did remind him of an unfortunate period in his own life.

He turned and looked out of the window into the darkness of the night. 'Maybe if you tell us what happened?' His voice was now unnaturally gentle.

Nicole grasped the cushion, wrapped her arms around it and held it tightly to her body like a shield. She had lost all her poise, all her self-control, all her skills of communication and all she was left with was fear and anger. But if she gave way to emotion now she would be lost. Angry tears built up within her and she struggled to retain some composure.

Why wouldn't these bastards stop treating her like a child and understand that she was serious? Scott was the biggest bastard of them all, sitting on the arm of the sofa and treating her like some sort of candidate for a mental ward. And these two policemen, particularly the younger one – supercilious bastard – looking at her as if she was some sort of freak. She was unable to prevent an angry tear from trickling down her cheek.

Ken wouldn't have treated her like this. He would have taken her in his arms and comforted her. How she longed for him now, longed for him to be here instead of Scott. It took something like this to make her realize what she was missing by holding on to her marriage for the dubious rewards of Scott's prospects. She made herself a promise that when this was sorted out she would employ a private detective and get shot of Scott. There wasn't a hint of doubt in her mind that he would provide her with ample evidence so that she would come out of any divorce better than him.

Anger and determination surged through her and she relinquished the cushion to pull herself out of the sofa.

'If you follow me to the kitchen I'll show you what the problem is,' she snapped, wiping her tears away with one furious swipe of her hand.

Nicole stalked out of the room, ignoring Scott's theatrical sigh and the pained expression on the younger policeman's face. She didn't look at them again until she threw the kitchen door open, stood back, and said, 'There. See for yourself.' She glared at them triumphantly.

The younger policeman scratched his head with his pencil, frowned, and then turned to stare at her. He seemed to be trying to suppress a smile, although she could see the perplexity in his eyes.

'Just exactly what are we supposed to be looking at?'

'The blasted animals, of course!' She had wanted to say fucking animals but didn't think she should, they were already looking at her as if she was unhinged.

'What animals?'

Nicole swung round and looked at the kitchen floor.

There was nothing there. The kitchen was as spotless as it usually was.

'But they were there! Laid out in a row like trophies. All dead.' She was unable to keep the horror out of her voice. Her eyes searched the room. She walked into it, but there was nothing. No animals, dead or alive. 'You bastard.' She swung round to face Scott. 'I told you not to move them.'

'But I didn't,' he protested. 'I haven't been back in the kitchen since I left you here.'

'I suppose they just got up and walked away.' Nicole's voice was bitter.

Scott regained his composure and raised an eyebrow. 'Whatever you say, darling, far be it for me to argue with you.'

Bill sighed. 'Let's go back to the lounge and I'll take your statements.' He raised his eyebrows as he looked at Andy and his expression said it all, bloody neurotic woman, bloody waste of time.

Andy's vintage Ford rolled through the security gates. 'Well, what did you make of all that?'

'Bloody waste of time if you ask me,' Bill replied. 'To think I got called away from what might have been a promising relationship to see to a neurotic bitch like that.'

He frowned into the darkness trying to visualize Julie's face, but from the short time they had been together all he could recall was her large, sad eyes that looked at him, but seemed to see someone else.

'Oh, I don't know. Granted it was a strange story and we've no evidence that any of it happened, but it does make me wonder.' Andy fell silent. 'What d'you make of the husband?'

'Bit of a smoothie. I wouldn't trust him with my wallet.'

'D'you think he set his wife up? Trying to give her a bit of a scare, or d'you go with her story of some nocturnal prowler?'

'I suppose it could be either, but I'm more inclined to go with the theory that she's a neurotic bitch who's looking for a bit of attention from hubby.'

'Doesn't explain the animals though.' Andy rummaged in his pocket for a cigarette. 'They both agree the animals were there when they got home.' Andy stuck the cigarette between his lips. 'And then they vanished.'

Bill grunted. He was not in the mood for vanishing animal mysteries. 'Not really Sherlock Holmes stuff though,' he said.

29

The crowds in Donovan's kept increasing and with each swing of the door, more people packed themselves into the crowded bar.

Julie narrowed her eyes. The clattering glasses, chattering voices, and strident background music jangled through her head setting her nerves on edge. The gathering pain building in her temples was becoming more than she could bear.

'Won't your wife be wondering where you are?'

Julie sipped at her drink trying to overcome the pain and accompanying nausea.

Harry swallowed the remains of his beer and then rolled the now empty pint glass between the palms of his hands. He contemplated it for a moment before he spoke, his voice barely audible over the noise in the pub. 'She's used to me. As long as I go home for a wee while to see Rosie to bed she doesn't worry, and I did that before I came out.'

He sighed. 'Sometimes I wish she'd bawl me out, but she never does. It makes me feel guilty in a way. It's as if she takes all the blame on herself, and I don't know how to make it better for her. I can't get her to understand that Rosie's just Rosie, and it doesn't matter that she's not like other kids. I feel I've failed her.'

Julie stretched her arm across the table and laid her hand on top of one of his.

'I'm sure she thinks you're a good man, Harry.'

Harry laughed. 'A good man? I just wish I was.' He contemplated his empty glass. 'I don't deserve her,' he mumbled.

Julie raised her glass to her mouth, but the thought of taking another mouthful was too much for her and she carefully placed it back on the table.

'I think I've had enough, Harry.'

The room tilted slightly and the crowds pressed in on her making it difficult to breathe. She would feel better once she was out in the fresh air.

'Think I'll get a taxi.' She rose from her seat, steadying herself with a hand on the wall, and pushed her way to the door.

'Maybe I'd better see you into the taxi.'

Harry seemed to be frowning at her.

'Nonsense,' she said, pushing the door open.

The fresh air slapped her in the face and her knees buckled. She staggered a few steps outside and leaned on the building for support.

'Oh God, I'm going to be sick,' she muttered, before sliding down the wall and collapsing into a heap on the pavement.

Ken stared after Claire as she stormed out of the kitchen.

'Damn,' he muttered to himself, 'what's come over the bloody woman.'

He raised the can of beer to his lips and gulped, but his eyes were troubled because, in his own way, he loved her. It was just that he wasn't used to her making so much fuss about any of his little romances. After all, who did they hurt? They just made life that little bit more interesting. He drained the can and, squeezing it flat, threw it into the rubbish bin beside the sink.

He was tempted to go after Claire, but as usual, he took the easy way out and reached into the fridge for another beer. It wasn't as if he'd been doing anything he shouldn't have tonight, he thought, deliberately forgetting his afternoon session with Nicole. So Claire had no right to be so uptight about it. Still, he had better end it with Nicole. Pity really, because she was hot stuff. He would tell Nicole tomorrow. Or maybe the next day, although he supposed it might be better to wait until Patrick's plans were clear and he'd filched all Nicole's ideas.

Ken sat down at the kitchen table and several beers later he was sure of what he was going to do and positive he would never look at another woman again. It was Claire for him, Claire and the kids and no way was he going to lose them.

Feeling pleased with himself he rose and walked through to the lounge, eager to tell Claire how much he loved her and convince her she had no need to worry about him straying again. From now on he was a home-bird.

The lounge was in darkness.

His heart jumped and fluttered inside his chest as he experienced a sudden twinge of irrational fear that she might have left him already. But he would have heard the door as well as her car starting up if that was the case, and he'd heard nothing.

He switched on the light thinking she might be sitting in the dark, but the room was empty. Toys lay scattered on the carpet and a solitary wine glass adorned the antique sideboard. Absent-mindedly he picked it up, but there was no ring mark on the polished wood so he laid it down again.

The silence in the empty room was broken only by the slow tick of the grandfather clock in the corner and he realized with a jolt that it was after midnight.

Breath whistled out of his lungs in a long drawn out sigh as his paranoia vanished. Of course, Claire would never leave him. She would have gone to bed, that was all. Probably too angry to say goodnight, he thought.

He turned towards the stairs. Maybe she wouldn't be sleeping. Maybe he could sweet-talk her, and tomorrow, or the next day, it would be goodbye to Nicole.

The bedroom was quiet when he entered, but he sensed Claire wasn't sleeping. He bent over her and extended his hand to stroke her hair. It was at that exact moment his mobile rang.

'Blast it,' Ken muttered under his breath. 'Who the hell can that be at this time of the night.'

He left the bedroom closing the door behind him and walked along the landing into the bathroom where he sat on the toilet seat to answer his phone.

'Ken. Is that you?' Nicole's voice sounded strange.

'Of course, it's me. Who else would it be?' His voice was sharp with annoyance. 'You almost woke Claire,' he complained.

'Fuck, Claire,' she said. 'I've had the most awful evening and I wanted to talk to you. You're the only one who can understand.'

Ken gritted his teeth and listened while Nicole told him what had happened. She finished by saying, 'Scott is the most selfish bastard out, he doesn't have a single bit of understanding or sympathy for me so I've decided I'm finished with him. It'll be you and me, Ken, what we've always wanted and never thought we could have. I'll talk to you in the morning and we can make our plans about when we'll tell Scott and Claire. Love you, darling.' The phone clicked as Nicole hung up.

Ken sat for several minutes, staring at the phone. He had never meant all those promises, surely she must realize that. He had only made them because he believed, just as she had, that he would never have to keep them.

What a bloody mess.

He shivered. Rising from his seat, he tiptoed to the bedroom where he quickly undressed and slid into the bed beside Claire, to lie wide awake for the rest of the night, staring into the darkness.

Harry stared at Julie in dismay. He couldn't leave her here. He would have to get her home.

He looked round him for a taxi, but the streets were deserted and he didn't have a mobile. Babs kept telling him to get one, but most of them were expensive and he never got round to it. He thought about going back into the pub to phone – but that would mean leaving her sprawled on the pavement and he couldn't do that.

Thoughts buzzed round his mind, popping in and out in no particular order. Babs always said he was no good at thinking out problems and she was right.

He bent down. 'Julie, Julie.' He shook her, but she only mumbled.

'Where d'you live, Julie? I need to know so I can get you home.'

Julie's head rolled limply as if she were a baby who hadn't yet developed neck muscles. It was hopeless. Harry knew she wouldn't come round for some time yet, so he hoisted her up until he could get her armpit resting on his shoulder. He wasn't a particularly big man and she was tall for a woman so he didn't have to stoop too far. But what now? Look for a taxi? But where could he take her? He couldn't go home to Babs with a strange young woman who'd had too much to drink. He doubted if even Babs would understand that. There was only one place and luckily it wasn't too far to walk.

'C'mon Julie, help me just a little bit,' he pleaded, as he steered her along the pavement, his shoulder buckling under her weight.

Julie's head lolled against his and she mumbled something incoherent as she lifted her arm, which had been dangling down his back, and wrapped it round his neck.

'Attagirl,' he said. 'Now just let's see your feet moving and we'll be there in no time at all.'

Harry ignored the curious stares of the few people who were on the street as they stumbled along the pavement. He kept his eyes fixed on his target, concentrating on putting one foot in front of the other and keeping hold of Julie so she wouldn't fall.

'Soon be there,' he panted, as the entrance to the alley grew nearer. But the last few yards felt like miles.

When he reached the entrance to the alley he propped Julie against the wall and, coughing and wheezing, tried to get his breath back. Several people passed by, but if they seemed a mite too interested, Harry scowled at them, and they soon hurried on their way. After a time his breathing became more even. He repositioned Julie on his shoulder and, with some difficulty, steered her down the alley.

Harry had to prop her against the wall again as he searched for his key and unlocked the door. He manoeuvred her inside but was unable to hold her up while he keyed in the alarm security number.

'Oh, Julie,' he murmured, 'what a state you've got yourself into.' Bending down he pulled her up. 'Won't be long now,' he said, as he half-lifted and half-dragged her along the passage.

The lift hummed gently upward sounding eerie in the silence of the store. The doors shushed open and Harry dragged Julie through them into a pool of darkness. The security lighting at the far end of the shop floor didn't quite reach the lift, making the shapes around them seem strange and menacing. However, Harry didn't need lighting to know his way around and he manoeuvred Julie through the avenues between the rows of furniture until he reached the bedding department.

'Which one? The best, of course,' he muttered as he inspected the display and, choosing one of the most expensive, he hoisted Julie into the bed.

She flopped, pulling him down with her so that he had to untangle himself from her arms. Her body sprawled where she'd fallen, her blouse twisted upwards under her breasts and her skirt had ridden so far up it exposed thighs, topped with cream lace panties that hardly covered anything. Harry drew in a long, shaky breath. She was a very attractive woman.

With trembling fingers he loosened the buttons of her blouse and slipped it from her shoulders, drawing in his breath at the amount of scarring on her arms. But, deciding it was none of his business, he turned his attention to her skirt which just slipped off after it was unfastened. With a deep sigh of regret, Harry grabbed a duvet from one of the displays and tucked it around her.

'Only the best for you, Julie,' he murmured, 'sleep well and I'll make sure I get back here in time to wake you before the store opens.'

30

Darkness was his friend. It moved with him as he slipped from shadow to shadow until he reached his own secret entrance.

Nobody knew he had a key, and nobody knew the alarm system no longer worked down here in the bowels of the building.

He was home.

He rested awhile in his secret, dark place, listening to the rats and mice scraping in the corners. They were his friends. He felt an affinity with them. Soon their soft rhythmic scrapings lulled him to sleep, but sleep was not natural for him and he woke again to the lullaby of familiar noises – the scrabbling, scraping sounds, the hiss of the pipes and the faint drip of water on stone.

The smell of the dark cradled him. It was a moist smell, like something on the turn, not quite rotten, but well on its way. Mixing with the fetid aroma was the familiar scent of oil and grease, entwined with something akin to paraffin or petrol.

His legs had stiffened under him. Leaning forward he massaged his calves, flexed his knees and rotated his ankles. It was time to go wandering again, while he thought about his next attack on the woman. He would leave a gift in her office. That would be nice.

The store, slumbering in silence as he walked through it, was his domain. During the daytime, it belonged to the people but at night it was his. He could wander wherever he liked. Do whatever he liked, in this place of dark secrets and shadowy corners.

Always he started from the bottom of the store and worked his way up. He particularly liked the food hall with its tall shelving units casting darker shadows than anywhere else in the store. He was there now running his hands along the shelves among the familiar objects. Selecting a packet of cheese he nibbled at it as he climbed the stairs, what he did not eat would do for the mice.

He liked enclosed spaces but had never felt safe in the lift. It was something to do with the motion and something to do with his lack of control over it. The stairs, however, reminded him of tunnels, particularly when they were dark. He liked the dark and he liked tunnels. Maybe he should introduce the woman to some of his tunnels. He had an idea this would increase her fear.

He wandered through the first-floor fashion department. It was another favourite of his. He liked to stroke the materials; rub his hands over the furs – pity they were all fake nowadays – and finger the silks, rubbing them against his face and imagining what it would be like if they were on her.

The door sighed shut behind him when he left, cocooning him on the stairs again. He climbed higher until he came to the next door which led into the furnishing department. Sometimes he came here to sit in their fancy chairs or lie in their fancy beds. They never knew.

Tonight though, there was a mound in one of the beds. He crept towards it, his footsteps silent on the carpet, until he stood alongside. He was curious. As far as he knew he was the only one who crept about the store at night, so who could be sleeping here.

He fingered the edge of the duvet and pulled it away from her chin. It was the other one, although what she was doing here he could not imagine.

He studied her. Her face was flushed with sleep and her short hair lay in a tousled mess on the pillow. There was something childlike about her. He stroked her hair back from her face with one finger following the shape of her head. Hardly touching her skin, his finger traced the curve of her neck – such a lovely, smooth, white neck – his finger hovered for a moment and then withdrew. She mumbled but did not wake, which was just as well because he did not know what he would have done if she had awakened.

He had a sudden urge to leave her a gift so he returned to the fashion department and selected the most expensive silk scarf on display. Then he went back to Julie's bedside and draped it round her neck.

He stroked her hair before returning to his mission of leaving the perfect gift in the bitch-woman's office. But after that, he would return and keep watch over the other one. It would be a long night.

31

By the time Harry got home he wasn't sure which part of his body ached most. He'd walked all the way from the town centre because the buses stopped running hours ago and he didn't have enough money for a taxi.

He hesitated, with his hand on the garden gate while he scanned the windows for a glimmer of light, and was thankful to see nothing but darkness. It was years since Babs had waited up for him to come home, but she never knew when to expect him nowadays and he couldn't tell her because he never knew himself. It seemed that as the pressures of his job increased, so did his restlessness.

Harry longed for the old days when he was happy at work and Babs could have set her clock by his movements. But that was in the days before Nicole rose to her elevated position. Maybe that was the reason she disliked him so much because he could remember when she was just a sales assistant. That was before she started balling Patrick Drake, and earned her promotion on her back. Oh yes, he knew all about high and mighty Mrs Ralston. She hadn't always been so powerful.

Sliding his key into the lock he opened the front door as quietly as he could, easing it shut once he was inside. He didn't put on a light because he didn't need it to feel his way up the stairs, and he was afraid it might wake Rosie or Babs. Avoiding the loose floorboard on the top landing he eased Rosie's bedroom door open and tiptoed over to her bed. She looked like an angel when she was asleep. He smiled and brushed his lips against her cheek before he sidled out the door again.

He wanted to relax in a hot bath to ease his aches and pains but decided not to in case the rumbling of the water pipes awakened his sleeping family. So he crept along the landing into his bedroom, slipped his clothes off and slid into bed.

Babs turned, mumbling in her sleep. Harry longed to reach out to her but knew the coldness of his body would wake her, and he didn't want to explain why he was so late. Not that Babs would reproach him, but the disappointment in her eyes haunted him and he was finding it increasingly difficult to face her.

Harry lay in the dark, eyes closed, but not sleeping. This was the time when all his worries collected and pressed down on him and tonight was no exception.

He didn't recall falling asleep, but the harsh clanging of the alarm startled him awake. He shot his arm out of the bed, feeling for the button to silence it before the noise woke Babs. But he didn't make it in time.

'You were late home last night,' she mumbled.

'I wasn't that late,' Harry lied, guessing she would have been asleep by eleven o'clock.

'I worry, you know,' she said, throwing the duvet to the side and swinging her legs out of the bed.

'I know.' He pulled her back and covered her up. 'You lie there. I'll get my own breakfast and bring you a cup of tea.' She hadn't realized how early it was and with a bit of luck, thought Harry, she'll fall asleep after her tea without noticing the time.

Babs didn't answer, but he could see the reproachful look in her eyes and he was glad to escape to the kitchen.

Drumming his fingers on the worktop he waited for the kettle to boil. He'd already decided not to bother with breakfast in order to save time. The cleaners started work two hours before he did and he had to get there before they arrived, if he didn't they might find Julie. But he had to take Babs her tea before he left so she wouldn't get up and question him.

'I'll be off then,' he said, moving the clock away and putting the cup on the bedside table. 'No need for you to get up yet, Rosie's still asleep.' He kissed her forehead and left.

158

Outside there was no one around except for a scruffy looking dog pawing at rubbish bags and raking through the spillage. He ran along the street, afraid he would miss the bus, but then had to stand and wait for five minutes.

Wind rustled round the shopping square sending pieces of paper, silver foil carry-out trays and leaves scudding across the paving stones. Ali was taking the steel shutters off his supermarket windows. Harry raised a hand in greeting to him, wondering if the man ever slept because he always seemed to be there.

The wind pummelled him making Harry pull his coat around his body. His blood must be getting thinner, he thought, for the mornings seemed to be colder nowadays. He was still shivering when the bus pulled up in a belch of fumes. He got on, huddling in a seat beside the heater, and relaxed. The bus would get him to the store in time to wake Julie. It wouldn't do for her to be caught sleeping in the furniture department.

It was still dark when Julie woke and for a moment she thought nothing in her life had changed. She was back in her Edinburgh flat and the last few months had simply been a nightmare from which she had now wakened. In her dream state she knew that if she got up she could walk to the old-fashioned casement window where she could look out on the Mile which was what everyone called the High Street. She liked the Mile, that long narrow street that led in one direction to Edinburgh Castle and in the other direction to the Palace of Holyrood. She'd been lucky to get a flat there in one of the old-fashioned tenements, though it cost her the earth.

She stretched her arm out expecting it to meet Dave's warm body sleeping next to her, but there was only empty space and a cold bed.

She remembered then. It wasn't a nightmare, it was real, and yet, when she'd been sleeping she'd had the strangest sensation Dave was sitting there watching her. The feeling of being watched was so strong that she struggled into a sitting position and looked around her. But, even in the gloom she knew she'd been mistaken, no one was there and even if there had been, it couldn't possibly be Dave because he was dead.

She turned her face into the pillow and scrubbed her eyes with the corner of the duvet cover.

Tiredness swamped her. Her eyes closed. If she slept again maybe the nightmare would go away.

But her eyes were full of grit, her tongue was sandpaper, and a hammer was beating inside her head.

If only she could sleep she would not want to wake up ever again – but it was impossible.

After a time she sat up. Her head swam and there was a nauseous feeling in her gut. She struggled against it, trying to figure out where she was, because she wasn't in her Edinburgh flat, nor was she in the Dundee one.

Where the blazes was she?

Gradually she acclimatized, although it only added to her confusion.

What on earth was she doing in a bed in the furniture department? Julie rubbed her forehead with a clenched fist hoping it would bring back a memory of how she got there, but it didn't work. She had a vague recollection of a noisy pub, of drinking a lot, of a man with nice eyes, but beyond that, nothing.

Her head throbbed with the effort of thinking. Someone must have brought her here. But who?

She shuddered.

Surely she hadn't been so drunk she had slept with someone. And if she had, where was he? Why couldn't she remember?

She must have had a real skinful last night. More than usual, because she'd never before suffered from amnesia.

She struggled out of the bed. She couldn't be found here when the store opened. How would she explain it? Particularly when she couldn't explain it to herself.

As she rose something fluttered to the floor and, bending,

she picked it up. There was a puzzled expression in her eyes as she looked at the silk scarf. It was beautiful, but it was not hers. She'd never seen it before. Maybe the man with the nice eyes had given it to her. She shook her head. She couldn't remember.

Julie shivered. The heating hadn't come on in the store yet and she was wearing only her bra and panties.

Looking around she spotted her coat, skirt and blouse folded neatly on the bed next to the one she'd been sleeping in. She grabbed them and headed for the elevator. She would get dressed in the toilets downstairs and after that she would worry about what might have happened last night.

32

Nicole woke with a raging thirst and a beating head. After the police left she'd drunk most of what had been left in the bottle of Glenfiddich. She wasn't usually a whisky drinker, but she'd been so upset and annoyed by the way they had treated her that she'd started on the bottle and kept going until it was almost empty.

'Oh,' she moaned, clamping a hand on her forehead. Why hadn't they believed her? Why did they treat her like some kind of lame brain? Smiling at her in that supercilious way some men have when they're talking to a woman. She hated that. It made her feel so inferior as if she were a child again listening to her father telling her she was stupid.

It was that sod, Scott, of course, filling their minds with ideas that she was paranoid, just a silly woman imagining things. She turned round ready to lambast him, but he wasn't there. His side of the bed was empty.

Nicole struggled into a sitting position, each movement sending a stab of pain through her temples. She looked at the clock, but couldn't focus.

The daylight filtering through the window stabbed at her eyes so she supposed it must be morning.

She sank back into the pillows, not caring what time it was. She would go in late – it would make up for all the extra hours she worked.

Her eyelids slipped shut, but the headache kept her from sleeping. She started to count the stabs of pain thumping through her head with the regularity of a pulse-beat but gave up because the effort of thinking was too great.

The bed undulated beneath her and the room wouldn't stay in one place. She tried to ignore the swimming sensation that made her feel she was floating. But when the wave of nausea hit, she forced herself to stumble from the bed into the bathroom. The white pile carpet swallowed her knees as she leaned over the toilet, but the porcelain was cool on her forehead. It helped to slow the room down until it had almost stopped spinning. She started to feel slightly better.

'That was some night you had!'

Nicole didn't need to look up to know that Scott would be smiling as he leaned against the door. One thing she knew she could never expect from Scott, was sympathy. Bastard.

'What d'you care,' she mumbled. 'You've never cared much before.'

'Of course, I care.' He sounded genuine, but when she looked up it was just as she expected. He was smiling.

Nicole struggled to her feet determined not to give him the pleasure of thinking she was suffering.

Acid burned at the back of her throat, but she swallowed hard, trying to ignore it. The hammer inside her brain continued its staccato beat and her eyes lost their focus for a moment.

She frowned, concentrating her gaze on a tile just above Scott's head until her vision cleared again and she was able to walk to the door.

Scott didn't move out of her way and she had to push past him. She continued her careful walk out of the bedroom, intending to go to the kitchen and make an assault on the coffee pot, and almost fell over a suitcase.

'Going somewhere?' Nicole struggled with the fuzz in her brain. She couldn't remember Scott mentioning a trip and she wondered if he was leaving her.

'Paris,' he said. 'I told you yesterday I'd be leaving early to catch the cross-channel ferry. I have a meeting arranged with one of the biggest distributors of software in Europe. If I can get them to distribute our software it'll mean big money.'

Nicole shook her head in an effort to clear it. Had he told her? She couldn't remember, but she didn't think so.

'I don't recall you saying anything.' She enunciated her words slowly.

'The condition you were in yesterday I'm not surprised.' Scott laughed, but it was without humour. 'Anyway, I've got to go. I just popped in to say goodbye.'

'When will you be back?' If he is coming back, she thought.

'Not sure. I might have to go to Brussels and Cologne as well, but I won't be away more than a week.' He moved past her and picked up the suitcase. He hesitated a moment. 'You'll be all right?'

'I suppose,' she murmured. It would please him if she begged him to stay, but she was damned if she would.

'Better get some clothes on,' he murmured as he brushed his lips against her forehead.

'Oh!' she looked down, she had forgotten she was naked. 'Yes, I suppose I'd better before Marika gets here.'

Scott was halfway along the corridor, but he turned to look at her. 'I forgot to say I gave Marika the day off, something to do with her sister being ill.'

'What the hell did you do that for? I need her here. Anyway, I didn't know she had a sister.'

'Well, too late now, and sister or not, she's not coming in today.'

He gave her a grin and with a wave of his hand he opened the door and left.

Nicole glared after him. 'I hope your bloody boat sinks,' she muttered.

Wrapping a robe around herself she staggered to the kitchen and the coffee pot.

The first sip of coffee burned its way inside her and she started to wake up. That was when she saw the passport sitting on the kitchen table. 'Let's see you get to Paris without that,' she muttered and, leaning over to pick up the briefcase from where she had thrown it last night, she stuffed Scott's passport inside.

The Nethergate was deserted when Harry got off the bus. Patrick Drake's store loomed at the other side of the road.

The plate glass windows at street level, with their attractive displays, beckoned with promises of further delights inside. However, the rest of the building had a menacing air.

He couldn't help looking upwards at the dark stone of the building, blackened through years of just being there in the city centre. The walls soared upwards like some mediaeval fortress until they reached the rounded attic windows, marching along the roof like ever watchful sentinels, overshadowed by the turret room in the corner facing the High Street.

Harry imagined it would be possible to see in three directions from the turret room, however, it was boarded up because the floor was unsound and he didn't know anyone who had ever been inside.

He crossed the road and walked down Whitehall Street until he came to the alley leading to the back door. It looked even more claustrophobic than usual, although he supposed he should be accustomed to it by this time.

His footsteps echoed and he had the impression he was the only living being there. He looked around for the tramp, but he wasn't in his usual place. Harry shivered momentarily, fearing the worst, but shook off his premonition. Tramps moved around, it was their nature. He'd probably got fed up with always being moved on. Still, there was a prickle of unease at the nape of his neck.

Harry never got used to the black silence of the store in the early hours of the morning and he always had the oddest feeling he was being watched. It was as if the store were a living entity, which hadn't woken up. But once it did, the odd little noises, the creaks and groans of the building settling, and the hissing of steam or water through the pipes, joined together in a chorus that was unnerving.

Harry flicked the light switch. At least he could get rid of the shadows. The spurt of electricity travelled both ways, up to the swinging, fizzing light and outwards along his finger with the slightest of shocks. He snatched his finger from the switch.

'Bloody electrics, it's time they were sorted before I get a real electric shock.'

He sighed at the thought of having to report it again. Mrs Ralston wouldn't be pleased and, as usual, she would make him feel it was his fault. 'Serve her bloody right if the store went up in flames.' He grinned at the thought and, after closing the outside door, hurried along the passage to the guardroom.

He shrugged his coat off and threw it over the back of the wobbly chair; the one he hadn't sat on since it unceremoniously threw him to the floor one morning. He'd felt a right pillock then, but luckily it was Julie who had come along and helped him back to his feet. She hadn't laughed at him and he'd always appreciated that because he knew plenty who would.

The concertina steel radiator felt barely warm when he put his hand on it so he gave it a kick. Just as he had expected, it rumbled and shuddered into life with the usual creaks and groans as the water squeezed through the pipes. He felt it again, absorbing the vibrations shuddering up his arm. The heat followed, with a spluttering fizzing noise, until the radiator became so hot he had to remove his hand.

Satisfied, he left the guardroom, it would be nice and cosy when he returned from waking Julie. He hoped she was all right and hadn't been sick, for that would take some explaining.

The sound of scampering paws broke the silence as he walked through the food hall. He would have to speak to Neil again. It was his job to keep the store free of vermin, but he hadn't been making too good a job of it lately.

Harry sighed. No doubt madam would blame that on him as well. She blamed him for everything else, whether or not it was his fault, so why would she act any differently.

His knees weakened and his corn throbbed, he couldn't afford to lose this job, but lose it he would. It was growing more likely as each day passed.

He didn't have to wait for the lift. It was sitting ready for him, as if he was expected, giving the impression the lift knew he was too weary to climb the stairs. The doors swooshed closed behind him and, with the smallest of jolts, it rose smoothly to the second floor.

Harry switched his torch on, it was too early for lights to be seen in the store, and headed for the middle of the floor so no light would reflect through the windows. He weaved between and around the furniture to the bedding area.

Stretching out his arm, he prodded the duvet that was humped in the middle of the bed, but it collapsed with the faintest breath of air for there was no body beneath it.

'Julie, where are you?' Harry didn't know why he was whispering because there was no one in the store yet. He raised his voice to a shout, 'Julie? Are you there?' The silence mocked him.

He shone his torch around, trying to pierce the shadows, but nothing moved. She wasn't here. Maybe she'd gone home, he thought, only she wouldn't have been able to get out of the store without setting off the alarms and if that had happened, he would have been called out.

She must be here somewhere. Absent-mindedly he picked up the duvet and replaced it on the bed he had taken it from the previous night. Satisfied that everything was as it had been before he'd left Julie in the bed, he walked back to the lift.

Harry left the lift on each floor and called Julie's name, but there was no answer.

Eventually, he returned to the guardroom where he put the kettle on and brewed his tea. He slipped his shoes off under the table and leaned back sipping the strong brew while he planned what to do next.

He came to the conclusion that Julie was probably hiding until the store opened, so he would look for her then.

Ken didn't want to wake up. He didn't want to go to the store today and most of all he didn't want to see Nicole.

'You were restless last night,' Claire grumbled as she reached for her dressing gown.

'Was I?' Ken was glad she was talking to him again. He

leaned over and hugged her. 'You do know I love you. Don't you?'

Claire wriggled free. 'What brought that on?'

She brushed her fair hair back off her face. Ken loved it when it was that way, all tousled and mussed. It made her look like a girl again. Like the girl he had first seen galloping her horse over the Yorkshire moors, her hair streaming behind her and her cheeks pink in the wind. He hadn't thought he would stand a chance with her because he was only a working class boy at that time, although he had no intentions of remaining working class. Despite that, he had pursued her relentlessly, as he did everything else, and when she agreed to marry him he thought he'd won something priceless.

He had been smitten then and he still was. If it had to be a choice between Claire and Nicole, then Claire would win every time. There was nothing else for it; Nicole was going to have to go.

33

Julie was holding her face up to the hot-air dryer in a not very successful attempt to dry it when she thought she heard her name called. However, with the noise the dryer was making she couldn't be sure.

Sighing in exasperation she grabbed a wad of toilet roll from the nearest stall and patted at the excess moisture. The dryer sputtered into silence.

Julie inched the door open and peered out. There was nothing to be seen other than the empty tables of the restaurant and the dark shadows of the still slumbering store, with only the faint hum of a refrigerator breaking the silence.

She closed the door and returned to the mirror where she applied her face powder and lipstick, which was all the makeup Julie ever wore.

It was what Dave had always said he liked about her, that she did not need to paint her face. And yet, he'd fallen for Nicole, who plastered herself with the stuff. Sometimes Julie wondered whether she would have held him if she had taken a greater pride in her appearance.

Julie pressed her forehead against the mirror as thoughts of Dave flashed through her mind.

What the hell was she doing in Dundee? Adrian was right she should never have come. She should have resisted the compulsion to get even with Nicole and should have buried the past when she buried Dave.

Standing back from the mirror she stared at herself. One way or another, she vowed, it had to end. She combed her hair, straightened her skirt and blouse, and left the ladies restroom.

Her office was dark and silent when she entered it, but that suited her because her head was still tight and she didn't think she could bear too much light.

The packet of paracetamol tempted her when she took it out of the first aid box, but after prodding one tablet out of the blister pack she resisted the urge to take more.

She slumped into her chair, rested her arms on the desk and laid her head on them, letting her mind drift away to happier times.

It had been the High School dance where she and Dave had first got together as a couple.

The band had been so atrocious she'd sat with Dave on the stairs outside the gym hall, giggling every time a wrong chord was played.

They had always seemed to be laughing. They found life so much fun.

Then, when they applied for the flat not thinking they would get it, the sheer joy they had felt when they knew it was theirs.

Dave had painted it himself to save money, although never having painted anything before, he didn't make a very good job of it. But that didn't matter, it was their flat.

It was after that he'd said, 'Let's get married. Let's be respectable.'

She had replied, 'It's not necessary.'

But he'd said, 'Don't argue,' before picking her up and spinning her around.

And so, they had married and for eleven years they had lived happily ever after. And then Nicole had come onto the scene, and everything changed.

At first, she hadn't been suspicious. He was a sales representative so he was away from home a lot. But then his periods away started to get longer and longer until she'd confronted him. At first, he had denied it, but then, after a time he had told her. He was leaving her for Nicole.

The damnable thing, of course, was that Nicole didn't want him. And so they both lost him, although Julie knew that she was the only one who suffered.

Julie lifted her head off her arms. Her eyes were wet. There were so many unshed tears that it was a relief to cry.

Maybe if she'd cried before, she would have been able to let Dave rest, although she doubted it. But now, in the darkness of her office the tears flowed.

She cried for Dave, she cried for herself and she cried for the life she had lost.

Maybe it was not too late. Maybe she could start again, learn to live without Dave and without all these gnawing feelings of hate that were eating her up.

Later she would phone Adrian, tell him she was coming home to Edinburgh and then finish it with Nicole. With a bit of luck, she would be back home before Christmas.

The piercing ring of the doorbell startled Harry out of a restless doze. He had stretched his arm out to silence the alarm clock before he realized where he was. His mind was fuzzy with sleep and for a moment he wondered how he'd got here, but then the memory of his early morning start and his concern about Julie crept back into his consciousness with an irritating niggle that something was seriously wrong.

The bell pealed again and he gave himself a shake, stretched out his legs, pushed his feet into his shoes and levered himself out of his chair.

'All right, all right,' he grumbled as he limped towards the back door. 'I'm coming.'

'Took your time, didn't you?' Betty looked him over. 'You look like death warmed up. Sleeping, were you? Lucky I wasn't madam, eh.' She poked him in the ribs. 'Don't look so worried, man. I won't be telling her.'

Harry watched her hurry up the corridor. She was surprisingly light on her feet for someone so large.

'Got to get the coffee on,' she shouted over her shoulder. 'Julie will want to take a cup to our friend in the alley.'

Harry opened the door again and peered out. 'Well I'll be damned,' he said, as he looked at the tramp sitting in his usual place.

The tea Harry had made earlier was cold. He looked at his watch. No wonder, he must have slept for an hour, although he had no recollection of dozing off.

He felt parched and bone tired. His back ached from his uncomfortable position in the hard chair, his legs were stiff and his corn was throbbing. If it had not been for his pride he thought he might have sat down and cried, but men didn't cry, or so his mother had brought him up to believe.

The sink in the corner of the room was cluttered and none too clean, but he stuck the kettle under the tap and waited while the water rattled into it. He was careful as he plugged the flex in and flicked the switch; he didn't trust the electric wiring down here. You just had to listen to all the odd fizzles and sparking noises coming from the lights to know things were not right. Some day the damned store would burn down, he just hoped that not too many of his friends were inside when it did.

He felt better once he had downed two cups of the strong tea he made for himself. Tar, Babs called it, while Harry responded that he wouldn't drink the cat's piss she called tea.

As he tended the door, opening it for one member of staff after the other, the thought of Julie was never far from his mind. He half expected her to come trotting along the passage with her handout for the tramp, but she never appeared and he couldn't leave his post until it was almost nine o'clock and time to open the store.

He detoured the food hall on his way to open up, but there was no sign of Julie. His worries grew.

Forcing himself to smile at the customers, he unlocked the front doors and tipped his hat to those who were waiting.

'You're late this morning.' The military-looking man with the well-groomed moustache, but rather shabby suit, snapped at him as he passed through the swing doors. He was always the first customer.

Harry hadn't quite sussed him out so he usually watched him closely, suspecting he might be a shoplifter. However, this morning, his mind was occupied elsewhere.

On his way back to the food hall he stopped at the restaurant and beckoned to Betty.

'Seen Julie this morning?' He held his breath as he waited for her answer.

Betty glanced up. 'Got a thing for Julie, have you?' She picked up a cloth and rubbed a tabletop. 'Wife'll have something to say about that, I expect.'

Heat crept upwards from Harry's collar into his face.

'Not at all,' he replied, his voice brittle, 'I just needed to let her know something.'

'Hmm.' Betty continued to rub at a non-existent dirty spot. 'She's in her office, but I wouldn't go disturbing her if I were you. She's got a pig of a headache.'

'Oh.' Harry's voice faltered, weak with relief. 'I'll catch her later then.'

He knew Betty was watching him as he walked away, he could feel her eyes boring into his back.

Ken was late so he didn't need to go to the rear entrance; instead, he scuttled into the store behind the major, which was his pet name for the old gent who was always first through the doors. He expected the security guard, damned if he could remember his name, to acknowledge him as he passed, but the man seemed to be lost in his own thoughts. Ken decided he would speak to him later because it reflected badly on the store if the staff were falling down on the job.

He glanced around him, ready to change course if he spotted Nicole, but couldn't see her anywhere. Maybe she was lying in wait for him upstairs, so it might be best if he avoided her office, particularly after her phone call last night about leaving Scott. He would have to shake her off because there was no way he was going to leave Claire for her. Claire was class compared with Nicole.

The lift was empty when he reached it. He got in and pressed the button to close the doors, but they seemed to take forever. He hadn't realized he'd been holding his breath until he exhaled in a massive sigh. He wasn't out of the woods yet, and wouldn't be until he got to his office without Nicole seeing him.

The doors creaked open at the executive floor and he looked swiftly up and down the corridor. The coast was clear so he scuttled along to his office, not relaxing until he was inside with the door shut.

'What a bloody mess,' he moaned as he slumped into his chair. How on earth was he going to get rid of Nicole? What would he do if she refused to take no for an answer? He couldn't bear the thought of a scene. But what if she'd already told Scott she was leaving him? He was no match for Scott and then there was Claire. How was he going to explain it to Claire?

He would just have to handle it. Ken shuddered. At all costs, Claire mustn't know.

34

After three cups of coffee, Nicole's nerve endings jangled and her body woke up. However, her foul temper remained, seething and boiling deep within.

'Bloody Scott,' she kept muttering over and over again, 'who the hell does he think he is?'

She rammed the dirty cup into the sink and kicked the dishwasher. 'Damned if I'm going to load that bugger,' she said, watching the cup pirouette in the base of the sink before toppling over and parting company with its handle.

Mounting rage forced Nicole's heart to thump – the pulse beats, pushing and forcing their way up into her throat until they almost choked her with their intensity. Her knuckles whitened as she gripped the edge of the sink trying to tame her rising fury. Eventually, she gave way to it and started to throw things.

First, she threw the dirty crockery Scott had left on the worktop. Once the crockery was exhausted she started on the wall units and threw everything she could touch. Eggs spattered on the wall; pickles and sauces joined them; flour; sugar; and jam helped create a colourful mural. Bread littered the floor; biscuits crunched beneath her feet while washing up liquid created a skating rink.

But the thing that gave her most pleasure was spattering Scott's favourite wine against the back door with a throw that could have launched a ship.

At last, she was spent and sank down into a sitting position among the mess covering the floor. That was when she began to laugh. It started with a giggle and gradually grew stronger until she had to wrap her arms around her body to contain herself.

Eventually, she wiped the laughter tears from her cheeks

with the back of her hands, and holding her sides she hefted herself up to a standing position.

She retrieved her briefcase, wiped it with the back of her hand, and then picked her way over the kitchen, slithering and slipping on the combination of flour, egg, washing up liquid and wine. She fought to keep her balance and when she came within reach of the door she leaned over to grasp the handle, easing herself towards it. Sliding sideways she pulled the door open and stepped through to the safety of the corridor. Without a backwards look, she pulled it shut behind her and left everything.

Stripping off her robe she let if fall on the carpet and headed for the shower. The spray stung her skin, hot and refreshing, and she turned this way and that to allow the water to penetrate every part of her body. Finally, she tilted her head back and lifted her face into the spray, enjoying the feel of the water dribbling down her forehead and cheeks, through her hair and over her shoulders. The hot water washed away the tightness in her muscles as well as the goo that covered her.

Feeling refreshed she wrapped herself in a towel and riffled through the clothes in her wardrobe. She selected a white blouse and a black jacket and skirt which was smart in its severity. Black tights and high-heeled shoes completed her ensemble.

Today, she decided, she would be professional even though her nerves were on edge after everything that had happened: the dead animals, the sense of being watched, Scott's scepticism and the disbelief of the police.

Damn them all to hell. It was up to her to impress on whoever was doing these awful things to her, that it did not affect her one little bit.

A myriad of small sounds: the patter of feet, the soft swing of a door, the hum of the lift, the rattle of trolleys being stacked in readiness for customers, all of these sent messages to Julie that the store was coming to life.

She eased her body out of the chair trying to ignore the sharp pangs piercing her head. A coffee would be nice and Betty would expect her to appear at the restaurant as usual. Better not disappoint her.

The door creaked slightly when she pushed it open and the sound, which didn't usually bother her, stabbed into her brain until she felt it would splinter into little pieces. She winced and crept out, into the food hall. Looking straight ahead she marched to the restaurant. Reaching it, she slumped onto one of the plastic chairs. Already she realized it had been a mistake to leave her office.

'Godalmighty.' Betty's voice, sounding unnaturally loud, made Julie shrink into the seat.

'Can you speak a little quieter,' she muttered. It hurt when she looked up so she kept her gaze on the tabletop.

'Must have been some night you had.' Betty patted her shoulder.

Julie winced as the blows vibrated up into her head.

Betty sat down opposite her. 'You look like death. Rough night, huh?'

Julie nodded. Pain stabbed at her temples and her eyes filled with tears.

Betty patted her hand. 'Can't let the staff see you like that so you pop back to your office and I'll bring you the strongest coffee you've ever had. That'll sort you out and in an hour or two the hangover will be a memory.'

Julie shuffled back to her office. She needed to phone Adrian, tell him what she had decided, but she would do it later, after the coffee.

It was two more paracetamol tablets, several coffees and another hour later before Julie felt able to face anyone. She still hadn't phoned Adrian. Later, she thought, maybe after I tell Nicole I'm leaving.

Customers clustered in the aisles inspecting and commenting on what was on offer, but the noise no longer impacted on her as it had done earlier and she was able to smile at them without pain.

Debbie, the assistant with the thick spectacles gave her a

scared look as she passed, however, Julie smiled and said, 'You're doing well, Debbie.'

The girl beamed and scuttled off to find some more work to do, maybe she wasn't too bright, Julie thought, but at least she was showing some keenness now.

After Julie finished her inspection of the food hall she walked to the restaurant, it was time for another cup of coffee.

Several of the tables were occupied, but Julie found a seat at the back. Over to her left, an elderly lady with blue hair stared into her teacup to avoid looking at the man with the military moustache who was trying to chat her up.

'D'you think we should interfere?'

Betty nodded in the direction of the couple as she placed two cups on the table and sat down.

Julie shook her head.

'Better to leave them. It's not as if she's a kid. I'm sure she'll be able to sort him out.'

'What about you, how are you feeling now?'

'Better.' Julie smiled. 'The headache has stopped thumping and I'm more like myself.'

She took a sip of the coffee. 'Ah, this is good. By the way, you weren't kidding when you said the coffee you'd bring me this morning was strong. It nearly took the top off my mouth.'

Betty grinned. 'I haven't looked after an alcoholic husband for years without knowing what to do.'

Julie looked over the rim of her cup. 'You never told me that before.'

'Wasn't any need before, was there. It's no business of the buggers who work in here and the less anyone knows about my private life the better pleased I am.'

'You don't mind me knowing then?'

'Naw, you're different Julie. I know you won't spread it around.'

Julie sipped some more of her coffee. 'Nicole hasn't been looking for me, has she?'

'Haven't seen her come in yet.' Betty frowned. 'It's not

like her though, she's usually always here trying to catch folks out.'

Fingers of wind combed through Nicole's hair as her sports car zoomed along the country road. Most days she tied her hair back with a scarf, but today she felt reckless and didn't care, enjoying the feeling of abandonment it gave her. The laugh bubbled up into her throat and she threw her head back to shriek into the wind. There was no one to hear her and even if there had been she wouldn't have cared.

Today would be the beginning of a new life, she told herself. Scott could go fuck himself. She would see her solicitor, change the locks on the doors and that would be that. She should have made the decision long ago.

When she reached the store she parked in front of the entrance even though it was a no parking zone. She slid out of the car and marched into the store, throwing her car keys at the assistant on the perfume counter.

'Find that lazy sod of a security man,' she demanded, 'and tell him to park my car.' Without a backwards glance she strode to the lift and pressed the button, tapping her fingers on the doors until they opened.

The executive corridor was empty when she left the lift, although she could hear the muted voices of the office girls and the churning sound of the photocopier. Turning away from the noises she walked along the corridor, stopping for a moment outside Ken's office, but there was no response to her tap. Strange, she thought, when she found his door was locked, maybe he's having a day off. A smile crossed her face as she continued on to her own office. Ken knew she was ditching Scott for him so he would probably be consoling Claire who would be distraught at the thought of Ken leaving her. She shrugged her shoulders everything was working out perfectly.

Her hand turned the doorknob and she entered the room. It took a moment for her eyes to adjust, but when they did, she screamed.

35

Ken had arrived at the store more than an hour before Nicole, so it gave him time to gather his thoughts and come to terms with what he had to do. But first things first. There was the project to prepare for Patrick.

He jabbed his finger onto the on-switch of his computer and listened as it hummed into life. It immediately went into a virus check, and while he waited, he leaned his elbows on the desk and let his mind drift.

He was happier now he'd made his decision. His problems were over and Nicole was history. Once rid of her, Claire would come round, she always did. And Nicole would be gone, from his life and from the store.

Ken was sure Patrick would agree with him when he suggested that Nicole was past it and that he was the best person to take the firm forward. After all, Patrick had returned to Dundee last night specifically to meet him, and Nicole hadn't been invited. He had never been more certain, Nicole's days were numbered. And with her departure, his problems would be over.

He leaned back in his executive chair, savouring the smell of the leather. Last night Patrick had been so positive.

'You have a great future with Drake's,' he'd said, patting Ken on the shoulder. 'I like the way you think. New ideas are the lifeblood of business.'

He'd smiled as he said it, that little tight-lipped smile that always reminded Ken to be careful because Patrick was a man with no scruples.

'What about Nicole?' Ken asked him, not really caring about her, but checking out where she stood with Patrick.

'What about her?' he had replied in an inscrutable tone that Ken interpreted as a signal of Nicole's demise in the company. 'You are the man I want in the driving seat,' Patrick paused, 'but no need to tell Nicole yet.' There was a cruel tinge to his smile this time.

'She won't be pleased. I expect she'll fight it.' Ken looked at Patrick, wondering if he would have second thoughts.

Patrick just shrugged. 'Another drink, Ken?'

The two men smiled at each other. Conspirators working for the good of the store and, of course, for themselves.

Ken liked his office on the executive floor. This was just as well, because even though he moved to a more elevated position in the company, which he expected to do very soon, it was doubtful if his accommodation would change. Still, he thought, looking around him, maybe Patrick would agree to a makeover.

He swivelled his chair around and sat for a moment in front of the computer, watching the cannibal fish on his screen saver gobbling anything that came near them. This suited his mood perfectly. It was what business was all about. His hand rested on the mouse, reluctant to move it and send the fish into monitor oblivion, but eventually, he gave it the slightest nudge and brought his project back onto the screen.

His concentration intensified and he became immersed in the fine detail of his plan. Already he had forgotten it was Nicole's ideas that initiated the plan. If he thought of her at all it was only to consider how he would handle her.

He didn't worry about Nicole. They'd had fun together, but now it had to end and he didn't see any problem with that. There would be no difficulties for him finishing the affair, knowing what he now knew. But for a brief moment, Ken felt pity for her because her fate was predetermined. However, he knew that given the opportunity Nicole would double-cross him without a second thought.

Ken worked for quite a long time before he heard the lift stop and the doors open with a noise that grated his nerves.

'Damned maintenance man, I reported that yesterday,' he muttered to himself as he closed the lid of his laptop, kicked his shoes off and rose from his chair.

However, he was glad of the noise because it signalled Nicole's arrival. He moved silently to the door and turned the key. He didn't have time to return to his desk before he heard Nicole stop outside so he stood still, afraid to move in case she detected a sound, although that was doubtful given the solidity of the oak-panelled door.

The handle turned and he held his breath. After a moment he heard her walk along the corridor to her own office. Ken breathed out, unlocked the door and returned to his desk where he was soon immersed in work.

Nicole froze. Another scream bubbled up in her throat, but it stuck there in a painful lump unable to escape. She forced herself to approach her desk, not believing what she was looking at. But there was no mistake.

'Oh, Freddie,' she moaned, biting her lip to prevent the tears gathering. She couldn't cry over a pigeon. Not her, not Nicole, who never let anything faze her because she had her reputation for toughness to maintain. But she loved animals and birds they were so defenceless and innocent, and there had been too many deaths already. Besides, Freddie had been special to her, maybe because he was so tame and she was always the one he came to. He had been there every morning, tapping on the window to attract her attention, and looking at her with those large sad eyes.

One tear escaped and trickled down her cheek. Had it been only yesterday that she'd crumbled one of her biscuits and scattered it on the windowsill for the bird? And now here he was crucified, his wings spread and secured to the desk by the brass tin-tacks skewering the tips of his feathers to the wooden surface.

Nicole reached out a finger to stroke him, hoping to feel a heartbeat or some other flicker of life, but he was cold and rigid. She hadn't really expected anything else, and yet, the shock vibrated through her, up into her throat where it stuck and throbbed until a keening moan escaped her lips. The sight of Freddie brought back other memories, hateful memories. The blackbird she had found on the seat of her car. The arrangement of small bodies lined up on her kitchen floor in some strange ritualistic sacrifice. Who was doing this to her?

The room shifted out of focus and her earlier nausea returned as she backed away from the desk. The sound of faraway voices and running feet in the corridor trickled over her, but nothing made any sense. She had the strangest sensation that she was encased in cotton wool. She continued to back away from the desk, but her movements were disjointed, her feet and body did not seem to be connected and she was floating. The world dimmed and faded away as she fell.

'Yes, Evelyn?'

Ken had become so engrossed in improving his business plan for the store he had been oblivious to the rumpus in the corridor until the senior administrative assistant burst in allowing the noise to soar to a level that was impossible to ignore. He turned to stare at her; he'd never seen her in this condition before. Usually, she was so calm and self-controlled.

'What on earth's going on?' He closed the file he'd been working on, slipped his feet into his shoes, and rose from the chair.

Evelyn's breath was coming in short gasps and she held her throat with one hand when she spoke. 'It's Mrs Ralston. We can't calm her down. I think you should come.'

Ken heard screams resounding along the corridor. 'Is that Mrs Ralston screaming?' He strode to the door.

Evelyn nodded. 'She's in hysterics and won't stop.' She backed out of the door. 'I've phoned the police, but I think someone should be with her.'

Ken halted. 'The police?'

'Yes. There's something in her room.' Evelyn shuddered. 'I can't describe it. You'll see when you get there.'

Ken started to walk in the direction of the screams, but then stopped as a vision of Nicole clutching him and sobbing on his shoulder hit him like a blow.

He remembered Patrick's offer, Claire's ultimatum, and his resolve to end it with Nicole.

How could he end it if he went to her now? Nicole would never let him go. He would mess up with Patrick, and Claire was bound to find out. He took another two steps then turned round as the urge to run and stay as far away from Nicole as possible overtook him. Whatever it was that had given her the screaming heebie-jeebies, he didn't want to know.

'I don't think it's a good idea for me to come,' Ken said.

He could feel Evelyn's eyes boring into him and wasn't sure what she knew, or guessed about him and Nicole.

'I'm not very good at calming screaming women,' he added. 'Besides she'd be better with a woman. I'll get her friend, Julie.'

He hurried to the lift muttering a little prayer of thanks that he'd been listening when Nicole talked about Julie. The knowledge had saved him from an embarrassing scene.

Ken rarely visited the food hall and wasn't sure where he would find Julie at this time of the morning. He wandered up and down various aisles, smiling at customers, while his eyes searched for a member of staff.

'Miss Forbes, where can I find her?' He smiled at the young girl to whom he'd addressed his question. Poor thing she didn't have a lot going for her, however, it was second nature for him to try to charm women.

The girl adjusted her spectacles and blushed. 'Try the office,' she stammered.

'And where would I find the office?' Ken raised one of his eyebrows. It was a trick he practised regularly because it seemed to have an effect on women.

She giggled and pointed to the rear of the food hall.

'Thank you,' he peered at her name badge, 'Debbie. You've been very helpful.' Ken sauntered down the aisle, aware that Debbie was watching.

The office was right at the back of the food hall, tucked

away in a corner so that if he hadn't been looking he might have walked past it without noticing it was there.

He turned the handle and pushed the door open without troubling to knock.

Julie's finger stopped in the middle of dialling the last number. It had taken her all morning to get herself in the right frame of mind to phone Adrian and now that she was ready, Ken had to walk into her office.

She replaced the phone on its cradle. 'Can I help you?'

Ken had never recognized or acknowledged her up to now and she wondered what he wanted. She knew he'd made advances to a lot of the women in the store and she toyed briefly with the thought that if she responded that would be a way to get back at Nicole. However, she dismissed the thought almost as fast as it occurred to her. There were some things she drew the line at, besides she didn't fancy him.

It wasn't that he was unattractive. There was an appealing quality about him. He had that little boy lost, hangdog kind of look that made him interesting to a lot of women. However, she got the impression he knew it and played on it. He looked at her now and she could feel him trying to exert his charm on her, but she decided she was having none of it.

'Can I help you?' she repeated in a slightly sharper tone. The annoyance she'd felt, when he came into her office without knocking, increased as he stood there looking at her. She had really wanted to make that phone call and if Ken hadn't disturbed her it would have been done. Now the chance had slipped away and she knew it might take her a long time to generate the courage again. Besides, she might change her mind about phoning Adrian and she did not want to do that.

Ken slid further into her office and closed the door behind him.

'I'm sorry to disturb you when you're busy,' he mumbled.

Julie's annoyance lessened and she almost believed him. There was a tone of sincerity in his voice that started her thinking she had misjudged him. However, she caught sight of a glint in his eye that seemed ever so slightly calculating and it rekindled her exasperation.

'Yes, I'm busy,' she said, not caring whether she offended him. After all, she was going to leave the job anyway.

She picked up her pen and rolled it between her fingers before starting to flick her thumb up and down on the button at the end of it making the ink-refill click in and out of the barrel in a staccato movement that reflected her impatience.

Ken sat on the edge of her desk and swung his leg. He leaned towards her making her draw back further in her chair.

Julie's dislike increased. The man had no manners, no finesse and didn't know when he wasn't wanted. The scars on her arms started to ache as her muscles tightened and she sighed with displeasure. It would be so easy to let her suppressed anger at Nicole spill over onto Ken. But she knew she shouldn't allow her emotions to take over, although she supposed that anger was maybe a healthier reaction than the bitterness she'd been feeling, which made her life an emotional desert.

Julie inhaled several times becoming calmer with each breath. At last, she was ready to listen to him. 'Yes? What is it you want?'

Ken seemed nervous as if he had sensed her dislike and annoyance. 'It's Nicole,' he said. 'She's having hysterics in her office.' There was a look that Julie thought might almost be pleading in his soft, brown eyes. 'I thought you might be able to calm her down, you being her friend and all.'

Julie stared at him. Help Nicole? It was the last thing in the world she wanted to do, but then Ken wouldn't know that. She was tempted to refuse, but curiosity grabbed her. If Nicole was having hysterics, she would love to know why.

36

When the darkness cleared, Nicole thought she'd gone mad. She had never considered herself capable of fainting or having hysterics, considering this to be a weakness, and within the space of a few minutes, she'd done both.

She sat with her back pressed against the office wall and her arms clasped tightly around her knees trying to make herself as small as possible. She tried to struggle up from the floor, but Evelyn's firm hand pressed on her head.

'Don't move,' the woman said, 'stay still and put your head between your knees. You'll feel better.'

Nicole's resentment flared. She had never liked Evelyn, thinking the woman was far too smart for her own good and she wanted to shake the woman's hand off her neck. But she didn't have the energy. Instead, she did as she was told and, because her throat was raw from screaming, nodded her assent.

'Take deep slow breaths,' Evelyn said. 'It'll make you feel better.'

Nicole nodded again. She hated having to agree to everything, but she didn't have enough strength to do anything else.

At last, she croaked, 'Ken, will someone fetch Ken?'

Evelyn's hand on the back of her head pushed a little harder.

'Ken's gone to fetch Julie. He thought she would be more help to you.' She didn't have to say, 'Useless men,' but the implication was there in the tone of her voice. 'I've also sent for the police. Whoever did this must be sick in the head.'

The room swirled. Bile burned in her gullet pushing acid into her throat, forcing Nicole to raise her head again. She pushed back against the pressure of Evelyn's hand.

'Water,' she croaked, in a voice that didn't sound like her own. She needed something to wash the taste out of her mouth and thin the acid bile.

'Nicky!' Evelyn snapped. 'Fetch Mrs Ralston a glass of water from the cooler instead of standing at the door looking gormless.'

The smallest and youngest of the office girls clustering around the doorway flinched as if she'd been struck. 'Yes, Evelyn,' she mumbled, scuttling out of the door.

Evelyn sighed. 'I don't know where they get them nowadays. Not a brain cell between any of them.' She glared at the other girls grouped around the open doorway. 'And you lot – back to work. We don't need you standing there gawping, we'll manage fine without you.'

The caustic tone in her voice was unmistakable and the girls, mumbling under their breath, scattered.

'They think I don't know they call me the dragon,' Evelyn confided in Nicole. A smile twisted the corner of her mouth before it was replaced by a frown. 'Where's that damned water,' she shouted. 'I could have gone to China for it by this time.'

'It's here, Evelyn.' The junior was almost running as she reappeared. She pushed the glass into Evelyn's hand, slopping some of the water over her fingers.

'Careful, girl, careful.' Evelyn grasped the glass. 'Now shoot off back to your work, like a good lass.'

She watched the junior as she fled up the corridor, then turning to Nicole she held the tumbler to her lips. 'Sip it slowly,' she warned. 'You've had a bit of a shock.'

Nicole grabbed the glass from her. 'I'm not a baby,' she croaked. 'I don't need help to drink.'

'Ah, you're coming round, I see. Back to your usual self.'

Nicole glared at her. 'What d'you mean by that little remark?'

'Nothing at all.' Evelyn stood up, towering over Nicole. 'Just trying to be helpful, that's all.'

Nicole struggled to her feet. 'When I want your help I'll ask for it, and believe me it'll be a cold day in hell before that happens. So just fuck off.'

Evelyn shrugged giving the impression she couldn't care less, although Nicole guessed the older woman was seething underneath her calm appearance.

'If that's what you want,' she said, her voice brittle and cold, then that's how it will be.' Evelyn turned and left the office, quietly closing the door behind her.

The room started to revolve again and Nicole leaned against the wall. Taking several, long, shuddering breaths, she tried to ignore the thumping in her chest.

At last, the spinning stopped and she was able to approach the desk where Freddie was laid out. 'Poor Freddie,' she said, 'you didn't deserve this.'

A tear dribbled down her cheek, but she made no attempt to touch the bird. Instead, she walked to the window and rested her forehead on the cool glass.

In the street below cars and buses moved in a graceless ballet while pedestrians, ant-like, went about their business. It was as if nothing had happened – and of course, for them, nothing had.

She opened the window, leaned out and screamed at them, 'Who is doing this to me?' There was no answer apart from the rumble of engines and the usual city-centre sounds.

Ken fidgeted. He stood up, straightened his tie, ran his fingers through his hair and adjusted his weight from one foot to the other. He had lost the cocky look he'd had when he opened her office door and really did look like a little boy who was unsure of himself.

Julie ignored him. She was damned if she would agree to his demands as soon as he snapped his fingers, even though she was consumed by curiosity.

She riffled through some of the invoices spread out on her desk and deliberately allowed the silence to continue so that his discomfiture would increase.

At last, she looked up at him. 'I would have thought she'd have preferred you to be with her and, as you can see, I have a lot of work to catch up with.'

'The work can wait.' Ken levered himself off the doorframe on which he'd been leaning. 'She needs you now.'

'What if I can't come now.'

Julie stared at him, challenging him. She could see the realization creeping over him that she wasn't the kind of woman who would do anything to please him just because he asked.

'I could make it an order.' Ken leaned over and placed the palms of his hands on her desk as he glared at her.

'And I could refuse.' Julie glared back. 'Oh, never mind,' she said, 'I'll go to her, but not because you're ordering me. If I didn't want to do it there's no force on this earth that could make me.'

She stood up and pushed past him to get to the door. 'Anyway, I still don't know why you can't help her, everything else considered.'

Julie smiled to herself as she walked away from him. She didn't look back, but she would lay bets that Ken would have a bemused look on his face. He wasn't used to anyone standing up to him or refusing him anything.

37

Cold air whispered through the open window lifting the ends of Nicole's hair and bringing with it relief from the overpowering heat that pervaded her office. She threw her head back and turned her face into the breeze until she cooled off and lost the clammy feeling that had contributed to her nausea.

She pulled back from the window, sliding it shut and muffling the street noises. Her eyes darted around the room, looking at anything rather than Freddie pinned to the desk.

The office was spacious, plush and comfortable. She had designed and equipped it with the best of everything. The paintings on her walls were originals; she particularly liked the McIntosh Patrick oil, which she was sure would gain value following the recent death of the artist. Her desk was antique mahogany and her chair the most expensive she could find at the time. The computer she hardly ever used was a top spec model and the red-buttoned, leather suite was the best money could buy, although not the most comfortable.

Eventually, she looked at the desk and poor Freddie. Now that she'd recovered from the shock she was able to look at him dispassionately, although that did nothing to dull the anger she felt over what had happened.

'Someone's going to pay for this,' she muttered to herself.

A shiver rippled up her spine.

She had that odd tingling at the back of her neck again, that feeling she had when she thought she was being watched. But there was no one here and there was nowhere for anyone to hide, but she couldn't shake off the feeling that there were eyes watching her every movement.

Maybe she was becoming as paranoid as Scott believed her to be.

She strode across the room to the well-stocked drinks cabinet, poured herself a generous measure of Scotch and, kicking off her shoes, sank down into the depths of the sofa. She gulped the drink. It would relax her, she thought, but it didn't. Instead, she felt more uptight, the prickly feeling in the back of her neck increased and the room felt increasingly claustrophobic.

'I've got to get out of here,' she muttered, bending down to slip her feet into her shoes.

She levered herself out of the sofa and hurried across the room, so desperate to get out she nearly fell over her briefcase. Grabbing it she hurried out the door so fast she was almost running. She breathed a sigh of relief when it closed behind her.

The corridor was empty, although in the distance she could hear the muted voices of the clerical staff and the familiar churning noise of the photocopier.

Nicole hesitated for a moment, expecting Evelyn to swoop on her again. She shuddered at the thought, while the fluttering sensation inside her chest increased in tempo making her gasp. She'd never experienced anything like it before. She inhaled silently, hoping to still the palpitations, then exhaled just as quietly, although she knew that Evelyn couldn't possibly hear the slight disturbance of air and that her fear was irrational.

Her footsteps were silent on the carpet as she approached the lift and she breathed more easily when she reached it. The doors creaked open before she put her finger on the button and with a startled glance behind her, she pushed herself inside almost knocking Julie over in her haste.

Bill Murphy was seriously fed up. When he transferred to the CID he had imagined life would become more exciting. Exciting, that was a laugh. No one told him he would have to sit in the office and type piddling reports about a piddling emergency that involved hysterical women who imagined bogeymen behind every bush and dead animals that didn't exist.

He jabbed at the keyboard with his forefinger. He hadn't joined the police to be a bloody typist either. Swearing under his breath he backspaced to delete the last word.

'Not finished that report yet?' Sue Rogers perched on the end of his desk.

Sue was one of the more attractive policewomen in the unit. A detective sergeant, like himself, he'd once had a brief fling with her before they mutually decided they would rather be friends than lovers.

'It's all right for you bloody women. You get taught this stuff, but what about us men. Eh? We just have to struggle with these bloody machines, nobody ever teaches us.' Bill swiped at the keyboard. 'Just look at that, will you? The damned machine's just told me I've performed an illegal operation. I'll be bloody arrested next for abusing a bloody computer.'

'You're a sexist pig, Bill Murphy, and bad-tempered with it.' Sue stood up and walked away leaving the faintest whiff of perfume behind her. 'I was going to offer to bring you a coffee, but you can whistle for it now.'

'Aw, Sue, you know I didn't mean it.'

Bill stood up and followed her to the coffee machine. 'I'm pissed off because I was pulled out on a job last night. Awkward timing it was … I think she was interested too.'

Sue placed the coffee sachet in the machine and her cup under the outlet tap before pressing the button. 'Vile stuff that,' she said as she watched the black liquid spurting into her cup. 'Don't know why I drink it.' She sipped, making a face. 'Get your own coffee then, lover boy.' Sue sauntered to her desk further down the room.

Bill filled his cup and followed her. 'Have a heart, Sue. You'd throw a moody as well if you'd been hauled away from a likely prospect to investigate some neurotic biddy who imagined she was being stalked and rambled on about dead animals that weren't there.'

'What's her name then, this likely prospect?' Sue looked at him over the rim of her cup.

'Julie.' Bill's voice softened as he said her name.

'Well, you'll just have to phone Julie. Otherwise, you're going to be a misery for evermore, although if I know anything about your previous likely prospects she won't last a week.' Sue sipped her coffee. 'Go and do it now and then you might become a human being again.'

'Can't.' Bill slumped into the chair beside her. 'I don't have her phone number.'

Sue stared at him. 'Address, or where she works?'

'Nope.'

'I don't believe it. The hotshot detective didn't get the basic information.' Sue laughed. 'You'll never live this down mate.'

Bill hoisted himself out of the chair. 'Thanks for the sympathy,' he said sarcastically. 'It was a great help.'

Back at his desk, he prodded the keyboard and wrote a few sentences. That would do it. The investigation didn't deserve much of a report. After all, it was only a woman trying to wind up her man, although the supercilious bastard probably deserved it.

As soon as the lift doors closed, Julie said, 'What's up? Ken asked me to come and see you. He said you'd had a bit of an upset.'

'Is that what he called it, an upset?' Nicole's voice was even.

'Actually, he said you were hysterical.' Julie studied Nicole, but she didn't look hysterical. 'Maybe he was exaggerating.'

'Maybe he was, but then maybe he wasn't. Anyway, how would he know?' Nicole's hand tightened on her briefcase. 'Bastard could have come to see for himself.' Nicole's scowl deepened. 'Men, they're all the bloody same. Only interested in themselves and what's in it for them. But as soon as there's trouble you don't see them for dust.'

Julie felt a tightening in her chest. She should have been pleased that Nicole was suffering, but instead, she felt a twinge of sympathy for the woman. She shook the feeling off. Nicole was only getting what she deserved. She used people but didn't like it when the compliment was returned.

Julie placed her hand on Nicole's arm in a supportive gesture, although she would much rather have twisted it behind her back until she screamed.

Nicole flinched as if she'd been scalded.

Julie withdrew her hand. Surely she hadn't gripped Nicole's arm by mistake. No, she couldn't have done. She was too careful. 'You're a bit nervy,' she said.

'So would you be if you'd been through what I've been through since last night.' Nicole's breath rasped out in a ragged gasp. She seemed to be in danger of losing her self-control.

'D'you want to talk about it?' Julie forced a sympathetic expression onto her face.

The lift jerked to a stop and the doors opened. Nicole flinched. She stepped out and then halted, as if afraid to move forward through the crowded store. Her eyes had a panic stricken look, darting here and there giving the impression she was looking for someone.

'We can go back upstairs if you want,' Julie suggested. 'It would be more private.'

'No!' Nicole grasped Julie's arm in a tight grip. 'He's up there. I'm sure he is.'

'The coffee shop then?' Julie started to move through the crowds and Nicole was forced to follow her.

'He might have followed me down.' Nicole cast an anxious glance over her shoulder. 'Can't we go to your office. He won't be able to see me there.'

'Okay, but it's awfully small compared to what you're used to. You might find it a bit claustrophobic.'

Julie could feel Nicole's panic. The air of control she had displayed when she got into the lift had vanished and Julie guessed it had been a major effort for Nicole to maintain that façade even for the shortest time.

Nicole stumbled after Julie, like a child following her mother, only Julie didn't feel particularly motherly. Whatever had happened to Nicole, as far as Julie was concerned, was well deserved.

'You'll be safe here,' Julie said once she'd settled Nicole in the only spare chair in the office. 'I'll just pop out and get Betty to bring us coffee. You look as if you could do with it.'

Nicole started to protest, but Julie didn't wait to hear. She closed the door firmly and walked to the restaurant.

'What's up with madam?' Betty asked.

'Damned if I know,' Julie said, 'but bring us a couple of coffees. Oh, and you'd better let them know upstairs that she's with me.'

'Sure thing,' Betty said. 'I'm doing it for you though, not her.'

'Thanks.' Julie returned to her office.

Nicole seemed to have lapsed into a semi-trance that she was reluctant to come out of.

'What's it all about then?' Julie asked as soon as she was seated.

Nicole shuddered, and a tear rolled down her face.

'I've been having such a dreadful time and no one seems to care.'

'There, there,' Julie murmured feeling like a nanny comforting a child. It helped mask the pleasure she experienced to know Nicole was suffering. 'Start from the beginning and tell me all about it.'

Nicole relayed everything that had happened since the night before. The dead blackbird she found in her car. The animals laid out on the floor of her kitchen. Scott's refusal to understand, and his mockery of her. The policemen who didn't believe her, and now Freddie's death.

'He's lying up there on my office desk,' she moaned. 'He never did anything to harm anyone.'

Julie made sympathetic noises at all the right places and, as the story continued, she did start to feel some sympathy for Nicole's distress.

'Who's doing this to me, Julie?' Nicole lifted a tear-stained face and looked at Julie with a mute plea in her eyes.

Julie's thoughts whirled. Here was her opportunity to drive a further wedge between Nicole and her husband, just as Nicole had done to Julie. So she suppressed any compassionate thoughts she might have and said, 'You don't think it could be Scott. Do you?'

38

'The DI wants you in his office.' Blair Armstrong hovered at Bill's shoulder. He was uncomfortably close forcing Bill to push his chair back to escape the strong aftershave smell. The man was a prick.

'What's he want now?' Bill grumbled.

'He has a job for you, I suppose.' Blair grinned and wafted himself down the room to join a huddle of detective constables gathered round the coffee machine.

Bill snorted as he rose from his chair. He wasn't in the mood for another case. He was still tired from last night's episode.

Andy looked up as Bill entered the office. 'I've got something for you. You'll love this one, it's just up your street.'

Bill could have sworn there was an amused look in the inspector's grey eyes. 'You're up to something,' he said, taking a deep sniff of the faint aroma of cigarette smoke, wanting to remind Andy about the no smoking policy, but not daring to, because he knew where his superior's sensitive spots were. Bill sometimes thought he knew Andy better than Andy did himself. It had its uses.

The two men had joined the police force together and been friends ever since. It had been a race to see who would make inspector first. If it hadn't been for the hassle with Evie and then the nasty divorce, which had distracted Bill for a time, it might have been Bill sitting behind the desk and Andy standing in front of it. Both men realized and accepted this and it hadn't interfered with their friendship. Still, Bill knew where to draw the line and made sure he didn't overstep it.

Andy ignored the sniff and grinned at Bill. 'Just as I said

this one's right up your street.' He waited for Bill's response.

Something was tickling Andy's funny bone, Bill recognized the signs, but refused to take the bait. Andy would tell him when he was ready and had stopped trying to play games.

He turned to the window and stared out. Police cars huddled in the car park far below, just waiting for a call out. The sight reminded him of his early days in the force and depressed him. Thank God the Courthouse was on the other side of the building and he couldn't see it from here; that would have been even more depressing.

Surely there's another and better life than this, he thought, as he looked up and watched the clouds scudding across the sky. It was too nice a day to be incarcerated in this glass-fronted mausoleum. Maybe he should develop a headache and go home. The only problem was that there was nothing to go home for, no one waiting for him and nothing in the fridge that was not out of date. It was at times like this he realized what he had lost when Evie left, even though they could no longer stand the sight of each other. He supposed it was the human contact he missed and nowadays he only got that at work.

Eventually, the silence became unbearable. 'I finished last night's report,' Bill said, immediately regretting it because he'd fallen into the oldest interviewing trap there was of breaking the silence first.

'You mean, you think you finished the report.' Andy toyed with a piece of paper on his desk and his look of amusement increased.

Bill gave up on his cloud watching. He hooked a chair with his foot, pulled it to him, and straddled it with his legs. He wriggled himself into a comfortable sitting position and leaned his elbows on the back of the chair so that he could stare at Andy.

'You don't mean it's not finished?' There was an anguished note in his voice.

'You could say that.' Andy was enjoying himself.

'But the woman's an out and out nutter. You said so yourself when we were on our way back last night.'

'Maybe so, but another complaint has been phoned in.' Andy passed the piece of paper to Bill.

'A dead bird? Aw, come on Andy. We went through all that last night and there was no trace of any animal either dead or alive.'

'If you read the note more carefully you'll see today's complaint was called in by a member of her staff who claims to have seen the body.' Andy drummed the fingers of one hand on his desk. 'Maybe she's not the nutter we thought she was last night. Maybe there's something in it.'

Bill wasn't convinced. 'I suppose we'll have to go out and investigate,' he muttered. A hard knot was gathering somewhere in his middle and he popped a Rennie into his mouth.

'Take Rogers with you.' Andy flicked his hand in a gesture of dismissal.

'You're not coming?' Bill heaved himself out of his chair.

'No. I have something else on. Besides, it'd be better to have a woman along, particularly if Mrs Ralston is upset.'

'Jammy sod,' Bill muttered as he left the office. He continued muttering under his breath until he reached Sue's desk.

'I see you're still in a happy frame of mind,' Sue said without looking up. 'Have you come back to pester me or is there a purpose to your visit?'

Bill glared at her. 'Don't you start needling me,' he muttered. 'It's going to be difficult enough without that.'

'What is?'

'The job we're going out on.' He grinned at her, but there was nothing happy about his grin. 'Grab your coat and I'll introduce you to some real detective work.'

'What's it about then?' She stared at him. 'I don't trust you. You've got that evil look on your face. The one you get when you think you're scoring off someone.'

'Never mind that, just get your coat and I'll brief you in

the car.'

Sue's response when he told her the details of the previous night's investigation wasn't what he expected. Instead of sharing his view that it was a waste of time she became thoughtful.

'Sounds as if this Mrs Ralston was quite distressed.'

'Hysterical, more like,' Bill muttered, unwilling to change his first impressions.

'You're an unsympathetic bugger, Bill Murphy. No wonder you can't keep a woman interested for any length of time.'

Bill's hands tightened on the steering wheel. What did she know about it? True, when he met a woman it was all passion and lust, which quickly fizzled out. But it was always him who ended it, never the woman. It was just that Evie's face and her carping tongue got in the way, shattering him with flashbacks when he least expected it. After all who wanted to turn over in bed to see his ex-wife's eyes staring at him from another woman's face.

'What's the husband like?' Sue's voice prodded him out of his thoughts.

'He's a big lad. Bit of a ponce though, if you ask me. Wears an earring – looked like a diamond – in one ear, and has long hair.'

Sue laughed. She had one of those infectious laughs that made you laugh with her and, despite himself, Bill grinned.

'I know, I know,' he said, 'I'm an ignorant, prejudiced sod who makes snap judgements. But you know I can't abide blokes who wear earrings.' He pulled the car over and parked it at the kerb. 'Should be a security guy waiting to meet us,' he said, as he got out.

The building soared above them, and Bill craned his neck to look up at the Victorian frontage.

'I love these old gothic buildings,' he said to Sue. 'They remind me of something from a Vincent Price movie. You know, all dark and brooding and hiding secrets.'

'Didn't know you were a horror fan,' Sue said, crossing the pavement to stand beside him. 'And are you really old enough to remember Vincent Price?' she mocked.

Bill snorted. 'Come on, let's look for the security guy.'

They found him standing inside the store, watching the revolving doors, obviously on the lookout for them. He was an older man wearing the smart blue uniform of a security officer, a well-worn shirt and scuffed shoes.

Bill nodded at him to draw his attention, but his eyes slid over them in a dismissive glance.

'Expecting uniforms, were you?' Bill flashed his identification in front of the man's face and then stared at him. 'I know you from somewhere.' He searched his memory for some kind of clue, but the man's blue uniform was throwing him.

'I don't think so,' the man replied, although Bill could have sworn a look passed over the man's face that indicated he recognized him. 'If you follow me I'll take you to the executive floor,' he said, 'they're expecting you.'

It had only taken Bill a few minutes to remember who Harry was, but the old guy evidently didn't want to acknowledge their connection so he let it rest for the time being. He would find him before he left the store and, even if he had to lean on him, he would make sure the old guy told him how to find Julie, for he hadn't been able to get her out of his mind. He was sure she'd been interested in him and yet she'd given him the brush off. Bill wasn't going to let it rest.

The lift was quiet and smooth, soaring up with hardly any sensation of having left the ground. Bill watched as Harry turned a key in the button pad. He raised his eyebrows in a silent question.

'Customers don't have access to the executive floor,' Harry explained. 'Only people with a key can get up there.'

'I see,' Bill murmured, thinking that this would narrow the field of suspects. 'So, who are the people with keys?'

Harry didn't look up. 'There'll be a list in the office. But basically, only the executive staff, the clerical staff who work here and of course the director, who isn't actually based here, but visits regularly.'

'What about maintenance staff?'

'I keep spare keys for that. They have to ask me and I book a key out to them when it's required.'

The lift doors rasped open. 'Sorry,' Harry apologized. 'Neil, the maintenance man, was supposed to have looked at that. Probably just something caught in the runners.'

He stood aside while Sue and Bill stepped out into the corridor. 'I'll take you to the main office and introduce you to Evelyn. She was the one who asked you to come.'

Harry left the two plain clothes police officers with Evelyn and hurried back to the lift.

He was feeling confused because he had recognized the male officer immediately as being the man Julie was sitting with in the pub last night. He'd seemed a nice enough bloke at the time, and Harry wasn't sure why he hadn't admitted to Bill that he'd met him before. It was probably foolish of him. Eventually, Bill would remember and then he would have to plead a bad memory or too much drink. The problem was that Harry didn't know whether Julie wanted to see Bill again, particularly when she'd been so dismissive of him last night.

Harry left the lift and walked through the food hall, but couldn't see Julie anywhere. He sidled up to Betty at the servery counter in the restaurant. 'Seen Julie around?'

'She's in her office with Mrs Ralston. You'll have to wait your turn.' Betty grinned wickedly.

Harry scowled at her. 'You've got an evil mind. I just need to let her know there's someone in the store she might want to avoid.'

Harry left Betty pondering his comment and walked to the aisle nearest to Julie's office where he hovered in the hope he would be able to warn her when Nicole left.

39

Faint light filtered through the grating allowing him to see the spider come to investigate this strange creature invading his home.

It was beautiful.

Little crawling things fascinated him. He loved them. He had to possess them.

Absent-mindedly he reached out a hand and, lifting the spider between his finger and thumb, squashed it.

The spider was his creature now in the same way as the pigeon was. It had only taken a moment to twist the neck of the bird and watch the life fly out of the wing tips. The artistic bit though, that had taken slightly longer.

His left leg felt heavy and he wanted to exercise it to restore the circulation, but he did not dare move too much. He did not even dare to lift his head, although his neck had long since stiffened with the position he held. It would not do to let her know he was there, watching her.

He wriggled his fingers and rested his chin on his arm. It was the most he could manage to do without making a noise, for the walls and roof of his hiding place restricted him. It was like being in a coffin. Not that he objected to that. He liked the closed in feeling and the sense of security it gave him.

She was uneasy. He could tell. It was the way she sat on the edge of the sofa and gripped her glass, the way she gulped her drink, the way she looked around her as if she guessed he was somewhere nearby.

He closed his eyes to remember how she had reacted when she first entered the office. The memory was delicious. Her shock; her hysterics; and, something totally unexpected, her fainting fit. Eventually, he was getting to her, wearing her down. It would not be long now until the final action when he removed her power.

Only then would he be able to rest.

The clatter of the glass against the wood of the drinks cabinet made him open his eyes. The woman was heading for the door.

He smiled to himself as he noted the panic in the fast way she walked, the way she almost fell over her briefcase when she grabbed it and the way she scanned the corridor before she left the room.

He slithered backwards along the duct as silently as he could. When he reached another air vent, one that allowed him to see along the corridor, he watched her until she entered the lift.

It was safe now. Her office was empty. He could do what he needed to make her doubt her sanity. She was already on the edge; it would not take much more.

The soft scraping noises he made, as he crawled along the duct to the woman's office, did not concern him. The man in the office next door had already made himself scarce, which was typical of him, so that room was empty. And if the clerical staff heard anything they would think it was the central heating or rats. None of them would be brave enough to investigate the air vents.

He hooked his fingers into the wire mesh frame and removed it before silently dropping onto the carpet. It only took him a moment to retrieve the bird and return to the coffin-like passage that was one of many weaving throughout the building like a gigantic maze.

A few moments later he hauled himself up into the turret room above the woman's office. He sprawled, flat out and panting, on the dusty floorboards in the old, forgotten room, which perched in isolation on the corner of the building. It soared above the roof like some castle battlement in a fairy tale.

He could imagine Rapunzel leaning out of the corner window to let her hair down to an admirer far below. For a moment his mother's voice sang in his mind, reading the old familiar story.

She had made him believe that all women were princesses just waiting for their Prince Charming.

She lied to him and paid the price.

The room smelled of dust and mould, a tantalizing aroma that never failed to arouse him. It reminded him of long forgotten vaults and catacombs, chambers holding the remains of people, once important, but now crumbling to dust. Places where the air had not stirred for centuries. This room reminded him of all these things.

It had been sealed so long it was doubtful if anyone remembered it was here, unless, of course, they took the trouble to look up from the street. He was glad it was sealed though, for it made the perfect hideaway. Somewhere he could be alone to think.

This was his secret chamber where he was the only living thing. And, of course, he could access the roof space of the rest of the building from the trapdoor in the corner of the room.

His breathing was less ragged now and he pulled himself up onto his knees and then to his feet. The effort this took caused him to tighten his grip on the bird's body.

Apologetically, he stroked the bird, whose spirit was now joined with his. He laid it on the floor in a patch of light in front of the window.

'Soon you will have company,' he murmured, visualising the woman lying spread-eagled in the middle of the room. No sunlight for her, only the innocent deserved a place in the sun.

It was time to go; time to return to the darkness and plan his next move.

He lifted the trapdoor and lowered himself into the roof space.

40

'It couldn't be Scott. He'd never do that to me.'

Nicole twisted her fingers together, gripping them until the knuckles whitened. The problem was she was no longer as sure of Scott as she'd previously been. She remembered the ridicule he'd heaped on her ever since she'd started to feel she was being watched, and even after he'd seen the evidence of the dead animals he'd still refused to support her. He had allowed the police to think she was imagining things. Why would he do that?

'It was just a suggestion,' Julie murmured.

The walls pressed in on Nicole, restricting her breathing, making her head spin, and Julie's voice sounded so far away it didn't register.

If it wasn't Scott, who could it be? Who hated her enough? Nicole's thoughts were all jumbled up in her head and she was having a problem thinking straight.

'I don't know what to do,' she mumbled, looking at Julie with a mute plea for help.

Julie leaned over, placing her hand on Nicole's knuckles. The hand was warm and comforting, and gradually Nicole's fingers loosened.

'Don't worry,' Julie said. 'Your friends won't let you down.'

Nicole's lips quivered as she tried to smile. 'I don't know what I'd have done without you.'

It was hard for Nicole to admit she needed anyone, but once she had said it the walls started to recede and the tightness in her head lessened so that she was able to think again. She would find out who was doing this to her and she would make them pay. They would be sorry they ever crossed her.

'I feel better already,' she said. 'Let's go to the coffee shop and get coffee and the biggest cream cake they have. I feel like company and if the sod who's doing this is anywhere around he'll see I don't give a damn for him and his little jokes.'

Julie smiled. 'That's the spirit. Show them what you're made of.'

Despite what she said and thought, Nicole's senses were reacting to everything around her. She stared at everyone, convinced that if anyone was watching her she would know. That was why she noticed Harry hovering among the produce aisles in the food hall. Immediately she saw him, she knew he was watching and waiting for her.

Her breath hissed through her clenched teeth. 'It's Harry,' she muttered, impervious to Julie's flinch of pain as she grasped her arm. 'That's who it is. I might have known. I might have guessed. He's such an insolent sod and he hates me.' She glared at Harry and wasn't surprised when he turned and walked away. 'See what I mean. He's just been waiting his chance to get back at me. Well, I'll sort him.' Her breathing shortened until she was almost gasping. 'He's fired,' she hissed. 'I'll get the wages clerk to give him his P45 tonight.'

'You're fired, Harry,' she screamed at his retreating back. 'Don't be here when I come back.'

'Don't be too hasty,' Julie murmured. 'You don't know for sure that it's Harry behind all this, only minutes ago you thought it might be Scott.'

'It's not Scott. I never ever thought it was Scott.' Nicole snapped. 'Anyway Scott's gone to France, so there's no way he could have killed Freddie and left his body for me to find. It's obvious. Harry's the only one who could have done that.' She removed her hand from Julie's arm. 'Well, are you coming for that coffee or not?'

Bill studied Evelyn. 'You're in charge of the office?' She was older than the other girls, maybe in her forties or fifties.

It was hard to tell. The woman was tall, unsmiling and evidently enjoyed her position of power over the typists.

She fingered a gold chain that circled her neck. 'Yes, I'm in sole charge of the clerical staff.' One of the girls giggled making her frown. 'Staff aren't what they used to be,' she sighed.

'Is there somewhere quieter we can talk while my colleague interviews the rest of the girls.'

Sue tightened her lips but took a notebook out of her purse.

'There's the mailroom next door.' Evelyn stood up and smoothed her skirt. 'We could talk there.'

There wasn't a lot of space in the room even though it was quite large. It was crammed with stationery cupboards; boxes of paper piled almost to the ceiling; two photocopiers; and a fax machine; while one wall was almost completely taken up with pigeon-holes overflowing with letters, bills, notices and all the detritus of a busy office. It reminded Bill of the stationery office back at the station.

Bill perched on the shelf in front of the pigeon-holes while Evelyn leaned against a photocopier.

'Tell me what happened this morning,' he said, smiling at Evelyn whose face immediately took on a pink tinge.

She focused her eyes on a spot just beyond his left shoulder and started to recite. 'I arrived at half past eight as usual. I like to be early so I can sort the mail and allocate it to the appropriate department or manager.'

'Yes, yes,' Bill said. 'If we can start with when the incident happened.'

'Of course.' Evelyn appeared flustered for the first time. 'It was after Nicole, Mrs Ralston that is, arrived. I heard her get out of the lift and go to her office.'

'What time would that have been?' Bill scribbled in his notebook.

'Oh, I don't know, maybe ten o'clock, maybe half past. It was late for her; she usually gets in much earlier. I heard her tap on Mr Moody's door, but I didn't hear it open or any voices. He was in though, I know that.'

Evelyn hesitated as if she wanted to add something, but instead she carried on.

'It was only a minute or so later that I heard her scream – I thought something must be terribly wrong because she's always so composed, so proper, you know – so I ran along the corridor to see what was wrong. I thought maybe, you know, it might be rats or vermin of some sort.'

She fingered her gold chain.

'We've had a bit of bother, lately. Scratching noises in the walls, that sort of thing – we're not overrun, nothing like that,' she added hastily. 'But we thought we'd better catch it early before it became a problem, so we were taking care of it.'

'And was it?' Bill cut her off in midstream.

'Was it what?'

She looked puzzled for a moment.

'Oh I see what you mean – rats. No, it wasn't rats. I wish it had been. I could have coped with that better.'

She paused before continuing to speak in a voice so low Bill had to strain to hear her. 'It was worse than that really.' Her eyes glazed and she stared at Bill, although he was sure she wasn't seeing him.

'Just tell me in your own time,' he said gently.

She started, and her eyes seemed puzzled. It was as if she'd been somewhere else and his voice had pulled her back to the present.

'Of course,' she said, taking a deep breath. 'Well, when I got there the first thing I saw was Mrs Ralston lying on the floor – I didn't see the other thing right away. I was too busy pulling Mrs Ralston over to the wall so I could get her in a sitting position. Anyway, she started to come round, although I don't think she knew what she was doing right away. She kept pointing to her desk and muttering Freddie. Well, I didn't know who Freddie was, but I thought I'd better look at what she was pointing to.'

Evelyn broke off and started to breathe deeply. There was something reflected in her eyes, which might have been horror.

'You're doing fine,' Bill murmured. 'But I need to know what you saw.'

Evelyn's head moved from side to side as if trying to rid herself of an image.

'I don't know why I'm so upset,' she said. 'It's not as if I haven't seen dead animals before, but this, it was so deliberate. How anyone could do such a thing.' A tear slid down her cheek. 'It was a bird, you see, just a pigeon. I mean, we've all seen dead pigeons you just have to walk in the square across the road,' she paused, her hands gripping the edge of the photocopier. 'But this pigeon.' She swallowed. 'It had been crucified, spread out on the desk with tin-tacks pinning it down.'

She looked at him with some kind of mute plea in her eyes. 'It had to be deliberate. Don't you see?'

'Yes, I see exactly what you mean.'

Bill chewed the end of his pencil while he tried to puzzle out what it all meant. Maybe he had been too easily convinced last night that Mrs Ralston had imagined it all and there had never been any dead animals. According to Mrs Ralston, her husband had seen them as well so what was he playing at by saying it was all in her imagination. Or had last night been imagined, but today's episode been real, and if so was it Mrs Ralston herself who had put the pigeon there. If that was the case she was some sick woman.

'D'you think you're up to letting me see it?' Bill hesitated to say pigeon because of the effect it had already had on Evelyn.

'Yes, of course.' Evelyn pushed herself away from the photocopier, smoothed her skirt and turned towards the door. 'This way.'

She led him along the corridor, through a set of glass doors and into a more luxurious corridor. The carpet was thicker, the wall decorations looked more expensive and the ceilings had the original ornate mouldings of a century before.

'This is the executive suite,' Evelyn explained. 'The director has an office here as well as the assistant directors and some of the managers.' She gestured with her hand to a door they were passing. 'That's the boardroom and we also have several conference rooms.'

Coming to a halt, she said, 'Here we are. This is Mrs Ralston's office.'

Bill went into the room before Evelyn, hoping to spare her from seeing the dead bird again. He crossed to the desk, his feet silent on the deep pile carpet, and looked around. There was nothing there.

'You're sure the bird was on the desk?'

Furrowing his brow, he looked round the room. He noted the leather sofa; the drinks cabinet, still open and with a used glass sitting on top of it; the leather swivel chair and the mahogany desk with nothing on top apart from a few papers and a laptop.

Evelyn, who had been hovering in the doorway, crossed the room to stand beside him.

'Well, that's strange.'

She fingered her necklace, turning it round and round on her neck. 'It was there this morning. See, there are the holes the tacks made.' She shivered. 'Weird that's what it is,' she muttered. 'Weird.'

Bill traced one of his fingers over the tiny holes in the desk.

'Where is Mrs Ralston? Maybe she can throw some light on the removal of the bird.'

'I heard her go down in the lift about half an hour ago. She didn't want me to stay with her, you see. I asked Ken, Mr Moody that is, to be with her, but he thought Julie would be better able to calm her down.'

'Julie?' Bill wondered if it was the same one he'd met last night. It was possible, he supposed, given that Harry worked here.

'Julie's her friend. She's the section manager of the food hall. If she's gone to Julie, that's where she'll be, the food hall.'

'Perhaps we can ask Mrs Ralston to come back up here?'

Evelyn regained her composure and, smoothing her hands

down her skirt, said, 'Certainly, I'll see to it right away.'

'Oh, before you go, just one thing.'

Evelyn turned. 'Yes?'

'Was Mrs Ralston alone in this office before she went downstairs?'

'Yes.' Evelyn smiled grimly. 'She practically threw me out, didn't want my help.'

'I see,' said Bill, noting the unspoken word – bitch.

Harry wasn't entirely sure whether he was shaking with rage or cold. He was not a man given to strong emotions, but now, as he leaned against one of the freezer cabinets, the sound of Nicole's voice resounded in his ears and his rage mounted.

How dare she fire him? He hadn't done anything wrong. If it hadn't been for Julie being there he wasn't sure what he would have done.

His fists clenched. He had never hit anyone in his life, but he had been very near to it when Nicole's voice soared over the shoppers' heads, making them turn and stare. That was the worst of it, everyone had heard her.

He didn't hear Betty coming towards to him. 'She's gone now. Come and have a cup of coffee, Harry.' Betty's voice was quiet and full of sympathy.

'I'm okay.' Harry removed his shoulder from the freeze cabinet and stood upright, although his insides were churning at the memory.

'I heard what she said.' Betty grasped his elbow. 'There was no need for it. And anyway, she can't fire you just like that. She needs a reason.'

'Since when did Mrs Ralston need a reason for anything.' Harry's voice was bitter. 'And how am I going to tell Babs.' His shoulders slumped as despair swallowed him into its black hole.

'Come and get that coffee. It'll calm you down.'

Harry didn't resist when Betty guided him towards the restaurant.

The roasted smell of the coffee was more pleasurable than the actual taste, which was bitter on Harry's tongue. He took his cap off and laid it on the chair next to him, it no longer mattered if he was improperly dressed. A band of sweat lined his forehead where the edge of the cap had rested and he rubbed it with his fingers, tracing them upwards to where his hair had started to recede.

He pushed the cup away from him.

'No offence, Betty, but I'm not in the mood.'

He grabbed his cap and stood up. 'I'll be off then.' He turned the cap round and round between his fingers, leaned towards Betty to hug her, but drew back at the last minute as he thought better of it. She might misunderstand. 'The sooner I'm gone the better.' He turned away from her, feeling as awkward as a schoolboy saying farewell to a favourite teacher.

'Take care, Harry.'

His shoes were heavy and pressed on his corn, which was throbbing again, as he lumbered out of the restaurant and through the food hall to the back exit. He could feel Betty watching him and wanted to turn and wave to her, but couldn't bring himself to do it for fear the tears, that were pressing on his eyelids, would spill over.

It didn't take him long to gather his possessions together. A spare pair of shoes, his old teapot, cracked mug, his screwdrivers and other tools he'd brought in, and the old clock that didn't keep very good time. He packed the lot in a couple of plastic bags and let himself out the back door.

41

Julie couldn't understand why she wasn't happier now that everything was falling into place.

She had wanted to destroy Nicole, make her suffer, erode her confidence and fragment her life in the same way that Julie's life had been destroyed when Dave died. And now, when success was within her grasp with Nicole showing all the signs of being on the verge of a nervous breakdown, she was worried.

Maybe it was because there had been ramifications she hadn't foreseen. Harry, for example, that had never been in Julie's game plan, and she knew she would have to do something about it. But it was more than that. It was the feeling she'd been part of something shameful, something she should never have started, something that had taken root and developed until it was beyond her control. How had that happened?

She pushed the feelings away, burying them in the deep part of herself that hated Nicole, telling herself Nicole deserved all she got. She had brought it on herself, nothing was too bad for her.

So, she gritted her teeth and smiled her sweetest smile, while she steered Nicole up the stairs to the ground floor coffee shop.

The department store was busy with customers, although it was the lull between morning coffees and the beginning of lunches. It was the time when most people started to think about having a meal. The basement restaurant had a reputation for serving excellent cooked food, so the ground floor coffee shop was not too busy. Julie spotted an empty table at the back where it was relatively quiet and she steered Nicole towards it.

Julie treated herself to a cappuccino, while Nicole ordered an expresso, saying it would calm her nerves. Julie agreed with her, although she thought it might frazzle Nicole's nerves even more than they were already.

Everything was working out beautifully, she thought, as she watched Nicole lifting her cup with hands that shook so much she spilt coffee on the front of her immaculate white blouse.

'D'you think it was wise to sack Harry?' she murmured, tracing the creamy froth on top of her coffee with a finger.

'Of course,' Nicole snapped. 'The man's a menace.'

Julie sucked the froth from her finger. 'What about the unions? Mightn't they be trouble?'

Nicole frowned and clattered her cup into its saucer. 'After what he's done, I doubt if the union will be interested in his case.'

'You're sure it's him then?'

'Of course. Who else could it be?'

'What if it's not him? What if it turns out to be someone else?' Julie leaned over the table and grasped Nicole's hand. 'It wouldn't do to make a mistake. He could take Drake's to a tribunal, you know. And somehow, win or lose, I don't think Patrick would like that.'

Nicole glared at her. 'I don't suppose he would,' she snapped. 'But it's not going to happen. He's guilty.'

'Guilty or innocent, he could still take the firm to a tribunal.' Julie sipped her coffee while she watched Nicole's reaction. She had never seen her so strung out before. 'After all,' she added, 'an employment tribunal wouldn't be interested in what Harry's done if it's not connected to his job. What they would judge it on would be whether or not disciplinary procedures had been followed.'

Nicole choked on her coffee, spluttering the crumbs of her cake over the table.

Julie smothered her glee as she passed her a paper napkin. 'It might be better if you had a word with Harry before it's too late,' she murmured.

'I refuse. I absolutely refuse.' Nicole wheezed. 'I can't

speak to that man. Not after what he's done.'

'We don't know he's done anything.'

'You speak to him then. But as soon as I've checked this employment thing out, he'll be back out that door quicker than he can blink.' Nicole stood up. 'I'm going back upstairs to see what's delaying the police.'

Harry had never been so tired in his life. His shoulders slumped under the weight of his despair. If that wasn't enough his corn throbbed with an excruciating pain inside a shoe that seemed to be getting progressively smaller. The bus queue outside Primark was so long he couldn't get on the first bus, and now this one was so full he had to stand.

He muttered under his breath as the woman next to him brushed against his toe. The pain flared and he transferred his weight onto his other foot in an attempt to relieve it.

The bus swung round a corner. He staggered and grabbed the back of a seat to stop himself falling. Anyone seeing him would think he'd had a drink, but so far he had not.

He fought the tears welling up in his eyes. A grown man, what would anyone think if they saw him crying. But, what was he going to tell Babs? She would understand, of course, she always did, but that wasn't the point.

He stared out of the window, so engrossed in his thoughts he almost missed his stop.

The shopping square looked different in daylight. It looked more dilapidated reflecting the deprivation of the area. Rubbish blew in the wind, tramps squatted in corners, yobbos clustered outside the shops just waiting for a chance to nick something. The shopkeepers were not daft though and kept a careful watch on their stock. Harry knew that some of them kept knuckledusters behind the counter, although he thought that was asking for trouble.

Ali was sweeping debris from the front of his shop and raised a hand in greeting. Harry moved his arm to respond, but it seemed too heavy to lift and he let it fall back to his side where it hung useless and limp. Lowering his chin into his coat collar, he averted his eyes and plodded homewards. No sweets for Rosie today, from now on he would need all his money just to live.

The door closed with the quietest of clicks after Harry let himself into the house, but Babs heard it and came to meet him.

'You're home early,' she said, as he struggled out of his coat. 'Here let me take it. I'll hang it up for you.'

'Don't fuss, woman,' Harry muttered.

Babs hung the coat on a hook in the closet and turned to look at him. She frowned. 'You don't look well,' she said. 'Have you been sent home?'

If only it was as simple as that, thought Harry. 'No love, it's worse than that.' Tears gathered in his eyes, shining like the dew that clings to grass early in the morning.

'She hasn't sacked you, has she?'

Harry couldn't interpret the look on Babs' face, but it made him shrivel up inside. 'Yes, she has,' he grated. 'But she's not getting off with it. If she thinks I'm going to lie down and take it, she's got another think coming.'

By the time Nicole left the lift on the executive floor she was in a foul temper. Julie hadn't been any help to her with all her premonitions of what might happen because she'd fired Harry. The woman should learn to mind her own business. Still, it might be better to play safe rather than sorry, so she'd allowed her to tell Harry he still had his job. She could always renege and blame it on Julie once she found out how she could fire the blasted man without any of the repercussions Julie had suggested.

Voices rumbled from the clerical office, but Nicole turned her back on it and headed for the glass doors that led to the inner sanctum and the peace and quiet of her own office. It was only when she reached it and had her hand on the doorknob that she remembered what was inside. She bit her lip and drew back. How could she forget?

She shuddered and retraced her steps to Ken's office, but

it was still locked. Damn, that meant she would have to return to the main office and face the typists and clerical assistants.

Evelyn popped her head out of the office just before she got there. 'Ah, there you are. I tried to page Harry to let you know the police wanted to see you, but he's not responding.'

Nicole glared at her. She didn't like the woman's tone of familiarity. Getting too uppity by half, she thought. She'll be the next one to go. She smiled grimly. 'About bloody high time they were here,' she snapped. 'Did they think I was going to wait around all day until they decided they had time to come?'

'Mrs Ralston?' the voice was deep and familiar. 'Perhaps we can talk somewhere more private.' He emerged from the office.

Oh, God, not him again. She'd had enough of his insolence last night. 'Constable . . . I'm sorry I don't recall your name.' Nicole decided she wasn't going to let him get the better of her this time and kept her voice aloof.

'Bill Murphy, ma'am, and it's detective sergeant.'

'And your inspector . . . is he with you as well?'

He smiled. 'No, ma'am, sorry to disappoint you. But I've brought along Detective Sergeant Sue Rogers. Thought she might be of more use, being a woman and all.'

The young woman who followed him out of the office was taller than Nicole, but she had a friendly face and sympathetic eyes. 'Call me Sue,' she said holding out a hand.

Nicole grasped it. 'Nicole,' she murmured. She decided she liked Sue.

'Is there somewhere quiet?' Bill raised his eyebrows and turned to Evelyn.

'Of course.' Evelyn's face turned pink again. 'One of the conference rooms should suit. Follow me.' She led the way through the glass doors into the executive corridor. Opening one of the polished oak doors, she said, 'Will this do?'

Bill smiled at her. 'This will do just fine, Evelyn.' Bill waited until Evelyn left and then gestured in the direction of the chairs clustered around the circular conference table. 'We'd be as well to make ourselves comfortable.'

Nicole glared at him. The bloody man was taking charge. Who did he think he was? However, she sat down, rested her arms on the table and clasped her hands.

'Well, let's start then and get it over with,' she said. 'Not that I suppose you'll believe me any more than you did last night.' Her tone was sarcastic. 'But I think you may have to change your tune because we have the evidence today.'

Bill Murphy stared at her as if he was weighing her up.

Silence, only broken by a faint hiss from the central heating, descended on the room. Nicole wriggled in her seat as she looked from Bill to Sue. Their faces were inscrutable, and Nicole started to reconsider her initial liking for the woman detective. She was just like all the others. Her clasped hands tightened until her knuckles were white, while her feet did a little jiggling dance beneath the table. Damn them, her nerves were starting to get the better of her.

'What are we waiting for?' she demanded. 'What d'you want me to tell you?'

Sue leaned forward after exchanging a glance with Bill. 'Let's start from the beginning.' She smiled encouragingly. 'Just tell it in your own words.'

Nicole slumped back in her seat and her voice flattened as she described how she had come to work that morning and found Freddie, the pigeon, crucified on her desk.

'You came in late. I gather that wasn't usual for you.'

'No. I'm usually in much earlier.'

'Why was this morning different?' Sue raised an enquiring eyebrow.

'Scott, that's my husband, left for Paris on a business trip, so I was delayed.' Nicole didn't bother to tell them the real reason for the delay was the row they'd had. It was none of their business.

'I see.' Sue jotted in her notebook.

'Why do you think this is happening to you?'

'It's obvious, isn't it? Someone's trying to frighten me.'

Nicole's skin prickled under the intensity of Bill's stare.

He wasn't nearly as sympathetic as Sue was.

'But it's not going to work.' She raised her voice to quell the tremor that threatened to take over.

'I can understand your distress. I'd feel the same way in your shoes.'

Nicole blinked at Sue as the tears gathered behind her eyelids. The woman's sympathy was getting to her, making her feel sorry for herself.

'Have you any idea who might want to frighten you?' Sue looked up from her notebook.

'It's Harry, that's who it is.' Nicole's fingers strayed to her hair. Her voice was firm and sure. But Sue made it all sound so horrible, and when she thought about how pathetic Harry was, she wondered if he really had the gumption to sustain the persecution.

'Harry?'

'He's the security guard. He doesn't like me.' But, Nicole wondered, did he hate her?

Bill cut in. 'Well, we'll interview Harry, of course. As well as some of the other people who are in contact with you. But for now, maybe we'd better inspect the scene of the crime.'

Nicole thought there was a note of irony in his voice, but shrugged it off as her imagination. To her horror, however, when they reached her office and Bill stood back to let her enter, there was no dead bird. She stared unbelievingly at the desk, it was like last night, first there were dead bodies then there were none.

She caught her breath. 'You don't believe me,' she muttered, placing her hands on the edge of the desk to bear her weight.

'On the contrary, we do believe you because other people saw the bird. But now we have to question, what happened to the bird? Who removed it?' There was an inscrutable expression in Bill Murphy's eyes as he looked at her. 'When you were the last person in here.'

42

'She's upset,' Sue said. 'Somebody's playing tricks on her. I don't like it.'

'You're sure about that, are you?'

Bill turned a chair around and straddled it. They had returned to the conference room to compare notes.

Sue perched on a chair after pulling it round to face him. 'Yes, I'm sure. But what about you?'

Bill traced his finger along the top of the chair-back. 'What I think is that she's doing it herself.'

'Why would she do that?'

'To attract her husband's attention – maybe to get him to return from France.'

Sue snorted. 'You're like all men, think a woman just wants a man to look after her.'

'Well, they're not all like you, Sue love.' Bill grinned. 'A rampant feminist if I ever saw one. I do believe you'd abolish men if you could.'

'That doesn't warrant an answer,' she snapped. 'Anyway, I don't see our Mrs Ralston as a poor, defenceless woman just waiting for some man's attention. She wouldn't have got where she was in her career if that had been the case. No, someone's definitely trying to frighten her, but what I don't like about it is all these dead animals. It indicates a sick mind.'

'Yes. And the sick mind's probably hers. But I suppose we'd better carry on with the investigation just on the off chance you're right. So, who are we going to see next?'

'I want to interview this Harry. See if there's anything in her suspicions.'

Sue pushed herself out of her chair.

'OK, you do that, and I'll see Julie. Mrs Ralston seems to

confide in her. She might have some ideas.'

Sue smiled mischievously. 'You can ask Evelyn to set it up. She seems to have taken a shine to you.'

Julie was sorting through last month's invoices when the telephone summons came. 'I'll see them down here,' she said. 'I'm busy and it'll save me wasting too much time.'

'Sorry, Julie. They want you up here. They've commandeered the conference room for their interviews.'

The phone line was so clear Evelyn might have been standing at Julie's elbow.

'Oh, all right. But it's a nuisance. Tell them I'll be there in five minutes.'

'Before you hang up, Julie. I've been trying to raise Harry and I can't find him. They want to see him as well.'

'I'm not surprised you can't find him. Mrs Ralston sent him home about a couple of hours ago.' Julie hung the phone up before Evelyn could ask any questions.

Julie started to shuffle the invoices into one neat pile. Thank goodness she wouldn't have to do this much longer.

She ached for her old life in Edinburgh, and it was time she laid Dave to rest. There was a limit to how much mourning she could do, and at the end of the day, he didn't really deserve her tears, not after what he had done to her. Not after he had betrayed her with Nicole. Anger flared briefly making her grit her teeth, but the anger was not as red hot as it had previously been. Maybe she was getting over him at last.

She stood, smoothed her skirt, put her jacket on and combed her dark-brown hair, although, with the short, sleek style she had adopted, there was rarely a time when it was untidy. She was feeling better already, more like her old self before she came to Dundee.

There were two people in the conference room. The first a young woman, tall with short reddish-brown hair and eyes that seemed to smile all the time, nodded a greeting to her. 'You'll be Julie.' She smiled as she held out her hand. 'I'm

Sue Rogers, we just wanted to ask you a few questions.'

It was the second person who jolted Julie out of her feel-good state of mind. It was the man from the pub who had rescued her from that weasel of a guy chatting her up last night. The man she'd snubbed.

Her memories of that night were so vague she hadn't thought she would know him again. But she recognized him instantly. She could also tell that he remembered her. It was in his eyes and the way he moved towards her and pulled out a chair for her.

Sue had a slightly bemused look on her face. 'D'you want me to carry on with the questions, Bill? Or would you prefer to do it yourself?'

'No, no. You carry on.' Bill perched on the edge of the conference table keeping one foot on the ground. He was so near to her their feet were almost touching.

Julie looked away from him not sure how to react in this situation. Maybe he was annoyed because she'd snubbed him and now, the way things were, she couldn't tell him she'd regretted it almost immediately. He'd been nice to her, but her anger about Dave had got in the way.

A breath of a sigh escaped her lips, just another lost chance among so many lost chances.

'I understand you are Nicole Ralston's friend.'

Julie had forgotten about Sue, but she looked at her now as she answered. 'I suppose you could say that, although we don't meet socially.'

'Is it a work relationship then?'

'Yes, you could say that.' The palms of Julie's hands were damp, but she resisted the urge to wipe them. She couldn't tell these people the truth because if they knew how much she hated Nicole they might think she was responsible for her harassment.

'These incidents,' Sue paused, 'of dead birds and rodents being left where Mrs Ralston can find them. What can you tell us about that?'

'I'm afraid I only know what Nicole has told me. I haven't seen anything myself.' Julie hated herself for allowing a note of scepticism to creep into her voice.

Sue seemed to be weighing her up. 'Mrs Ralston thinks she is being stalked. What do you think?'

Julie hesitated. 'I'm not sure. Her husband thought she was paranoid and to begin with I thought the same, but now I'm not so sure.'

Sue waited until the silence became unbearable to Julie.

'I did think, to begin with, that her husband might be having her watched . . . because of her thing with Ken Moody.'

'Thing with Ken Moody?' Sue exchanged a glance with Bill.

'Yes, they're having an affair.' Julie squirmed in her seat. 'Maybe I shouldn't say.'

She twisted her hands together and a look of misery passed fleetingly over her face. However, she was not too concerned for there was still a part of her that enjoyed scheming against Nicole.

Nicole paced up and down her office. She'd never been any good at doing nothing. She'd always needed to keep busy, but now, she couldn't settle to do any work and didn't know what to do.

The office wasn't the same either. It had this faint aura of menace even though Freddie was no longer there. But she supposed that was part of it.

She was fragmenting, like the pieces in a broken mirror. She couldn't think straight and her thoughts were jumbled.

Who removed the bird? And why? Maybe it was someone trying to discredit her. But why would they want to do that? She didn't know and couldn't figure it out. Whatever they were up to was working though. That policeman as good as said she'd removed Freddie herself.

She stopped her pacing to kick the waste paper bin. It clanked across the room until it struck the wall. It should have made her feel better, but didn't.

Maybe she should just go home. But what was waiting

for her there? More dead animals?

She slumped onto the leather sofa and put her head in her hands, tearing at her hair and moaning. After a time she sat up. This won't do, she thought. I'm not going to let this bastard get the better of me. She crossed the room to the drinks cabinet and poured herself a large shot of whisky which she gulped faster than she should have, choking and gagging as it burned her gullet.

She combed her hair, powdered her face and reddened her lips, before she went in search of Ken. I'll find him, she vowed, even if I have to hunt him down at his house.

However, it was easier than that because as she walked along the corridor she met him coming out of his office.

'I need to speak to you,' she said.

Ken started. 'I'm just going in to see the police. It'll have to wait.'

'Fine,' she said. 'I'll wait.'

She settled herself in his office but left the door open so that she would hear him leaving the conference room. She didn't have to wait long.

'Who told them about us?' Ken demanded after he left the conference room. He sounded annoyed.

'I don't know,' Nicole replied. 'But anyway it won't be long before everyone knows.'

'What d'you mean?'

'Well, I thought we'd agreed you were going to leave Claire. I've already arranged to change the locks so Scott can't get back in. We've burnt our boats, my love.'

Ken fidgeted with his tie and tugged at his collar.

'You haven't told her yet. Have you?' Nicole glared at him. 'What a coward you are.'

'I need more time,' Ken mumbled.

'Tell her tonight. If you don't I will,' Nicole snapped. The expression on her face softened. 'Anyway, I need you to be with me tonight. I don't want to be in the house on my own, not with all this going on.'

'I don't know if I can manage,' Ken faltered. 'If I'm to tell Claire tonight she might be upset.'

'Oh, fuck Claire,' Nicole snapped. 'I'm tired of hearing about Claire. It's Claire this, and Claire that, and we mustn't upset poor Claire. What about me? I'm being threatened and stalked and nobody gives a damn.' Her voice faltered. 'I need you tonight. Don't fail me.' She laid a key ring, with a square button pad attached to it, on the table. 'That's a spare control pad for the gates. I'll see you tonight.'

Julie returned to her office, but couldn't concentrate on the invoices. She kept thinking about Bill Murphy, the way he'd looked at her, the way his eyes seemed to bore into her and the tone of his voice when he spoke.

It was a long time since she'd thought about any man and she couldn't understand why he was affecting her the way he did. It was no use thinking about him though, not now he was investigating Nicole's stalker. Julie realized, with a start, that she was now taking Nicole's fears seriously.

She didn't hear Nicole enter her office, but when she looked up, there she stood, wraithlike and pale, with shoulders slumped and a look on her face that was nearing desperation. Julie's emotions flipped, first one way then the other and she wasn't sure whether she wanted to laugh or cry. This was what she wanted, wasn't it? This was what she'd aimed for, the destruction of Nicole. Well there could be no doubts left that Nicole had been brought down, her self-esteem hammered into the ground, her confidence shattered.

'Nicole,' she said, meaning to tell her she intended to leave Drake's and return to Edinburgh before she started to feel pity for the woman.

'Come home with me,' Nicole whispered. Her eyes seemed larger than normal. 'I'm afraid.'

Julie combed her fingers through her hair. No, this was too much. Maybe she was suffering from remorse because the revenge she had planned had spiralled out of control. Things had happened for which she had no explanation, but she'd fed into them, increasing the emotional impact on

Nicole. So she was as much to blame as anyone for Nicole's state of mind. But she could never be a friend to this woman. So, although it would have been the easiest thing in the world for her to say yes, she closed her eyes and said, 'I can't. There's something else I have to do tonight.' She kept her eyes averted, unable to look at Nicole because she was so sure her lie would be patently obvious.

'Oh.' Nicole's voice was like a breath of air that had somehow escaped.

Julie opened her eyes and looked at her, but Nicole was already turning away. There was a defeated, helpless air about the woman. It showed in her posture and the look on her face. Julie almost changed her mind. She rose from her chair and extended an arm towards Nicole. 'I'm sorry,' she said and sat down again, feeling as miserable as the other woman looked.

After Nicole left, Julie sat for a long time just staring at the wall, not seeing or taking anything in. She didn't even register that Nicole had left her briefcase resting against the end of her desk.

Bill tucked his notebook into his pocket. 'Well, we've seen everyone we can see today. There's only the security man to interview and we can catch him tomorrow. Pity he left early.'

Sue had a faraway look on her face. 'D'you think she's in any danger?'

'Who? Mrs Ralston? I'd be more likely to think that once she finds out who's doing this, they'll need protection from her.'

'It's not normal, you know, dead animals. Most people won't harm animals. It's the batter the kids before harming the dog syndrome.'

'I know what you mean, but I'm not totally convinced that Mrs Ralston's as upset as she makes out to be.'

Sue studied him. 'Do you still think she's doing this herself?'

'Let's say I'm not convinced there's anyone else involved.' Bill smiled. 'It seems to me she's one tricky lady.' He levered himself out of the chair and rubbed his legs. 'God, I'm stiff. I think I'll walk back. You can take the car and I'll meet you there.'

'If you'd sit in a chair in the same way everyone else does you wouldn't get stiff.' Sue's eyes narrowed. 'This wouldn't be about that rather attractive witness we interviewed, would it? What's her name again? Ah yes, Julie. Anyone with half a brain could guess she's the same Julie you've been rabbiting on about all day.'

'As if.' Bill grinned at her. 'See you back at the station, Sue, my love.'

He escaped out of the conference room door, leaving Sue to tie up any loose ends. 'I'm off,' he said, popping his head into the main office. 'But before I go I'd like another quick word with Miss Forbes. Where can I find her?'

Evelyn reached for the phone. 'I'll ask her to come back upstairs. Shall I?'

'No need for that,' Bill said, smiling pleasantly and making Evelyn blush again. 'Just tell me where to find her.'

'If you're sure then.' Bill could hear a trace of doubt in Evelyn's voice. 'You'll find her in the food hall. It's on the basement floor.'

Bill whistled as the lift descended. He hadn't felt so happy for a long time.

It was the second time Julie had been disturbed in her office.

She hadn't done any work since Nicole left, although she was less confused and gradually returning to normal. She'd managed to push the guilt feelings away by telling herself that she owed Nicole nothing, on the contrary Nicole owed her a life, Dave's life. So when the knock on the door came she was feeling considerably more alert.

'Come in,' she shouted in response, thinking maybe Nicole had returned.

'Hi,' Bill said, standing there grinning at her. 'I didn't

think I was going to find you again.'

Julie hid her confusion by shuffling the papers on her desk. 'Did you have some more questions?' she asked without looking up.

'A very important one.' He pushed the door shut with his foot and sat down in the chair opposite her, although she hadn't invited him. 'When I left Donovan's the other night you never told me when we could meet again. So, I thought I'd come to arrange it now.'

Her pulse quickened and she was aware of her heart thumping so much it was almost choking her.

'I wasn't aware I'd agreed to meet you again.' She tried to keep her voice calm but wasn't making a very good job of it. 'Anyway, isn't that a bit unprofessional of you considering you've just interviewed me in connection with an investigation.'

'Ah, but I didn't interview you. Sue did. Besides, the police work with the entire population so does that mean we can never ask an attractive woman out.'

Julie laughed. 'I think you're stretching it a bit. Anyway, what makes you think I'd like to meet you again?'

'You'd be as well to say yes, you know, because now I know where to find you I'll never leave you alone until you agree. What about tonight?'

'Not possible. Nicole has asked me to keep her company tonight because she's alone.' Was that a lie, or wasn't it? She hadn't said she was going.

'Tomorrow then?'

'I don't know what I'm doing tomorrow.'

'Okay, I can take a hint.' He grinned and stood up. I'll be back tomorrow anyway, to interview the security man. 'See you then,' he said as he left her office.

She watched the door close and once again had that strange urge to run after him. She'd botched it again, but maybe not completely because he was coming back tomorrow to see Harry.

'Damnation,' she muttered. She'd forgotten to phone Harry.

Lifting the phone she dialled. After several rings, a woman's voice answered.

'Mrs Watson. This is Patrick Drake's department store. I'd like to speak to Harry.'

'I'm sorry, but Harry lost his job with you today so I really don't know if he'd want to speak to you.' The woman sounded distressed.

'Mrs Watson, tell him it's Julie on the phone.' She hesitated. 'I'm a friend of his.'

'It doesn't make any difference. He came home and then went out again. He was in an awful state.' Julie thought she heard the woman sob. 'And now, I don't know where he is or when he's coming back.'

'Mrs Watson, when he comes back tell him he's got his job back. I've spoken to his boss and it's going to be all right.'

'I'll tell him if he comes back.' The phone clicked down.

Damn, Julie thought, I should have phoned him earlier.

43

He waited until he was sure no one was left in the building. Then he crept out of his secret hiding place into the darkness of the early evening.

The stone steps up to the outside world were slippery with an accumulation of grease which had built up over many years. He climbed upwards, into that dangerous world of other people with staring eyes; eyes that shifted and moved away from him only to watch him when they thought he was not looking.

Smells wafted to meet him: interesting smells; rotting smells; smells of corruption and putrefaction – fascinating smells.

Rubbish blew down the deserted alley, fluttering and rolling until it gathered in the lowest corner, where it trembled and settled.

His fingers traced the cold stonework as he moved slowly up the alley. However, despite his attempts to blend into the shadows of the building where they were at their deepest, they were no protection once he came to the street.

He disliked the street intensely. There were too many people, too many eyes.

Eyes were everywhere, staring at him, spying on him when he was on his travels.

In these situations, he had often tried to pull his cloak of invisibility around him, but it did not work under the harsh street lighting and the flickering, shining eyes of passing traffic. And all he could do was scuttle through the streets, eyes down, until he found the darker, quieter places he preferred.

He knew it would be no different tonight, but he had his work to do, his mission to complete, which left him no option but to reveal himself. A premonition tingled in his bones. He had great faith in his premonitions, they came from the Greater Being. So he hesitated on the corner before sidling around it onto the street.

If he had not been so close to the wall he would not have bumped into the rowdy group of young men congregated in front of one of Drake's display windows. But he did, and it was too late to draw back.

Two of the men turned and glared at him.

'Watch where you're going, you fucker,' the one with the leather jacket said.

They clustered around him, surrounding him, pushing and prodding him and breathing their fume-laden breath into his face.

For a moment he was transported back in time to the ward, where he feared the lunatics were going to invade his body and take over his mind.

Desperation, like the clutching of firm fingers around his chest, almost stopped the beat of his heart. He was being suffocated. The dark was closing in on him. It was an unfriendly dark filled with bodies, not like the dark he loved.

He had to escape. He tried to push past them, but there were too many and they stood too close together.

'The bastard pushed me,' the guy with the tattooed forehead grunted.

'You going to let him off with that?'

'No way.'

The bodies smelled of sweat and filth. He knew he was being taken over and his panic mounted. If they took over his body and mind how would he complete his mission?

'Aw, leave him alone.' This man was a bit older than the others and he held out a bottle. 'Have a drink mate and we'll call it quits.'

He pressed his back into the cool glass of the window, shaking his head. Alcohol was Satan's weapon. He could not allow it to pass his lips.

'My drink no good enough for ye,' the older man roared. His eyes glared and his face twisted into a menacing mask.

'Ye see that fellas, he'll no drink with me. That's an insult, that is.'

His panic mounted. It was like an animal inside him struggling wildly to get out. He twisted his head from side to side. His eyes bulged. He tried to slide away from them, but his path was blocked. The feeling of invasion increased. He slipped a hand into his pocket and caressed the cold steel of the blade. Pulling it out, he waved it at them. They would go now.

'Bastard's got a knife,' leather jacket shouted.

The other one did not wait but swung his bottle.

The blow was sharp, bringing with it an exquisite pain. Somewhere far away he heard the window cave in. He floated for a moment, feeling something wet trickle down his forehead, before sliding slowly to the ground. A booted foot kicked his precious knife out of his hand, and he flexed his fingers feebly in a vain attempt to hold on to it. Then he was vaguely aware of the older man, the one with the glaring eyes, bending over him and forcing Satan's drink into his mouth and down his throat.

'No bugger refuses to drink with me,' were the last words he heard.

When he woke up he was no longer lying on the pavement. He was in a strange place. Somewhere he had never been before. There were bars on the windows and the door was made of steel. He tried to open it, but it was locked. He gave up and cowered on the bench-like bed with his knees drawn up to his chin.

For the first time in his life he had failed in his mission and surely this was his punishment.

44

Julie pushed herself beyond the pain barrier and her feet continued to thud on the pavement in a rhythmic pattern. If only life were as simple as running.

She was passing the darkest bit of her running route, the entrance to Balgay Park which, as usual, tried to seduce her with its solitude and shadows. There had been many times over the past six months when she'd thought she wanted to embrace the dark, that she would find peace there. At these times she was tempted to enter the shadows, but tonight she kept going, no longer sure whether she was running into the dark or away from the dark.

The repetitive beat of her feet was like music playing familiar chords over and over again. The breeze, wafting over her face and lifting the ends of her hair, a friend she had known for a long time. Even the street smells, car fumes, foliage, damp soil, and the odd whiff of animal urine, was pleasant.

Running was a solace for her, it cleared her mind and allowed her to think, or so she believed. Up until now, those thoughts had been angry thoughts of revenge. Destructive thoughts that threatened to destroy not only Nicole but herself as well.

She reached the crest of the slight hill and stopped to look at the spreading lights of Ninewells Hospital below. Bending over, she clutched her middle with one hand and a nearby lamp-post with the other.

The muscles in her legs quivered and ached now they were no longer being pushed beyond their capabilities, while each breath she took tore painfully from her chest leaving her weak and gasping. Her hand tightened on the icy, wet surface of the lamp-post. The hospital always had an effect on her, arousing mixed feelings of despair and anger, and tonight it looked the same as always, a conglomeration of buildings winking their lights into the surrounding darkness. A sight that usually reinforced her desire for revenge, but tonight, she just felt sadness.

Her breath rasped painfully in her chest, but it was only physical, not the intense, overwhelming emotional agony that had all but destroyed her. She was able to think of Dave now without suffering that searing pain, remembering the good times and the not so good times, and all that was left was sadness.

It all seemed so long ago. Maybe it was time to say goodbye to him.

Cold sweat trickled from her hair into the sweatband she wore round her forehead. Her shirt clung damply to her back. Maybe she should feel happy now she'd had her revenge, a revenge that was more complete than she'd ever imagined it could be. But it was an unsatisfying revenge, which made her feel soiled and dirty.

'Goodbye, Dave,' she murmured, turning her back to the hospital and forcing her legs to run again, away from the dark and into a new life. Tomorrow, she promised herself, I'll really do it. I'll hand in my notice. It's time I returned to Edinburgh and got on with my life. She smiled as she ran, no longer conscious of the pain. There was a lot she had to do so she could start living again.

Dusk was gathering by the time Nicole arrived home. Her nerves jittered, sending spikes through her body like breaking glass, making it difficult for her to handle her remote control and keys.

She skidded the car to a stop, as near to the door as she could take it, and, not bothering to lock or garage the car she bolted for the house door. Once inside she locked it and then inspected the house making sure all the other doors and windows were secure. Even then she didn't feel safe.

The kitchen was still a mess from the morning and she

tiptoed through the debris to inspect the fridge. There was nothing in there that she fancied, but then she decided she wasn't hungry anyway.

She percolated some coffee; then didn't drink it.

She wandered through the house but didn't know what to do with herself.

She turned the television on and turned it off again.

She rechecked the windows and doors.

She worried the ends of her hair, winding it round and round her fingers and pulling the ends into her mouth where she sucked it just as she'd done when she was a little girl.

Nothing helped.

Eventually, she curled up in one of the white leather armchairs, her feet tucked beneath her and her arms hugging her middle while she sang the words to a long forgotten children's song.

She thought she was going mad.

She must have dozed off, for when she woke it was dark outside. The external lights must have gone off or maybe she'd forgotten to put them on, but she didn't think so. The table lamp at the side of her chair spilled a pool of light onto her, but the dim shadows in the corners of the room seemed to move, expanding and threatening until she was almost ready to scream. She bit her knuckles until the blood came. She was sure she'd switched on the ceiling light when she came in, but maybe she hadn't.

The house creaked and settled in its silence. Even that worried her.

She steeled herself to get out of the chair and switched the light on. Maybe she would go through the house and put on every light, although she had a vague recollection she'd done that when she arrived home.

Her finger was on the light switch when she heard footsteps in the hall. At least it sounded like footsteps, but maybe she was mistaken about that as well. Maybe it was just her nerves.

She wrapped her arms around her middle, clutching her skin with pincer-like fingers to make sure she was awake.

But still, the footsteps came. Hollow and echoing and menacing.

The door handle turned, but she couldn't move.

The door opened.

She sighed, a long, low sigh of relief. 'Oh, it's you.'

'I'm sorry, but I found this when I came in.' The hands that cradled the body of Ralph, the big ginger cat, were gentle.

Tears flowed down her cheeks as she held out her arms for Ralph. His body was still warm, his fur still as silky as she remembered, but he was quite, quite dead.

'Oh, poor Ralph. Not you as well.' She cuddled the cat to her body and, turning her back, placed him on a cushion.

The hands circled her neck, gentle, but strong. The fingers caressed her skin.

'Stop playing around,' she said, 'you know how frightened I've been.'

The hands tightened, holding her in a bruising grip, and it was then she knew. She wanted to ask why, but it was too late. She struggled, desperate to break free, but the grip tightened. Then the lights grew dim. And soon there was only the dark.

It had been a pig of a day and it hadn't got any better. Now it had become a nightmare. Ken stared at Nicole's body, sprawled on the white carpet in an elegant pose that some might have thought artistic.

He knelt down beside her and stroked her forehead. Her eyes stared at him, blank, unseeing and partly blood filled. There were scratch marks on her chin where she had tried to pry the choking hands loose, and fingertip bruises on her throat.

Suddenly he wanted to be sick. He ran to the bathroom and hung his head over the toilet pan and retched. A mouthful of yellow bile burned his throat with a painful intensity that was worse than the pain that gripped his ribs. But still, he retched and retched, although there was nothing in his stomach.

The scene with Claire was still bright in his mind. 'That damned woman phoned here,' she'd screamed at him. 'Here of all places. Demanded you go and see her.' Cool, calm Claire had burned with an anger he'd never thought she possessed. Her anger had sparked his and he'd slammed out of the house without his dinner. He'd driven for miles, and walked along the beach for miles, before he'd come here.

He had used the keypad to open the gates, and then driven up to the house. That was his first mistake. When he found the back door open he'd come into the house. That was his second mistake.

He rested his forehead on the cool china of the toilet bowl unable to stop seeing Nicole sprawled on the lounge floor. At least now he was free, he thought, with grim amusement. Suddenly he felt like laughing and as the giggle started, it sounded, even to his ears, deranged.

Panic surfaced. It would be disastrous if he was found here with Nicole's body. It would be the end of his reputation and his career. Patrick Drake would never stand for the scandal. He had to get out.

Bile resurfaced in his throat as he levered himself up. He thought he might be sick again, but he swallowed hard. Grabbing a wad of toilet paper, he scrubbed the edge of the bowl, the sink and the taps before finally polishing the cistern handle, depressing it with his elbow, and then dropping the paper down the toilet to be flushed away.

He retraced his steps to the lounge and, taking his handkerchief from his pocket, he polished every surface he might have touched. Then with one last look at Nicole, he left the house.

His hands were shaking so badly when he got into the car that he had difficulty starting the engine, and then, when it finally roared into life, his driving was so erratic he nearly crashed into one of the gateposts. In his hurry he didn't bother to close the gates behind him, it no longer mattered. Nicole was dead.

45

'Slow down, take a deep breath and start again.' Bill was having trouble understanding the woman on the other end of the phone.

'She dead,' the voice screamed at him. 'You gotta come, come now . . .' The voice deteriorated into a garbled mixture of Polish and broken English.

Bill sighed, the sigh of a man at the end of his tether. He tapped a pencil on the piece of paper in front of him. At least switchboard had got her name and address.

'Listen, Marika. Who is dead?' He pronounced his words slowly in the hope she would do the same.

'Mrs Ralston, she dead, that who,' the voice screamed at him. 'You gotta come.'

The hair on the back of Bill's neck prickled, he had thought that only happened in books, but it was definitely prickling. Sweat ran down his back and his underarms were awash. So this was what impending doom was like.

'Okay, we'll come right away,' he said. He stared into space for several seconds after he laid the phone down. This case had been a flaky one from the start and he'd made a wrong decision, a mistake, which had resulted in disaster.

'Is something up?' Sue stopped at his desk on her way back from the coffee machine.

'Shit's just hit the fan, that's all.'

'Which particular shit would that be?' Sue perched on the edge of a spare chair and sipped her coffee.

Bill rearranged the files on his desk until he found the one he wanted. He threw it over to her. 'That one,' he said.

Sue opened it. 'Not another phone call,' she groaned. 'Not more dead animals. I can't bear it. I like animals you know.'

'Yes to the first. No to the second.' Bill waited a moment, then added, 'It's worse than dead animals. It's Mrs Ralston who's dead.'

Sue laid the file back on his desk. 'I worried about her, you know.'

Bill thought he detected a tone of censure in her voice. 'I know you did.' He tapped his fingers on the desk. 'Maybe we should have done something.'

'Such as?'

'Well, I don't know. Got someone to check on her. Put a watch on her house.' Bill's voice tailed off. 'Something.'

Sue snorted. 'You've got a guilty conscience because you didn't believe her. But there was nothing else we could have done. You'd have been blasted out of the water if you'd suggested a personal guard for her, and you know it.' She smiled sourly. 'It's called lack of resources, mate.'

'I suppose you're right.' Bill felt a little better, although he knew he should have taken the case more seriously. 'Let's go out there and see what's what.'

'Better tell the big white chief first, he'll want to know and it takes the heat off you.' Sue pushed her notebook and pencil into her handbag. 'I'll be ready when you get back.'

Bill hurried to Andy's office, tapping on the door after he was inside.

'Can't you knock first? I might have a bird in here with me for all you know.'

'Chance would be a fine thing,' Bill said. 'Having a fly puff at a fag is probably more like it.' He crossed the room and placed his hands flat on the desk. 'Something's come up. Remember that neurotic one the other night, that Mrs Ralston in the big posh house, friend of the Chief Constable and all?'

'I thought you had that one all sewn up.' Andy glared at him. 'Is she still giving us grief?'

'You could say that. Gone and got herself killed, that's all.'

Andy sighed. 'Chief Constable's not going to like that.' He scratched his head. 'You'd better get out there. Take someone with you. I'll get things arranged at this end and see the top brass here are kept informed.'

'Okay if I take Rogers with me? She's familiar with the case.'

'Yes, yes. Just get it started at that end. But keep me informed.'

The rush hour traffic was starting as they drove out of Dundee, but Bill was driving against the flow of it, so they arrived at the house within a reasonable time. However, it was not fast enough for Marika who met them at the door in full flow.

'Why you no come sooner? Why you take so long? Come, you see, Mrs Ralston, she dead.' Marika clasped her hands on her ample chest and sobbed.

It was all too melodramatic for Bill. He turned to Sue. 'I'll leave Marika to you,' he said. 'Find out what she knows.'

He strode into the house simply to get away from the histrionics. He stopped in the hall and looked around him wondering where the body was.

Marika pushed past him. 'I show. I show.' She waved her hands in the air before throwing the lounge door open. 'She here.' Tears poured down Marika's face.

Nicole Ralston lay on her back, sightless eyes staring at the ceiling. Her arms clasped a large ginger cat. A hiss of breath escaped Sue Rogers's lips and Bill heard her mutter, 'Another bloody animal. What's with this guy and animals?'

Marika started to mutter in a foreign language, her voice rising higher and higher until it was almost a scream.

'Thank you, Marika.' Bill stepped in front of her to prevent her throwing herself on the floor. The woman was like an engine cranking up and Bill didn't want to be with her when she eventually exploded. 'You go with policewoman. She ask questions. Okay?' Blast, he was at it now, speaking in broken English. He sighed disgustedly. 'Take her somewhere else,' he hissed at Sue, 'before I say or do something stupid.'

'I'm not sure you haven't done that already,' Sue

murmured sweetly as she ushered Marika from the room.

Bill pulled the door shut, he knew better than to enter and be accused of contaminating anything. The Scene of the Crime guys were a bit touchy that way.

Marika's voice, high and excited floated along the corridor, gradually lessening in volume as Sue's calming tones took effect. He knew he should join them, but he had no stomach for hysterics, so he walked along the corridor until he found a small study. He would square it with Sue later. In any case, he had to phone Andy to find out when he could expect the police doctor to arrive, and when the SOCOs would get here, and he couldn't do it with Marika yabbering in his ear.

Once he'd made the necessary calls he settled himself at the desk, poking into drawers and pigeonholes, and riffling through various letters, notes, invoices and papers.

Claire rose from bed just as the night started to turn into dawn. She hadn't slept and her head and eyes ached.

It had been after two o'clock when Ken returned home and slid in beside her. They'd had a dinger of a row earlier on and she didn't want it to start again so she hadn't moved and had kept her breathing slow and regular.

It was all this business about Nicole, and Ken's inability to end the affair that he'd probably entered into with very little thought.

That was Ken all over though, he would get involved with any woman who caught his eye and then drop them when he tired of them.

However, he'd never been involved with someone like Nicole before, someone who wouldn't let go. Claire knew he was having difficulty shaking her off.

That was what frightened her because she knew how weak he was. That was why she thought she might have to take matters into her own hands and why she had gone out looking for him after he left. She shouldn't have left the kids on their own, she knew that and felt guilty about it, but they had been sleeping soundly and hadn't come to any harm.

She looked in all the places she thought Ken might have gone, but couldn't find him. One o'clock struck on the church clock as she arrived home. There was nothing else she could think of to save her marriage so she'd gone to bed and waited, wondering whether or not he would come back.

The shower prodded her into wakefulness, the water rushing over her head and down her body in a wonderful cleansing waterfall. She stood under it a long time hoping that the streaming flow would wash away all the guilt, fear and jealousy.

Ken was sitting on the edge of the bed when she returned to the bedroom. His face was haggard and his eyes peered at her in a strange way.

'Are you all right?' She sat on the bed beside him. 'You look a bit strange this morning as if something's troubling you.'

She wanted him to take her in his arms and hold her close but was afraid to make the first move. He might not want her. And she didn't know how to talk to him anymore, which made all their conversations so stilted.

'If it's the argument, I've got over that, just as long as you finish with her.'

Fear gripped her. Maybe he was going to tell her their marriage was over. She towelled her hair hard to prevent her hands from shaking.

'It's finished.' His voice sounded flat and emotionless. Suddenly he clasped his head with both hands. 'Oh God, it's finished, really finished.'

Claire put her arms around him. 'There, there,' she said, in the same way she would have said it to a child. 'You'll get over it.' She patted his shoulder.

'You don't understand,' he muttered through his hands. He took them away from his face and stared at her with strange unfocused eyes. 'She's dead, and I found the body.'

Claire stopped patting him. Her heart was thudding dangerously fast and an icy coldness swept through her.

'What d'you mean. You haven't . . .' She couldn't say

what was in her mind.

'No. I didn't do it. I just found her.' Tears rolled down his face.

'Do what?' Claire's voice rose several decibels.

'Strangle her. I didn't, Claire. Honest, I didn't. You've got to believe me.' He clutched her hand and held it fast. 'What am I going to do? They'll think it's me.'

Claire stared at him. She'd never seen him so agitated.

'The police – did you phone the police?'

Her brain whirled as she tried to think what to do. Even if he had done it, she couldn't let them arrest Ken.

'No. I daren't. Don't you understand? They'll think it's me.' His body shook uncontrollably. 'They're bound to, aren't they?'

Claire loosened his fingers from her hand. It had become numb with the pressure of his grip.

'But they'll know you were there. You'll have left fingerprints.'

Despair seeped through her. The police weren't fools.

Ken stopped shivering and smirked. 'I'm sure I wiped everything before I left the house.'

Claire frowned. He sounded so smug and so sure of himself. Her doubts increased, and she wasn't sure what to believe.

Ken seemed to sense her slight withdrawal. 'Don't you see, Claire? I can't let them know I was at her house last night. They're sure to think I did it.'

Claire pulled him close to her, patting his shoulder again. Now that he'd returned to her it didn't matter what he might have done. She would get him out of it.

'That's all right, Ken. You couldn't have done it because you were here with me all last night.'

Ken nuzzled his face into her neck. 'I knew you'd stand by me,' he said.

46

Patrick Drake's Department Store slowly awoke from its silent, brooding, overnight hibernation where the only noise was the settling of old timbers and the hiss of radiators. That silence was now broken by the electrical hum of vacuum cleaners on carpets, and the clank and clang of mops and pails on tiles, as the army of cleaners prepared the store for the onslaught of staff and customers.

Julie stood aside as a bunch of cleaners came out the back door. They seemed a cheery bunch, laughing and joking together as they fastened their coats over their working overalls and lit up cigarettes for their much-needed puff now the work was finished. Their good nature lightened the gloom of a dreary morning.

Julie held the door open and watched them for a moment, weaving up the alley. Their day was finished just as hers was starting. They vanished around the corner and the alley was deserted again. Even the tramp was not there this morning. Julie had got used to seeing him and wondered if he'd moved on, maybe found something a little bit warmer and more comfortable now the weather was turning colder.

She shivered. There was a suggestion of snow in the air. She could smell it. She closed the door behind her and hurried into the store, noticing as she went that Harry's little room was empty. Julie hoped he'd got her message, but she would phone again, just to make sure.

Betty was bent over a cupboard, busy inspecting the stock when Julie crept up on her and planted her cold hands on the older woman's cheeks.

'Got the coffee on the heat then,' she said, as Betty squealed in protest.

Betty straightened. 'My, but you're chirpy this morning.'

'It's a beautiful morning,' Julie replied, grabbing Betty by the waist and swinging her into a dance around the servery.

'If you want that coffee, you'll let go right away. Anyway, why are you so happy now?' She grabbed two cups and held them up in front of her. 'When you were so goddamned down yesterday. What's happened since then?'

'I've made my decision, Betty. I'm going to hand in my notice and go back to Edinburgh.' She performed a little jig. 'I'll tell Nicole when she comes in.'

'I can tell you, madam's not going to like that. Not when she thinks she's got her hooks into you.' Betty sniffed as she poured the coffee. 'Besides, I'll miss you as well.'

'I don't give a damn what Nicole thinks. She can't stop me.' Julie accepted her cup from Betty. 'I do care what you think though, and I'll miss you too.'

Julie waited until after the store opened for the day before she phoned upstairs.

'Nicole hasn't come in yet,' Evelyn informed her, 'Ken's just arrived though. D'you want to speak to him?'

She was tempted to say yes, hand her notice to him and tell him she would be leaving, but that would be taking the easy way out, and Julie never took the easy way out of anything. She believed in facing her problems and dealing with them, after all, that was what she'd been doing since she came to Dundee.

With a bitter smile at the thought of the problem she'd been dealing with, Julie said, 'No I'll wait for Nicole.' Besides, she thought she might enjoy the look on the woman's face when she told her.

It was after lunchtime before she phoned Harry. She'd looked for him several times, but he hadn't appeared in the store so far.

'I'll just get him for you,' Harry's wife said.

'Julie.' Harry's voice sounded strained.

'I wondered whether you got my message to come back into work'

'Yes, Babs told me, but I wasn't sure. Not with Mrs

Ralston being so definite like.'

'It's all right Harry. I talked to her and she agreed she'd been a bit hasty. The best thing you can do now is to come in.' Julie hesitated. 'I'll make sure it stays all right with her.'

There was a silence on the other end of the phone.

'Are you still there, Harry?'

'You haven't heard then.' His breathing sounded laboured. 'It was on the one o'clock news.'

'Heard what, Harry?'

'Mrs Ralston's dead, murdered.' The words were flat and emotionless.

Julie's hand tightened on the handset she held to her ear. 'What did you just say?'

'She's dead, Julie. Dead.' Harry's voice echoed with anguish. 'They might think it was me, with her accusing me of stalking her, and then sacking me and all.'

'Don't be daft, Harry. You're not sacked, that was a mistake.'

'Some mistake,' he muttered.

'Come into work, Harry. Sitting at home's not going to help.'

'I suppose.' He sounded resigned. The phone clicked off.

Julie leaned back in her chair. From where she was sitting she could see Nicole's briefcase, still leaning on one of the desk legs.

Was it only yesterday Nicole had said to her? 'Come home with me. I'm afraid.'

She could still hear her own reply, 'I can't. There's something else I have to do tonight.' Only, she didn't have anything else to do. She could easily have gone home with Nicole. If she had, would Nicole still be alive?

Julie covered her face with her hands. It was her fault Nicole was dead, her and her silly revenge plan.

She should have believed Nicole when she shared her worries about a stalker, and if she were really truthful she would have to admit she did believe her. But instead of that, she'd played her little game of planting suspicion in Nicole's mind, that it was only a private detective employed by her husband. Nothing she should be scared about. Not like a stalker, for example.

Julie moaned. This would be on her conscience for a damned long time.

Evelyn broke the news to Ken at roughly the same time that Harry was telling Julie. 'It was on the news,' she said, adding, 'isn't it awful?'

Ken sat back in his leather, executive chair and feigned a look of surprise.

'It can't be true,' he said, although he, more than anyone knew it was. Every time he closed his eyes he could see her lying there, that terrible look on her face and those horrible bruises around her neck. Even when his eyes were open, he could see her. He wondered if he would ever stop seeing her.

Evelyn made a sympathetic noise. 'Everyone's upset,' she said.

She kept her face solemn, although Ken thought he could detect a glimmer of excitement in her eyes.

'I'd better tell Patrick. God knows what he'll think. But he needs to be told.' Ken reached for the phone. 'I'll do it now.'

Evelyn took the hint and left the room.

Patrick's voice displayed no emotion when Ken told him. He asked several questions, to which Ken had to admit he didn't know the answers. 'Get on to the police and find out what's happening,' Patrick snapped before he hung up.

Up to that moment Ken had been quite composed and had been pleased with the way he was handling things, so the shaking fit shocked him with its unexpectedness. He shook everywhere, his hands, his head, his body. He couldn't control it. Tears gathered in his eyes and forced their way down his cheeks until he was sobbing noisily.

Evelyn, who had been lingering outside, burst into the room. 'Oh, blast,' she said. She stuck her head round the door and shouted up the corridor, 'Somebody, get along here quick.'

Crossing the room she put her arms around Ken, rocking him and muttering soothing noises. That was when he started to scream.

'Phone a doctor,' she shouted to the girl who appeared at the door. 'He's gone into shock.'

'Maybe if you slapped him – I've seen them do that on the telly – maybe he'd come out of it.' The girl said.

Evelyn raised her head to look balefully at the girl. 'Just do what you're told,' she said. 'Get a doctor, fast.'

The Scene of the Crime Officers padded into the house in their white overalls and plastic overshoes. There was something about those bootees that always made Bill want to laugh, but he didn't dare because these men were so serious they wouldn't even laugh at the Sunday Post comic strip.

After a quick discussion with the men in white, Bill and Sue closeted themselves in the dining room. They had considered the kitchen, but one look at the mess there was enough to make them think again. It was enough to make Bill return to the lounge to suggest to Colin Wilson the SCO in charge that they might want to look at the kitchen as well.

'Some house this,' Bill said, sticking his hands in his pocket and walking over to the window. 'Not that I'll ever be able to afford anything like it.'

He turned to look at Sue. 'Well, did you get anything out of Marika?'

'Not that much.'

Sue consulted her notebook. 'Apparently, Mr Ralston isn't here he's gone off to France and she doesn't know where or how to contact him. Left first thing yesterday morning and gave her the day off. She says Mrs Ralston's been jumpy and short-tempered. She also said something about an intruder or trespasser. As far as today's concerned, she said the gates were open when she got here, which is highly unusual. And the house doors were open as well. She thought the house might have been burgled so she was looking around when she discovered Mrs Ralston. After that, she went into hysterics again, and I couldn't get anything else out of her.'

Bill turned his gaze to the window again. It overlooked the orchard. 'There's plenty of trees and bushes out there,' he murmured, 'ideal for anyone who wanted to hide.'

'Pardon?' Sue said.

He placed his hands on the window ledge and leaned forward. 'I forgot. You weren't here when we saw Nicole first. She spoke about having seen someone at the window, but when her husband investigated there was no one there. He thought she was paranoid.' Bill paused. 'I'm afraid we thought so as well. But it's possible there could have been someone out there.'

'Do you go along with the stalker theory then?' Sue joined him at the window. 'There's only one thing. How d'you know it's this window?'

'Elementary, my dear Rogers. They were having dinner at the time. Where do toffs have their dinner? Why the dining room of course, and that is exactly where we are now.' He grinned at her. 'Oh, I nearly forgot. Did Marika say how many people had control pads for the front gate.'

'As far as Marika knew there were only three people – Scott Ralston, Nicole Ralston and of course Marika.'

'So who left the gate open? Not Nicole Ralston that's for sure.'

47

There was a small window high up on the wall where he was able to see the stars and the gradual lightening of the sky as daylight crept in.

He had not slept, that would have been too dangerous, but sat all night curled up in the corner of the bench that was supposed to be a bed, watching the window and the sky beyond.

Confusion reached into the darkest corners of his mind wrapping his thoughts in dusty cobwebs. He did not understand why he was here in this enclosed space from which there was no escape. Nor did he understand why God was punishing him. But God always knew best so he accepted his situation without question.

When daylight seeped through the window a guard brought him a bowl of porridge, a mug of tea and some toast, but he did not eat or drink in case it was poisoned.

Then they came and took him out of the cell. He followed them without protest and allowed himself to be locked in the van that sat outside. He had no curiosity about where he was being taken. Everything that happened to him was God's will and He would not allow it without good reason. When they opened the door again he was in some kind of courtyard.

He stumbled out of the van and stretched himself, flexing his legs to relieve the cramp gripping his calves. Iron gates clanked shut and there was nowhere else to go but through a rather insignificant door at the side of the ominous, grey building in front of him. They went through it into a passageway leading to a large, open hall which reminded him of the halls of judgement.

The atmosphere in the courthouse stifled him for, even

though it was early, it heaved with people, their yabbering voices making as little sense to him as the screeching sound of migrating geese. Air moved in waves above their heads and he could see it being sucked down, becoming heavier as it became thinner, until it disappeared altogether into their ugly bodies. Soon there would be no air left. It would all be used up.

He did not like the guard, who had brought him here, staying by his side to separate him from the heaving mass, and prodding him into the inner sanctum.

Once inside nothing made any more sense. Not the ridiculous man who sat on his throne wearing some sort of white wig – maybe he did not have any hair – nor his cohorts who bowed and scraped to him. He was not God, although he seemed to think he was. He said peculiar things like 'drunk', 'disorderly', 'criminal damage'. The words made no sense. Nor did he understand when the white-wigged man said, 'Sentence deferred for reports.' But he nodded and smiled because that was the only thing to do when the world had gone mad.

He was not afraid though, for only God could call him to account and he knew that would never happen, as long as he had an uncompleted mission.

He scuttled through the streets, away from his place of imprisonment, only stopping when he reached the place where Satan's minions had attacked him. The store window was boarded over and he had a vague recollection of the sound of breaking glass.

His hand worried the lining of his empty pocket. He had lost his knife, his precious knife. A sense of foreboding overtook him. He dropped to his knees and crawled round the corner into the alley. It was not there. He sat back on his heels to think. The kick had been forceful, the knife could have gone anywhere.

He crawled out of the alley, eyes focused on the ground – oblivious to the people stepping around him – not hearing the snorts of disgust. There was a drain almost level with the place he had been attacked. Hooking his fingers into the iron slats he raised it and plunged his hand into the water at the bottom. His fingers curled around the knife. He had found it.

The morning was over by the time he crept into the store through his secret entrance and it was the middle of the afternoon before he found out the woman was dead.

He scuttled back to his basement, to the furthest away corner where it was at its darkest. The corner he shared with spiders and mice and small things that scuttled in the dark. Huddling into the corner, between hissing steam pipes, he raised his head and howled like a wolf in the wilderness.

It was not fair, it was not just. Someone else had taken the woman's life. They had no right to do that. It had not been their life to take. It had been his.

God's anger was bound to be great and terrible.

He would have to find out who had done such a terrible thing and make them pay. He would also have to find another way to make up for the loss of his mission.

The basement ticked and hummed and hissed, gradually soothing him until he was calm again. He would pick another target. It would have to be someone who served Satan just as the woman had; someone who had power and used it for their own benefit; someone who preyed on others; someone who had hate in their souls.

The face of the other one pushed into his thoughts. He had seen hate in her eyes and she did have power, how much he was not sure, that would have to be checked out. He would watch her and decide whether she was another of Satan's chosen ones and if she was, he knew what to do.

He pulled his knees up to his chest and hugged them. It would be difficult. He liked this one, which was unusual because he could not think of anyone he had ever liked before, with the exception of one of his doctors. Still, when God chooses someone to carry out his works that person also has to make sacrifices. He had made this sacrifice before when he found out the doctor had been chosen by Satan.

He would not fail this time either.

48

Colin Wilson popped his head round the dining room door. 'Ah, there you are,' he said. He had taken off his white boiler suit and overshoes and was munching a sandwich.

Bill's stomach growled. It had been a long time since breakfast. 'You finished then?'

'We've done as much as we can for the time being.' Colin chewed reflectively. 'Strange about the cat though.'

'What's strange about it? There's a history of wee dead animals littering this case.'

'Makes you sick,' Sue muttered, 'don't know how you can eat that sandwich.'

Colin ignored her. 'It's strange because the cat was placed in her arms after she was dead.'

'How d'you make that out?'

'The scratch marks on her chin and neck. She would only have got them if she'd struggled and she would've needed both of her hands free to do that.'

Colin stuffed the last bit of sandwich in his mouth. 'Weird bugger you're dealing with. Hope you find him.' He turned back to them just before he left the room. 'Oh, I forgot to say, the doc's finished with her as well and if I'm not mistaken that's her getting loaded into the meat wagon now.'

'What say we pop down to the village and get a sandwich,' Bill said, watching the last car swing out of the drive. His stomach churned out another growl.

'Better finish up here first,' Sue said. 'It'll let Marika get away.'

'Where is she?' Bill had forgotten about the Polish maid.

'In the kitchen tidying up the mess. It seems Mrs Ralston had a bit of a temper tantrum this morning.'

'D'you think she should be tidying it? Crime scene and all that, you know.'

'The SOCO guys went over it and said it was all right. Nothing there to indicate it had anything to do with the crime scene. And it was annoying Marika. She seems to think she would get the sack if she left it like that.'

Bill frowned. 'Well, I suppose if they gave the go ahead.'

'What about the house search then? Where d'you want me to start?'

Bill was not sure what would be gained by searching the house, particularly if it was an intruder who had committed the crime. However, it was standard procedure, and anyway, it might give them some insight into what kind of person Nicole Ralston was, and why she would attract the attention of this sicko. So he said, 'You start with the bedrooms at that end of the house. Once I've looked at the murder room again, I'll start from this end, and I'll meet you somewhere in the middle. Don't suppose we'll find anything we haven't found already, but you never know.'

'What about the grounds.' Sue nodded her head towards the window.

'Colin and his boys went over that with a fine-tooth comb this morning, but I don't suppose it'll harm to have a walk around. Okay, let's get going, the sooner we start the sooner we can get something to eat.'

The search was unsatisfactory, although Bill did find an address for Scott's business premises.

'Burger and coke first,' he said to Sue, 'then we'll see what we can find out here.' He handed her the piece of paper with the address. 'You drive.'

The business was situated in a small unit off Brown Street. 'Doesn't look like much,' Bill said. 'I thought he was supposed to be some kind of high flying business man.'

Sue studied the plaque on the wall. 'They say there's money to be made from software development. Look how well Grand Theft Auto and Lemmings did. Those games were designed in Dundee.'

Bill snorted. 'Computer games aren't my forte. I've better

things to do with my time.'

'Okay, no need to take the hump, better see what they have to say inside.'

'Be with you in a moment.' A boy who looked hardly old enough to have left school looked up from the computer he was working on. He tapped a few more keys before turning to grin at them. 'I was at a tricky bit.'

'We're looking for Scott Ralston.' Bill fumbled in his pocket for his warrant card.

'Not here.' The boy peered at the card. 'Police is it? What's Scott done then? Left his Beamer where he shouldn't have?'

Sue laughed. 'No, nothing like that, we just need to speak with him.'

'Fraid you're out of luck then. He's off to France. Paris I think he said, lucky sod.'

'How can we contact him?'

The boy turned his attention back to the computer. 'Haven't a clue, but maybe Karen will know.'

'Somebody looking for me?' A young girl emerged from the tiny cubby hole that seemed to serve as an office. Bill had the impression she'd been listening behind the door.

'How can I get in touch with Scott Ralston?'

Karen shrugged. 'Your guess is as good as mine. He just takes off and nobody knows where he goes.'

'But surely he leaves word about how to contact him.' Bill was getting exasperated, and Sue was no help. She was peering over the young guy's shoulder and watching the computer screen.

'Nope,' the girl said. 'He's the boss. Does what he likes. He phones in every second or third day though.'

'What about a mobile number?'

'I can give you that okay, but it won't do you any good. He keeps it switched off all the time – says he doesn't like interruptions when he's at meetings. To tell you the truth he's a bit weird about mobiles, says they turn your brain to mush.'

'You weren't much help in there,' Bill grumbled as they

left and got in the car.

'Oh, I don't know. Ricky was quite helpful. Apparently, Mr Ralston has what you would call an extra-marital interest. He goes to Manchester regularly to see a girl called Emma.'

'I suppose he's having it off with his secretary in there as well.'

Sue laughed. 'She's not a secretary. She's a Jill of all trades. Works on the computers and keeps the accounts. That sort of thing.'

By mid-afternoon, everyone in the store knew about Nicole's death and rumours abounded.

Depending on who was talking, she had been shot, had her throat cut, been garrotted, raped, strangled or drowned; and that it was an accident, suicide or murder. Ken Moody had been sent home in a state of shock, and Patrick Drake had arrived demanding answers that couldn't be supplied. His face had been thunderous when he arrived. It was worse when he left.

Julie sought shelter in her tiny cupboard of an office. She still hadn't informed anyone she was leaving and didn't know how she could, after what had happened. It seemed to her as if there was a conspiracy to keep her in Dundee.

She thought longingly of Edinburgh and her job in the art gallery. Her job? That was a laugh because Adrian had informed her it would not be hers any longer if she stayed in Dundee. She didn't want to stay in Dundee, but it seemed as if every time she made a plan to leave something happened to prevent it.

She reached for the phone and started to dial Adrian's number. She owed it to him to explain what was delaying her this time. But what would she say? 'Nicole's dead – murdered.'

She could imagine his response, 'What have you done, Julie?'

She hadn't done anything, but would he believe her.

Slowly she replaced the receiver. The time to phone Adrian would be after the murderer was identified.

The cold fingers of a shiver rippled up her spine lodging itself in her shoulders and neck.

There was a funny smell, like grease or oil, and she had the oddest sensation she was being watched, although the door was still shut and there were no windows in her cubicle of an office.

She flexed her shoulders and did some neck stretching exercises. It was probably stress or maybe a guilt reaction triggered by Nicole's death.

The exercises relaxed her muscles but did nothing to relax her mind. Her forehead was tight, it seemed to be continually tight nowadays, and a headache was starting to gather.

Unable to concentrate on work she tidied her desk, locked the confidential papers in her filing cabinet, shrugged her coat on and left the office.

'My,' Betty said, as she passed the entrance to the restaurant. 'Finishing on time tonight, are we? Must have a heavy date.'

Julie forced a laugh. 'Sorry, Betty, nothing like that. It's just that I don't have the stomach for it after today's news.'

'Yeah, I know. It's a bitch, isn't it?'

Julie hurried through the food hall with her head down. She was not in the mood for conversation and when the exit door banged shut behind her, she sighed with relief.

Her feet clattered as she climbed the half set of stairs that led to the rear corridor. The stairs went higher, all the way to the top of the building. However, they only began at the food hall basement, although Julie was aware there was a lower sub-basement. Harry was probably the only one who knew how to get down there. There was a lot about this building that no one but Harry knew, and Julie wondered if he'd returned to work as she'd advised.

The light was on in his little room and she stuck her head round the door. 'Ah, there you are, Harry. You came in then.'

259

'Yes, I thought about what you said and I suppose they can only fire me again if that's what they want.'

'It'll be their loss if they do,' Julie said. 'But don't you even think that way. This is your job and you do it well.'

'Thanks, you're always nice to me.'

'I'll be off then, but you look after yourself.'

The alley had never seemed so ominous. For the first time Julie realized the high walls at each side gave it a tunnel effect and she was glad Harry remained standing at the door until she reached the safety of the street.

She pulled her coat around her, grasping the collar with one hand so the wintry draught couldn't find an entry point, and hurried in the direction of the Nethergate and High Street. If she hurried she would catch a bus before the rush hour queues started to accumulate.

'Tilly, Evening Tilly!' The newspaper seller bellowed as she passed him.

She rummaged in her pocket for some loose change. There might be something about Nicole in the newspaper.

'Ta, miss.' The man touched his flat cap in an old-fashioned gesture and she nodded her thanks as he handed her the Evening Telegraph, noticing as she did so, the crutch under his arm.

'Never mind the change,' she muttered and hurried off along the street to catch her bus.

Julie managed to get a seat near the front and, once she was settled, riffled through the paper until she found what she was looking for. But it didn't tell her any more than she knew already, simply stating the body of a woman had been found in a house outside Dundee and the police were investigating.

Her shoulders tensed and her neck stiffened. It was that feeling again, the feeling that someone was watching her.

She shrugged her shoulders to loosen them. She was being silly. It was probably just someone reading the paper over her shoulder. People did that all the time on buses.

The newspaper crackled as she folded it and tucked it down the side of her seat. Once that was done she glanced over her shoulder, but the two High School kids behind her seemed to be too engrossed with themselves to bother reading any newspaper, and no one else in the bus seemed interested in her.

I'll soon be as paranoid as Nicole, she thought, but she could not shake off the feeling.

Once the doctor had examined Ken, standing over him while he swallowed a tranquillizer, Evelyn took charge. 'I'll drive you home,' she said, 'and get a taxi back.'

'But Patrick will expect me to be here,' Ken protested.

'I'll handle Patrick,' Evelyn said.

Lassitude was creeping over Ken swamping his muscles with cotton wool. It was an effort to move.

His tongue stuck to the roof of his mouth, making it difficult to argue with Evelyn. Home suddenly seemed very attractive and, in any case, he could not remember why he wanted to stay here. It was not a nice place.

Later, Ken could not have described how he got home. He was aware of Evelyn driving as he relaxed in a pleasant limbo beside her. He floated into the house while Evelyn whispered to Claire, and then he crashed out on the sofa in the lounge.

He might have slept for minutes, or hours, or days, Ken had no way of knowing. When he woke he was floating again in a pleasant, if somewhat disorienting, haze, and didn't know where he was. The room was vaguely familiar, but it kept altering in size as the walls swayed back and forth, while the ceiling seemed to extend to the sky. Even the air moved around him in waves of light. Colours assaulted his senses, brighter than anything he had ever experienced before and he could hear his breathing and the rustle of the upholstery beneath him in minute detail.

'You're awake.' The voice was so sweet and caring, he wanted to cry.

She knelt beside him. 'Are you all right?'

Her aura shimmered and shifted, outlining her body with

scintillating colours that moved when she moved. She was an angel.

'Of course, I am.' He beamed at her and reached out a hand to stroke the rainbow round her head. 'Everything's all right now.' He didn't know why he just knew it.

Claire started to cry. 'That must have been some drug that damned doctor gave you, but you've got to pull yourself together. What if the police come?'

'Let them come.' Ken grinned. 'I have nothing to hide. And now, I've got what I want. I've got my darling Claire.' He sighed and then giggled.

'And Nicole's gone, gone, gone.'

For once in her life, Claire was speechless.

49

Bill arrived in time to see her start on her run but had been too tired to follow her, so he sat on the stair to wait.

Someone, further up in the building, was frying onions and the smell whetted his appetite. All he'd eaten today had been a burger after he'd left the crime scene.

He shouldn't be here. It wasn't the cleverest thing he'd ever done, but he couldn't resist it. There was something about her that drew him.

His breathing deepened and he was on the verge of sleep when the door at the foot of the stairway opened. That was when he remembered why the place seemed so familiar. He'd been here before. This was where they had found the hanging man. But that had been months ago.

He sensed her hesitation as she peered into the darkness and, using the stair banister for leverage, he hoisted himself to his feet intending to go down to meet her.

'Who's there?'

Her breath came in short gasps, sharpening her voice with anxiety. He also thought he detected an underlying note of fear.

'It's all right, Julie. It's me. Bill Murphy.' He snapped on his lighter so that the flame illuminated his face. He hadn't smoked for a couple of years but still carried the lighter. It came in handy when he was interviewing the punters and wanted to give them a fag to loosen them up.

She started to climb the stairs. 'What are you doing here?' She passed him and slid her key into the lock.

Bill followed her into the small living room. It was a bit of a mess. There were dirty dishes on the table, an ancient dusty sofa and chairs to match, a cooker, partially hidden behind a curtain. The door to the bedroom was ajar and he could just glimpse the unmade bed. Somehow he'd imagined her as a tidy person, someone who would pick up a pin if it fell to the floor. He'd never for a moment visualized her in such tawdry surroundings.

She collapsed on one of the armchairs. 'Well?' Her breathing was still laboured.

'I wanted to see you again.' It sounded lame, but it was the truth. 'Besides I thought you might be upset at your friend's death.'

Julie bent over and, grasping one of her legs behind the knee, she flexed it. After several swings of her leg, she transferred her hands to the other leg and started to exercise that one. 'I'll stiffen up if I don't do that,' she explained.

After she finished exercising her legs she kneaded them with her hands using the same motions that Bill remembered his mother doing when she was making pastry.

Finally, she leaned back. 'Who said she was my friend?' She stared at him challengingly.

'Why, Nicole did.' Bill returned her stare.

'Well, I suppose she was entitled to think what she wanted,' Julie said. 'But I never regarded her as anything more than a colleague. So I really don't need you to be concerned about me.'

'You said you were going to be with her last night.' Bill was finding it difficult to justify his presence in her flat.

'Something came up,' Julie said. She thought for a moment. 'D'you think she'd still be alive if I'd been with her?'

Bill couldn't decipher the emotion behind the words and wondered if she was blaming herself.

'No, either the killer would have waited for another chance, or,' he hesitated, 'you'd both be dead.'

'Oh,' she said. She pummelled her knees. 'D'you want a cup of coffee or tea or something. I don't have alcohol in the house.'

'Tea would be all right.' Bill was sick of drinking coffee. It seemed to be all he'd been doing recently.

'Fine,' she said. She rose from the chair and walked to

the sink to fill the kettle.

Bill watched her. She had the grace of an athlete and, even without makeup and with her face streaked with sweat, she was beautiful.

He wanted to hold her and caress her. He wanted to remove the sweatband from her forehead and kiss the damp brown hair that had sculpted itself to her head. He wanted her. But he didn't know what to do about it because he didn't want to screw everything up before it even started.

He stuck his hands in his pockets and studied the photographs on the mantelpiece above the electric fire.

'Who's this?' He removed his hands from his pockets to lift the silver-framed picture.

She looked over her shoulder. 'That's Dave, my husband.'

'Ah,' he said, 'I didn't know you were married. You don't wear a ring.'

'No. But I still feel as if I'm married.' She washed two mugs under the tap and dried them on a reasonably clean towel. 'He's dead.' Her voice was little more than a whisper and she didn't look up.

The towel squeaked as she polished the second mug over and over again. The old-fashioned clock on the mantelpiece ticked loudly. And the building creaked and groaned as only old buildings do. Bill watched her hands polishing the mug with fingers so stiff and rigid it was a wonder it didn't break, but he couldn't see her face.

Bill replaced the photograph on the mantelpiece. 'How long's he been gone?' For some reason, Bill didn't want to say the word dead.

Julie turned the tap off and turned to face him. 'Gone, or dead?' There was a harsh quality to her voice giving him the impression he'd touched a nerve.

'Both, I suppose.' This was a complication Bill hadn't anticipated and he needed to know.

'He's been dead for four months, but he was gone long before that.' There was a bitterness and finality in her voice that hadn't been there before and it sounded as if she were closing a book. Cutting herself off from a part of her life that still hurt.

'I'm sorry . . .'

'No need to be sorry.' She clattered the mugs onto the table.

'I meant, I'm sorry for asking. But I had to know if I stood a chance with you. Do I Julie?'

'When you see this you might change your mind.'

She pushed the sleeves of her sweatshirt up, exposing her scarred arms.

Bill stared. 'What happened?' he whispered.

'I was going through a bad patch, but that's over now.' She pulled her sleeves down and turned away from him.

'I don't care, Julie. That's in the past and doesn't alter who you are now.' He grasped her hands. 'As far as I'm concerned you are the most beautiful and interesting woman I've met for a long time.'

There was a strange faraway look in her eyes and she seemed to be looking past him, rather than at him.

At last, she exhaled a sigh that fluttered through her teeth with the softest of sounds. 'Why not,' she whispered, more to herself than to him.

Bill shook her gently. 'Does that mean yes?'

Her eyes widened. She was looking at him now, although there seemed to be sadness deep within them that he couldn't quite fathom. 'It means perhaps, maybe, I'm not sure, but we can give it a try.'

Bill drew her to him until they were standing close together. 'Ah, Julie,' he said, 'I've wanted you since the first time I saw you sitting there, so alone, in that crowded pub.'

'I know,' she said, allowing him to pull her into the circle of his arms.

He bent his head, nuzzling her where the damp strands of hair met her neck. She smelled of sweat mixed with perfume; he'd never smelt anything sweeter. He lifted his head to look at her. There was a tear trickling down her cheek. 'We don't have to,' he said, 'if you don't want to.'

'The damnable thing,' she said, looking at him, 'is that I

266

want to. I want to very much.'

Bill knew, when he took her, that this wasn't something that came naturally to her, and he was glad. However, she responded with a passion that bordered on desperation and he wondered, just briefly, if he was the man she was seeing behind her closed eyelids.

Julie woke first the next morning and lay staring at the ceiling. She hadn't meant to let things develop this far, but something had happened between them when he had stood in her flat last night. It was something mysterious that she didn't quite understand and couldn't explain to herself, but when he'd touched her, a delicious, shivering sensation had travelled through her as if every nerve in her body had been sensitized.

Maybe it was because no man had touched her since Dave and her body was crying out for a replacement of something she'd once had that was very fine. Maybe it was the stress of everything that was happening just now, and she needed comforting. Or maybe it really was a physical attraction to this man.

She hoisted herself up onto her elbow and looked at him. He was nothing like Dave. His features were stronger, his hair darker, his nose slightly misshapen and his body was firm and hard. The slightly cruel twist of his mouth had softened as he slept and the worry lines appeared less. She realized, with a shock, that she wanted him again. She wanted to wake him and run her fingers through his hair and over his body until he was aroused. Her reaction astonished her because she had rarely taken the initiative when she was with Dave, and to think of doing it now with Bill, whom she'd only known for a few days, was out of the question. She lay back and breathed deeply, but the feeling remained.

It was a long time before he woke. He turned to face her, a worried expression on his face. She smiled at him and his worry lines receded. He reached for her, cradling her in his arms. She relaxed, enjoying the closeness and the warmth, wondering if he would want to make love again. She wanted to give him a sign, but could not, so she just snuggled up to him and enjoyed his warmth and maleness.

'You don't do this very often, do you?' He nibbled her ear.

'I've only ever been with one man before,' she said, blushing at her lack of experience, and knowing that she was an exception in this modern age. Her mind flashed to Nicole with her many affairs, but look where it had got her.

'I'm glad,' he said. 'I haven't met many women lately who could say that.'

He pulled her even closer. 'Again?' He stroked her back with his hands.

The shivers started, deliciously engulfing her body, so, not trusting herself to speak, she nodded.

This time it was slower and more intimate than the mad passionate abandon both had experienced previously, and far more satisfying.

Julie lay back on her pillow. She was happier than she'd been for a long time. The bed heaved and she glanced over at him. 'Where are you going?' She couldn't see his face as he bent to retrieve his clothes from the floor.

He leaned over and stroked her face. 'Sorry, love. I've got to go.' He kissed her forehead. 'There's a case conference this morning and I have to be there.'

A vague, troubled feeling seeped through her. He didn't have to tell her the case conference was about Nicole. She knew.

'Got to go,' he said, kissed her again and left.

Julie lay for a time, her head cushioned by the pillow and her limbs covered by the duvet. She realized he hadn't said anything about seeing her again and her former feeling of satisfaction dribbled away. She also realized that neither of them had mentioned the word love.

Suddenly she felt dirty and rose from her bed to jump into the shower and wash away the feeling that she'd been a one night stand.

50

He thought he was immune to anger. It was unworthy of him and clouded his judgement. But then he was rarely, if ever angry.

He was angry now. The anger had fizzed and bubbled in him ever since he had heard about the woman's death. She had been the chosen one and someone had stolen her from him.

Now he had chosen another to take her place, but he had to justify to God that she was a worthy successor, or God might make him pay for losing the woman.

This one, however, was more sensitive. She had sensed his presence almost from the beginning. It was not difficult to discern she was uneasy by the way she looked around her office as if she was expecting to see someone. Of course, she never thought about the air conditioning duct. And then, on the bus, it was obvious by the nervousness in her every move and the way she looked at the other passengers. She had not seen him though, sitting four seats behind her, because he was invisible.

He would have to be careful with this one. It would not do for her to identify him before he completed his mission. Maybe that was a good thing because it meant he would be able to speed up the process.

Watching her had been easy until she arrived home and went upstairs to her first floor flat. He knew she lived upstairs because he had crouched at the outside door and listened to her feet on the stairs.

His anger grew, for how could he continue to watch her here. There were no balconies, bushes or trees to assist him in his job, only the open street, a glass bus shelter, or the lobby and stairs, where he could easily be seen. It was not in his interests to be seen yet.

He slipped into the darkness of a doorway in the building across the street and waited until he saw her light come on and her shadow cross the window. When her light went off he got ready to follow her again, but she appeared at the door in a jogging suit and started to run. He stayed where he was because he knew she had to return.

He was there when the policeman arrived.

The policeman sat in his car in the dark, waiting and watching.

It made his anger boil up zapping his brain with electric shocks until it became unbearable. He clasped his hands to his head forcing the interference to bend to his will.

When he was calmer he concentrated on willing the policeman to leave, but his magic powers had deserted him and the policeman stayed.

The door opened at his back.

'Get the fuck off my doorstep.' The man's voice was rough and brooked no argument. The dog with him growled.

He scuttled along the street until he came to a shop doorway that was not protected by a steel shutter. He slipped into the dark recess and watched the man drag his dog along the street, muttering as he went, 'Bloody tramps.'

He relaxed on the cold wall. This was a better hiding place. It was dark, clammy and smelled of urine as well as the indefinable smell of decay and rot. He could still see the window of her flat and her street door from where he stood. But the policeman's car was now empty.

Cold seeped into his bones. He shivered. Maybe he should have run behind her, plotted her route. It would be useful to know where she ran to, where she could be intercepted. But that would have left him vulnerable to discovery. That was not part of his plan.

At last, she came back. She was running easily as if she had only just started out. He saw her enter the stairwell, saw her hesitate, heard her query the dark. She was cautious. He watched the light appear in her window, like a signal from God. But now there were two shadows.

When the light eventually went out and the policeman still had not left he knew he had to do something. So he moved his cramped, cold limbs and crept across the road and up her stairs where he pressed his ear to her door. He heard nothing, but he could imagine their animal sounds and writhing bodies.

She was no better than the woman who preyed on men. She deserved her fate.

It was time to send her a present.

51

Claire's hands cradled the cup of tea which had long since grown cold. It was very early in the morning – she'd been up all night – and the kitchen was quiet except for the occasional hum of the fridge-freezer motor.

The supper dishes lay piled on the draining board. She hadn't had the energy to load them into the dishwasher last night and no longer cared. Life had suddenly become too complicated and what had happened was, in many ways, beyond her comprehension.

She'd gone over and over things until her mind was reeling. But despite trying to rationalize the situation and find excuses, the one factor that remained unchanged was her conviction that Ken had murdered Nicole.

She'd been surprised the police hadn't come yesterday to question him, although if they had, that would have been a disaster. But she supposed they were gathering their evidence. That meant they might come today or tomorrow, and when they did, what was she going to tell them?

It was all bloody Nicole's fault of course. If she hadn't been such a bitch, grabbing other people's husbands because she wasn't satisfied with her own, this would never have happened.

Even in death, she wouldn't let go. But he belonged to Claire. She was Ken's wife and the mother of his children.

With a start, she realized she hadn't given the kids any thought since last night. Maybe she should check on them.

The tea slopped over the sides of the cup as she pushed it away, while the effort of standing sent blood rushing to her head and she grabbed the edge of the table to stop from falling.

She teetered and swayed as the giddiness hit her, and she

held on to the table with desperate fingers until the room stopped revolving.

Tiredness swamped her. Her teeth chattered, her legs and arms quivered, even her bones ached.

She pushed herself away from the table, forcing her legs to support her weight. However, it took all her energy to place one foot in front of the other, and she needed her hands to grip the banister to pull herself up the stairs.

The furthest away bedroom was Catriona's, but Claire always checked on her first because she was the baby of the family. Catriona was fast asleep, looking more angelic than she did when she was awake. Claire tiptoed over to the bed and pulled the quilt over her shoulders and under her chin.

Catriona doted on her father and any doubts Claire had about supporting Ken vanished at that point. She would lie for him if necessary, if only for the sake of the children.

After checking on Jake and Charlie, Claire opened her own bedroom door. Ken was snoring softly, smiling in his sleep and looking more than ever like a little boy. Claire lay down on the bed beside him, fully clothed, and slung her arm around the hump in the duvet where his middle should be.

She slept very quickly, at peace with herself now her decision to support him was made.

Several miles away on a local authority housing estate, Babs also sat in her kitchen, restless and sleepless and worried about Harry. The heating was off because they couldn't afford to keep it on all the time and she'd pulled her heavy winter coat on over her dressing gown.

She knew she shouldn't worry and that Harry could never have had anything to do with Mrs Ralston's murder, but Harry was scared and worried. He was convinced that because of the trouble with his boss, her firing him and all, he would be the prime suspect.

'Don't you see, Babs,' he'd said. 'They'll say I've got a motive.'

She'd never seen Harry crying until last night. He'd

always said men should be strong and men shouldn't cry, no matter what. But Harry wasn't strong, she knew that. He needed her and he needed his Rosie. Without them he always said, life wouldn't be worth living.

'They can't do anything to you without proof,' Babs had said. But she was afraid to ask him where he'd been the night Nicole was murdered.

'Proof,' he'd said bitterly. 'Unless they find out who did it they won't look very far. Nicole's already told them she thought I was the one stalking and playing tricks on her. And I can't prove it wasn't me. After all, I hated her enough.'

'Oh, Harry. Don't say that. Hating someone isn't proof of murder.'

'Isn't it?' Harry's voice had been bitter. 'I can't even give them an alibi for last night because I don't know where I was.'

'What d'you mean?'

She'd never seen Harry look so shamefaced before. 'Just what I say, I went out and got blootered, didn't I. I got so drunk I don't know where I went or when I got back here. All I know is that I woke up in my own bed in the morning.'

'But you must have come straight home after the pubs shut, Harry, because you were here just after midnight.' Babs' fingers had been crossed firmly behind her back. It had been well after four o'clock before Harry had staggered into the house.

Babs shivered and, pulling her coat around her body until it gripped her like a straitjacket, wondered what the penalty was for perjury.

Ken woke with a headache pounding his temples. His mouth was full of cotton wool and his eyes ached. 'Ooh,' he moaned through lips that were thick and rubbery.

'You look like death warmed up,' Claire mumbled as she hoisted herself onto her elbows.

'I feel like death, never mind the warmed up bit,' he complained.

'I feel as if a road roller just rolled over me.'

'Patrick called last night,' she said, swinging her legs out of the bed.

Ken buried his head in the pillow and moaned.

'It's all right, I told him the doctor had sedated you and you were in no condition to speak to him. He'll understand.'

'Patrick never understands anything.' Ken's voice was barely audible, muffled by the pillow. 'It'll be a black mark against me.'

'You shouldn't worry,' Claire said. 'Your opposition is gone and you're the only one left able to do the job. He's going to need you.'

'For a time maybe,' Ken muttered, 'but as far as he's concerned I'll have fallen down on the job.'

He raised his head from the pillow and looked at her with an agonized expression on his face. 'He never forgets.'

Claire stood over him, looking down as he sat on the edge of the bed.

She had an odd expression on her face that Ken couldn't interpret, and a sudden feeling of dread, that she might be thinking of leaving, rushed through him.

He grasped her hand. 'As long as we're together we'll be all right. Won't we?'

Claire nodded and looked away from him.

'Won't we?' he repeated.

He needed her, now more than ever before. Oh, God, he prayed, don't let me lose Claire now. Not now after everything that's happened.

'Of course, we'll be all right,' Claire said.

He let go of her hand and she walked over to open the bedroom curtains, letting in the watery daylight.

She turned to him. 'You'd better get dressed and go to work. We don't want people to be curious.'

The weak light pierced Ken's eyes with all the brilliance of a floodlight. He clasped his hands to his head again, hoping to soothe the beating pain.

'I suppose,' he said.

'I'll go down and prepare breakfast for you.' She stopped

with her hand on the door. 'Will tea and two paracetamol be okay?'

Babs was not beside him when Harry woke. He slid a hand over to her side of the bed, but there was not even the slightest bit of warmth there and he wondered how long she'd been up.

It was cold outside the bed, but he rose quickly. It was the only way to do it otherwise he would be tempted to remain there forever, hibernating like the animals. But he wasn't an animal; he was a man, a man with responsibilities, a man on whom others relied.

The pipes in the bathroom shuddered and thumped as he filled the bath. He had often thought about installing a shower, but couldn't afford it. The water barely covered the bottom of the tub when he turned the taps off and got in. Babs wouldn't appreciate it if he used all the hot water. Once his quick scrub was over he jumped out and hurriedly dressed. Only then did he open the curtains, although as yet, there was very little daylight.

'I heard you moving around,' Babs said when he entered the kitchen. 'So I put the kettle on.' She laid a hand on his shoulder. 'You don't look very great.'

'I'm okay, Babs. It's just that everything that's going on is getting to me.' Her hand felt warm and comforting on his shoulder. He turned his head to nuzzle it with his chin.

'I know, but you mustn't forget that no matter what happens I'm here for you and so is Rosie. As far as both of us are concerned you're the greatest man that ever lived.'

'Thanks, Babs,' he said, 'you're the best.'

Babs turned to the cooker and, lifting a pot, she ladled porridge into a bowl. 'Eat that,' she said. 'You're going to need all your strength.'

Harry's stomach turned when he looked at the plate. He wasn't hungry. 'Thanks,' he said, forcing a smile. He poured milk on the porridge, lifted his spoon and ate.

52

Andy nobbled Bill as soon as he arrived. 'In here a minute,' he said, ushering Bill into his office and closing the door.

'What's up?' Bill fidgeted. He'd been hoping to get a cup of coffee inside him before the meeting, and the bacon roll he'd brought was cooling off.

'Grant, bleeding, Donaldson. That's what's up.' Andy glowered. 'Of all the sods they've chosen to attach to us, it had to be him.'

Bill forgot about his bacon roll. He didn't like the Crime Management Unit at the best of times. They always wanted things done by the book and he preferred the old-fashioned way of just getting on with the job. There were too many bleeding meetings nowadays. They got in the way of the work.

'It can't be that bad,' Bill said. He didn't know Grant Donaldson very well, but he'd always seemed like a straightforward kind of man. Not like some of the younger high-flyers.

'I've worked with him before.' Andy's voice held something ominous in its tone. 'We don't gel, and I'm the one who'll have contact with him.'

Bill tried to sidle out of the office. 'If that's all then?'

'Stay where you are,' Andy snapped. 'We need to get our act straight before the briefing so that we're the ones doing all the talking. It's the only way to stay ahead or he'll take over the whole damned thing.'

Bill nodded. So that was it, Andy didn't want anyone encroaching on his case. It made sense.

'Come on, we'll get a head start in the conference room before anyone arrives.'

Bill tossed his bacon roll into the waste bin. It wouldn't

be worth eating now anyway.

By the time the briefing meeting started, Bill and Andy had the tables rearranged to suit themselves, photographs pinned to the display board, and names and diagrams scrawled on the whiteboard. Two chairs were positioned at one side of the boards and another solitary chair sat at the other side.

Sue Rogers was the first to arrive, closely followed by Blair Armstrong and Sid Low. Several other officers wandered in and positioned themselves around the room. Last of all was Colin Wilson in deep conversation with a tall, heavily built man who looked as if he was some kind of executive rather than a police officer.

Andy smiled a greeting. 'I've kept a seat for you here,' he said to the tall man, pointing him to the single chair off to the side. He waited until the newcomer was seated before he said, 'I'd like to introduce Grant Donaldson who has kindly agreed to join us. Some of you may know him already, but for those who don't, he's from the Crime Management Unit. I think everyone else knows each other, so let's get started. Bill, maybe you want to kick off since you've been working this case from the start.'

Bill stood up. 'Nicole Ralston,' he said pointing to the photograph on the display board. 'Found, by her maid, yesterday at her home, apparently strangled. Time of death thought to be about midnight – this was indicated by the medical examiner, but is still to be confirmed following the post-mortem. Mrs Ralston had been in touch with us prior to this with complaints she was being stalked. An investigation of her complaints was carried out and interviews held, but these were inconclusive.'

He turned to the whiteboard. 'Suspects – not a lot at the moment because we've been looking for a stalker rather than a murderer. But the options we've got are; number one, the stalker who may or may not be known to her; number two, the husband who, we are told, is in Paris on business; number three, a lover or lovers, there has been some suggestion that Mrs Ralston had a certain weakness for men;

number four, the unknown factor that always has to be taken into account in every investigation.'

Bill looked at Colin Wilson. 'Anything from forensics yet?'

'Not a lot,' Colin said. 'The forensic team are still examining things like fibres. We also took some samples from the grounds that might give us information about the stalker. Plenty of fingerprints throughout the house, but we'll need to match them with those who have a right to be there. I thought we might get something from her neck, it's a bit dicey but sometimes you can get a fingerprint from skin, but no joy. It's possible he wore gloves of some sort.'

Grant Donaldson opened his mouth to speak.

'What about witness interviews?' Andy snapped out. 'Who have we spoken to?'

Sue stood up. 'I've spoken to the maid, Marika. Apart from discovering the body, she wasn't much help. She did give us information about Mr Ralston's whereabouts, although it was very general. She also volunteered the information that Mrs Ralston had a temper and that she thought the marriage wasn't particularly happy.'

'Have we contacted the husband yet?'

'I've been in touch with his firm,' Bill said, 'but apparently he moves around a lot on these trips and seldom leaves an address, so that was no go. I've also left a message on his mobile, although his staff told me he rarely uses it. They did say that he usually phones in every second or third day, so if he hasn't contacted us by that time they'll be able to get word to him that we wish to interview him.'

'Anyone else got anything to contribute?' Andy looked around the room. 'Okay, things seem to be going to plan so let's get the next part of the operation underway. I want to know everything about Mrs Ralston, her background and her secrets. Find out if there's anything in her past that might have a bearing on the case and if so, check it out. I also want to know about her movements yesterday, what time she left work and whether she went straight home. I want to know who saw her, which means house to house enquiries in her neighbourhood and on her route home. I realize there are no near neighbours, but you never know what might turn up. I want a thorough house search as well as a search of her office. We'll also need officers to interview her friends and work colleagues. Find out when her husband will be back and check out his movements. Oh, and find out if anyone else has been stalked.'

He turned to Bill. 'I'll leave the arrangements to you, Bill. Allocate the tasks whatever way you want.'

'Sure,' Bill said.

'Is there anything you'd like to contribute, Grant?' Andy smiled at him in a pseudo-friendly way.

'No, I think you've covered it very well.'

It was impossible to tell from Grant's voice whether he was pleased or not.

Julie's mood fluctuated between euphoria and despair as she readied herself for work and travelled to the town centre. Despair was winning when she alighted from the bus in front of Primark.

Directly across the wide street, Patrick Drake's store brooded over the Nethergate in one direction and the High Street in the other. It was an old-fashioned edifice whose facade was gothic and age-darkened, in direct contrast to the sparkling glass frontage of the new mall. No wonder the store management were worried.

She turned into the side street leading to the back alley, that dismal, narrow close that had to be negotiated before she reached the rear entrance.

The large display window, just before the alley, was still boarded up. Julie stopped. This was unusual because Drake's liked window glass to be replaced immediately. She would mention it to Harry when she went in. He wouldn't want anyone to think he was falling down on the job, particularly considering recent events.

The alley seemed longer, darker and narrower than she remembered; the buildings flanking each side higher, the tramp, sitting close to the rear entrance, more menacing.

Julie dug her hands into her pockets to feel for her key, but it wasn't there.

Her heels clacked loudly on the stone as she hurried towards the back door. The feeling of being watched had returned and she swivelled her head to look at the tramp. But his head, as well as his body, was totally enclosed in the old blanket he had wrapped around himself.

Time seemed to stand still and she thought Harry was never going to open the back door. She jiggled nervously from foot to foot. If he didn't hurry up she would have to return up the alley.

When the door finally opened Julie slipped inside glad to be within the safety of the store even if it was only this eerie back corridor with its fizzing electrics and dancing shadows.

'I was beginning to think you weren't there,' she said.

'Sorry, Julie. My foot has been giving me gyp. It kind of slows me down.'

There was a slump to Harry's shoulders that was more pronounced than previously.

Julie looked at him with sympathy in her eyes. 'This has taken a lot out of you,' she murmured. 'But don't worry, it'll pass over.'

'I hope so. I'm not sure how much longer I can go on with this hanging over me. After Mrs Ralston's accusations, I feel everyone's looking at me and whispering. I wouldn't care, but I haven't done anything.'

'I know, Harry.'

Julie continued up the corridor and was almost at the connecting door before she remembered the window. She half turned. 'While I'm remembering, Harry, the side window's still boarded up. Can you check it out?'

'I'm going to be doing that as soon as everyone's in and the store's opened.'

Ken drove into the car park under the bridge. As usual, it was almost full.

Often he had met Nicole here and they had sauntered along the road together, but he wouldn't be doing that anymore.

A quick pang of grief struck him unexpectedly, making him draw in his breath and fight back the tears that threatened to come. It made no difference that he'd intended to end the affair, he still felt something for Nicole.

He climbed back into his car and, resting his hands on the steering wheel, he lowered his head onto them and gave way to tears.

It was almost an hour before he managed to compose himself enough to leave the car, and he was still in a daze as he walked to the store.

53

Patrick Drake stepped out of the Rolls Royce moments before the store opened. Several people were clustered on the pavement outside and Patrick, who could always make an educated guess about what a customer would spend, mentally weighed them up.

It was a game he played and he was rarely wrong, which was why he'd been so successful in business. Even in the early days when he'd only had a market stall he had known who to concentrate on and who was a waste of time. As a result, his rise in the business world had been swift and profitable.

He concentrated on the game now, his gaze flicking from one person to the other.

The old man, leaning on his cane and fingering his moustache with his other hand, had evidently seen better days judging by the shabbiness of his clothes. He would be going inside to get out of the cold and was probably only worth the price of a cup of tea.

Two harassed looking young mothers with toddlers in tow would be heading for the food hall or children's wear. They wouldn't waste time but might spend a pound or two.

The blue haired granny was a typical candidate for the makeup or perfume counter. Someone should tell her she was wasting her money and would look better with less of a face mask, but it wasn't going to be him.

The young man, dapper in his business suit and with his briefcase swinging at his side, was probably a travelling salesman, or representative as they liked to be called nowadays, so he wasn't worth spending time on.

Patrick recalled it had been some time since he'd handled a rep, although he had considerable experience of dealing with them. He'd particularly enjoyed the games he played with them and on them, particularly the cocky ones, for they were the ones he liked to take down a peg or two and he knew just how to do it.

There was movement inside and the small crowd surged forward. Patrick watched carefully as the security man unlocked the doors, noting the way he welcomed those waiting, tipping his hand to his cap as the first of the customers trickled in.

Leaning against the car, Patrick was convinced he looked like any other bystander, as he puffed on his cigar and deliberately allowed time for the small influx of people to subside. While he waited, he took the chance to admire the window displays.

This had been his first department store and he'd never lost his affection for it. But profits had been consistently dropping since the new shopping mall had replaced the previous uglier mall.

He turned and looked across the street, comparing the ultra modern frontage of the Overgate Centre with the gothic building that housed his department store.

It made him wonder whether he was allowing sentiment to get in the way of a change and whether this was why he was losing customers. Perhaps modernizing his present store was a non-starter as there was only so much that could be done with such a large building. It was maybe time to put out feelers about space within the new extension that was being planned for the Centre.

However, he would need to be convinced of the profitability of any potential move before he took a decision.

He dropped his cigar to the pavement grinding it under the sole of his shoe before he turned round to smile tightly at the chauffeur.

'That'll be all for now, Frankie. I'll phone you when I'm ready to go, but I expect to be in the store most of the morning.'

He smiled again, a thin-lipped cruel smile.

'I'm sure the staff will appreciate my presence – showing

my concern and all that.'

The security man seemed startled to see him, but he stood to attention, touched his cap, smiled, and said, 'Good morning, Mr Drake.'

'Good morning. I'm afraid I don't recall your name.'

'It's Harry, sir. Harry Watson.'

'Of course, I remember now. I've been watching you, Harry. You're doing a good job. Keep it up.'

As Patrick strolled on into the store a warm contented feeling surged through his body. It had been just a few words of encouragement, but the man had responded to it like a dog being stroked.

Patrick hadn't felt so good for a long time. He would have to come to the store more often. He would also have to speak to Ken about the security man's uniform. No use speaking to Nicole anymore, he thought, with a wry twist of the dark humour he was renowned for. The man's uniform was smart enough, and he obviously looked after it, but his shirt was threadbare and his shoes, although well polished, were obviously worn. He would suggest to Ken that shirts and shoes should also be provided.

Instead of heading for the lift as he'd intended, he descended the stairs to the food hall. Normally he left store inspection to the assistant directors and the section managers but, he thought, maybe it was time he took a more personal interest.

He hovered at the edge of the restaurant area surveying the functional chairs and tables, turning over in his mind the various possibilities for improvement.

'Can I help you, Mr Drake?'

He hadn't heard Betty approach him from behind. 'Just considering,' he said. 'It's Betty, isn't it? I remember you from the old days when I was here more often. You must have been with us for a long time.'

'More years than I care to think about, Mr Drake.'

'There doesn't seem to have been much change over those years, Betty.' He thought for a moment. 'What d'you think of a complete makeover? A new servery. Upgrade the furniture. Swank the place up a bit.'

'I did have some ideas I put forward last year, but there wasn't any money at the time.'

'Tell you what, Betty. You work out a plan for upgrading the restaurant and send it to me and we'll see what we can do.'

He moved on leaving Betty staring at his retreating back.

A youngish woman, late twenties early thirties, he guessed was approaching him.

'Mr Drake.' she said. 'Julie Forbes, section manager of the food hall.' She held out her hand and shook his with a business-like shake.

'I don't think I've previously had the pleasure. I would have remembered,' he murmured.

She was very attractive, short brown hair framing a perfectly shaped face. Large, grey eyes which, on closer inspection had small flecks of green intermingled with the grey. Long neck and delicately shaped shoulders that were at odds with her athletic frame. Oh yes, he would have remembered her.

'Maybe you can walk me round the food hall and tell me how it's doing. Whether you've made any improvements and any further areas of development you've identified.'

He spent a pleasant half-hour with Julie, making a mental note that a promotion might not be out of order, before moving on to inspect the other departments in the store. Gradually he worked his way upwards until he reached the office floor.

Betty waggled a cup in the air to attract Julie's attention.

'Does that mean what I think it means?' Julie said as she joined Betty at the servery.

'I think we deserve it,' Betty said. She filled the cups with frothy white coffee and pointing to a table nearby said, 'Let's sit, shall we.'

'He seemed quite nice.' Julie sipped her coffee appreciatively.

'About as nice as a cobra,' Betty said. 'All charm, but watch out for the bite. I'd guess he's getting ready to do a management shake-up and I don't give much for Ken's chances now Nicole's gone.'

'That's a bit cryptic, and if I didn't know you better, I'd say it was also cynical.' Julie studied Betty over the rim of her cup.

'Cynical for sure, I've been around too long and seen too much. That old blighter knows everything that's going on. He knew about Ken and Nicole and I'd guess he was playing a game with them. A great one for games is our Mr Patrick. A great one for a pretty face too. You watch out for him, I saw the way he was looking at you.'

Julie laughed. 'He was only interested in what I'd been doing with the food hall and wants to know what other plans I have in mind.'

'Oh yes,' Betty said. 'We've all been there, just make sure there's plenty of folk around when you give him feedback about your plans or you'll find his plans are taking over. And I don't think they would have anything to do with the development of the food hall.'

'Oh, you don't know that, Betty. It's all part of the mystery he likes to surround himself with. The stories about him are only a rumour.'

'It's more than a rumour,' Betty said grimly. 'Just take it from me, I know.'

Julie put her cup down in the saucer with a clatter. 'Betty, you didn't, you haven't?' she looked at her friend while her mind turned over the thought that had just sidled its way in. 'Betty, I do believe you're blushing.'

'Believe what you like. Anyway, it's a long time ago – the best part of twenty years. Just mind what I say. Watch out for the old blighter, he looks harmless, but there's some as knows better.'

Patrick looked around the boardroom table. The room was packed with representatives from every department in the store, and now that the last of the stragglers had arrived he could get started. Evelyn had made a good job of arranging this meeting in the least possible time. He smiled at her, noting with interest the pink tinge creeping into her cheeks.

'You sit at my side Evelyn, and maybe you can take a note of the meeting.'

Evelyn was an asset, worth keeping because she would support him in anything he wanted to do.

He was not so sure about the rest of them: Miss Smithers, for example, the woman was a pain in the neck, questioning everything, although admittedly she had a good record in the electrical department and at least she could be relied on for her honesty; then there was the new girl Julie, an unknown quantity, but with possibilities and the added benefit of looks. He wouldn't mind a session or two with her, but that could wait. First, there was the business.

'Everyone knows what has happened and I'm sure everyone regrets it.' Patrick surveyed the staff sitting around the table. His eyes lingered for a moment on Harry, the security man, who was looking decidedly uncomfortable, probably understandable under the circumstances. It hadn't taken Patrick long to find out about the bawling out Nicole had given him, although Patrick didn't intend to let that influence any decision he might make.

'In the circumstances, I'm sure everyone will want to pay their respects.' He didn't elaborate on how this might be done.

'No doubt the police will be back and I want everyone to co-operate fully,' he paused, 'however, I'm sure you'll all keep the good of the store in mind.'

He continued his pep talk finishing with, 'Of course, we will now have to look at some restructuring and I'll be doing this over the next few days. I'm sure you will understand the reasons and co-operate with any decisions made.'

His eye lingered on Ken. The man was looking very shifty, no doubt worrying about what the outcome of any investigation would be and its possible effect on his marriage. Maybe there was more, Patrick wasn't sure. In any event, Ken's days were now numbered. Patrick didn't forget or forgive anyone who let him down, and Ken had let him down yesterday.

He placed his hands flat on the table top, levering himself up.

'I think we can close the meeting now, and I know I can rely on everybody to remember where their loyalties lie.'

He smiled at each one of them as they filed past him, waiting until Julie was within reach. Leaning over, he placed a hand on her arm.

'If you could just hang back a moment Julie, I'd like a few words.'

It was time to start putting his plans into action.

54

Grant Donaldson hadn't taken long to swing into action once the briefing meeting was over. Bill suspected the man knew they'd tried to gag him and, although he'd played along, he was now asserting his authority.

'We'll set up the largest conference room as an incident room,' Grant said.

'But the Chief Constable,' Andy spluttered. 'It's booked for him.'

Grant waved his arms. 'That's all taken care of.'

'We could use one of the incident rooms downstairs,' Andy protested.

'I prefer to set up my own.' Grant brushed Andy's objections away as if they were of no importance. Andy eventually gave up and, muttering under his breath, retired to his office to brood.

The incident room didn't take long to set up. The previously prepared whiteboard and display boards were the first things to be moved to their new abode. The technicians installed computers, a phone system was established, staff requisitioned, and desks moved in. The resultant noisy chaos gave Bill a headache.

He sat behind his desk, morosely considering the cardboard box with his bits and pieces in it. It was not that he'd objected to his desk being moved in here, and he'd got a good position in front of one of the windows, it was just that he hated the upheaval of the move.

'Are you trying to hypnotize that box into unpacking itself?' Sue enquired, perching herself on the end of his desk.

'I could think of better things to do,' Bill muttered through gritted teeth. 'Why couldn't we have continued working from our own offices? It would've saved wasting time on this removal.'

'It's what's called modern policing, Bill. Get everything together in one place and the investigation's more coordinated. It saves missing anything.' Sue poked a finger into the box. 'What a load of rubbish you've collected. Throw it out and you won't have to unpack.'

Bill made a rude noise and, leaning over, pushed the box out of her reach.

'You know, Bill. For a guy who's only thirty-nine, you're a right old fart. You want to move with the times.'

Blair Armstrong and Sid Low barged into the room, shrugging off their coats and hanging them on the coat rack.

Where Grant had acquired a coat rack was beyond Bill who usually threw his jacket on the back of his chair.

Both men headed in the direction of Bill's desk, the aroma of Blair's aftershave reaching it before he did.

'Present for you.' Blair grinned, throwing an address book and photograph album on Bill's desk. 'The big white chief said for you to look over them. See if there's anyone you recognize from your previous investigation.'

'Where'd you get them?'

Bill turned the pages of the album. The photographs were of men, some of them with Nicole and some not. Some of the poses verged on the pornographic.

'House search.' Blair grinned.

Sue looked over Bill's shoulder. 'But Bill and I looked over the house yesterday and we didn't see these.'

Bill scowled at her. He would have preferred Blair not to know that.

'Didn't look hard enough then, did you.' Blair smirked. 'Actually, we found these in a little secret compartment at the back of her wardrobe.'

Bill remembered the wardrobe, a large walk-in affair the size of a small room. 'Good work,' he said, although it made him sick to his stomach to admit it.

'Leave you to it then.' The two men sauntered away.

Sue pulled a chair over to Bill's desk. 'Let's go through it,' she said.

'Panting does not become you Sue, so take that salacious look out of your eyes and study this professionally.'

Bill ducked as Sue swung her arm at him in a mock slap.

'This chap here.' Sue tapped a finger on the photograph. 'I saw a portrait of him in that conference room at Patrick Drake's department store, although mind you, he looks a bit different without clothes. D'you think it might be Patrick Drake himself?'

'Could be.' Bill slipped the photograph out of its plastic pocket and laid it on the desk. 'We'll stick the ones we recognize on the display board.'

They leafed through several pages. 'Nobody here I recognize,' Sue said. 'The poses are interesting though.' She turned a page. 'Wait a minute. I think I saw this guy in the gents section when I was having a nosey around the store after the interviews.' She slipped his photograph out of the book. 'And isn't that the other assistant director, what's his name, Ken somebody or other.'

'Ken Moody,' Bill murmured, but he was not looking at that photograph. He was looking at another one, a man he'd last seen in a silver-framed photograph on Julie Forbes's mantelpiece. His finger hovered, but he didn't withdraw it to join the others. The man was dead after all. He snapped the album shut. 'Let's look at the address book now,' he said, his eyes already searching for the F's.

Julie stood to the side, trying to hide behind Patrick, but couldn't help noticing the curious glances of the other staff as they left the room. Ken was the last one to leave and the look he darted at her was poisonous.

'Close the door behind you,' Patrick instructed him. The sharp click of the wood as it closed reflected Ken's displeasure to those in the room. 'Not a very subtle man,' Patrick said, as he turned with a smile to Julie.

Julie kept her face impassive as she looked back at him. It helped mask the anxiety she was feeling.

'Sit down,' Patrick murmured. 'You'll be wondering

what this is about.'

He leaned towards her. 'Quite simple. Nicole's death has left me with a problem. I need two assistant directors to manage the store in my absence and now I'm left with only one. You can no doubt see, Ken has been very upset by what has happened and, quite frankly, I think he's going to be of limited use to me for a time so I need to fill the gap right away.' He paused. 'I would like to offer you the opportunity of filling one of the assistant director posts with immediate effect. What do you say?'

Julie stared at him. Whatever she'd expected it certainly wasn't this. 'But, I have no experience,' she blurted.

Patrick patted her hand. 'You're bright. You'll learn,' he said.

'No, I can't. I have other plans.'

She thought of Edinburgh and the gallery. It seemed to be getting further away.

'I insist,' Patrick said. He frowned. 'I am accustomed to getting my own way, you know.'

She would have to tell him. 'My plans involve moving back to Edinburgh and I had intended to hand in my notice.'

'Nonsense,' he said.

'You can't prevent me leaving,' Julie blurted.

'Maybe not, but you'll have to stay until the investigation into Nicole's death is completed in any case. So you can move your personal belongings up to this floor immediately and I'll arrange for temporary office space for you until the police give me the go ahead to use Nicole's office again. You never know, you might like the job and change your mind about returning to Edinburgh. Anyway, run along for now, and remember, you start work tomorrow on this floor in your new role. Evelyn will make sure you get everything you need.' He opened the door and ushered her out.

Julie stood for a moment in the corridor trying to order her thoughts. Everything had happened so quickly. She was sure she hadn't agreed to the proposition, and yet, he just expected her to do it.

Ken was standing at the door to his office.

'Well,' he said with a sneer in his voice, 'I take it you're going to climb the ladder the same way Nicole did. Doesn't give us poor blokes a chance, does it?'

'That doesn't even warrant an answer,' Julie snapped and marched to the lift.

When she reached her office, Harry was already packing her belongings into cardboard boxes.

'I believe congratulations are in order,' he said.

Julie stared at him. 'How did you know to start packing my stuff?' she whispered.

'Evelyn instructed me to do it as soon as we came out of the meeting.' Harry rammed some stationery into the box. 'What d'you want me to do with the files, Julie?'

'Oh, put them in as well. I have some work to finish off, and no doubt I'll have to do both jobs anyway.'

She slumped down in her chair. 'He must have been damned sure I'd agree to do the job.'

'Of course, he was.' Betty poked her head round the door. 'Nobody refuses Patrick. Wasn't that what I was telling you earlier. You just watch out for the next move, and be ready to run.'

'There's a wee parcel here, Julie. Somebody must have left it on your desk. D'you want me to pack it or are you going to open it now?'

'Give it here,' Julie said. 'If you pack it I'll probably never find it again.'

'Maybe it's a good luck token,' Betty said.

'Have you been up to something behind my back?' Julie shook the package. 'It doesn't rattle.'

'Oh, go on. Open it. Don't keep us in suspense.' Betty moved closer.

Julie stuck her fingernail under the tape sealing the package and ripped the paper off to reveal a small box. She prised the lid off and looked inside.

'Oh, shit,' she said.

The other two sets of eyes reflected the horror she was feeling.

55

Bill was the only investigating officer in the room when the call came in. Blair and Sid were swanning around the countryside in search of anyone who knew Nicole or who might have seen her on her way home. Kath and Jim had gone to visit Marika again; Jim was a dab hand at languages, although Bill didn't think that included Polish. Sue had taken Jill Marshall and gone back to the store to speak to everyone in an attempt to find out what Nicole was like as a person. Everyone thought they knew the answer to that one, but still, you never knew what they might dig up.

'You said your name was Betty Cooper.' He scribbled on the pad of paper in front of him. 'And you're the manageress of the restaurant. Okay Betty, just tell me in words of two syllables what exactly was in the box.'

Bill's sense of unease mounted as Betty spoke. 'I see, Betty. Can you stay with Julie for the time being? You've got her in the restaurant. That's fine, keep her there. I've got two police officers in the store just now. I'll get one of them to you immediately. Try not to handle the box too much, it could be evidence.'

He listened to the crackle of the phone. 'Yes, I can understand why you don't want to handle it, but I just thought I should tell you.'

He stuck his finger on the disconnect button and immediately redialled. 'Detective Sergeant Murphy,' he said. 'Can you ask Detective Sergeant Rogers to come to the phone please?' He listened for a moment. 'I don't give a damn. Get her to the phone.'

'What's up?' Sue said a few moments later.

Bill explained. 'You're on the spot Sue, so can you check it out? Get hold of the package and have it sent over to forensics. You know the drill. And, you never know, if things work out this might be our lucky break.'

It was only seconds after he replaced the phone in its cradle before his excitement turned into dread. The stalker had a new target and it was Julie.

'I'll leave you to continue here,' Sue told Jill Marshall, 'while I go and interview Miss Forbes.'

She gathered up her notebook and pencil and slipped them into her shoulder bag.

Sue found Julie sipping coffee in the restaurant. A heavily built woman wearing an attractive uniform-style overall with Patrick Drake monogrammed on the pocket, sat at the table with her. Sue guessed this must be Betty.

'I'm Sue Rogers. I interviewed you yesterday.'

She held out her hand for Julie to shake.

'Can I call you Julie? It makes it less formal. And you'll be Betty.' She shook hands with the older woman.

'I'll get you a coffee,' Betty said, standing up.

Sue nodded and turned back to Julie. 'I understand you've received some sort of package.'

Julie shivered, although to Sue's eyes she was not as upset as she'd expected her to be.

'Yes,' she said and went on to explain what had happened.

'I see. And you don't know how the package got into your office and on your desk.'

'That's right.'

'Harry was in your office when you got back.' Sue inspected her notes. 'That's right isn't it?'

'I know what you're thinking,' Julie said, looking directly at Sue. 'But it wasn't Harry. I trust him. And anyway it would be difficult to find a more honest and straightforward person than Harry. So I won't have anyone accusing him.'

'Any other ideas about who it could be?'

Julie shook her head.

'Anybody you've upset recently? Any enemies?' Sue

probed, still thinking Harry was the most likely prospect.

'Not really,' Julie said. 'Although I don't think Mr Moody is too pleased that Patrick Drake is promoting me.'

'Mr Moody? You mean Ken Moody the assistant director?'

Julie nodded.

'What about the package? What have you done with it?'

Betty plonked a cup of coffee in front of Sue.

'I've got it in one of my cupboards behind the servery,' she said. 'Julie didn't want to look at it, so I took it away. Nasty thing it is.'

Sue stood up. 'I'll need it, of course. We'll get forensics to check it out, but that means I'll need fingerprints from everyone who's handled it.' She looked at her notebook. 'That'll be you, Julie and Harry.'

'I'll go get the package now,' Betty said.

'It would be better if I collected it. Save getting more fingerprints on it.'

Sue rummaged in her handbag, removed a pair of latex gloves and put them on. 'I don't suppose you've got a plastic or polythene bag,' she said, 'I didn't bring any evidence bags with me.'

'I'll pop over to groceries and get one,' Betty said.

While she was gone Sue turned back to Julie. 'I take it this is the first package you've received.' She was sure it was, but thought she'd better check. 'Nothing else?'

Julie shook her head and seemed to hesitate before saying. 'I've had this feeling someone's watching me. It's crazy because there's never anyone there. It's just one of those feelings when the hair at the back of your neck prickles.' She shook her head. 'It's probably just nerves because of what's happened.'

Betty came back with the bag and took Sue behind the servery.

Sue lifted the lid of the box and looked at the body of the rat inside. 'I'm not surprised Julie got a shock,' she said. 'I don't think I would like to have received this when I wasn't expecting it.' She popped the box with its wrappings inside the polythene bag and returned to the table.

'Be careful, Julie,' she said. 'Try not to go anywhere on your own and keep your doors locked at home.'

'She didn't even drink her coffee,' Betty said, after Sue left.

'I'm sure she didn't mean to offend you.' Julie smiled at Betty, although the smile was simply bravado because the dead rat had upset her more than she wanted to admit. After the box was opened she'd put a brave face on it, but she couldn't bring herself to keep the box anywhere near her, so she'd asked Betty to look after it until the police came. Now Sue had taken possession of it, she didn't have to worry anymore, but she couldn't get the image out of her mind.

'What about you, Julie?' Betty sat down on the seat beside her. 'Are you going to be okay?'

'I'll be fine.' Julie sounded more confident than she felt.

'You live alone, don't you?' Betty's brow creased with a worried frown. 'I'd ask you home with me, but there's my old man. He wouldn't like it.'

Julie leaned over and patted Betty's hand. 'I'll be all right, honest. You don't need to worry about me. And anyway I live in an upstairs flat so nobody's going to peer through my windows. And I'll make sure I lock my door.'

Julie could see Betty wasn't convinced. 'What about when you're going home?'

'There are always plenty of folks around, Betty. You know that. Anyway, I'm a damned good runner.'

'I don't like it just the same. Betty's hand closed around the pepper shaker she'd been fiddling with. 'You stick that in your pocket, it's better than nothing.'

'Well?' Bill snapped the address book closed as Sue and Jill entered the room.

'We've already popped the package into forensics and they've promised to do a rush job. Should get the results tomorrow sometime.' Sue perched on the end of Bill's desk and updated him on her interview with Julie and Betty, while Jill crossed to her own desk to write her notes into a report.

'Does Julie have any ideas who might have sent it?'

'She says not. I did suggest the security guy because he was in her office when she found it, or rather he found it and gave it to her. But she flew up in a blue light at the suggestion.'

'It's probably to be expected. She seems to be friendly with him.' Bill wondered, not for the first time, what their relationship was.

'Bit old for her I would have thought,' Sue said. 'Anyway isn't she the one you had your eye on?' She leered at him.

'Don't know what you mean,' Bill blustered.

'Oh, come on, I wasn't born yesterday.'

Bill shifted position in his chair. 'D'you think it's the same person who was sending wee dead animals to Nicole Ralston? I mean, this one was wrapped up, the others weren't.'

Sue considered. 'I would guess so,' she said. 'I can't see the possibility of anyone else doing it. I've advised her to be careful, but she doesn't seem to be so spooked as Nicole was, so maybe she won't be such an easy target.'

'No,' Bill murmured, thinking there was a lot more to Julie than appeared on the surface. 'Maybe we'll get a lead from forensics,' he said, although there was a chill deep within him.

'Let's hope so. We have to catch this guy before he does any more damage.' Sue hoisted herself off the desk. 'Well, I'm for the off. I'd suggest you do the same.'

'Sure, I'll finish what I'm doing first and won't be long behind you.'

He concentrated on some papers, pretending to be busy until the room was empty. Then he sat back and stared at the address book where he'd found the initial clue to Julie and her background. It hadn't taken much detective work to find out the rest. Oh no, Julie was not what she appeared to be and he didn't know what to do about it.

56

Julie's bravado fled as soon as Betty left her at the bus stop. It was the rush hour and there was a long queue, which she joined.

'I'll be safe here,' she'd told Betty. 'You don't have to wait with me.' But now she was alone she wasn't so sure.

An icy wind whistled along the street, plucking at the edges of coats, and chilling fingers and toes.

She shuffled her feet, fidgeted with her buttons, her gloves and the edge of her coat.

Her neck and back muscles ached with tension and she shrugged her shoulders several times to rid herself of it.

However, her nervousness increased with each minute she had to wait and, although she was thankful for people around her, she was afraid that one of them might be the unknown stalker.

All the way home she imagined eyes watching her, footsteps behind her and menace everywhere, and she didn't relax until she was inside her flat with the door locked behind her. She had to admit she was spooked, so spooked she'd bought a mobile phone, although she'd never felt the need for one before, considering them to be a yuppie status symbol or a kid's toy.

The journey home had been a nightmare of suspicion, making her tense and on edge.

Now her muscles ached with pent up energy and she longed to run it off. But there would be no running tonight because the dark was now her enemy instead of her friend. It held terror instead of relief. Even the familiar street outside seemed menacing, forcing her to cross the room to the window to pull the curtains with quivering fingers until they closed and forced the darkness, with its flickering shadows and images of dark street corners, to remain outside.

She hadn't realized until tonight how much she hated this room with its grubby paintwork and peeling wallpaper. It was tawdry and squalid, and not what she was accustomed to. She longed for the tasteful furnishings, the fine art on the walls and the light décor of her comfortable flat in Edinburgh. Why on earth had she ever left it? She had to get back to her old life or she would go mad. Maybe she already had.

A scuffling noise whispered in the silence. She conjured up a vision of a horrible, crouching shape waiting for her on the stairs – a shape that even her imagination couldn't visualize.

She stared in horrified silence at the door, thinking she saw the knob move. Imagining she heard shuffling feet. She closed her eyes, waiting for the sound of splintering wood.

Her paralysed fingers tried to close over the mobile phone, although she didn't know if she had enough strength to dial.

Time slowed. Her breathing became shallow, each breath more laboured than the one before.

She wasn't sure how long she stood there. It seemed an age, before she heard footsteps on the stairs and the knocking started. Low at first and then louder.

Her heart thudded in her chest until she was sure whoever was outside could hear it. Her lips were dry and her tongue stuck to the top of her mouth.

She wanted to call out, to scream, but she had no voice. She'd thought she was brave, thought she could respond to any threat. But she'd been wrong. And now, it was too late.

'Julie, open the door, I know you're in there.' Bill's voice broke the silence with a thunderous crash.

'Bill,' she said, feeling stupid, 'is that you?'

She walked to the door and opened it with unsteady hands. Relief swamped her and she almost fell into his arms. She wanted to tell him how afraid she'd been; wanted to confide in him; wanted his protection.

She felt him stiffen and realized she'd flung herself at

him. She pulled back, flustered, afraid she might frighten him off. But she needed him. She needed him badly.

Bill pushed her into the room and closed the door.

'What are you playing at, Julie?' His voice was cold making her shrink back into herself. She shouldn't have rushed at him. After all, they had only just met.

He turned from her and stared at the photograph on the mantelpiece. He picked it up and held it in his hand for a moment, before thrusting it in front of her face.

'Dave, tell me about Dave?'

The photograph wavered and her eyes closed against the tears that threatened to come.

'I told you, he's dead,' she said in a tiny voice that wasn't much more than a whisper. 'I don't want to talk about him.'

'I bet you don't,' he hissed. 'But I do. Shall I tell you what I know?'

Julie stared up at him her eyes wide and suddenly afraid.

'David Chalmers,' he said as if he was quoting from a piece of paper. 'Travelling salesman. Married Julie Forbes in 1996, left same Julie Forbes in June 2007 for a woman he had been having an affair with, namely Nicole Ralston. Committed suicide in July 2008 when same Nicole Ralston rejected him. Have I got it right so far?'

Julie nodded. Her brain was whirling and her thoughts were in a jumble. She slumped into one of the chairs and pulled her feet underneath her. If she could have curled up and died, she would have.

'Here's where it gets interesting,' Bill snapped. 'David's wife, Julie, reverts to her maiden name, gives up her job as Managing Director of an art gallery and comes to Dundee to work in a department store.'

Bill looked at her. 'Quite a change, wasn't it, Julie? Then she becomes friendly with Nicole Ralston, the woman who drove her husband to suicide.'

Bill stopped and drew a long breath. 'Why, Julie? Why?'

Julie bent her head onto her knees. 'I don't know why,' she mumbled.

'Julie.' He bent down and took one of her hands in his.

'Don't you realize this puts you in the frame for Nicole's murder?'

She pulled her hand out of his as anger spurted through her, making her shake with the heat of it. She lifted her head and glared at him.

'What right do you have to pry into my affairs?' she snapped. 'It's none of your business. But you had to find out about me, didn't you? It wasn't enough to sleep with me. Oh, no. You had to know, didn't you?'

'It wasn't you I was investigating, Julie. It was Nicole's contacts, past and present. You were just there.' Bill looked away from her.

As quickly as it had erupted the anger seeped out of her leaving behind despair.

'What are you going to do about it?' she muttered, not looking at him.

'I don't know, Julie. I'm going to have to think about it.'

He replaced the photograph on the mantelpiece and walked to the door without looking at her. 'Remember to lock it behind me,' he said.

Julie shuffled to the door, turned the key in the lock and then stood, her head pressed to the wood, silent, but screaming inside.

Claire, apparently calm except for the force she used to clatter the plates inside, stacked dirty dishes into the dishwasher. She looked across the kitchen table, her glance flickering past Ken to the plate of food he was playing with.

'Aren't you going to eat that?'

The kids had long since finished their meal and gone to pursue more interesting things in the playroom. Only Ken remained, pushing the food round and round on his plate.

'Not hungry,' he said, shoving the plate away.

Claire snorted. She lifted the plate and scraped the two complete chops, potatoes and peas into the waste bin.

'I thought you liked lamb chops,' she muttered.

Ken didn't reply. He looked awful, grey-faced and

shrunken, with a dead look in his eyes she didn't like.

'They'll soon be here,' she said. 'You'd better pull yourself together.'

'I don't know why they wanted to see us here,' Ken muttered, getting up from the table. 'I could have gone to the police station.'

'They're just trying to make it easy for us, they said. Besides, they want to see us together and they know we have kids.'

'Since when were the police considerate about things like that?'

Claire took his arm. 'Let's just go through to the lounge and you can get settled before they come.'

The lounge was tidy, but Claire busied herself plumping up cushions and rearranging ornaments.

When the doorbell rang she gave a final look around and, glaring at Ken, said, 'Don't slump. Look alert. Remember you've nothing to hide.'

'Detective Constable, Blair Armstrong, and my fellow officer, Sid Low. I hope we're not too late.'

Blair grasped her hand but held on to it a fraction longer than Claire liked. She smiled at him, thinking he might be susceptible to female charm.

'Come in,' she said, 'we've been expecting you. My husband's in the lounge.'

'Just a few questions, for the record.' Blair was looking at her legs. 'First of all I need to know your movements on Wednesday, 26th November 2008.'

'Why that's easy, inspector . . .'

'Constable, ma'am.' Blair corrected her.

'Oh, I'm sorry, I always get things wrong.'

She smiled at him and looked away as if in embarrassment, but not before she saw him readjust his position on the chair and straighten his tie. In another situation, she would have laughed at him. But for now, it was better if he thought she was a silly female.

'Your movements?' he prompted her.

'Oh, yes. As I was saying – constable – that's quite easy.

We were here at home all evening. Watched the telly, although for the life of me I can't remember what was on.'

Claire had mugged up on the programmes and knew perfectly what had been on that night. She would probably be able to answer any question on the content and get off with it. She wasn't so sure about Ken though.

'Didn't much matter to Ken what was on anyway because he fell asleep in his chair. Not that he would remember or admit that. We went to bed after the ten o'clock news. And that's about it really.' She smoothed her skirt over her knees.

'I'm afraid we don't lead a very exciting life.'

'I see.' Blair leaned forward. 'That seems to cover what we need, but I'll have to ask Mr Moody some questions of a more personal nature. Maybe he would prefer it if you weren't here.'

Claire frowned. 'You mean about his affair with Nicole. I know all about it. Can't say I was very pleased but the woman chased him, and Ken's not the strongest person in a situation like that. Are you, Ken?' she reached over and clasped her husband's hand. She could see from the policeman's expression that he thought she was a martyr.

'Right then, Mr Moody.' Blair seemed to have lost some of his previous confidence. 'How would you describe your relationship with Mrs Ralston?'

Ken glowered at his feet. 'We went out a few times, but it was starting to get intense, so I ended it.'

'Intense! In what way, sir?'

'Well, she started to think it was more serious than it was. It was only a fling after all, but she started to want more. I told her she'd made a mistake and there was no way I would leave my wife for her.' Ken stopped and looked at Claire.

She smiled at him and nodded her head.

'I also told her I'd go to her husband if she didn't stop pestering me. I can't say Nicole was all that pleased about it, but she had to accept it. In any case, I think she already had her eye on somebody else.'

'Have you any idea who that might be, sir?'

'Not a clue,' Ken said. 'We were barely speaking by the

end.'

Blair asked a few more questions before saying. 'I think that will be all for now, sir. We may want to speak to you again though.'

Ken and Claire watched the policemen drive off.

'I think that went quite well,' Ken said.

'Yes,' Claire said. 'I'm not sure you didn't go a bit too far though with that comment about Nicole being interested in someone else.'

'Oh, I don't know,' Ken said. 'It'll take the heat off me if they're hunting around for someone else.'

57

The taste of his disappointment was bitter in his mouth. Even the air around him in this claustrophobic place seemed tainted.

He longed for the security of his hiding place deep beneath the store beside his only companions, the creatures and crawling things that also inhabited the dark places. But he had not been able to move because there had been three of them in the office. They clustered like witches around a cauldron, looking at the package he had left for her.

He was the instrument of God. His plan should not have failed, but it had. He had delivered his gift to her in the same way he had delivered gifts to the woman; the one who had cheated him; the one who was dead. But this one was not responding in the same way.

Where was the fear? Where was the distress?

Without fear and distress there was no point in providing gifts, but how could he move to the next stage without them?

It had not been part of the plan to have other people there. She should have been on her own.

He had watched her face when she opened the package, but apart from a blasphemy, there was no response, no fear, no distress. The most she had shown was distaste, which was not the same thing at all. Then, if that was not enough, they had removed the gift so he could not claim it back. And claiming it back was part of the ritual.

It was as if they had stolen part of his soul.

At the first opportunity, when the office was empty and the door closed, he wriggled back along the duct to the next grating, the one overlooking the food hall.

But it was as if the fates were conspiring against him. He could see, but could not hear. She was sitting in the restaurant area which was well out of hearing range of any of the ventilation shafts.

The fat one remained with her, the busybody who had taken his gift from her and hidden it. After a time the policewoman joined them and she, in turn, took the gift away.

At this stage in any mission, he should have been feeling the familiar build up of excitement, the forerunner of completion when he would offer his ultimate gift to God.

The gift of the chosen one's power.

But the doubts gathering in his mind made him dispirited and discouraged.

Had he been mistaken?

If he had been allowed to complete his previous mission she would never have been chosen. Was God punishing him for failing? And if he did complete a mission on someone who had not been chosen, someone who did not have enough power to make the gift to God worthwhile – did that mean he would have to pay the ultimate price and donate himself to God?

He remembered the sandwiches and the tea and the little tokens of kindness he had witnessed. He also remembered her refusal of Patrick Drake's offer of promotion, a sign that she did not want power. But then she had been forced to take it, a sign she did want power. Then there was last night with the policeman, surely proof that she, like the other one, used sex for power.

What he needed now was more proof that she was the chosen one and he could only resolve his dilemma if he continued watching her.

His mind was still muddled when he followed her home. He felt rather than saw her eyes examine the travellers in the bus, but he kept his head down, studying a newspaper he had no interest in.

Later he had hovered outside her door, but the intense silence signalled to him that she knew he was there. And then, when the policeman came he had barely had time to tiptoe up the stairs to a higher landing. He sat on the stairs, smiling to himself. Surely the policeman being here was proof that she was evil. If she was not evil she would tell him to leave.

A door opening higher in the building forced him to scuttle down the stairs, past her door, through which he could barely hear raised voices, and down another flight of stairs to the entrance door to the building. He did not need to open the door very far to slide around it. After a quick look along the street, he scurried to his hiding place of last night. From that vantage point, he could watch her window until the light went out.

He had hardly taken up his position when the policeman left the building, slamming the door behind him. Anger surrounded the man like an aura. She must have told him to go.

He flexed his fingers and stuck them into the coat pocket where he kept God's implement. The blade was sharp and it needed a sacrifice, but he did not dare contaminate it with the wrong sacrifice or he would never be able to use it again. Because then it would be Satan's tool.

He waited until her light went out before leaving. Still confused, still looking for proof.

58

Bill spent a sleepless night. His confrontation with Julie had done nothing to relieve his mind and he still didn't know what to do. However, as he tossed and turned he knew he would have done anything to have her warm body lying beside him.

Eventually, he rose, washed and shaved, and went into the office, ostensibly to work. He was the first to arrive and he wandered aimlessly around the room looking at the photographs, flow charts, and the list of suspects marked on the display boards, but not registering anything.

The paralysis in his brain did not improve when he sat at his desk. If anything, it became worse and the urge to bang his head on the wooden surface was almost too much to resist.

He was still staring moodily at the address book on his desk when the others started to drift in. The noise of their feet, voices and the whir of computers powering up played a noisy tune in his head.

'You look like death.' Sue plonked her rear end on the corner of his desk. Sometimes Bill thought she preferred that to sitting in a chair at her own desk.

He grunted, threw the address book into a filing tray with a gesture of disgust and started to play with a pencil, turning it round and round before stabbing dots on a piece of paper.

'Worried about Julie, are you?' Sue whispered. 'Maybe we should ask for surveillance in case our weird friend tries some funny tricks.'

The bleakness in Bill's eyes increased. Anything could have happened to Julie after he left last night, but he'd been so angry at her deception, and angry with himself for having been sucked in, he hadn't given it a thought. 'You don't think . . .'

'Don't worry, I phoned the store. She's there. Apparently went in early.'

Sue tapped a fingernail on Bill's desk and looked at him with narrowed eyes.

'Maybe she's another one who couldn't sleep.'

Grant Donaldson stopped beside them. Bill hadn't seen him coming.

'Briefing meeting,' he hissed. 'It might be helpful to the investigation.' The sarcasm in his voice was barely masked.

'Sorry, sir.' Sue stood up. 'Coming, Bill?'

The two of them walked over to the other side of the room where everyone was clustered around the display boards.

Blair Armstrong was finishing his feedback.

'What were your impressions of them?' Andy was frowning.

'He was more nervous than she was, but she doesn't seem to have much up top. Pretty little piece though.' Blair looked thoughtful. 'I thought they were both lying through their teeth.'

Sid Low chipped in. 'I'm not sure about Blair's assessment of Mrs Moody. I thought her simple act was just that, an act. I think you'll find the lady's very clever, probably more so than her husband.'

'So,' Andy said, 'Ken Moody's still in the frame as a suspect. What about Mrs Moody?'

'I'd say she was the jealous kind,' Sid said. 'Do anything to keep her husband.'

'Any word from the victim's husband yet?'

'There was a phone message this morning from his place of business. He's expected to return from France on Monday. He'll come into the office as soon as he gets back.'

'Have you checked out his movements yet?' Andy scribbled on the whiteboard.

'Didn't think there was any point until after we'd found out where he's been for the last few days. But it's down as a task still to be done.'

'Thanks, Jill,' Andy said. 'Bugger's not in any hurry, is he?' He added a note to his previous scribble before looking up.

'Bill, you've been going through the stuff we removed from the house. Did you get anything from it?'

'Some photographs and addresses.' Bill studied his fingernails. 'We're following up the leads.' He knew he should have provided the information he had gleaned about Julie, but there would still be time if other leads did not work out. He caught Sue's curious glance but ignored it.

'Sir.' Sue pushed herself to the front of the group. 'I wondered if we should provide surveillance for Miss Forbes. She might be in danger, and it could pay off if it leads us to the murderer.'

Andy gave her a sharp look. 'Where is she just now?'

'In the store, sir. I checked this morning.'

'So she should be safe enough for the time being. Can you lean on the staff to keep tabs on her and phone us if she goes anywhere?'

'Yes, sir. But what about after work, sir, that's probably when she'll be at her most vulnerable.'

'That's very true.' Andy smiled at Sue. 'I admire your concern and the keen way you pursue your duty so, in the circumstances, I'll allocate it to you.'

He turned away grinning. 'You and Sid can commence your surveillance from, say five o'clock, before the store closes until, let's say, midnight. After that, Blair and Jill can take over until morning when you'll be back on duty again. Is that satisfactory?'

'I suppose I asked for it,' Sue said afterwards. 'But the bugger didn't need to enjoy it so much.'

Out of habit, Julie went to her office in the food hall, but it had been stripped of everything apart from the bare desk and empty filing cabinet. It now looked more like a largish cupboard than an office and had a deserted air.

She sat for a moment in her chair trying to feel something

at the loss of her private space, but there was no regret, nothing. But then it never had felt like her office, her private space, she had left all that in Edinburgh.

She was starting to feel she would never see Edinburgh again, but Adrian had promised to keep her job open until Christmas, and this was only the 29th of November. She still had time.

It was with a sigh that she entered the lift and used the key she'd been given to reach the top floor where the executive offices were. She supposed she'd better show willing and start work there, at least until all this fuss was over.

Bill's voice still echoed in her mind, 'Don't you realise this puts you in the frame for Nicole's murder?'

At some level, she supposed she'd known this, but she'd pushed it down somewhere deep within herself and ignored it. Oh yes, she had wanted her revenge on Nicole, but that had not included murder.

The lift doors grated open and she stood for a moment before she plucked up the courage to enter the main office. It was certainly a lot more luxurious on this floor; deep carpets instead of cord, works of art on the walls instead of posters and, as she entered the main office, she noticed that even the clerical assistants had mahogany desks instead of veneered chipboard.

The office manager, Evelyn, hurried over to greet her and introduce her to the typists and clerical staff. She took Julie on a tour of the clerical suite pointing out where everything was, where the various facilities were and where the financial staff, accountants, clerks and such like had their offices. Finally, Evelyn ushered her through the glass doors to the executive office area where the carpets were even deeper and the artwork more valuable.

'I checked with the police and they said it was all right for you to have Nicole's office.' She swung the door open.

The room was large with a massive desk, leather swivel chair, double-door filing cabinet, deep-buttoned leather settee and armchair, coffee table and drinks cabinet. Julie had seen smaller lounges.

'I hope you don't mind having Nicole's office. After what's happened,' Evelyn said, her voice tentative. 'But Patrick said you had to have it.'

Julie smiled. 'And what Patrick says goes, I take it.'

She didn't like the office, didn't want to be here and most definitely didn't want to be reminded of Nicole. But on the other hand, she didn't want to upset Evelyn.

'It'll be fine, Evelyn,' she said.

'I've sorted out your stuff and put it in drawers and the filing cabinet. I hope that's all right.' She sounded anxious. 'Oh, and your briefcase is on the desk. I didn't want to open it.'

'That's fine Evelyn, I'll call if I need you.'

Julie waited until Evelyn left the room and walked over to the desk. It wasn't her briefcase. It was Nicole's. She sat down and stared at it. She should give it to the police, but then there might not be anything important inside. She leaned over and snapped the locks open, took a deep breath and lifted the lid.

It contained very little. Some sheets of paper, a file labelled Development Plan and right on top a passport. Julie fingered it. Although she hadn't said anything to Julie, maybe Nicole had been planning to go abroad.

She laid the passport on her desk. She should give this to the police maybe it would be a clue to Nicole's death. What if she'd been planning to run off with Ken, for instance?

Julie turned the passport round and round teasing the pages between her fingers until she came to the photograph, but it wasn't Nicole's face that it pictured. It was the face of a man, handsome, with longish hair and a strong chin.

Scott Ralston the name said, but how could it be Scott's passport if he was in France? Unless, of course, he wasn't there.

The possibility that he might never have left Dundee flitted across her mind, but she dismissed it. There was probably some logical explanation.

She put her hand out to the phone, but just then her door

opened.

'Settling in are we?' Ken lounged in the doorway and she hurriedly pushed the passport into a drawer.

'Yes thank you,' she said keeping her voice level and ignoring the sarcasm she thought she could detect.

He crossed the room towards her, leaned on the desk and threatened, 'Don't think you're going to get in my way. Patrick already has me marked for greater things so just be careful.'

She had no intention of letting him know he frightened her. Keeping her voice cool, she said, 'The last thing I'd want to do would be to get in your way. In fact, there is a distinct possibility I might not stay too long with this firm. So I'd be obliged if you would leave my office.'

Once he left she relaxed, leaning back in her chair until the shaking subsided. Ken Moody, she decided, was a dangerous man underneath all that boyish charm.

She had completely forgotten about the passport.

Sue parked the car outside the back entrance of Patrick Drake's Department Store at exactly five o'clock.

'I really mucked it up for you tonight, Sid. I'm sorry.'

'That's okay,' he said. 'I didn't have anything on anyway. Besides, it's overtime. Not often you get that nowadays.'

'I suppose so. But I'm starting to think it would've been better if I'd kept my mouth shut.'

'What and lose the chance of nabbing a murderer? It's our big chance, Sue. Could mean promotion if it works out.'

'Yeah,' Sue said. 'As long as we don't fall down on the job and, instead of rescuing the damsel, we have us another body. Mind you, I don't know what they could demote you to. Office cleaner maybe?'

Sid grinned. 'You sure this is the way she'll come out?'

'Sure, I'm sure. I checked it with the security guy. All we have to do now is sit and wait.'

59

The day passed in a flurry of activity leaving Julie no time to think She hadn't noticed the passing of time until she heard the sound of feet in the corridors, the slamming of doors, and the hum of the lift.

She looked at her watch, tempted to leave as well, but Patrick expected her to read the Development Plan before Monday's meeting. 'I'll look forward to your comments,' he'd said, so she couldn't avoid reading it.

There was also her office to sort out, although she supposed that could maybe wait.

And there was the little matter of being in the store on her own, although it was not so long ago she'd spent the night there and been safe enough.

She shrugged her shoulders. She couldn't go through life scared of every shadow. In any case, she was probably safer inside the store than outside on the street. There was always the security system for added protection. Usually, it was Harry who provided this. He stayed in the store until the last person left and if anyone was working late, he checked their workplace at regular intervals.

She reached her hand for the phone, but hesitated before she lifted the receiver. It would be better to go downstairs and let him know. She didn't want him to think she'd become uppity now she was part of the executive staff.

Except for a few security lights, the store was in darkness.

Julie took the lift to the basement rather than the first floor because she knew her way around the food hall and it held no terrors for her. She clattered up the half flight of stairs, banged through the access door and into the back corridor.

Light streamed from the doorway of Harry's small room, shafting across the corridor, brighter than the illumination from the fizzing ceiling bulbs. Music thumped, something modern and catchy, a good indication Harry was there.

Harry was standing in front of the sink filling his kettle when Julie reached his door. He turned round to look at her.

'Working late tonight, Julie?'

'You must be a mind reader, Harry.'

'It doesn't take much mind reading when you're standing there with no coat on.' Harry grinned at her. 'Want a cup of tea before you start?'

'No thanks, anyway I only came down to ask if you'd wait back for me. I shouldn't be any later than about eight o'clock.'

'That's okay, Julie. I'm not doing anything later tonight anyway, so I'm just as well here. I'll let your guardian angels know you're working on.'

'My guardian angels? What d'you mean, Harry?'

'Oh, I thought you knew. You've got a police guard. Two nice officers sitting in a car at the top of the alley waiting to escort you home.'

Julie was thoughtful as she returned to her office. She hadn't known about the police guard and wasn't sure how she should react to this bit of protection if that was what it was. Somehow or other she had a suspicion that Bill was behind it and that he was looking out for her.

Her steps quickened into a jaunty stride. Maybe their relationship could be rescued. She slowed as it suddenly crossed her mind that maybe she was being followed rather than protected, which meant she was under suspicion. But no, she quickened her steps again. They wouldn't have made their presence known to Harry if that was the case.

The executive floor had a deserted feel, but once Julie was in her office with the door closed she felt safe and secure. She opened the Development Plan file and started to study it. She'd also found some of Nicole's notes which she referred to from time to time.

Harry checked on her once and she lifted her head, waved

and smiled. The next time she looked at her watch it was almost seven o'clock.

She stretched her arms above her head, did some neck exercises and then went to the executive loo, a luxurious facility with marble floors, tiles, gold-plated taps and fluffy towels. Ten more minutes, she thought, as she washed her hands, that should do it and then I'm off home.

A slight sound sent her nerves zinging into overdrive.

She opened the door, but there was nothing to be seen. Probably Harry checking up, she thought, but the back of her neck was prickling.

'Thanks for letting us know,' Sue shouted to Harry as he hurried back down the alley.

'That's a bummer,' she said to Sid. 'She's working late. Eight o'clock the security guy said.'

'Maybe we should go and come back then. What d'you think?'

'I suppose we could,' Sue mused. 'Bill wouldn't like it though. He's got a thing for this one.'

'Bill doesn't need to know.' Sid grinned at her. 'I won't tell him if you don't.'

'I don't know. What if she finishes earlier than that? We'd miss her. Then he'd know.'

'Yeah, I suppose.' Sid lapsed into a gloomy silence.

Ten minutes later Bill tapped on their window. 'She not out yet?'

Sue rolled the window down. 'She's working late until eight o'clock. The security guy let us know.'

Bill stared up at the darkened store. 'Not sure I'd like to be locked in there by myself.'

'Security guy's in there with her.'

'Is that Harry? The one Mrs Ralston accused of being the stalker.'

'Jeez,' Sue said, 'I never thought about that.'

She got out of the car and stood beside Bill as they looked at the store together. 'Mind you, he'd be stupid to try anything with us being here.'

'I suppose you're right,' Bill said. 'But keep an eye on it. If she's not out by eight o'clock let me know.'

'Sure thing.' Sue returned to the car, less confident than she had been.

The store had been quiet for a long time before he discarded his disguise and emerged from the toilet where he'd been hiding since before closing time.

The food hall was deserted and dark and he moved silently between the aisles, feeling his way to the door that led onto the stairs. He didn't want to risk using the lift, it would make too much noise.

Pausing on the stairs, he listened. Faint music drifted upwards. He followed the sound. Everything would be lost if he was seen and he wanted no witnesses.

The corridor was quiet enough and, although she felt foolish, Julie crept along as quietly as she could. Her office door was open, but maybe she'd left it that way. The rustle of papers, however, was certainly not her imagination.

All of a sudden she knew. It was Ken, poking and prying into what she was doing. It was like him. He was a nasty piece of work, and he wasn't going to get off with it.

'What the hell d'you think you're doing?' Her voice tailed off as the man turned round. It wasn't Ken. He was tall, extremely attractive, and looked just like his passport photograph. 'You're Scott,' she said. 'But what are you doing here? And why are you going through my papers?'

'I'm sorry, I thought this was Nicole's office.' He looked confused and apologetic. 'I was just looking for something,' he murmured, 'something that belongs to me.'

Julie instinctively knew what he was looking for. 'Try the top right-hand drawer,' she said.

He moved behind the desk and slid the drawer open, removing his passport. 'Ah,' he said. 'Thank you.' He held it in his hand while he gave her a puzzled look. 'How did you know what I was looking for?'

Julie didn't answer his question. 'I thought you were supposed to be in Paris.'

She walked towards the desk, keeping it between them, although she had no sensation of danger.

'No. I went to Manchester instead.' His voice was slightly flustered, although his eyes were steady and focused on her. 'Why did you think I was going to Paris?' He sounded puzzled.

Something about his attitude unnerved Julie. She didn't know what it was, but it left her feeling distinctly uneasy.

'Nicole told me,' she said. 'Why would she say you were in Paris when you weren't?'

'Why indeed,' he said. His voice was light and soothing, but the expression on his face had tightened. 'What else did Nicole tell you?'

Something in the tone of his voice unnerved her. 'You shouldn't be here, you know,' she said, reaching for the phone. 'I'll just contact security and get you shown out.'

'I wouldn't do that,' he said pleasantly, laying his hand on top of hers to prevent her lifting the receiver. 'I'd prefer to see my own way out. As you say. I shouldn't be here.'

The feeling of unease niggling at Julie's insides increased and the back of her neck was prickling again. 'Have you spoken to the police?' she said. 'They were trying to contact you.'

'Oh, yes,' he said. 'I'm seeing them on Monday. That will be soon enough.'

Julie wriggled her hand out from underneath his. 'I really must call security,' she said, keeping her voice steady as she tried to mask her nervousness. 'How else are you going to get out of the store?'

'Same way I got in,' he said. 'I'll hide until the store opens again and leave like any other customer.'

'I can't let you do that.' Julie focused her eyes on his but didn't like what she saw there. She reached for the phone, but his hand slammed down on hers and he ripped the wire out of the wall.

'You have no choice,' he said, his face bland and pleasant, but his voice menacing.

Julie's nervousness had now turned into alarm and, pulling her hand free, she backed towards the door.

He remained where he was, watching her and smiling. 'You wouldn't even get the length of the corridor,' he said, his voice soft and gentle. 'So why don't you come and sit down, like a good girl, and I'll tell you all about Nicole.'

Julie leaned her back against the door, her fingers feeling for the doorknob. She grasped the knob ready to turn it and run, but she would need a head start, so she relaxed and smiled back at him as if she agreed. Slowly she turned the handle and as she did so her hand brushed the top of the key. With her other hand, she worked it loose, blessing the day that Patrick had decided to keep the traditional features of the building.

'And if I do stay here,' she murmured, 'what will happen to me?'

'Ah,' he said. 'Now there's the dilemma because you were Nicole's friend, her confidante, and I'm sure you've guessed why I had to come here.'

Julie's hand tightened on the doorknob. She pulled the door open, shot through it and rammed the key into the keyhole at the same time as she slammed the door shut. She turned the key until the lock clicked. The door vibrated as he slammed against it and she bounced backwards almost falling. For the briefest moment she stood, staring at the door, paralysed, and then she ran. Ran for her life.

She reached the lift door and punched the button.

'Hurry, hurry,' she muttered, listening to the thudding of his fists on the door. Then the sound changed. He seemed to have found something heavy to batter the door with and she could hear the first sounds of splintering wood.

Her eyes watched the lift doors, willing them to open. If the lift didn't hurry she might have to run for the stairs. That was when she realized she didn't have a key for the connecting doors on the stairs, she still had the lift key in her pocket, although it wasn't needed on the way down, however, she wasn't sure if the same key would fit the doors. If it didn't she would be trapped on the stairs. There were fire doors, but she didn't know where they led.

The splintering noise of the door breaking increased and she was on the point of running to the fire doors when the lift doors slid open.

Thankfully she got in. The doors seemed to take forever to close, and she watched in agony as they slid shut in slow motion. Feet thudded along the corridor as she pressed the button for the basement. If he caught her in the confined space of the lift she would have nowhere to go.

'Start, start,' she shouted, jumping up and down. The sound of fists thumping on the lift doors echoed down the lift shaft. Thinking they would slide open again, she grabbed the small fire extinguisher from the wall prepared to use it on him. But the lift was already sinking to the basement.

She thought the lift would never reach the bottom, and then it seemed to take an age before the doors slid open. She hurried out, but not before she propped the fire extinguisher between the doors to prevent them closing.

Julie didn't even consider the phone in her old office. It was not an option for her because of the sudden aversion she had developed to small, enclosed spaces where she could be trapped. Her best option, she thought, was to get out of the store, and to do that she would need a key or her mobile phone, both of which were safely tucked away in her handbag on the executive floor. She would be mad to try and go back for them. Besides, Harry would be able to let her out, and even if he wasn't in his room she knew where he kept the spare keys.

She sped through the food hall, out onto the stairs and up to the back corridor. High above her, she heard footsteps thudding downwards. The connecting door to the back corridor banged shut behind her and Julie ran to the stream of light and the welcome noise of music coming from Harry's room.

'Harry,' she gasped, as she rounded the corner into the

room, but that was as far as she got. Harry was slumped forward on the table, blood oozing from the gaping wound on the back of his head. She knelt down beside him and grasped his wrist thinking there might be a flicker of a pulse, but she wasn't sure. One thing was certain there was nothing she could do for Harry and nothing he could do for her.

She had to get out of here, right now. There was a fluttering sensation behind her breastbone and she knew she was hyperventilating. Her breathing rasped in her chest until it was expelled in short, sharp gasps. It was a sure sign her panic was building.

'Slow down,' she told herself, speaking aloud to reassure herself. 'Get the key.' She stood up and darted over to the key box, but there was nothing in it.

She looked around the room but could see no signs of keys anywhere.

She tried the phone hanging on the wall, but it was dead.

'I'm sorry, Harry,' she said as she knelt down beside him, 'but I'm going to have to go through your pockets.'

No keys.

She sat back on her heels. Nothing else for it she would have to go back up to the shop floor. If she managed to reach the first floor she could set off the fire alarms. Why hadn't she thought of that before? Try to attract attention. She thought of the police sitting outside in their car, so near and yet no help to her if they didn't know what was going on.

Hope seared through her. She wasn't going to make it easy for him.

With one last look at Harry, she left the room and turned to go back up the corridor.

The access door opened and Scott appeared. He was in no hurry as he closed the door behind him. He leaned against it, smiled at her, and said, 'Looking for these?'

A set of keys dangled from his fingers.

60

The smell of fish and chips permeated the car. Sue wiped her greasy fingers on a tissue. 'I'll never get the smell out of here,' she complained.

'You didn't say that when I offered to nip out and get them.' Sid popped the last chip into his mouth and screwed up the paper wrappings.

'No, and I won't object when you get out of the car and bin this lot.' Sue tossed her greasy wrappings onto his lap.

'You just take advantage of me, you do,' Sid moaned. But he got out of the car and trotted down the street to the nearest waste bin.

'What time is it anyway?' he asked when he returned to the car.

Sue turned the key in the ignition to light the dashboard. 'Quarter past seven,' she said, switching the ignition off.

'Is that all.' Sid groaned. 'Another three-quarters of an hour to go.' He leaned back and closed his eyes. 'Wake me if anything happens.'

Sue snorted. She was starting to think this surveillance was a waste of time.

Julie froze, watching the keys swinging from Scott's fingers. What was she going to do now? At her back was the door to the alley, the way out. But it was locked. In front of her was the access door to the store, but Scott blocked her way.

She licked her parched lips with a tongue that was almost as dry and started to retreat along the corridor, into the shadowy part where one of the fizzing bulbs had probably failed.

Scott laughed. 'There's nowhere for you to go, Julie.' He

started to walk towards her, slowly, tormenting her.

Still, she retreated, a vague memory of a partly open door niggling away at her. Was it a memory or wishful thinking? But just as she'd decided it must be wishful thinking, there it was, swinging partly open with stairs beyond that led down into darkness.

Without giving it a thought she pushed through the door and clattered down the stairs. Down and down, seemingly forever, into the dark.

The place frightened her almost as much as Scott did, but it was the only place she could go if she wanted to escape from him.

Her feet skidded on the greasy surface and she slid down the last few steps into a cavernous, gloomy space filled with strange shapes that were barely distinguishable. Pipes and machinery stretched in all directions giving no indication where the walls or any doors might be. She imagined she heard breathing, but it was only the hissing of steam pipes, spurting and rattling.

The back of her neck stiffened and prickled, but that was probably a reaction to Scott who was now outlined in the door. If he came down maybe she could circle around him and get back up the stairs. With that object in mind, she felt her way further into the basement. Further into the dark.

Her eyes were getting used to the dark, but it only made the vague shapes of the metal objects, machinery and pipes seem surreal and threatening in the shadowy gloom.

The floor was uneven and greasy beneath her feet and, although still moving as fast as she could, she trod carefully for fear she might slip and make herself vulnerable.

Her hearing became super sensitive.

Small, scurrying noises sounded in the darkness and she imagined rats and mice everywhere. She shuddered at the thought, remembering the rat in the box.

Her eyes strained to see beyond the shadows.

One of the shadows moved, but she convinced herself it was her imagination. Scott was the only one in the basement with her. He was the one she had to be afraid of. And he was behind her. Her nerves tightened until they reached screaming pitch.

Scott's footsteps clattered on the stairs. He was coming for her.

She retreated even further into the dark, into the place of machinery, hissing pipes and the scurrying noises of the unknown.

However, she dared not lose sight of the small square of light that was the door at the top of the stairs because it would be easy to get lost down here and that might prove fatal.

Scott reached the bottom of the stairs and was moving forward, searching for her.

She wedged her body behind a machine and held her breath. He passed, so close to her she could have reached out and touched him. He moved on.

'I can hear you breathing,' he said. 'You can't hide from me.'

But he was moving further away. Dare she move and run for the stairs.

She stood still. Convinced it was a trap. He wanted her out in the open again. She huddled further into the corner. If she stayed quiet long enough maybe he would give up and go away.

Something scurried over her foot and up her leg. She cut the scream off before it erupted, but was unable to prevent the gasp it turned into.

Scott stopped. He was on his way back.

She decided to make a dash for the stairs and stood up, ready to run. But he was there, blocking her way. She tried to back away from him. But the machinery at her back prevented any escape.

'Ah, there you are, Julie?' He bared his teeth in a smile.

His arm reached out to her and his fingers circled her throat. 'Such a lovely soft neck,' he murmured.

His fingers tightened.

It was like looking into a snake's eyes they hypnotized and fascinated her. She froze, unable to move. Cold sweat made her blouse stick to her clammy skin.

She tore at his hands as they tightened even more, digging her nails into his flesh, trying to force the constricting fingers away from her neck. But it was no use.

Her eyes widened and she struggled to breathe as her airway narrowed under the pressure of his hands.

She could make out his shape, the gleam in his eyes and the whiteness of his teeth as he stood over her.

But there was another shape behind him. It loomed up out of the gloom and swung its arm in a curving motion.

Scott's hand loosened from her neck and he crumpled at her feet. His hands made one last scrabbling motion towards her legs, and then he was still.

Julie didn't stop to think. There was a man lying in front of her with a knife protruding from his back and a tall thin shape standing behind him. She ran.

She ran as she'd never run before, scrabbling up the stairs, along the corridor, through the access door, down to the food hall and over to the lift. She grabbed the fire extinguisher to release the doors. Got in and sent it up to the first floor. Still holding the extinguisher she got out and, leaning into the lift, she jabbed the button to send it up to the top floor. Hopefully, whoever was following her would think she was still in it.

There was no sound of feet behind her, but that meant nothing because this one was silent.

Bending low, Julie scuttled crab-like between the counters and over to the window displays. Her only chance was to attract the attention of the police waiting outside.

She crawled into the display window, the one nearest to the top of the alley because she knew that was where the police car was parked.

The moan erupted from her throat before she could stop it. There was no glass, only wooden boards. She had forgotten about the broken window, which wasn't repaired yet.

There was no way she could signal the police from here.

She was keenly aware her moan must have been heard

and didn't know where her assailant was. Maybe he was behind her, waiting outside the display area.

Her hesitation was only momentary. If he was there she would clobber him with the small fire extinguisher, which she still held. It might not be a lot of protection against a knife, but at least it was something.

Gripping the extinguisher she held it out in front of her as she stepped out of the display window and hoisted herself into the next one.

She could see the police car. She waved. They didn't see her.

A slight noise brought the panic streaming back through her and she screamed.

She raised the fire extinguisher ready to clobber anyone who climbed into the window behind her, but the noise seemed to be coming from the other window.

In desperation she hammered on the glass with her fists, but still, they didn't see her.

The noise was nearer now, behind her. She turned. Froze for a second as she stared into his ice blue eyes. There was death in those eyes.

He took a step towards her.

She raised the fire extinguisher over her head and brought it down with all the force she could, on the plate glass of the window.

The window exploded out onto the pavement.

Sid's eyes snapped open. 'Bloody hell! What was that?'

Sue was already out of the car and running to the window. 'Phone for reinforcements,' she shouted over her shoulder to a still dazed Sid. 'And get Bill.'

'Oh, thank God, thank God,' Julie screamed, as she jumped from the window and collapsed into Sue's arms.

Sue put her arms around Julie's shoulders and helped her into the car. 'You're okay,' she said, 'you're okay.'

61

Bill's car skidded to a stop. He jumped out, his feet crunching on the glass littering the pavement, and ran to Sue's unmarked car parked just in front of him.

'Is she okay?'

Ever since receiving the phone call he'd been afraid. Terrified that Julie had been hurt and blaming himself for not taking better care of her. His chest heaved with the effort of breathing.

'A few cuts and bruises, but she'll live.' Sue had her arms around Julie who was shaking and panting. 'I think she's in shock though, so I've sent for an ambulance.'

'She doesn't look okay to me.'

Bill leaned into the car for a closer look. 'Julie,' he said. 'Can you tell us what happened?'

She looked back at him, her eyes wide and frightened. 'In there,' she whispered. 'Scott . . .' she covered her face with her hands.

Three police cars arrived, sirens blaring and blue lights flashing. A crowd was starting to gather, gaping at the shattered window and the police activity.

'It's all right, take your time.' Bill turned to Sue. 'Check out who's here. Get someone on crowd control. Station someone at each exit and then organize a search of the store. Apprehend anybody at all who is inside, doesn't matter who they are, even if it's the big boss himself.'

Sue climbed out of the car and Bill got in the back seat beside Julie.

'It's okay, Julie,' he said putting his arms around her. 'You're safe now.'

Julie took her hands away from her face. 'I didn't think I was going to get away.'

Bill uttered soothing noises, holding her close. 'I know you're upset Julie, but I need to know who's in there. What are my officers looking for?'

'Help Harry,' she whispered, a pleading look in her eyes.

'Was it Harry? Is that who we've to look for?'

'No, you don't understand. Harry's been hurt. I don't know if he's dead. Help him. Please.'

Bill beckoned to Sid who was standing close to the car. 'Julie says the security man's been hurt, maybe dead. Get someone to look for him.'

Sue returned to the car. 'I've checked every door and exit, but they're all locked tight. Had to move a courting couple out of the alley. Believe it or not, they didn't hear a thing. Found an old tramp sleeping down there as well, poor sod, so I moved him on. Told him the Cyrenians would give him a bed, but he didn't seem to be interested. We're ready to go in and search now.'

Julie looked past Bill to Sue. 'You must get help for Harry before it's too late.' Her voice was clearer than it had been earlier.

Sue bent over so she could lean into the car. 'Is Harry the only one we're looking for?' Her voice was urgent. 'It would help us if we knew what's in there.'

'Scott.' Julie shuddered. 'I think Scott's dead. He was chasing me. I think he would've killed me, but there was someone else.' Julie's eyes widened. 'I don't know who he was. I only saw a shape, tall and thin with icy blue eyes. They reflected the light, but they were flat and dead.' She shuddered.

'He stabbed Scott as he was going to . . . going to . . .' She shuddered again and covered her face with her hands. 'He saved me from Scott.' Her fingers muffled her voice. 'But then.' She took her hands away. 'I ran because I knew he didn't do it to save me. He wanted me himself.' Julie burrowed her face into Bill's jacket.

'Just one more thing,' Sue said. 'Where do we look?'

Julie raised her head. 'The back corridor, Harry's in the porters' room. The sub-basement, there's a door leading off the back corridor that takes you down. Scott's down there.' Her body shook. 'The other one was right behind me when I came through the window. That's when I saw his eyes. I don't know where he is now.'

Sue patted Julie's hand. 'We'll find him, don't worry. And we'll get help for Harry.'

Sue organized the search of the store. They soon found Harry who was suffering from a severe concussion, but were unable to find any keys, the ambulance men had to stretcher him out through the broken window. Julie was taken to hospital, in the same ambulance, suffering from shock.

Scott's body lay in the sub-basement. The police surgeon certified his death, apparently by stabbing, although no knife was found. His body was removed to the police mortuary.

No trace was found of the mystery man.

Patrick was informed and asked to come to the store, but he delegated the task to Ken who made his reluctance plain to everyone who was there.

'Sulky bugger,' Sue said to Bill later when she was reporting back. 'I don't know what the women see in him.'

Hospital sheets, white, cold and unnaturally smooth, never felt like any other kind of sheets. That and the myriad of hospital sounds, scurrying feet, swishing doors, trolley wheels and the muted sounds of nurses chatting and comparing notes, meant that Julie's sleep was fitful. There was also the smell, a mix of antiseptic, cleaning fluids, and that other indefinable smell peculiar to all hospitals.

She awoke to a bleak, grey day, but Julie's private room overlooked an inner courtyard with a square of sparse grass, so even the brightest sunshine would have looked grey in this room.

She closed her eyes trying to remember her dreams, confused dreams where she was running away from Dave through interminable corridors. There was something or someone, which she could never quite reach, just out of sight.

The door creaked open.

'You're awake then.'

The nurse approached the bed, her white uniform straining tightly over her hips. The nurse's fingers were short and fat, but they held Julie's wrist in a professional grip while she checked her pulse rate.

'You'll do,' she said, a smile breaking the severity of her features. 'I'll ask your visitor to come in. He's been waiting quite a long time for you to wake up.'

Julie pulled herself up the bed, pushing one of the pillows into a more comfortable position, and wishing the nurse had given her the opportunity to comb her hair.

Bill peeked around the door. It was as if he expected her to tell him to go.

'I would have got you flowers,' he said, entering the room, 'but it's Sunday and the florist in the hospital concourse isn't open yet.'

Flowers reminded her of hospitals and death and Dave. She didn't want to be reminded of these things and she would be out of this place as soon as she could escape.

'What would I want with flowers,' she said. 'They're not really my scene.'

Bill pulled a chair close to her bed. 'I don't really know a lot about you,' he said.

'That's not what I heard,' she said, a bitter tone in her voice, 'when you were giving me my life history the other night.'

'Ah, that, yes.'

The silence that descended was oppressive. Julie stared out of the window, wrestling with her feelings for Dave and her feelings for Bill. The two men were so unlike each other, but then that was a good thing because she knew Bill would never be simply a replacement for Dave.

'You asked me why,' she said after a time, 'and I never gave you an answer.'

'It's not important,' Bill said. 'It was just that I couldn't get my head around it because of Nicole's murder.'

Julie hooked herself up on the pillow with her elbow.

'Did you think I murdered Nicole?' Her voice was very quiet.

'It was a possibility,' he said, not looking at her, 'but in my heart, I knew you could never do such a thing.'

'I'm not sure I deserve that.' Julie sank back onto the pillow. 'You see the reason I came to Dundee . . .'

'I don't want to know.'

'You need to know because I don't think I'm the nice person you think I am.'

She looked away from him. 'It was revenge,' she said. 'I wanted to punish Nicole for taking Dave away from me and for making him do what he did.'

I shouldn't have told him, she thought, he won't want me now.

'I had to be honest with you,' she said. 'Although I haven't been honest with myself. If you want to leave I'll understand.'

'I don't want to leave, Julie. What's in the past is in the past and I know you couldn't have done anything really bad. The only thing I want to know now is where do we go from here?' He reached over and clasped her hand in his.

'You have to give me time, Bill. It's too soon.'

She saw him smile. 'Anything you want. And Edinburgh's not too far away.'

62

Wind whistled along the platform at Dundee Railway Station, but he did not feel the cold.

There were other passengers, but they paid no heed to him, a shabby man with a backpack, waiting for a train. No doubt they would keep their distance. People seemed to do that with him. Not that he minded for he was a solitary man.

His mission was complete, maybe not in the way he originally planned it, but it was complete nonetheless.

To begin with he thought he had failed. The death of the woman had been unexpected. He should have been the one to strike her down, but that was not to be. Someone else had a prior claim – someone who was more of a devil than she was. Only he had not seen it right away.

He knew he was there for a purpose. To strike down Satan's chosen one. He was God's tool. If he was unable to deliver the woman to God then there had to be another. He had to identify the one that God wanted.

God was testing him.

The chosen ones had always been women. That was what led him astray. He had been looking in the wrong place, and that was why he had tried to mould the other one into becoming Satan's chosen one.

He should have listened to his inner voice. The one that told him she was kind and good. Instead, he had looked for all the evil aspects in her character. And he had found them.

It was only at the final moment that he had come to understand. The moment after he struck down the man. The moment when his hand had been raised to strike her down.

The flash had almost blinded him and he'd had to close his eyes. The gift had already been given. It had not been a woman who was Satan's chosen one this time. It had been a man.

God was testing him.

And so he had let her live. It would have been easy to end it for her in the seconds before the window crashed out onto the street, but he had held back. He had watched her go in a blinding flash of light.

God had been testing him.

It had been easy to slip away. He had left Neil's boiler suit hanging on a hook in the basement, donned his tramp's rags, crept out of the store by his secret way and sat in the alley until the police moved him on.

Neil would not be missed. They would simply replace him with someone else and it would be as if Neil never existed. Well, in a way he had not.

The tramp would not be missed either. No one misses a tramp.

The train drew up to the platform. He got on and settled in a corner seat. Glasgow was a big city. There were bound to be many of Satan's chosen ones there.

It was time to continue with God's work.

Also by Chris Longmuir

DUNDEE CRIME SERIES

Night Watcher
Dead Wood
Missing Believed Dead

KIRSTY CAMPBELL MYSTERIES

Devil's Porridge
The Death Game

THE SUFFRAGETTE MYSTERIES

Dangerous Destiny

HISTORICAL SAGAS

A Salt Splashed Cradle

NONFICTION

Nuts & Bolts of Self-Publishing

CHRIS LONGMUIR

Chris Longmuir was born in Wiltshire and now lives in Angus. Her family moved to Scotland when she was two. After leaving school at fifteen, Chris worked in shops, offices, mills and factories, and was a bus conductor for a spell, before working as a social worker for Angus Council (latterly serving as Assistant Principal Officer for Adoption and Fostering).

Chris is a member of the Society of Authors, the Crime Writers Association and the Scottish Association of Writers. She writes short stories, articles and crime novels. Her first book, Dead Wood, won the Dundee International Book Prize and was published by Polygon. She designed her own website and confesses to being a techno-geek who builds computers in her spare time.

www.chrislongmuir.co.uk

Ingram Content Group UK Ltd.
Milton Keynes UK
UKHW010620130423
420098UK00006B/489